"YOU ARE THWARTED, O'NEILL."

The pirate smiled. Katherine grew uneasy. Instinct warned her the time had come to leave the table. Too late. He pulled her forward and his mouth claimed hers.

Molten heat pooled in Katherine's body. Her body shook. She grew dazed. She made a sound, but it was raw and only partly a protest.

He tore his mouth from hers, unsmiling, eyes ablaze. Then the hall was filled with thunderous applause. Lusty male cheers and hoots sounded amidst female giggles and whispers.

"If I am thwarted," he said to her quietly, "then what, pray tell, was that?"

Praise for Brenda Joyce's
AFTER INNOCENCE

"Keeps the reader on an emotional seesaw... Her characters are fresh and wickedly sympathetic."

Publishers Weekly

Other Avon Books by
Brenda Joyce

THE BRAGG SAGA

INNOCENT FIRE
FIRESTORM
VIOLET FIRE
THE FIRES OF PARADISE
SCANDALOUS LOVE

THE DELANZAS

SECRETS
AFTER INNOCENCE

THE DE WARENNE DYNASTY

PROMISE OF THE ROSE

BRENDA JOYCE

The Game

AVON BOOKS ◆ NEW YORK

THE GAME is an original publication of Avon Books. This work has
never before appeared in book form. This work is a novel. Any similarity
to actual persons or events is purely coincidental.

AVON BOOKS
A division of
The Hearst Corporation
1350 Avenue of the Americas
New York, New York 10019

Copyright © 1994 by Brenda Joyce Senior
Inside back cover author photograph by Volkmann © 1994
Published by arrangement with the author
Library of Congress Catalog Card Number: 94-96267
ISBN: 0-380-77573-5

First Avon Books Printing: March 1995
First Avon Books Special Printing: November 1994

AVON TRADEMARK REG. U.S. PAT. OFF. AND IN OTHER COUNTRIES, MARCA
REGISTRADA, HECHO EN U.S.A.

Printed in the U.S.A.

RA 10 9 8 7 6 5 4 3 2 1

This one is dedicated to everyone at Avon Books, but especially to:

Bob Mecoy and Mike Greenstein, for being my biggest champions.

Tom Egner and Darlene DeLillo, for those wonderful, fantastic, fabulous, extraordinary covers.

Denis Farina, for his incredible support.

Bruce Brill, who made me the promise every author longs to hear.

Debby Tobias, a go-getter who's gone to bat for me with great enthusiasm—thanks!

Susan Hecht, for her wonderful support and for being so nice.

Mary Kate Maco, my publicist, for being so wonderfully receptive.

Michelle Hinkson, for her enthusiasm and support of my sometimes wild publicity schemes.

Brian McSharry, for handling my end-of-deadline hysteria with utter kindness, without blinking an eye.

Marie Emmich, for tying up so many loose ends with complete enthusiasm!

And also, to my agent, Aaron Priest, without question the best agent in town.

And finally this one is dedicated to Maggie Lichota. Thank you. For pushing me beyond any and all limits, for challenging me and for being the most thorough editor I have ever worked with.

PROLOGUE

Whitehall, 1562

*T*he queen was nervous. With two dozen of her most favored courtiers, all clad in silk and brocade, she waited for the O'Neill.

She was very young, just about to turn thirty, and had been ruling for a scant four years. Intuitively she understood that her advisors were right and that Ireland must be brought to heel—but it seemed a huge and hopeless task. The Irish lords were barbaric, immersed in petty rivalry and bloody warfare, and still steeped in their ancient Gaelic culture. O'Neill was the worst of them, she knew. Yet it seemed as if the savage Irish chieftain—one of her most intractable enemies—was finally about to submit to her royal will, coming before her on bended knee.

The queen was splendid, and it was commonly held that she was quite attractive. Her brocade gown had a low, square neckline, but a huge ruff framed her ivory-hued face. Her full skirts were held up and out by a farthingale, which was now in vogue, and sewn into the pattern were thousands of tiny white pearls. A chain of gold encrusted with pearls and rubies was worn as a belt around her narrow waist. About her neck she wore a huge gold necklace with a ruby pendant, and rubies dangled from her ears. Her heart-shaped coif was of black silk, embroidered with gold thread and pearls. Elizabeth might have been only thirty, and she might have been nervous about receiv-

1

ing Shane O'Neill, but her expression was implacable, her presence outstanding, and she looked every bit a monarch.

All her courtiers were almost as fabulously garbed as she. Clad in colorful doublets with puffed shoulders and slashed sleeves, in tight hose and exaggerated codpieces, dripping gem-set rings and long gold necklaces, they comprised a brilliant and gaudy sea of spectators. And standing right beside her were her three favorite advisors: her cousin, Tom Butler, the earl of Ormond; Sir William Cecil, her secretary of state; and Robert Dudley, the Master of the Horse.

Just as the courtiers began to whisper amongst themselves, she heard him coming and thought to herself, marry, I can not believe this happens—the O'Neill yields at long last!

Not the O'Neill, she corrected herself. The earl of Tyrone. He was coming to submit, to take on an English title, to become a part of the fabric of the English kingdom. Sir Henry Sidney, the leader of her troops in Ireland, had convinced her that O'Neill's surrender and the regrant policy was the only way to civilize the savage Irish—force them to bended knee, then regrant them their lands with English titles, privileges, and duties.

The crowd gasped.

Elizabeth gasped.

The O'Neill had appeared. A man close to six feet six inches tall, and hugely built, he wore a saffron cape lined in ermine and it swirled about his shoulders. Some Celtic kind of brooch pinned it in place. Beneath the cape he wore only a coarse, dark, knee-length tunic. His calves, ankles, and feet were bare. His heavy belt was studded with gold, an immense sword was sheathed there, and a long, dangerous-looking Irish dagger winked amongst the folds of his clothing. Over his left shoulder he carried an Irish battle-ax that appeared to be six feet long.

Behind him marched twelve barefoot men with shaved heads, who were almost as tall and as broad as the O'Neill. They, too, carried battle-axes but wore wolfskins over old-fashioned leaf mail.

The crowd moved back, toward the walls of the royal

chamber, as if afraid. Elizabeth began to sweat. If the O'Neill lived up to his bloody reputation and ran amok, undoubtedly everyone within the hall would die this day.

And then a deafening howl split the chamber and the O'Neill threw himself down upon the ground at Elizabeth's feet.

The queen jumped in shock. Both Ormond and Dudley stepped in front of her protectively while reaching for their ceremonial swords. Then she began to relax when she realized that, undoubtedly, she was witnessing some kind of ancient and barbaric form of submission to her authority. But the O'Neill was now spewing gibberish. Was he mad? She exchanged a questioning look with Robin Dudley.

"He speaks Gaelic, savage that he is," Dudley murmured, the color returning to his aquiline face. "Mayhap he seeks to trick us with this show. I know well that his tongue can form the English word with cunning ease." Dudley grimaced. "The Grand Disturber could do no less than make this display, but what does he wish to gain?"

Elizabeth had no idea what O'Neill's bizarre behavior foretold, and did not answer, unsure of what to do. She did not understand a word of what this huge, savage man was saying, and she looked helplessly at Ormond and Cecil. Yet they were as flustered as she, because O'Neill was defying all protocol. But then a movement brought her attention back to the high drama unfolding at her feet. Another dozen or so of O'Neill's followers had entered the hall behind the wolflike soldiers, but had hung back by its entrance. Except for one young man, who had detached himself from the group and was now moving toward Elizabeth.

He paused before her, beside the prostrate O'Neill. He was almost as tall as the Irish chieftain, but he was young, perhaps seventeen, and his broad-shouldered frame, while sinewed and hard, had yet to flesh out. While Elizabeth noted all of that, she was stricken by his face. Thick streaked gold hair framed the most handsome countenance she had ever seen, and her pulse raced. Somehow he seemed familiar. But then she met his cold gray eyes, and she shivered. What manner of man was this?

He bent one knee. "Your Majesty, if it pleases you, I shall translate what the O'Neill speaks."

Elizabeth recovered. She straightened her shoulders, giving the youth an imperious look. "We do believe you mean the earl of Tyrone, sirrah," she said.

His cool gaze fastened upon her. He did not speak.

And so it begins, she thought, a flicker of excitement sparking in her veins. The O'Neill was appearing to submit, but the youth's failure to respond told her that a war of wit and will was about to follow. And the delight that tingled down her spine had little to do with the O'Neill, but with this extraordinary youth instead. "You may introduce yourself to Us."

He rose from bent knee and bowed. "Liam O'Neill."

Elizabeth's mind moved with startling speed. "Not—not Mary Stanley's son—not the O'Neill's son?" In her shock the forbidden Gaelic title had slipped out.

His smile was sardonic. "The very same."

She inhaled sharply. She had known Liam almost since the very day of his birth. Mary Stanley had been en route to Ireland with her husband, an official of the Crown, when her ship had been set upon by pirates. Raped and impregnated by O'Neill, she had been promptly rejected by Sir Stanley, who had sent her back to her own family in London. Queen Catherine, Henry VIII's last wife, had pitied her, been kind to her, and Mary had become one of her ladies-in-waiting. Images flashed through Elizabeth's mind of a beautiful yet solemn baby, then of a grim, withdrawn young boy. Elizabeth forced herself out of the past. "What year was it that your father claimed you and took you from London?"

That mocking smile again. "It was seven years ago." His tone dropped, and the frost left his eyes. "How fare you, Bess?"

She felt Dudley stiffen, saw, out of the corner of her eye, his hand clench his sword. She touched his arm lightly; "The little boy has become a man," she said, not softly, pushing a note of asperity into her tone. But her heart fluttered, just a bit. "An impertinent one."

He bowed again, his expression closed, all warmth gone.

"Translate," she snapped, furious now, with him, with his murdering father, with herself.

"Shane O'Neill begs your pardon," Liam said briskly, without emotion. "He is the lawful and legitimate son of Bachach, while Matthew was born of a locksmith married to a woman named Alison, and great deceit was made upon all. Matthew is not and has not ever had the right to claim succession, but justice has been done, making it clear that there is but one lawful heir to the lands in question, that legitimate and rightful heir being the O'Neill."

There was a moment of silence. Elizabeth looked down at Shane O'Neill, still lying upon the wooden floor, wondering how to address him, then at his fearless son. "Is not Matthew dead?" she asked, although she already knew the answer. He had been murdered by Shane O'Neill. Rumors also abounded that many of O'Neill's cousins had died strangely accidental deaths. And gossip also held he had imprisoned poor Bachach, his own father, in order to usurp the O'Neill chieftaincy and lands, and that Bachach was dead now, too.

"Yes," the son said. He offered no explanation, and no sign of guilt flickered in his eyes.

Shane suddenly rose to his feet. Elizabeth did not move, but the three men standing beside her all flinched. Elizabeth focused on O'Neill. She must grant his pardon, as she and her Council had planned. But she was at a loss. How in God's name should she address him? It was clear he would resist the English title of earl, and she was not certain now that she should grant him the earldom anyway. He was clearly defiant—clearly dangerous. Yet a truce must be reached.

Dudley leaned close to her. "You must not address him as the O'Neill. Nor must you insult him."

Elizabeth's jaw tightened.

Cecil whispered, "As he will not accept our title—we must think of another appellation of distinction, something he will think grand."

Elizabeth shot a glance at the pair standing before her, the shaggy-haired bearlike father, a notorious murderer, a rapist, a savage, and the lean, golden Adonis-like son. Shane was grinning, his eyes gleaming. Liam was expressionless. She now noticed that Liam was dressed exactly like his father, in a coarse cloak and tunic, his feet bare. She recalled the small boy in doublet and hose and leather shoes, a red plume waving from his hat. A wave of pity washed over her. But then their gazes met, his mocking, and she chased away any sympathy she might wish to feel. He was unquestionably a savage now, like his father, undoubtedly dangerous and not to be pitied at all.

Cecil said in a low tone, "O'Neill the Great. I wager he will love that."

"That's hardly enough," snapped Ormond. " 'Tis no different from the O'Neill."

"It matters not," Dudley countered. "He is here—he has obeyed the queen, more than obeyed, in making himself prostrate."

Elizabeth smiled at the O'Neill. "O'Neill the Great," she said in a loud, carrying voice, aware of the surprise of the crowd and of Shane's open pleasure, "cousin to St. Patrick and friend to the queen of England, we hereby grant you pardon and welcome you warmly to Londontown, wishing you God bless."

Shane's smile faded. His succession to the O'Neill lands had not been recognized—and he as well as everyone else knew it.

The tavern consisted of a single, malodorous smoke-filled room. Too many unwashed bodies had been crammed into the establishment night after night, year after year, and too often those drunken patrons had relieved one need or another without adjourning upstairs or outside.

Now the room was as crowded as always, but no Englishman had remained once Shane's frightening and savage horde had arrived. The Irishmen quaffed mug after mug of ale, singing tunes either lewd or victorious while mauling the buxom serving girls as they passed.

Liam sat alone in a corner, watching the celebrations

from afar. He was still on his first mug of ale, and rarely did he sip. He did not sing, did not smile. His gaze moved over the familiar faces crowding the room, as always, coming to settle upon his father as if purposefully seeking him out.

Shane was standing, toasting the yellow-livered, spine-less queen, his words treasonous and should any of the maids or the proprietor care to inform upon the events of the evening, Shane might very well find himself in the Tower. His father was courting disaster with his actions now, and his son did not care. He was only Shane's son by the fact of his mother's violent rape, by the coincidence of the blood running in their veins. And although, seven years ago, Liam had thought Shane to be invincible, he now knew that no man was immortal and a man like Shane, who lived so dangerously, invited death. Liam knew he would shed no tears on the day his father met his Maker, knew there would only be relief.

Shane was all wolfish smiles, downing his tenth mug of the night. Ale did not affect him—nothing affected him. Shane finished his toast, his men cheering. He reached out and seized one of the passing maids. The girl was attacked so unexpectedly that, crying out, she dropped her tray and all the mugs it contained. Shane promptly placed her on his lap, one arm a manacle around her waist, his other hand inside her bodice, scooping up her breast. His men laughed at the sight of the woman's naked flesh.

Liam stiffened. In his mind he saw his mother, pale, blond, bitter, and stunningly beautiful as she had been when he had last seen her, when he was ten years old and being taken away by the father he had never known. He shook her image free and faced his father and the serving girl, wishing she would receive Shane the way the Irish girls did, with lusty eagerness. In Ireland Shane was a hero.

But the maid looked terrified, twisting ineffectually while Shane laughed and squeezed her nipple. The girl began to cry.

Liam was on his feet. He wasn't afraid of his father, although he had every right to be. He had stopped being

afraid many years ago—the fear had been beaten out of
him. He shoved through the crowded tables, and Shane
finally saw him coming. He ceased stroking the girl, anticipation lighting his eyes. She also saw Liam, and she grew
utterly still, her eyes wide.

"Release her," Liam said.

Shane barked with laughter, shoving the girl off of his
lap so abruptly that she tumbled to the floor. He rose to
his full height; the girl scurried away. Liam tensed, prepared for the inevitable. No man, not even his son, could
challenge the O'Neill without paying the bloody consequences. Shane's meaty fist swung out. Liam blocked the
blow but staggered backward under the incredible impact.
His father weighed 240 pounds and there was no fat on
his massive frame. They both knew that Shane was far
stronger than Liam, but what only Liam knew was that
one day the scales would tip in his favor. He would make
certain of that.

And he looked forward to that day.

Liam was off-balance. He took his father's next blow
in his gut, doubling over in pain. But he did not cry out.
Stoic acceptance of pain had also been beaten into him.
Another blow took him squarely in the jaw and sent him
flying backward onto a table. Liam fell hard on the wood
surface, sending mugs of ale and plates of food to the
floor, blood spurting from his mouth.

Shane towered over him. "Come, boyo, surely you have
not had enough?" he mocked. "Surely you do not yet
taste the sourness of defeat?"

Liam forced himself to sit up and slide to his feet. "One
day," he said, low, "I am going to kill you."

Shane laughed. "You'll have to make haste, if you think
to be the one to send me to my Maker."

Father and son stared at each other, Shane grinning,
Liam expressionless. Except for his eyes. They blazed
with hatred.

Shane shoved his bearded face close to his son's. "You
are weak," he growled. "To fight me over a worthless
woman, an English slut? She means naught! You think to
succeed me as the O'Neill? Hah! No Irishman will ever

proclaim you their chief, not with that weak English blood running in your veins! I do not wish for you to succeed me!''

Liam said nothing, wiping his bloody mouth with one sleeve. But his father's brutal words were a blow he could not help but feel. Still, he said, ''Leave the yellow-haired wench alone. The dark one is willing—she has been servicing our men all night.''

''Weak!'' Shane spit. ''I take what I want, when I want it, and I am the O'Neill!''

Suddenly another huge fist swung out and Liam's head exploded with pain. When he opened his eyes, he was on the floor, and bright lights danced sharply before him. The sounds of the tavern washed over him, drunken laughter and song, raucous conversation. Slowly he sat up, then levered himself to his feet. His father was dicing, the dark-haired whore hanging on to him. Despite the painful throbbing of his head, Liam smiled grimly. The little serving maid had fled. It was a small victory, but it was a victory nonetheless.

I

THE PAWN

1

Normandie, January 1571

*S*he had been forgotten.

Katherine knew that there was no other possible explanation for her having languished for almost six long years in the Abbé Saint Pierre-Eglise. Beneath her knees, the stone floor of the chapel was hard and as cold as ice. She murmured the prayers which she knew by heart but thought instead of the fact that none of the letters she had sent home to her father in Munster had been answered, not one. Finally, in despair, last summer she had sent a missive to her stepmother, Eleanor. That, too, had failed to elicit a response.

Katherine choked on both fear and despair. It was prime, the beginning of a new day, and although she prayed with the other sisters of the convent, today was the day that her life *must* begin anew. Today was the day that she must gather up all of her courage—today she would confront the abbess about her situation.

She had no choice. She was eighteen, and growing older with every passing moment. Another year had concluded, and in a few more months Katherine would be nineteen. She could not grow old in this secluded convent. She could *not*! She wanted to live. She wanted a husband, a home of her own, children. She was of the age when by now, she should have already had one or two or even three sturdy babes tumbling about her skirts. Oh, God. How had they forgotten her very existence?

Six years ago she had been too numb with grief to care when Eleanor suggested, no, insisted, that she enter a convent. Her family had been in disarray after suffering tremendous losses in the Battle of Affane back home in southern Ireland. Three hundred of her father's most loyal troops had been massacred by the forces of Tom Butler, the earl of Ormond, on the banks of the Blackwater River, and her father, the earl of Desmond himself, had been wounded and captured by Butler. But Katherine suffered more than just the defeat of her kinsmen and the capture of her father. For she had lost her betrothed that day.

Hugh Barry had been fatally wounded in the ghastly fray. Katherine had been betrothed to Hugh from the cradle. The Barrys were kinsmen, and she and Hugh had grown up together, Hugh being but a year older than she. He had been her childhood friend, her childhood sweetheart; he had bestowed her very first kiss on her. His death had destroyed her dreams, and with them, it seemed, her future.

Numb with grief, Katherine had obeyed her stepmother, glad to have a reprieve in a faraway convent before another marriage could be arranged. Losing Hugh had been especially difficult for Katherine to bear because the year before Affane, her own dear mother had died. The earl of Desmond had been Joan FitzGerald's third husband, and Katherine was their first and only child. Mother and daughter had been close. Katherine had yet to cease missing her.

But she had thought that a new marriage would be swiftly arranged, that she would spend but a year or two in the nunnery, and that she could be wed on her fifteenth birthday as planned. Yet Eleanor had only written to her once, later that first year, explaining that she was with the earl, who was imprisoned in the Tower and awaiting the queen's pardon. She had received no other word from her father or her stepmother in five and a half endless years.

And the truth of the matter was that Katherine was afraid.

The prayers were finished. Katherine crossed herself, murmured "Amen," and rose. She hung back, allowing the other ladies to file out ahead of her. They were all noblewomen like herself. Some were widowed, others were too poor to make marriages, or were one daughter too many for the family to bear. Silk and brocade gowns rustled as the ladies left the chapel. Outside it was frigidly cold, and Katherine gripped her worn, fur-lined mantle more closely to herself. She paused in the courtyard as the noblewomen entered the dining hall, where fresh breads and warm cakes, meats and cheese, and ale and wine were being served.

"Will you do it?"

Katherine turned, shivering, more from her nervousness about what she had to do than from the cold. She faced her dear friend and only confidante, Juliet, who would leave the convent in February, in spite of the winter weather, for her guardian had ordered her home to Cornwall. "Yes."

Juliet, startlingly fair of skin but dark-haired with a full, rosebud mouth, looked Katherine directly in the eye. "Surely the abbess will give you permission to leave now. How can she refuse you yet another time?"

Katherine's heart pounded harder. Immediately she took Juliet's hand. "I am afraid she will refuse my plea again," she admitted. Katherine had already petitioned the abbess twice before for permission to go home. The abbess had refused, explaining that not only did Katherine not have her father's permission, she had no escort, either.

Juliet smiled. "It would be wonderous to travel together. Oh, how I hope the abbess listens to your plea and judges fairly!"

Katherine flinched. She was very desperate, but she was not hopeful. Although the abbess was kind and well intentioned, and generally of a soft nature, she was a firm administrator, as she must be to oversee a nunnery filled with ladies entrusted to her care by rich and powerful families. But Katherine's will had never been stronger.

She must convince the abbess that she should return home now, even without her father's permission. She had prepared her arguments. It was 1571. A new year. A time for new beginnings.

The two girls crossed the courtyard, Katherine too preoccupied to speak or even notice the bitter winter chill, while Juliet chatted about how happy she was finally to be going home to Thurlstone. The dining hall rang with laughter and good cheer as the ladies enjoyed their first meal of the day. The gems in their rings glinted as they gestured to one another. Servants, many of whom had come with the noblewomen to the nunnery from their homes, waited upon them so that they did not have to rise for any reason. Lady Montaignier, the countess of Sur-Rigaud, had four small dogs panting with expectation at her feet. Ruby brooches in the form of small ribbons adorned their curly-haired heads. Indeed, all of the ladies were so well dressed and so thoroughly bejeweled, so catered to, so pampered, that had a visitor not known he was at an abbey, he would have thought himself to be in some great noblewoman's hall.

Katherine herself was one of the few exceptions. Her gowns were old and extensively mended. She had had nothing new since her fifteenth birthday—the year the funds she had arrived with had run out.

Fear slid over Katherine again. The abbess had been paid handsomely upon her arrival six years ago and had expected more funds to be forthcoming, as needed for Katherine's upkeep. When Katherine's pension was gone, the abbess had written to Katherine's father, but her subtle request for monies had been ignored. The earl had not bothered to respond to the abbess's letter. Other, more direct requests had gone unanswered. Fortunately the abbess had generously allowed Katherine to remain at the convent despite the fact that she had no pension.

Katherine's stomach churned. Whenever she thought about the earl's failure to communicate with the abbess over the matter of her support, she grew terribly dismayed.

Knowing her father, Katherine assumed that he must be at war with the Butlers again. It would be unlike Gerald to let the massacre of Affane go unavenged. He was too busy to think about his only daughter. Perhaps Eleanor was responsible for their ignoring her. She was but a few years older than Katherine, quite beautiful, and Gerald adored her. And she did not like Katherine.

Katherine's apprehension grew. She knew her father would not be pleased to see her when she arrived at Askeaton Castle, unbidden and unexpected. Perhaps he'd even be angry if Eleanor had indeed whispered against her in his ear. However, Katherine was willing to risk his wrath for the sake of realizing her dreams. But first she must persuade the abbess to allow her to leave the nunnery without her father's permission. It was a monumental task.

After the meal was done, Katherine and Juliet exchanged conspiratorial glances and separated. Katherine hurried not to the dorter where she slept, but to the antechamber where the abbess worked. Her anxiety increased. So much was at stake in the interview she would soon face. Katherine could not lose.

For she could not remain at the abbey any longer. She could not. Life was passing her by, and it was grossly unfair. This could not possibly be her fate. Her fate had to be something far more.

The abbess's plump face registered worry and concern. "You wish to go home." She sighed.

Katherine stood before the delicate mahogany secretaire where the mother superior was seated. "I cannot remain here. I am not suited for this life. I must return home, remind my father of my existence. Surely then he will arrange a marriage for me." Her gaze was direct but pleading. "Mother Superior, all I have ever wanted is a husband and a home of my own and several children. I am already eighteen. In another few years no man will want me."

The abbess doubted that. Katherine was an extraordinary beauty, in spite of her tall stature, with her perfectly oval face, her fine features and flawless ivory skin, her startling green eyes and dark wine red hair. She rose to her feet, the color returning to her cheeks. She was in a quandary.

A terrible quandary. She studied Katherine. "My dear, you have a few years left, trust in that, before you are old and gray."

Katherine began to protest.

The abbess lifted her hand, cutting her off. "I am well aware that you are not suited to this life. I have been aware of it almost from the first day you arrived here, a wild vixen of thirteen. I have no doubt now that you would be a superb wife. Clearly you are endowed by nature to bear many healthy sons. But what you ask is impossible. To send you home without your father's permission? I cannot do it!" But even as she spoke guilt twisted inside of her. For she knew Katherine would never receive her father's permission to leave. And she also knew what awaited Katherine—and was terribly uneasy.

Katherine wet her lips. When she spoke, her tone was strained. "Do not misunderstand me. I am very grateful for the charity you have bestowed upon me in allowing me to remain here. I am unhappy, but I am so grateful. You have been nothing but kind to me."

The abbess winced, but Katherine did not appear to notice.

"There is another reason for me to return to Ireland," Katherine continued urgently. "I am afraid that something is amiss. How could my father forget to send my pension to you? It makes no sense. I must return, I beg you, Mother, to learn why I have been forgotten like this. I cannot stay here. Perhaps my father needs me. Or—perhaps he is truly too busy to think of me at all."

The abbess felt a deep pang of sympathy for her young charge. Gently, the older woman said, "If your father needed you, he would send for you, my dear."

But the abbess did not know what else to say, or what to do, and she stroked her rosary, very worried. If ever there was a time to tell Katherine the truth, it was now, yet she had agreed to deceive her, for the girl's own peace of mind. The abbess had had little choice, for it was either that or release Katherine unprotected and impoverished onto the streets. It had been wrong then, and it was still wrong now, to withhold all the facts from her. But now, even more, the abbess did not dare tell Katherine the truth. Fear prevented her from doing so, fear and some higher sense that Fate was at her mysterious work here.

"I have been here for five and a half years," Katherine implored. "I never dreamed when I arrived that I would not be sent home after a year or two. Please, I must leave. I know that once I am home, all will be well, that Father will immediately seek to rectify my circumstances." Her gaze locked with the abbess's. "I can return with Juliet. There will never be a better time."

The abbess looked at her beautiful, intelligent, willful charge. "I would counsel most of my ladies to trust their fate to God," she said slowly, "and they would heed me. But you would not."

"I cannot obey you," Katherine said softly. "Not if you order me to remain."

And the abbess made up her mind. Not because Katherine had been unhappy for so many years, and it hurt her to see any of her ladies so distressed. Nor was it because if any woman deserved to live in the outside world, it was a woman like this. It was because she understood Katherine's meaning exactly. She knew her charge too well. If the abbess denied her permission to leave, Katherine would run away. The abbess almost swooned in terror at the very notion. A woman like Katherine traveling alone and unprotected, dear God. She would wind up terribly abused, perhaps even a concubine in some Turkish lord's harem. Their gazes held for a long moment. It was clear that Katherine would not take no for an answer. This, then, was the best and safest way.

She sighed. "I will allow you to leave, Katherine. But I must caution you. The world outside is not as it appears. You may return home only to be gravely disappointed. Perhaps your father will even send you back."

"Oh, Mother, thank you!" Katherine was smiling widely, ignoring the thinly veiled warning. "Thank you for your concern, but he will not send me back, I promise you that!" Impulsively she embraced the abbess.

"Very well," the abbess said. Beaming, Katherine thanked her again. After she was gone, the abbess returned to her desk, picked up a quill, and dipped it into an ink-horn. She no longer smiled. Her face was lined with worry. She was too soft. She should have refused her charge. But then Katherine would have run away, and the abbess would not allow that. The convent was not a prison, and the world was hardly a safe place.

The abbess trembled. It was not too late to tell Katherine some of the truth—or even all of it. Except . . . she did not dare. Like a puppet on a string, she must obey her own masters. And trust to a higher Fate.

The abbess bent over the parchment and, very carefully, she began to write, explaining in great detail what had just occurred and what Katherine was about to do.

Juliet's guardian had sent six men to escort her home. With his men came a short letter in which Richard Hixley expressed some disapproval about the fact that Katherine would travel with his niece. It was not difficult for Katherine to understand why. Juliet was a rich English heiress, and Katherine was but an Irish one. This was not the first time she had encountered snobbery from the English. Some Englishmen considered the Irish naught but a race of savages.

It did not matter. What mattered was that she was finally going home, and in the past month, time had crept by at an infuriatingly slow pace. Katherine could not wait to set foot upon the fertile ground of southern Ireland. She could not wait to reach her home, Askeaton Castle, a stout stone fortress built in medieval times and set upon an island in the River Deel.

The convent was less than a half day's carriage ride from Cherbourg, where the small ship they would cross the Channel in awaited them. The road to Cherbourg was not well used, and the hours again dragged by. But toward nooning the monotony of their short trip was broken. A group of traveling players passed them on the road. One of the men was darkly handsome, and quite bold and brazen. He only had eyes for Katherine. He wished to make her acquaintance, and did not seem willing to take "no" for an answer. Katherine tried to ignore him, but was flattered and bemused by his interest. Finally, professing undying grief, making his talent for theatrics quite clear, he had doffed his plumed hat and he and his troupe of players moved on.

The girls and their escorts arrived at the harbor and were quickly boarded onto the ship. The man in charge of their party, Sir William Redwood, advised them to remain within their cabin for the duration of the short Channel crossing. He informed them that they would set sail at first light the next morning and come abreast of Dover if the winds were favorable by the next night, or, at the outside, by dawn of the following day. Juliet thanked him prettily, and then the two girls were left alone in their cabin.

Katherine walked to a porthole and stared out at the dusky water of the bay. Twilight was creeping over the harbor. A star twinkled vaguely. She was trembling with elation. Home. Before it had been a dream. Soon it would be reality. She was on the precipice of a new beginning— and she could barely wait for the happy future that was surely hers.

Katherine had been sound asleep. Now she jerked up with a cry. She had been dreaming of the meadows in springtime in Munster. In her dreams, Hugh had been alive and she had been a young bride. She shook her head, to free herself of the foolish dream, noticing the bright sunlight streaming through the cabin's single porthole. It was well past dawn from the look of it. They had set sail some time ago, but neither she nor Juliet had been awake or aware of it. Katherine was perplexed and faintly uneasy. What had caused her to awaken so abruptly? And what were the strange scratching noises above her head?

And then she heard a sound she had never heard before. A deafening boom. No one had to inform her as to what it was. She knew, instantly. It was a cannon.

Katherine's heart seemed to stop. She prayed to Jesus, God, and Sweet Mary that she was still asleep, still dreaming. And then another boom sounded, even closer and more loudly than the one before, and she knew, dear Lord,

that it was no dream. *Oh, God—they were under attack.*
"Juliet!"

She raced to the porthole as Juliet shot upright, but
could see nothing but an incredibly bright winter sun hanging over the endless, amazingly calm gray seas. If ever
there had been an illusion of a perfect day, this was it.

Another boom sounded, and this time Katherine heard
the sound of wood splintering before she clapped her
hands to her ears. It had sounded as if an entire mast had
been shorn right off the deck.

"We are under attack," Katherine cried, turning to face
Juliet, who was sitting motionless, as white as death, upon
her bunk.

"Who?" Juliet croaked. "Who would attack this ship?"

Katherine's dazed mind began to function. Juliet was a
rich heiress, and she herself was the earl of Desmond's
daughter. Oh, God. Pirates infested the waters of the Channel, as well as those off of France, Spain, and both England and Ireland. Preying upon any cargo of value, even
if it be human. "Oh, God, have mercy," Katherine
whispered.

Juliet slid to her feet and ran to the porthole.
"Katherine?"

Katherine could not speak. And then from the deck
above she could hear men shouting in panic, and the word
they shouted was "Pirates!"

"There is nothing to see!" Juliet cried, peering over
Katherine's shoulder.

Then another explosion made the girls cling to one another as the ship bucked like a wild horse. They tumbled
to the floor together, rolling across it. Men were shrieking,
and something huge and hard crashed against the deck just
above them. The ship groaned as if alive and in great pain.
Muskets were firing now, and Katherine could smell the
acrid powder. She prayed it was the crew firing, defending
the ship from the marauders. Then she realized that a man
was shouting, "Fire aft! Fire aft!" and soon the cry was
taken up by some dozen others.

Katherine and Juliet gripped each other, both pale with
fright. "What are we going to do?" Juliet whispered.

Katherine tried to think through her thick, cloying fear. "We must stay below. With the door barred." Images of the dirty, savage pirates descending in a vicious horde upon them assailed her. She felt faint.

"But—what if the ship goes down? We will drown! What if it is sinking even now!"

Katherine realized then that, no matter what happened, they were in the gravest jeopardy. If the ship sank, and they remained below, they would die. If they went above, looking for Sir William and the others, they might very well die as men were undoubtedly dying even now. And if the ship were captured . . . Katherine did not want to think about it. She must not think about it, or she would lose her very fragile control, and give in to mindless terror. She must be calm.

"We are not sinking," Katherine said as normally as possible. "If we were, we would hear the men screaming in terror."

"Yes, you are right," Juliet said. Her fingernails were digging into Katherine's wrist even through the sleeve of her nightclothes. "And the ship has righted itself."

Katherine climbed to her feet, legs apart, and braced for any sudden lurching. "We will stay below here," Katherine decided as Juliet also rose. "Until something happens to make us think the ship is sinking. Then we will go up. Together. Not before."

Juliet nodded, speechless, gripping Katherine's hand.

Katherine inhaled, forcing herself to appear calm. Then she turned to the porthole and froze. A ship had appeared in her line of vision, a big black galleon, its huge white sails billowing, black guns and cannon glistening in the sunlight. It was racing toward them. Nothing she had ever seen had appeared more threatening, more lethal. Even as Katherine watched, it came closer and closer still.

Juliet saw the pirate ship, too, and she whimpered.

The two girls stood at the porthole, unable to move, stiff with terror, vainly trying to fight panic, listening to the explosions tearing apart their ship, explosions which were coming with increasing frequency. The vessel had begun to list again badly to starboard. Chaos seemed to reign on the deck above. The battle seemed to go on forever. Time stood still.

And then, abruptly, the cannons stopped.

Katherine and Juliet were gripping one another's hands so tightly that they were locked together. The two girls' eyes met. Suddenly they disengaged their numb fingers. "Is it over?" Juliet whispered.

Katherine did not know—but then the sound of musket fire began in frenzied earnest. And shouts, raised and triumphant. And their ship lurched hard, as if pushed. And suddenly swords clanged, again and again, viciously.

"They have boarded," Katherine cried, now mindless with fear. "They have boarded us!"

Juliet sobbed once, her hand against her mouth.

Katherine swallowed hard. "Juliet—you know what will happen to us."

Tears filled Juliet's eyes. "But afterward . . . we will be ransomed."

"Will you want to live without your virtue?"

Juliet inhaled. "I don't know. Katherine, I am only fifteen. I do know that I don't want to die."

Katherine knew she did not want to die either, but she had heard stories, and she imagined that, a few hours from now, both she and Juliet would wish themselves dead. "We have no weapons," she said with surprising calm, closing her eyes briefly.

"We cannot fight pirates," Juliet responded.

"Not to fight them," Katherine said, regarding her friend. "But to end our own lives."

Their gazes held. They did not speak again. There was nothing to say. Even if they could find the courage to kill themselves before the pirates plundered the ship and captured them, they had no weapons with which to do so. There was nothing for them to do, then, but be brave and await their fate.

An hour later it began. Someone tried to open the door to their cabin. When he failed, he called out in a foreign tongue. Katherine and Juliet did not speak, did not move, did not even breathe for fear of being detected. The intruder stomped away.

Both girls were now dressed, having realized that they had no wish to be captured in their nightclothes. Juliet turned to Katherine. "He was speaking Gaelic. Could he be Irish? Or was he a Scot?"

"I am not sure," Katherine said unsteadily. Suddenly tears formed in her eyes. "If you think the fact that I am Irish will spare us if they are Irish, you are wrong. Pirates are not loyal to anyone, Juliet, except themselves, surely you know that."

"Sssh!! He is coming back!"

The girls froze, arm in arm, as two men spoke to each other outside their door. And then an object was banged upon the door and wood splintered. The blade of an ax appeared through the shredded wood.

Katherine pulled Juliet closer. She was older than her friend and somehow she felt responsible for her. She would protect Juliet if she could. But her knees were still horribly weak, and her legs were shaking.

A hand darted through the wood and the bolt was shoved aside. The door burst open. Two seamen in black breeches and plain tunics burst into the room. They were huge men, carrying swords and wearing daggers, their weapons and clothing splotched with blood. The pirates froze, surprised to see the girls.

Then they exchanged glances. One of them was huge and baldheaded, and he stepped forward, his gaze going from Katherine to Juliet and then back to Katherine again. Katherine stepped in front of Juliet. She and the bald pirate stared at one another. Katherine was tensed, awaiting his lecherous assault. But it never came.

He only spoke to the other pirate, and when he did, he spoke in Gaelic, which Juliet could not understand but Katherine could. He said, "We'll bring them above to the captain. He'll be pleased with this."

Katherine's heart was in her mouth, beating a mile a minute. "Who is your captain?" she asked with false bravado. "I demand to see him immediately!"

If the seaman was surprised that she had understood

him and spoke Gaelic herself, he did not show it. "Don't fret, lass. The captain is waiting to meet you."

Katherine took Juliet's hand, hoping to give her courage to face their impending ordeal, but then the pirates separated them, each man grabbing one of the girls. Katherine cried out, attempting to jerk free of her captor, but he took her elbow firmly in his hand. And he pulled her forward and into the narrow hall and up the stairs, Juliet following with the other man.

Katherine gasped when they stepped out upon the deck. It was unnaturally still. But the pirates were everywhere, clad in their short breeches, wielding their long swords. She saw that the French crew were all in irons, and that several of the men had been wounded, perhaps seriously. Sir William Redwood and his men were also bound in manacles and under guard. Sir William appeared unhurt and furious. But relief filled his eyes when he saw that the girls were still unharmed.

Katherine's gaze swept the deck. Part of the stern had suffered from the fire, the wooden deck charred and blackened, smoke still hanging in the air. Sections of the ship's railing had been destroyed as well. One of the largest masts had been shorn in two, and lay like a huge broken tree across half of the middle decks, the great canvas sail forming puffy piles around it. And then when she gazed at the topmost deck, she saw him.

Without being told, she knew that he was the master of these pirates.

Katherine stared, her heart beating madly. He stood on the forecastle in pale hose and thigh-high black boots, a loose white linen shirt, its laces open, fluttering about him. He was a huge man, far taller than Katherine, broad of shoulder, narrow of hip, long and powerful of leg. His hair was gold, cropped short, and it was brighter than the sun. He had one hand on his sheathed sword and he stood easily, riding the ship the way the ship rode the swells of the sea. He surveyed the deck below him as if he surveyed his kingdom.

Katherine felt his power and saw his arrogance and she

hated him for all he had done and for all he was about to do.

And then she realized that he surveyed her as well.

Across the charred deck, his cool questing eyes held hers. Katherine froze. Never in her life had she been more vulnerable. He stared, and between them she felt an invisible tightening, as if a powerful cable was being winched tight and tighter still. Katherine could not breathe.

Slowly, he smiled. And she felt as if she were some pitiful earthbound hare and he the great gyrfalcon, slowly circling above her, preparing himself for the kill.

Katherine dug in her heels as the sailor abruptly propelled her forward, toward him, and marched her across the decks. "No," she said, raw panic chasing away any show of courage which she might make. Raw panic, and raw fear.

The golden pirate watched her, no longer smiling.

"No," Katherine cried again, balking like a mule.

With the slightest inclination of his golden head, he signaled his sailor and the man jerked her forward and hauled her up the set of steps to the deck where he stood. The boat was rocking and Katherine was weak, not just with terror, but from the terrible ordeal of withstanding the long battle, and when the sailor released her, her knees finally gave way and she sank down onto the deck at the pirate's feet.

Katherine gripped the wooden floorboards, willing herself to rise, but her body would not obey and she could do no more than look up.

He gazed down at her from his incredible height. The wind whipped a few short gold curls away from his stunning face, revealing high, hard cheekbones, a strong, determined jaw, and an arrow-straight, finely chiseled nose. The wind did not cease, pushing at his loose, open shirt, molding it against his body. A wide swath of his broad, bronzed chest was revealed by his open laces, while the fine linen fabric outlined the length of his torso, his concave stomach, and the narrowness of his hips. The fluttering of his shirt also revealed the very heavy bulge of his manhood between his thighs. Katherine sucked in her breath, praying he was one of those fops who still wore a codpiece. If not, he would kill her when he raped her.

Glinting gray eyes met her gaze—and Katherine could not look away.

"I am Liam O'Neill," he said, his smile hard and satisfied. "The captain of this ship."

Katherine could not respond—could not remove her gaze from his.

Something began to smolder in his eyes. His smile widened—but it was far from reassuring. "What is it that I have captured? Such a pretty prize. A veritable treasure, it seems, a gem amongst so much lead and ore. Come, sweetheart, come."

And he reached down for her.

2

*B*efore Katherine could react, the golden pirate was bending over her and, with a grip of steel, pulled her to her feet.

Her wide eyes locked with his. Satisfaction gleamed there. Abruptly Katherine regained her senses and she yanked her arm back. To little avail; his grip was not broken. He smiled, his teeth flashing white.

"Unhand me!" Katherine cried, rising hysteria sounding in her tone.

Surprise filled his gray gaze—quickly followed by amusement. "As you wish, mistress."

The instant she was free she backed away from him, rubbing her wrist, never taking her eyes from his face. He regarded her with lazy anticipation. He was supremely confident. Katherine realized that she was shaking visibly. How could he not be certain of victory? He was the captain of the pirates, the king of this thieving lot, and she was his helpless prisoner. Her glance shot to the right, to the cold winter gray swells of the sea.

"There is no escape, mistress," the pirate said softly. "Unless you think to jump to your death?"

That thought was just occurring to her. He recognized her intent in that same moment. As Katherine turned with the intention of hurling herself to a watery grave, he leapt upon her. She was pulled against his muscular body from behind—and wrapped in his embrace.

She screamed in impotence and fear and anger, twisting,

desperate to escape. His iron grip only fueled her anger and encouraged her to increase her futile efforts at resistance. She grew so faint from her exertions that she feared she might collapse in his arms. Finally he grew bored. Abruptly he tightened his arms around her, and she was forced to become absolutely still.

"Better," he breathed against her neck and ear. "I can not allow you to escape, mistress; in truth, you have only succeeded in whetting my appetite further."

Katherine trembled. Would he rape her now—on the deck—publicly? "Please."

"Please, what?" His arms were still wrapped around her waist. When he spoke, his mouth brushed her neck, and sparks of unwelcome sensation seemed to ignite there. His body, pressed against hers, was far too warm, and far too hard. Katherine had never before been held by a man. It was shocking. It was terrifying. Katherine found it difficult to breathe. "Please, let me go." She was acutely aware of every male inch of him.

He turned her to face him. "Come, sweetheart, I am not going to hurt you. Do not be afraid."

Katherine jerked her arm free of his. But suddenly she was hopeful, and it showed in her eyes.

His beautiful mouth curled. "You misunderstand me. I will not hurt you, but surely you do not think to dissuade me from the pleasures of your body? Have you not heard it said that all is fair in love and war? Do you not understand that to the victors go the spoils—and that you are, by far, the loveliest treasure I have won in some time?"

Katherine stood very still. "This is not love."

His pause was brief, barely discernible. "No."

"And to attack a small ship like this, 'tis not war. 'Tis piracy, 'tis savage aggression," Katherine cried.

His gaze was hooded, but his teeth glimmered white again. "But I *am* a savage, fair lady, and wars of words, while amusing, cannot deter me from your charms and my *evil* design."

Katherine was rigid, anger flaring and mingling with her fear. "How does one argue with a savage?"

"A difficult task," he agreed.

"You must release me! My father—"

He cut her words off. "No."

Katherine looked into his cold gray eyes and knew that she would not be able to move this man. Hatred welled up within her. *"Damn you."*

His response was a flash of white teeth and a short, rich chuckle. "From the lips of a near nun?"

"You play God with my life!" she shouted furiously.

"I am only intent on bedding you, mistress, not murdering you."

" 'Tis the same."

His glance grew speculative. "You would jump to your death before lying with me? Or perhaps, afterward?"

Her glance strayed to the sea. She knew she did not have the courage to do it, but she lied. "Yes."

"Suicide is a greater sin than fornication." His glance impaled hers.

He blurred before her very eyes. "Then perhaps you will feel some remorse in the end."

He tilted up her chin. "How very foolish you are. I will not let you jump to your death. And I shall show you just how foolish you are."

"No," Katherine said, shaking her head. "No. There is nothing you can do or say to convince me to lie with you."

His smile dawned, slow and bright. For a moment he did not speak. "On the morrow, Katherine, you will be whispering words of sweet, undying love in my ear whilst begging me not to leave your bed."

Katherine gasped. She was incredulous. She could only stare up at his beautiful, arrogant face.

He turned to the big, bald pirate who had brought her up from below. "Escort the ladies to the *Sea Dagger,* Macgregor. And if a single hair is missing from either of their heads, *your* bald pate will roll into the sea without further ado."

"Aye, Captain," Macgregor said, apparently unperturbed by the threat.

And as the brawny sailor took her arm and escorted her across the deck toward the warship that was hooked to the trader, Katherine was relieved. Their first confrontation was over, she had not been raped—she had thus far survived.

But he had made his intentions clear. She was being removed to the pirate ship and sometime this evening he would take her to his bed. She had gained but a momentary respite.

But a brief respite was better than none at all. Some of Katherine's fear began to subside. Surely, if she were very clever, she could extricate herself from a fate worse than death.

Macgregor left Juliet and Katherine in the captain's cabin alone. Katherine was shocked. Juliet was also agape. This was a pirate's den?

The cabin was intricately paneled in teakwood. Dozens of beautiful rugs covered most of the gleaming oak floor. Under one of the cabin's five portholes were some half dozen oversize Turkish pillows, embroidered and tasseled. A small tufted ottoman in emerald green silk made it appear that someone, perhaps the pirate captain, actually reclined Muslim-style upon those pillows.

A large, nearly black, wood dining table, its heavy pedestal boasting four clawed feet, graced the far end of the room. Six leather-backed Spanish chairs surrounded it. One end of the table was used as a desk, for it was covered with maps and charts, inkhorn and quill, and books.

One wall boasted a bookcase almost as high as the ceiling. Every inch was crammed with leather-bound volumes. Another wall held an exquisite pine armoire. Two delicate French chairs with embroidered blue cushions were on either side.

At the other end of the cabin was a bed. It was fit for one of the state rooms at Hampton Court. The canopy was a royal purple damask, the underside pleated gold silk. The curtains were of royal purple velvet, pulled back by heavy red-and-gold cords. Gold-and-red down quilts covered the bed, and embroidered pillows similar to those Katherine had worked upon in the convent were strewn about it. Katherine did not recognize the coat-of-arms above the headboard, but noted the fleur-de-lis and recognized that it was French.

There was also a large, boldly carved chest at the foot of the bed. She recognized the Celtic design atop the padlocked lid instantly—the chest had come from her homeland. And upon the walls of the cabin were numerous works of art.

Katherine turned to face Juliet, who stood in front of the door. "What kind of place is this?"

"Katherine—undoubtedly this very room is a testimony to all the ships the pirate has plundered."

Katherine realized that Juliet was correct. This room was evidence of many years of savage theft and bloody mayhem committed upon the high seas. This room was proof positive of his evil pirate ways. Then Katherine saw the bed.

She had remarked it before, of course. But in passing. Now she stared at it. Riveted. In her mind's eye she saw herself upon the soft mattress, thrashing, the pirate on top of her, ravishing her, laughing. She cried out and rushed across the room, past Juliet. Wildly she tried the door, but it was barred from the outside.

Juliet put her arm around her. "Katherine, what are we going to do?"

"I don't know. I am so afraid." Katherine looked around, then finally chose to sit in one of the heavy Spanish chairs. Her eyes widened when she grasped the chair and it did not move. It was tied down to the floor. She realized that everything in the cabin must be similarly secured. She slid into the chair and closed her eyes.

She felt extraordinarily tired, but her heart was pounding, too, in anticipation of the horror that was to come and from knowing that she must still attempt to defend herself. For she did not believe the pirate's declaration that he would not hurt her; such a statement, coming from such a man, was ludicrous. Katherine knew that she must reveal herself as the earl of Desmond's daughter immediately. Surely he would leave her virtue intact once he learned her identity, and give her over to her father for a handsome ransom.

Katherine recalled the pirate's smoldering gray eyes. She had never seen a man look at her in such a way before.

She shook. Instinct warned her that the pirate would toy with her as a cat did a mouse, then take her, ransom or no. She crossed herself, praying that she was wrong.

A moment later he entered the cabin. Katherine jerked upright as he closed the heavy door behind him. Juliet darted to where Katherine sat, but he did not even glance at her. His gaze slid over Katherine. Clearly he undressed her with his eyes. Katherine's breathing was shallow. Her heart felt as if it might leap right out of her breast. She flushed in response to his insolence.

Finally he turned his gaze from her to Juliet and crooked his finger. "You, my lady, come."

Juliet froze.

Katherine was horrified—what did he intend for her younger friend? Surely he would not abuse them both? She was on her feet, in front of Juliet. "S-she stays w-with me."

He raised one of his brows and laughed. "How brave you are, mistress. But you do not give orders upon my ship. Lady, come."

Juliet did not move, and Katherine gripped her arm, preventing her from obeying him. "What do you intend?"

He held her eyes. "Not what you are so obviously thinking, sweetheart. I have no need of your friend—your charms will occupy me well this night. But unless you wish an audience, the lady leaves."

Katherine swallowed, her color higher. She did not release Juliet. "C-captain."

He looked amused.

"You surely think to ransom me?"

His gaze moved from her eyes, to her full mouth, then down to her bosom, flattened by the current style of dress. Katherine's nipples were tight. From breathing so hard and fast. Did he now notice the shabby state of her clothing, or the charms he had so recently referred to? " 'Tis not what you must think!" she cried in a rush. "I am no serving girl; I am the daughter of an earl!"

He lifted one tawny brow slightly.

"I swear upon the cross and all that is holy," Katherine said frantically, "I am the earl of Desmond's daughter."

He said, "Lady Juliet. Do you wish to be removed in a forcible manner from this cabin?"

Juliet shook her head no, freed herself from Katherine's grasp, and quickly walked toward the pirate. Katherine was panicked, aware that her fate was soon to be sealed. The captain of the *Sea Dagger* opened the door. Macgregor waited there with supreme indifference. Juliet was handed over to the seaman, and then the door was closed and the pirate faced Katherine, a slow smile spreading across his face. He moved toward her.

Katherine lost the last of her good sense. As he came forward she flew toward the door. He caught her easily as she tried to rush past him, and a moment later she was pressed against the very door she wished to escape through. But his huge hands held her shoulders firmly, pinning her to the wood, and one of his thighs was suddenly between her legs, much too intimately. Katherine could not move.

"So foolish, sweetheart. I am not going to hurt you. I would never hurt a flower such as you. Pluck, yes. Hurt, no."

Katherine tried to compose herself in the face of his soft, seductive tone—no easy task when pressed against his formidable body. "I am the earl's daughter," she said desperately. "He will kill you for this trespass."

"Desmond can hardly kill me," he said easily. He did not appear to be moved at all by the fact of her parentage.

"Then you do not know him," Katherine insisted.

"I know him," he said, and then he touched her face with one hand. His palm stroked her cheek and jaw. Katherine froze, wishing he would cease his butterfly touch.

"And soon I will know you," he whispered, his mouth coming close to hers. "Soon I must know you."

Katherine gasped then, for his huge phallus brushed against the joining place of her thighs.

He murmured, "You are a great beauty, mistress, the kind of woman to haunt a man's dreams."

Katherine's gaze flew to his. He had not moved away

from her and she was acutely aware of his virility, and what would soon happen if she did not somehow defend herself. And for one single moment, she did not, could not, move.

Abruptly she writhed and jerked against him, but he only tightened his grip upon her. "You have hardly dreamed of me, pirate, for we have just met!"

He grinned briefly. "I am going too fast. That is not my intention." But he did not move away from her. "Relax, sweetheart, relax. You cannot win in any love play that occurs between us. I am far too experienced. I am not going to hurt you. I am going to please you."

Katherine was frozen but a moment. "You think to steal my virtue and not hurt me? 'Tis impossible! And a man such as you could never please me—not in any way."

He laughed. And as he laughed, he slid one arm behind her, drawing her even farther into his embrace. Again he touched her face, his fingertips fluttering across her skin. "Foolish—innocent—green."

Katherine trembled. His tone was far too soft. "Release me," she whispered.

"I can—and shall—please you, darling, in every possible way." His regard held hers.

She could hardly guess at his meaning, but she blushed. Crazy, jumbled images of a man and woman entwined rushed through her mind, the man big and bold and blond.

"There will only be one moment of pain," he murmured. "And then there will be so much pleasure that you will forget all else but your desire."

"No! Never!" she cried, forcing aside her imaginings.

His answer was a smile. "Taste me," he said, and then he bent forward and brushed her mouth with his.

Katherine was unyielding. She tried to beat at his chest. But it was impossible. Quickly he caught her wrists, immobilizing her fully. His mouth was firm but gentle. He began to tease the seam of her lips with his tongue. Katherine realized that she was not breathing. When she did not open for him, he began, very gently, to nibble on the fullness of her lower lip. And all the while his manhood pulsed there between her legs, where he had lodged himself.

Her pulse pounded so hard she thought her heart might explode.

Katherine finally gasped for air, no longer able to deny her lungs. The pirate made a thick sound deep in his throat while he filled her completely. Katherine cried out, struggling anew, to no avail. His tongue swept the depths of her mouth. It was a stunning act of possession.

Katherine's knees gave way and she sagged, but his iron grip prevented her from falling to the floor. And suddenly he tore his mouth from hers.

Dazed, Katherine stared into his eyes. She could not yet move. No one had ever hinted to her that such a kind of kiss was possible.

Katherine realized that she clung to his broad shoulders, and she tried to push him away. He allowed her to put a small distance between their heated bodies. She forced her thoughts away from the hot, hard feel of him, and spoke. It was not true, but she said, "My father will not pay a ransom if you abuse me."

He smiled, bent his head, and kissed her neck. Katherine gasped. His mouth moved around her throat, forming an imaginary necklace with his kisses. Her heart beat harder, so hard he must surely hear it. He lifted his head, smiling again. "There shall be no abuse, sweetheart. I would never abuse a woman such as you."

"You do not take me seriously!" she cried.

"No, I take you very seriously, indeed," he murmured, holding her gaze.

Katherine could not guess at his meaning, but was certain there was more to his words than she could comprehend. "Then free me, unharmed," she said.

His gaze flickered over her face, then over her breasts. "I cannot."

Katherine cried out. "Why not?" It was a demand.

His jaw flexed. He was deadly earnest now, and it was hard to believe that just a few moments earlier he had been smiling. His fingers brushed her jaw once again. "Because you are the loveliest woman I have ever seen, and I want you very badly."

Katherine was incredulous. "But you cannot have me!

I am not a pretty red apple, to be plucked and devoured on a whim. I am Katherine FitzGerald, daughter of the earl of Desmond, a noblewoman born and bred. *You cannot have me!*''

His gaze held hers, brilliant, diamondlike. It was a moment before he spoke. ''To the contrary, not only can I have you, I shall,'' he said. ''You do not seem to understand. We are not in Desmond. We are on my ship. On the open sea. I am king here, master of everyone and everything you see. The moment you passed into my hands, you belonged to me. Katherine, I have no intention of hurting you. I do not rape virgins. You fear me now, but before the night is through, I shall prove your fear misplaced.''

For a moment she stared at him, speechless. Just past his shoulder she saw the big bed. ''Think of the ransom I can bring! S-surely that is worth more than a passing pleasure!''

The corners of his lips lifted ever so slightly. ''Did you not hear a word I said? I have no wish to ransom you.'' He lifted her chin. His gaze moved to her lips. ''Ransom is the last thing on my mind.''

Fully aware that he intended to kiss her again, she shouted, ''Let me go! *Please.*''

He stared at her, something flickering in his eyes. His fingertip skidded across her cheek again. Then he looked directly into her eyes. ''You do not understand. And I am sorry, Katherine, to be the one to inform you of the facts, but even if I wished to ransom you, which I do not, a ransom is impossible.''

Katherine tensed, suddenly far more afraid than she had been before. ''What are you saying?'' she whispered.

He hesitated, then grew brisk. ''Your father is the queen's prisoner, has been such for many years.''

Katherine stared, unable to make a sound, unable even to breathe.

His gaze searched hers. ''FitzGerald was convicted of high treason, his lands and title forfeit. In fact, there is no earl of Desmond, no earl, no earldom, just a prisoner in disgrace.''

Katherine stared at him in shock and disbelief.

3

*K*atherine's mind screamed, *It cannot be true!*

The pirate broke into her thoughts. "So you see, Katherine, your father can neither pay a ransom, nor help you."

She met his gaze, her green eyes wild. "I do not believe you. You are lying!"

He remained calm. "I am not lying. I speak what the whole world knows. I speak the facts."

Katherine refused to believe him. She could not believe him. Her father a prisoner of the Crown, stripped of his lands and title? Oh, God! No, it could not be possible.

His tone became more gentle. "But your father is alive, Katherine. He was not hanged. I believe he still resides in Southwark, where he is under house arrest."

Katherine jerked, her bosom heaving. "Southwark?" She was numb. Southwark, not Desmond. Her father was a prisoner of the Crown, forced to remain in London—in exile.

"Understandably you are shocked," he said, watching her closely.

And Katherine hated him. She hated him for his indifference, for his intentions, and for having harbored and then revealed such ugly news. For having revealed the horrible truth. "You understand nothing about me," she snarled. Tears welled up in her eyes. "Get away from me!"

His jaw tightened. Coolly he turned away from her. Immediately Katherine sagged against the wall, beginning to shake. If her father was a prisoner of the Crown, stripped of all that he possessed, then her departure from the convent had been all for nothing. If her father were in such disgrace, in such exile, then she herself was reduced to disgrace and exile, too. For without a title and a dowry, no man would want her. Suddenly she had no future, no dreams, no hope. Suddenly she was Mistress Nobody.

"Drink this."

Katherine looked up wildly, saw the pirate handing her a glass of brandy. "No."

"How headstrong you are," he said softly. "Do not be a fool. Drink." And he gripped her chin and pushed the rim of the glass to her lips.

Katherine choked when he tilted the glass, succeeding in getting a few drops of the fiery liquid down her throat. She swatted his hand away. Brandy splashed over his bronzed skin. His mouth tightened, anger appeared in his eyes. "I am not a gentle man. Nor am I kind. But I am trying to go slowly with you," he said. "To tame you as I might a wild mare. I have no wish to break you, Katherine. Despite the fact that my lust remains huge."

She took a deep breath. "I am not a horse, to be bridled and trained."

"But you are a woman, one without a protector, and like all women, you need a man, both to protect and firmly guide you."

"And you think to be that man? To be my protector?" she shouted, furious. "To rein me as you will?"

"I am not giving you any choice."

Livid, Katherine tried to push past him, but he caught her with one powerful arm, crushing her to his chest. He set the brandy down without releasing her. Katherine stiffened instantly. The last place she wished to be was in his arms, pressed against his hard, aroused body. She squirmed to separate herself from him.

"I have a very lusty nature," he said very softly. "And I suspect we suit each other."

"We do not suit! Take your lust elsewhere," she hissed.

"No."

She looked into his hard gray gaze and understood him

completely. He did not care for her or her feelings. He knew she had no family, no name, to protect her now. He was conscienceless, and would take advantage of her predicament. Nothing would, or could, stop him from ruining her when he chose to do so. It was but a matter of time.

Katherine wished she could think clearly. She still had to fight her way through a maze of shock and disbelief and fear. Surely there was a way out of her dilemma. After all, she was Katherine FitzGerald. Surely there was something left, some small amount of hoarded money, some secret parcel of land. There were her uncles and kinsmen. And there was her proud, ancient name. "Unhand me," she said.

He did as she asked.

Aware that her heart was racing again, Katherine backed away from him. He did not move, watching her with eyes at once cold and hot. The coldness, she knew, came from his lack of a heart. The heat came from his loins.

Katherine put the heavy dining table between them. She gripped the back of one of the Spanish chairs. Perhaps, just perhaps, he lied, although she no longer thought so. It would explain why there had been no pension for the past three and a half years, why her father had not answered any of the abbess's inquiries. In any case, she must now learn all that she could. "Tell me about my father."

He shrugged gracefully and stalked toward her. Katherine froze, but he was not pursuing her. He settled one lean hip upon the edge of the table and faced her. "What is it you wish to know?"

"Everything." Her voice shook. "I cannot believe that he has been convicted of treason. That he is a prisoner . . . in disgrace."

The pirate regarded her intently, so intently that Katherine looked away. Finally he spoke. "After Affane, Butler imprisoned your father at Clonmel. The queen ordered them both to court, and your father was immediately tossed into the Tower. He remained there for two years. The queen and her Council were undecided about what to do with him. She was angry with Tom Butler, of course, for his part in their feud, but he was pardoned."

"Of course," Katherine said stiffly. Tom Butler, the earl of Ormond, was not just her father's hated enemy, but Queen Elizabeth's cousin and thus a favorite of hers as well. Katherine leaned forward, toward the pirate captain, her hands splayed out on the table, almost touching his. "But why?" she cried earnestly. "My father has transgressed before—but was always pardoned! Why did the queen not pardon him when she pardoned Ormond?"

"The queen was younger when she pardoned your father," Liam said flatly. "And reluctant, I believe, to take on the issue of Ireland. This time she felt she must begin to bring the Irish lords to heel, especially your father, who refused to accept her authority on his lands. Do not forget, Ormond is a loyal subject. Nonetheless, her Council was divided. Factions formed. Some, led by Dudley and Sir William Cecil, favored a pardon and the return of your father to Desmond. Others, led by Ormond, favored his removal—forever."

Katherine clawed the table. "And Black Tom Butler won."

He nodded. "But with your father's help. After two years, he was allowed to reside in Southwark, under guard and with restrictions. As you can well understand, he tried to escape, but the sea captain who was to aid him turned Judas. I believe the queen herself was most happy that they finally had some substantial charge with which to rid themselves of Desmond. He was tried for treason and convicted, his lands and title forfeit, two years ago. As far as I know, he is still under arrest at St. Leger House in Southwark."

Katherine was dazed by what he had told her—dazed and dismayed. The refrain drummed through her brain: she was Mistress Nobody now, Mistress Nobody. "You are telling me that my father has been a prisoner ever since Affane."

He nodded, watching her. "In the end, the need to bring southern Ireland under the Crown's control, once and for all, won the day. As your father was the most powerful lord in Ireland, and the most defiant, his fate was doomed the moment Butler took him prisoner at Affane."

Katherine closed her eyes, giving in to a moment of despair. Her father had been in one prison or another ever since she had left southern Ireland for France. For six years, he had been confined. And he had lost everything. How unjust it was. "I cannot believe this," she whispered. "Dear Lord, I cannot." And now she had lost everything, too. Now she had no future. No gentleman would want her—no one but this pirate would want her now.

"You must face the truth if you wish to survive." His piercing tone brought her eyes to his face. His gaze held hers. "Listen closely to one who knows. I am a man of the sea, without either clan or country, and in order for me to survive, I must know every happenstance of import worldwide—and my actions are directed accordingly."

She stared at him unblinkingly. "You are an O'Neill. I do not understand you. You have a clan, you have a country. And if you have chosen otherwise, then that was your stupidity."

His smile was grim. "My father was as Irish as you are, but my mother was an Englishwoman. I was given no choice in the matter. Stupidity had little to do with the union between my parents, violence had everything to do with it. The O'Neills consider me as English as the queen. The English think me a savage like my father."

He spoke flatly, without self-pity or regret. Katherine stared at him, and his meaning hit her, hard. Their situations in life were similar. Like her, he had a useless name, and did not have a powerful family behind him. He survived by facing the truth and weathering any storm that should arise. He was advising her to weather this particular one, now. "So I can only survive now by welcoming you into my bed?" she said bitterly. "After all, I am the perfect victim for a man like you. There is no one to challenge you for aught that you do to me, no one to demand satisfaction when you ruin me. There will be no political storms engendered by your abduction of me, or by your abuse."

His eyes were bright with undisguised interest now. "An intelligent woman," he murmured. "Beautiful, headstrong, and intelligent—how very rare."

Despite herself, Katherine flushed. His words could not

possibly be flattery, even if they sounded like such. The ideal woman was neither headstrong nor clever, but chaste and demure and given to obedience in all matters great and small. But he was smiling at her as if he were most pleased with his discovery. Katherine lifted her chin. "I will not be your victim. I do not believe I am without a single protector in this world. I do not believe that you can do with me as you will and walk away freely from such heinous deeds."

His jaw flexed and he rose to his towering height. "You are a victim, Katherine. You are a victim of political circumstance." His stare was hard. "But I did not decide your father's fate—I did not pronounce his guilt and sentence him accordingly. Do not blame me for your father's rash actions and the queen's determination to end his defiance. I did not take away your inheritance, your name, or your station in life."

"I blame you for *your* rash actions," she cried scornfully, her fists clenched.

His smile flickered. "I am *never* rash." He started to walk around the table toward her. Katherine backed up—against the wall. Her pulse rioted as he paused before her. His smile was dangerous. "But you are right about one thing."

She did not want to know his thoughts, and kept silent.

His gaze slid over her face. "You do have a protector, Katherine, one single protector in all of this world, and that is me."

She gasped. "But you will not protect me from yourself!"

He chuckled then, the sound rich and amused. "You have misconstrued it all. You do not need to be protected from me. My intention is not to hurt you. My intention is to protect you from the rest of the world, to provide for your needs, to pleasure you. I only wish that you come to me willingly. There is naught else for you to do, Katherine. You have no other choices in this life." His gaze turned to smoke. "The moment I first saw you, I knew you would become my mistress."

"No," Katherine said tightly. "My answer to you is

no! I am not about to become your *mistress!*" It was exceedingly difficult for her to say that horrid word.

"You will change your mind when you have calmed down, when you have had a chance to reconcile yourself to fate and circumstance."

"I will never change my mind! My father may be a prisoner, but my dreams still live!" And Katherine knew it was true. Nothing could kill her dreams, not even the unkind facts of life, not even this unkind man.

"Your dreams are dead," he said softly. "Killed by circumstance. Killed by fate."

"No!" She blinked back hot tears. He stared at her, but she hardly saw him. "Damn the Butlers!" she said bitterly. "Damn the Council—damn the queen!"

"Katherine! Sweet Mother of Christ! What has he done to you!" Juliet cried.

The pirate had left her when she began to weep. Exhausted, Katherine had finally subsided into a heap on the bed she had been determined to avoid. She had not been aware of the passage of time, nor of Juliet's entering the room. Now, as Juliet hugged her, she sat up slowly. Her head ached from the long debate she had waged with the pirate, and from her equally arduous defense against him. She was also exhausted from having spent every moment since he had left her alone analyzing the choices and alternatives left to her. So far, there did not appear to be any of significance.

She returned Juliet's embrace. "I am fine," she whispered. It was hardly the truth. "He did not—" Her voice cracked. "He did not take my virtue."

"Thank God," Juliet breathed, her look dark with concern. She smoothed curling red hair from Katherine's face. "Did he . . . hurt you?"

Katherine hesitated. "Not really." She was still aghast at her body's treacherous sensuality, and even now, she could not shake his too-golden image from her mind. "Are you well? Unharmed?" she asked.

Juliet nodded. "The crew has been ordered to stay away from both of us."

Katherine's gaze was inquiring.

"I was so afraid, Katherine. But apparently these devils have some souls after all. The bald one, Macgregor, told me the captain does not, generally, allow mayhem or rape, and that we especially need not worry. In fact, the French ship was released. None of the crew, I'm told, were harmed."

Katherine was contemptuous. "You mean he did not force everyone into the sea? I do not believe it!"

Juliet did not seem to hear. Lines of strain were etched onto her face. "What does he plan for us then? Ransoms?"

Katherine recalled all that Liam O'Neill had said. Her jaw tensed. "Juliet, my father has lost his lands and title and he is a prisoner of the queen."

Juliet started. "Oh, Katherine!"

Katherine's face crumbled. "I do not think he lied." She tried to imagine her powerful father stripped of all he had and reconciled to an inglorious exile. She tried, and failed. Surely her father, her bold and clever father, had a plan for recovering all he had lost. It could not be exactly as the pirate had said. "I fear there will be no ransom for me."

"But what will he do with you, then, if he does not wish to use you?" Juliet asked.

Katherine looked into her friend's eyes. "You do not understand. He has every intention of using me."

Juliet stared, her brow furrowed, clearly unable to comprehend Katherine.

Katherine had forgotten how naive and sheltered Juliet was. "He intends to seduce me, to make me a willing prisoner of his passion."

Juliet gasped. Hot pink color flooded her cheeks. "What are you going to do?" Juliet cried.

"I do not know," Katherine replied. Then, grimly added, "Fight."

Both girls suddenly froze as they heard the bolt being moved aside. They stared at the door, watching it open slowly. But only a young boy of no more than ten or eleven entered the cabin, carrying a covered tray. Clearly he brought food. The aroma of succulent beef stew made both girls sit up straighter. Their stomachs rumbled. They had last eaten a light supper in their cabin on the French ship the night before, and already darkness was falling on the day.

The boy glanced at them. "The captain ordered me to bring you something to eat." His accent marked him as French. He set the tray down on the dining table, whipping off the linens covering it. "You need something, I am Guy."

Katherine stared at the boy. It disgusted her that the pirate would take on a lad so young. In all likelihood he had been abducted from his home and then sold to the pirate. The boy was far too thin to be healthy. And from the look of him, she doubted he was happy. "Thank you, Master Guy."

He scowled. " 'Tis Guy, nothing more."

"Guy," Katherine called, before he could leave. "Where is this ship headed?"

"North." He turned and started for the door.

Liam O'Neill launched himself off of it, startling Katherine. She had not heard him enter. Their glances held for a beat longer than necessary, as if they were intimate lovers, not strangers and enemies. Katherine colored, looking away.

Liam moved to the table but did not sit down. "Come, ladies. 'Tis hearty fare we have here. Boeuf bourguigon, vin rouge, Cook's freshest baked bread and hot apple tart."

Katherine wanted to refuse. Juliet glanced at her, also rebellious. But both girls were starving and as one they slid to their feet. Shoulders squared, Katherine crossed the cabin, Juliet following, careful to keep her eyes cast ahead and not on the pirate. She knew he regarded her— only her. She did not fool herself. She knew they were in the midst of a grave war, one she must absolutely win. The hairs at her nape tingled and prickled with unease. She sensed with a sinking heart that the war had hardly begun.

She slid into a chair. It was only after she and Juliet were seated that he took his own place at the table's head. "Where are you taking us?" she asked.

His hesitation was barely discernible. "I am taking you north, to my island home."

Katherine lost all interest in her food. She stared at him, hating him. He stared back.

"What about me?" Juliet whispered, breaking the silence which simmered between them.

The pirate did not even look at her. "You will be returned to Cornwall," he said.

Katherine pushed her plate away. She was agonizingly aware that the sky had turned dusky blue, and that the first stars had emerged into view. Soon he would take her to his bed. Afterward he would take her to his island home.

She was going to have to escape.

When they finished eating and their plates were removed the cabin was uncomfortably silent. Katherine dared to look up. The pirate held a glass of brandy, sipping it, regarding her from under long, dark lashes. In the golden lantern light his eyes gleamed silver. Behind his head she could clearly see the four-poster bed.

Katherine glanced away, too late. He said, "I understand that you two ladies were traveling from a convent."

Katherine barely looked at him. "Yes."

"Surely your family did not summon you home?"

Katherine knew he spoke only to her. What did he care? Her hostility increased. "I was not summoned home. But now I know why my father forgot me. His troubles are so vast." Still, she was upset that neither he nor Eleanor had seen fit to send her the terrible news of his conviction and imprisonment.

"I was summoned home," Juliet inserted. "And 'twas convenient for Katherine to join me."

"It is unusual, is it not, for a lady to decide to leave a nunnery without her family's permission?" The pirate stared at her.

Katherine's temper erupted. "I decided to take my fate into my own hands. I had no intention of growing old in the nunnery."

"Indeed," he murmured, his tone like the stroke of a feather upon her skin.

Katherine flushed, suddenly aware of how disobedient, ungenteel, and independent she must seem. Of course, it did not matter what he thought. But her tone of voice sounded defensive. "Father did not answer my letters. I did not know of his plight. I only knew I must return to Ireland."

"Many ladies wish for nothing more than the soft, predictable life of a nunnery."

She stared. "Not I."

He smiled at her. It was an arresting moment. His expression was intimate, warm. "I am glad," he said. "You are by far the most intriguing woman I have ever met, Katherine."

She clasped her hands in her lap, looking down at them, breathless. He did not even try to hide his desire. He did not care that Juliet was a witness to his intent. He was immoral, despicable—and Katherine was afraid, no matter how she tried to hide it.

And she knew she was hardly intriguing.

His gaze caressed her bent head. Katherine looked up sharply and their gazes collided. Panic bubbled in her breast. Behind his disturbingly handsome face, Katherine kept seeing the bed. How was she to avoid imminent ruin? How?

He smiled. "Lady Juliet, let me escort you to your cabin."

Juliet tensed and did not move.

Katherine gripped the table. Her eyes were wide, wild. "Surely Juliet stays here—and sleeps with me?"

He rose lazily to his great height. His smile was as languid. But there was nothing casual about the glitter in his smoky eyes. "Lady Juliet?"

Juliet got to her feet, darting Katherine a frightened glance. Katherine found herself standing, begging. "Please. Let Juliet stay here. With me."

His glance slid from her face down her body. He did not condescend to answer her, instead taking Juliet's arm and guiding her to the cabin door. Katherine watched in horror. He opened the door, called out to the sailor. Juliet threw one last, despairing glance at Katherine and then she disappeared. The pirate closed the door, slowly turning to face her.

"What will you do with me now?" Katherine cried, no longer trying to hide the panic she was feeling.

He crossed his arms and leaned against the door. "I am going to seduce you, Katherine."

Katherine tensed in expectation as he suddenly moved toward her. He took his time. He was in no hurry, but then, he was confident of his ultimate victory.

Katherine detested his arrogance as much as she detested everything else about him. She clenched her fists at her sides. It crossed her mind that when she struck his handsome face, she would be deeply satisfied.

"I am not going to murder you," he murmured, his tone spun silk.

"No, you think but to destroy me instead."

He smiled at her, reached out to touch her face.

Katherine raised her fists and punched at his cheek and jaw.

He ducked, his reflexes so fast that her knuckles did not even scrape his skin. A second later he had caught both her wrists in his hands, immobilizing her. Amazement showed in his eyes.

She did not move, did not speak, did not dare even to breathe. Her chest heaved. She watched his face, trying to guess what he would do next. She knew he was considering his options carefully.

But he took her by surprise. As quick as a snake, he lifted her under her knees, into his arms. Katherine began to struggle wildly when she saw that he strode to the bed. This was happening much too fast!

He sank down on the plush mattress, Katherine still in his arms. "Sssh," he said. "Be still. I am only going to kiss you."

He lied of course, and even if he did not, Katherine had no intention of obeying him. She jerked her head back, so his lips found the soft underside of her throat instead of her mouth. Instantly she knew that had been a grave mistake.

Unruly sensations that were hardly unpleasant swept her as he nibbled and kissed the sensitive skin on her neck. Katherine fought a gasp. She heard him chuckle, then froze as his hand swept over her breast. Immediately her nipple peaked. Katherine cried out, trying to pull his wrist away.

He ignored her efforts to dislodge him much as he might ignore a buzzing fly, and shifted her onto her back upon the bed, leaning over her, his mouth claiming hers before she could move or protest. Katherine struggled even more, digging her fingernails into his collarbone to keep him away. He did not seem to notice. He was vastly patient. His mouth was exceedingly soft and undemanding, stroking her lips lightly, feathering them, teasing them. How expert he was. Unbeknownst to Katherine, her gyrations slowed, then ceased. Her fingers uncurled, her body becoming increasingly pliant. His mouth firmed, taking advantage instantly, the tip of his tongue darting against hers. Unwittingly Katherine's lips parted.

Liam growled low in his throat, the sound distinctly erotic. Katherine heard a funny, mewling sound escape her as he shifted his heavy male weight on top of her, while deepening his kiss. Katherine was aflame, the fire spreading from her heavy limbs to her throbbing loins. Her body was aching now, her blood pounding, insistent, while her mind did not want to function.

He understood. He laughed against her mouth, the sound sensual, thick, raw. He began to rotate his hips languidly, slowly, caressing her with his shaft. Katherine flung her head back, tearing her mouth from his, crying out. He pressed himself against her far more urgently, far more dangerously.

"Katherine," he whispered. "Sweetheart." His hand had insinuated itself under her skirts and petticoats, caressing her thigh through the thin linen of her crotchless drawers. And then his palm swept upward dangerously high, brushing the soft, swollen flesh at the apex there.

Katherine was dazed, but his caress was shocking her back to her senses. Dear God. His thumb was stroking the seam of her lips now, tracing the heavy outline, touching her bare skin.

One coherent thought seized her. She must resist. If she did not resist now, he would do far more than stroke her where no one had ever trespassed before—he would steal her virtue before she even knew what he was about.

He tore his mouth from hers, gasping her name again. "Katherine."

Katherine inhaled, forced herself to action. She pounded both fists against his broad shoulders. "No!"

Startled, he froze. His smoky gaze was somewhat unfocused and puzzled as it met hers.

Katherine heaved at his body, and when that failed to dislodge him, she aimed her knee at his bulging groin. He understood her intention at that precise instant, shifting his hips just in time to avoid her attack. In doing so, he was off-balance. Katherine pushed against him hard and rolled and then scrambled away from him, sliding off the side of the bed to the floor.

She herself was dazed and out of breath. She paused only for a moment, but it was a moment too long. As she crouched, about to lunge to her feet, he reached down and gripped a chunk of hair at her nape. Katherine cried out.

He leaned over the bed, his face close to hers, using her hair like a leash. His eyes were wide, incredulous, furious. His mouth was drawn into a tight, angry scowl. Katherine's lips curled in an answering snarl—but tears filled her gaze.

And as the tears began to fall, unwanted, an affront to her pride, his grip eased. His expression changed. He cursed savagely and released her. Katherine sagged to the floor.

She heard him slide to his feet. She fought for her self-control and finally found it. Hugging herself, she lifted her gaze upward. A mistake. It was impossible not to notice how enlarged he was. Katherine flushed, looked anywhere but at that, wishing she could forget the excitement he had somehow engendered in her own body, wishing she could ignore the unfamiliar and unsteady pounding of her pulse now. "I hate you," she said raggedly.

"You did not hate me a moment ago."

The anger and the tension in his tone forced her to meet his gaze. The gray fire in his eyes frightened her. Katherine had never witnessed such stark hunger before. She shrank back against the leg of the bed. For a moment she could not look away. And because something she was resolved to ignore flared to life inside her, something strong and heated, she cried, "I hated you then just as I hate you now, O'Neill!"

An unpleasant smile formed on his lips. "You are turning a pleasant seduction into something far worse."

"A *pleasant* seduction?"

"Aye—a seduction pleasant for both of us." His gaze darkened visibly. "Do not try to deny it."

Fear stabbed at her as she finally comprehended his entire meaning. "What do you mean, something far worse? Do you threaten me with rape?"

His nostrils flared. "Some *ladies* happen to enjoy a modicum of force. Perhaps you are of that persuasion."

Katherine's eyes widened.

"Do not look so surprised. But then I am forgetting that you have been locked away in a convent for six years." His smile was twisted. "However, before you succumb to hysterics, let me tell you that I do not rape. Not before, not now, not ever. Not even if provoked."

She did not believe him and she meant to laugh scornfully, but instead, she emitted a choked, pitiful sound. "You just said you were happy to oblige those women who ..." She could not continue. She was still shocked to think that some women actually liked it when a man was forceful, brutal. Images assaulted her, images of this golden pirate ravishing a faceless woman who was feverish and eager.

"I can be rough, or I can be gentle. If you but tell me what it is you want." His eyes held hers.

"I ... I want you ... to leave me alone."

His laughter was harsh. "You want me inside you sweetheart."

His graphic words stunned her for a moment. "You are a savage, a pirate, a man who preys upon those weaker than himself." She crouched on the floor, staring up at him. "You are preying on me just as you have preyed on those other women. I do not want you!"

"Other women have welcomed me into their embrace."

Katherine laughed. "Then they were whores and sluts."

He bent over her, angry. "I do not lie with pox-ridden whores. My last mistress was a dowager countess."

She regarded him, unwilling to believe him, but he was so angry that she thought he spoke the truth. How had he seduced a countess? Katherine just could not fathom it. No matter that he was so strikingly attractive.

"Some women are not afraid of passion," he said, watching her closely. His chest heaved. "But then, they are not convent-bred, teary-eyed virgins."

Katherine cried out. She lurched to her feet, livid, ignoring a small inner voice that told her to retreat. "I am not afraid of passion," she shouted. "I want nothing more than to be with a man—a noble man, a good man—a man who is my husband."

He stared at her, unspeaking, his shoulders rigid. Finally he said, "And who is this paragon?"

Katherine lifted her chin. "I have not found him yet."

His laughter was cold and cruel, derisive.

Furious that he was laughing at her she cried, "I have been in a convent for six years, so how could I have found him? Know this. I do not yearn for an ungodly, murderous, thieving pirate."

Fire leapt in his eyes. He was holding a bottle of brandy. He lifted it to his lips and swigged from it, not once, but several times, yet all the while his smoldering gaze remained upon her. Katherine regretted her words, knowing she had pushed him too far. She feared he might snap and become the savage beast again, and force her to his will.

He stared at her coldly. "I must be mad," he said. "To have embroiled myself with one such as you."

"Then release me."

There was no hesitation. "No."

"Please."

He did not respond.

Katherine's breasts heaved. "Then rape me and be done with it."

His glance skewered her. His face contorted. The bottle went flying. Katherine flinched and cried out as the brandy smashed against one of the walls. Then, to her horror, he was upon her.

How she regretted her rash, stupid words, her incitement! She screamed as he bent down to her. He lifted her and tossed her onto the bed. Katherine bounced and came up scrambling away from him. He caught her foot and yanked her down, hard, on her face. And then he was on top of her, pinning her in place.

Katherine froze. He was as still as she, except for the pulsing of his body against hers and the short, heavy labored breaths coming from his chest. "Shall I rape you and be done with it?" he asked in her ear.

His breath licked her flesh. Katherine shook her head, terrified, and acutely aware of how easy it would be for him to lift her skirts and do the deed. Fear did not override the heavy, throbbing sensation of his flesh wedged against hers.

"Shall I rape you and be done with it?" he demanded.

"No!"

He rolled off of her and left the bed.

Katherine jerked into a sitting position, then hurled herself across the bed and into the farthest corner away from him, pressing her back into the wood-paneled wall.

He stared at her, unblinking. Steel glinted, flashing.

Katherine sucked in her breath, her eyes frozen upon the long, lethal dagger that appeared in his hand.

Neither of them moved, neither of them spoke. Suddenly the dagger flew from his hand. It landed in the wall beside her head, inches from her cheek. Katherine stared at the quivering blade, fear running down her body in rivulets of sweat. Then she blinked and their gazes clashed hard. His eyes glittered savagely.

He whirled. With long booted strides he crossed the room and yanked open the door. A moment later it was kicked closed from outside. She heard the bolt being thrown, locking her inside.

Katherine turned her head and stared at the dagger, imbedded in the wall. She covered her face with her hands, beginning to shake. His promise was crystal clear.

4

*K*atherine knew that she must not antagonize him.

It was late. She had no idea of the exact time, but she guessed that it was close to midnight. She was not asleep. There had been no way, despite her exhaustion, that she could sleep while waiting for the pirate to return, while preparing to engage in yet another battle. Instead, she had sat on the bed, in the far corner, her spine pressed to the wall, exactly as he had left her.

A few moments ago he had returned to the cabin. Katherine watched him silently now, wide-eyed and wary, but he did not look at her as he crossed the chamber, his graceful stride a bit looser than usual. Katherine thought that she detected a whiff of brandy. Was he drunk? Katherine did not care for that thought. She recalled from her childhood at Askeaton what liquor did to men, and she tensed even more.

Still he did not look at her. The pirate opened the armoire, abruptly shrugged off his shirt. Katherine managed to smother a gasp, faced with the nakedness of his broad, bronzed, rippling back. She could not help but notice how his breeches clung to his high, hard buttocks. "What are you doing?" she cried in alarm.

He turned to her, his gaze direct, but strangely soft. "I am changing my shirt."

Katherine refused to look at the hard slab of his chest, lightly furred with golden brown hair, or at his flat, hard stomach. To her great relief, he shrugged on a snowy white tunic. She realized that the odor of brandy came from the shirt he tossed carelessly aside.

Her eyes were riveted to him now. He paused in the center of the cabin, his legs braced in a seaman's stance. "We must reach an understanding, you and I," he said.

He did not slur his words. She was further relieved. He was sober, or close to it. Carefully she regarded him, not yet responding. She knew now that she must not incite either his temper or his lust.

His gaze flickered over her face. "You are very, very beautiful, Katherine. Do you know that I dream of you at night?"

She sat up straighter, realizing that he was drunk after all, for he had but met her that morning. "There are many beautiful women in the world."

"True," he said, and somehow that agreement disappointed her. He rested his hands on his narrow hips, betraying some lingering tension in him. "There are many beauties in the world, but are they willful and intelligent?"

Her gaze darted to his eyes. "Do you mock me?"

He chuckled then, the sound rich and warm. "No, darling, I do not."

She froze. Katherine did not like the sound of his laughter or his endearment, and she stiffened against the wall.

"You are still afraid of me." His jaw flexed. His gaze was no longer as soft. "I must apologize for my behavior."

Her eyes widened. The pirate was apologizing for his bestial actions?

"You are far too enticing, but still I should have controlled myself. The only defense I can make is that I did not expect such spirit from you." His stare penetrated hers.

"That is no defense. A gentleman would never have assaulted me as you did."

The corners of his mouth lifted, but the expression somehow seemed ripe with self-derision. "But as you have said, I am a savage."

"Can you deny it?"

"I would not bother even to try." His gaze had grown darker now. "You are very adept at provoking my temper. Never have I met a woman who angered me so." His

temples were throbbing, his expression strained with distaste. "I have never touched a woman in anger before."

Katherine could not help but laugh scornfully. He was
not just a pirate, but an O'Neill. They were a savage clan,
almost a race apart, coming from the farthest reaches of
northern Ireland. She thought of the infamous Shane
O'Neill, who had been chieftain of his clan until his murder some years earlier. Katherine had seen him once, when
she was but nine years old. She still remembered how big
and dark and ugly he had been, how frightening and fero-
cious. "This from the mouth of an O'Neill?" she cried.
"O'Neills are known for their violence against women!"

His gaze, razor-sharp, found hers. She pressed her spine
harder against the wall. She must control herself! She must
not arouse him!

He did not speak. He inhaled deeply, turned his back
on her, his fists still on his hips. When he finally faced
her again, he said, low and strained, "I do not want to
fight with you. I did not capture you to fight with you."

She swallowed hard, knowing full well why he *had*
captured her.

"Katherine, let us stop this war. There is no sense to
it. You desperately need a protector, and I am more than
eager to be one. Surely, by now, you must realize that
you have no other choices. And once you have lived with
me a while, you will see that it is far from an unpleasant experience."

Katherine forced aside images that were coming to her
in a steady stream now, of him and her, heated and entwined. And feelings she did not wish to recall, sensations
she had never experienced before, all of it, she wished to
forget forever. "I want to go home."

His gray gaze softened and he hesitated. "You have
no home."

She swallowed the lump in her throat, thinking of
Askeaton Castle, thinking of Castlemaine and Shanid. "I
want to go to my father." Her voice quavered, and she
thought she sounded like a foolish, frightened child.

The pirate stared at her, emotion she could not identify
seething in his eyes. "So you wish to return to FitzGerald

to live with him and his pretty wife in exile, in poverty, in disgrace?''

Her breasts rose and fell. "I wish to marry. I wish to marry an Irishman and return to Ireland. I want children and a home of my own. My father will find me a proper husband. I am certain of it.''

"Will he, indeed?" Liam asked gently.

"Yes!"

"And what marriage can you now make, *Mistress* FitzGerald? You wish to wed a farmer or a clerk?''

She could not imagine marrying a farmer or a clerk; the very idea was so shocking that for a full minute she could not speak. And how she wished he would stop looking at her like that, as if he felt some sympathy for her plight. "My father will arrange a marriage befitting my station.''

"Your station in life is gone.''

She hugged herself. "Stop! I insist you release me so I may go to him!''

"But you are my prize," he countered, serious and unsmiling. "I have won you at sea. You belong to *me* now. And I cannot give you up.''

She was desperate. "Why not?''

His only answer was an impenetrable stare.

Katherine clenched her fists and beat the coverlet. "Damn you!''

A smile crossed his features. "Convent-raised and cursing yet again? Come, Katherine, 'tis most unladylike.''

She glared at him. "Go back to your dowager countess.''

The smile remained. "Do you think to dissuade me by showing me your ill nature? Such a ploy is doomed.''

Katherine stared, dread consuming her. "So you will keep me against my will.''

His gaze held hers. "I intend to change your will, Katherine.''

"You are a savage! A pirate! A bloody savage O'Neill!" she cried. "You will never change my opinion of you! Perhaps, in time, you might enslave my body . . .'' She could not continue. Tears spilled down her cheeks.

His expression was grim, his jaw rigid, his eyes twin

black flames. "I may be a savage, a pirate, and an O'Neill, but you are mine now, and you have no choice in the matter."

"No! I refuse to believe that."

Finally he moved toward her and stood over the bed. "I am your fate, Katherine. How shall I convince you of that?"

"I would have to see with my own two eyes that Desmond is no more. I would have to hear with my own ears that a ransom is impossible."

Liam regarded her for a long, thoughtful moment. "Then so be it, Katherine," he said.

Katherine huddled into her fur-lined cloak as the long-boat pushed through choppy seas. The last hours of the night were bitterly cold and thick with fog. Three seamen accompanied her and the pirate, two of whom wielded the huge oars. Macgregor sat beside her, perhaps to prevent her from trying something futile or foolish. But Katherine had no intention of jumping to a watery death, not now, not when luck had finally come her way. Nor did she intend to try to escape. She would wait now, for her father to gain her freedom.

Liam O'Neill stood at the prow, as if oblivious to the cold, the dark, and the bucking boat. He seemed one with his vessel, one with the sea. Katherine stared at his broad, cloak-draped back, unable to prevent herself from wondering what kind of man he was. Then she told herself it did not matter. Soon she would be free of him and would be left with naught but unpleasant memories.

The entrance to the Thames, where different currents collided, was terrifyingly rough. Katherine had to bite her lip to keep from screaming when the small boat rode the crest of a wave up and up and leapt high into the air, then plummeted steeply down into the pits of the sea. She gripped the seat she sat upon as the small boat reared up again. To her shock and amazement, O'Neill had not moved from the prow, and stood there supremely indifferent to the dangerous ride. Once he turned and glanced back at her. In the dark, misty night, Katherine saw that he was smiling, as if enjoying himself, his teeth a white glimmer in so much dark and shadow.

Katherine bowed her head and prayed. He was insane, they were all insane, and she would soon die, it seemed. But after a while, she realized that the boat no longer crested and plunged so wildly. Indeed, the small boat bucked almost rhythmically. Katherine lifted her head, opened her eyes. They were in the river now, and the waves had subsided into much calmer swells.

The longboat soon scraped a sandy shore. The sailors jumped out, thrashing through the water, pulling the vessel up onto safe ground. O'Neill had leapt out as well. He turned and waited for the longboat to come abreast of him. Katherine slowly stood up. He reached for her and lifted her out of the ship and onto the loamy beach.

She jumped out of his embrace and looked around, wondering where they were. Far from London, of course, which was many miles from the mouth of the river. She realized the audacity of the pirate. If he were caught in England, he would be tried for his many crimes and sentenced to death. If he were lucky, his fate would be a simple beheading. If not, he would be hanged, drawn, and quartered. How daring it was for him to venture onto English soil—how daring and how foolish.

Yet she knew that he was not a foolish man. Katherine stole a glance at him. Liam spoke to his men in low, crisp tones. His face appeared carved in stone. His profile was glorious and uncompromising. His men scurried to obey him instantly. He was a pirate, a man she abhorred, but unquestionably, he was a commander of men. Katherine decided that arrogance would explain his daring in coming to shore, that and supreme self-confidence.

Liam nodded to Macgregor and Katherine was led up the beach by the Scottish sailor, following the pirate. The other two seamen remained behind. The crenellated roof of a castle suddenly winked out at them from the swirling fog, not far distant. As they approached, the mist parted and closed repeatedly, revealing the castle's stone outer walls. The sky was lightening. Dawn was stealing upon them.

Keeping her voice very low, unsure if detection were to her advantage or not, Katherine whispered, "Where are we, O'Neill?"

" 'Tis Tilbury Castle you see," Liam said in equally low tones. "You wait with Mac."

"But where do you go?"

He ignored her, disappearing into the shadows.

Many minutes passed. Katherine knew he could not enter the castle, for the gates would be closed until the sunrise. But there must be a village nearby. Undoubtedly he sought transportation for them. Again she thought of how bold he was—to steal horses and vehicles out from under the nose of castle and castellan. Katherine was amazed. Bold and arrogant he might be, but grudgingly, she had to admit the extent of his courage.

But he returned without any conveyance. Astride a large dark horse, his cloak swirling, he appeared a midnight highwayman. Two other horses on lead lines foamed at their bits. Katherine was heaved upon the smaller gelding before she could blink. In another moment they were cantering down the road toward London.

"Can you ride?" he asked, his knee brushing hers.

" 'Tis late to ask, is it not?" Katherine retorted, finding her seat and grateful to be riding astride and not sidesaddle.

He smiled at her. "An Irish lass like you must know how to ride, Katherine. I would be sorely disappointed otherwise."

She met his gaze for a brief moment, thinking him mad to be enjoying the affair. Then she decided to concentrate on the task at hand. As a child, she had been a good rider, but that had been many years ago. And it was still so dark, making it very difficult to see. Katherine decided to let her mount have its head.

But how suspicious this predawn journey would appear to any passersby. Katherine threw a glance over her shoulder at the disappearing castle. A chill crept up her spine. What would happen if they should be captured by the queen's men? Would she not be released? The thought was intriguing.

Yet her father was the queen's prisoner. What would Elizabeth do with her, the daughter of a man deemed a traitorous earl? Would she be confined in Gerald's prison in Southwark? Would her capture also mean the loss of her own freedom, the ruin of her future?

Katherine decided to make no efforts to draw attention to herself and her party. For now.

They rode hard and fast for several hours. The fog lessened. The sun crept into the graying sky, a burning ball of orange. London soon loomed ahead of them. Towers, spires, and a multitude of rooftops and chimneys pierced the cloudless sky, the huge, soaring Cathedral of St. Paul in the midst of it all. Katherine glimpsed Liam's face. He still rode beside her, Macgregor behind. She looked for a trace of fear on his features, and saw nothing but resolve.

They rode through one gate and clattered down one deserted street after another. The city would soon awaken, but they saw no one. Sometimes groups of drunken men could be heard on another thoroughfare, singing bawdy tunes and laughing uproariously. Liam seemed to know these streets like the back of his hand. It made no sense.

They skirted the walls of the Tower. Katherine was in disbelief. She decided he was mad after all. No man who defied the queen's authority for his livelihood would dare to come so close to the dreaded place that might well one day become his destiny. No man, no matter how bold, no matter how arrogant.

They galloped over London Bridge and turned east. They had entered a rowdy neighborhood of breweries and brothels. Several well-dressed gentlemen were leaving one such house, and Katherine pretended not to see several half-naked women standing on the street corner. One plump doxy waved at the pirate, even calling out to him, her words both shrill and suggestive. Katherine's face and ears burned. Liam appeared not to have heard the graphic proposition.

Suddenly they came upon a square building, a depot of some kind, that blocked the street. Liam rode to the left, Katherine automatically following. On the other side was a large two-storied house with a steep, pitched roof of timber, surrounded by stone walls. Liam abruptly pulled up his mount and slid to the ground. "Wait here," he ordered Katherine and Macgregor.

He strode not to the front gate but around the side of the wall, disappearing from view. Fifteen minutes later the front gate was opened. Liam stood in the shadows cast by it, his mantle pushed back over his broad shoulders, revealing the fact that he now wore a jerkin over his shirt as well as his breeches and thigh-high black boots. He gestured impatiently. Katherine spurred her mount forward, her heart dancing with sudden, wild elation. And at long last she was to see her father—at long last!

Katherine slid from the horse and hurried to the front door, well ahead of Liam now. She banged upon it. When there was no response, she banged again.

Suddenly a woman demanded from within, "Who goes there at this ungodly hour?"

"Eleanor!" Katherine cried. " 'Tis I—Katherine FitzGerald!"

The door was unbolted and pushed open. Eleanor stared at Katherine in disbelief, then glanced at the pirate. "God's teeth! What do you here?!"

She was a small, slender woman of extraordinary beauty. Light brown hair framed an oval face unblemished by pox or scars. When she spoke, white teeth were revealed, with no gaps between them. She was a Butler, the daughter of Baron Duboyne, and she was exactly three years older than Katherine.

"I have come home," Katherine whispered, smiling tremulously.

But Eleanor did not smile in return. "This is hardly a home," she said bitterly. Then she stepped aside. " 'Tis a surprise you've made for your poor father—and him not well. Come inside." Her body stiff with reluctance, she gestured for Katherine, Liam, and Macgregor to enter.

But Liam turned and spoke sharply, "Stay outside, Mac. A whistle shall suffice if any visitors appear."

Macgregor nodded and disappeared, moving with surprising speed and grace for a man so big and brawny.

Eleanor closed the door behind them. "You should have told us you were coming," she said sharply.

Katherine said, "I wrote many letters. Did Father not receive any of them?"

"I received several of your missives, but did not wish to disturb his peace of mind with the selfish demands of a spoiled daughter. He has enough problems, God knows."

Katherine was rigid. " 'Tis hardly selfish to ask to go home and to be wed."

"And what will your dowry be, pray tell?" Eleanor said caustically. "Two cows and a piglet?"

Katherine did not believe what the other woman was suggesting. She knew very well that Eleanor disliked her, she always had, from the first day she had arrived with Gerald at Askeaton Castle, a lovely, laughing bride. The memory was still painful for Katherine, not because Eleanor had been so pretty or so happy, but because her own father had also been filled with joy, smiling from ear to ear. Katherine's mother Joan had been buried less than a month. "Everything cannot be gone," Katherine said. "Surely there is something left for a dowry."

"Everything has been taken away or destroyed," Eleanor cried with rage. "I have had to beg alms from my neighbors! We live on bread and mead!"

Katherine refused to believe what she was hearing. "Where is Father? I must see him now!"

"Gerald sleeps, but I will wake him as O'Neill is with you. Both of you, wait here." Abruptly Eleanor shoved past Katherine, holding up a glass-domed candle, and began to climb the narrow stairs.

Katherine glanced at Liam, perplexed that Eleanor knew him. Then she recalled that her father, many years ago, had had some dealings with the O'Neill chieftain, Shane. In truth, Ireland was a small world if one were native born. Undoubtedly Eleanor's father, Baron Duboyne, had trafficked with the O'Neills, too. But what kind of business could Duboyne have possibly had with this man?

But she was distinctly uneasy as she waited restlessly in the dark hall for her father to appear. Was Gerald's situation even worse than she had feared? The rushes on the floor smelled foul and overused. It was too dark to see, but Katherine had the unhappy feeling that the hall was quite bare. And now she recalled Eleanor's well-mended, threadbare nightdress and robe. The stepmother she remembered of five years ago had always been resplendent in furs and velvets and jewels. In fact, Katherine could not recall seeing a single ring upon Eleanor's fingers, and her heart sank.

Katherine became aware of Liam's probing regard. She turned her back on him abruptly, beginning to shake. If all Eleanor had said was true, then dear God, what would happen to them all? And what would happen to Katherine herself?

She glanced up, unwillingly meeting Liam's unflinching gaze. And Katherine was afraid of what lay ahead.

"Wake up!" Eleanor cried, lighting a candle and setting it down on the chamber's single small chest, which was beside her husband's narrow bed.

Gerald sat up, rubbing his eyes, nightcap askew. "God's blood, woman, what is amiss? Is the house afire?"

"No," Eleanor cried, sitting down beside him and gripping his arms. "Gerald—your daughter is here!"

Gerald blinked, finally awake, a slender man with startlingly fair skin and midnight black hair. "My daughter?" he echoed.

"God has finally heeded my prayers!" Eleanor cried ecstatically. "For he has sent your daughter to us—with none other than the Master of the Seas!"

Gerald started. "What are you babbling about, Eleanor? Have you gone mad?"

"I am hardly mad!" Eleanor was jubilant. " 'Tis Liam O'Neill! The infamous pirate, Shane O'Neill's son, is standing outside this very door just down the hall! Oh, Gerald! At last! At last God has delivered to us a great and wonderful opportunity—do you not see?"

But Gerald had flung his feet to the floor and he lunged upright. Facing the door, his expression was no longer annoyed. And then, he smiled. "Yes, dearheart, I do see. Send for them," he said.

* * *

Liam's touch upon her shoulder made Katherine jump and then spin to face him. "Come," he said, not unkindly. "Your stepmother calls."

Katherine did not want his sympathy or his pity—and that could not be what she saw in his eyes. Her heart beating wildly now, Katherine hurried past Liam up the dimly lit stairs and down the hall to the master chamber. Her father was standing in the center of the small, bare room in his nightclothes. At the sight of his darkly handsome face, Katherine cried out. Gerald smiled and pulled her into his embrace.

And Katherine clung to him. She closed her eyes, leaning her cheek upon his chest. He was thin, but he felt warm and strong. Surely he would solve her terrible plight.

"Katie—are you all right?"

Katherine smiled at him wanly. "Yes. I am . . . unhurt."

Gerald's glance strayed briefly to Liam, but then he gazed at his daughter. "How you have grown up!" Tears suddenly filled his eyes. "How beautiful you've become, the image of your dear mother—I would never have known."

Six years ago Katherine had been tall and skinny and hardly pretty. She flushed with pleasure at being compared to her very beautiful mother. "I am not like her," she whispered.

But her father was looking at the pirate. "Aye, you are much like her."

Katherine looked from her father to Liam, watching as they stared at one another in a strange silence now. She could not help but compare them. Gerald was not just thin and gaunt, but so pale, far paler than she'd ever seen him, and she did not think the pallor was due solely to his confinement. There were deep brackets around his mouth and eyes, as well, as if he perpetually scowled. Then he eased her aside with a grimace and moved stiffly to a chair. Katherine understood the heavy facial lines now—she realized that he limped and lived in pain.

Her gaze flickered back to the pirate. Liam O'Neill was powerfully built, strong and young. He was golden in color, even his skin, from being perpetually out of doors and in the sun. He towered over Gerald and everyone else in the room. He exuded an undeniable presence, at once masterful and indomitable.

"Father—what happened to your leg?" Katherine asked.

He lowered himself awkwardly into the chair. " 'Tis my damnable hip. It never healed as it should have after Affane. 'Twas a musket ball. Cold winter nights are the worst. This is not too bad." He smiled slightly at her.

Katherine dropped to her knees before him. "Father— how can this be? All has been forfeit to the Crown? And you are exiled to such poverty? Is there no hope, no chance of justice?"

His black eyes blazed. He gripped the chair. "There is little hope, Katie, and none from the queen."

Katherine sucked in her breath. Until this moment, she had hoped, deep inside herself, the way a child might, that it was all a pack of monstrous lies. Or that her powerful, invincible father would have a plan to undo the wrongs done to him. She told herself that she would not cry. Once Gerald FitzGerald, earl of Desmond, had been the most powerful lord in Ireland, like his father and his father's father before him. He had been born to power, born to wealth, and born to the knowledge that forever he would wield it over Desmond and the other Irish lords. This was the grossest injustice Katherine had ever faced.

"Katie, my exile is no easy fate. I live for my return to Ireland. I think of naught else. But I do not want you to cry, darling. At least I am no prisoner in the Tower. Thanks to Eleanor." He smiled at his wife. "Last year she came from Desmond and she moved heaven and earth to gain an audience with the queen, and finally convinced Elizabeth to remand me to Sir Warham Leger." His glanced settled on Liam. "How did you get past my guards, O'Neill?"

Liam smiled. "Easily enough. They were preoccupied with dice and ale. Now they dream of drink and gaming."

Katherine wiped her eyes with her fist.

"What do you with my girl, O'Neill? The two of you together, 'tis a surprising sight."

Liam placed his hand on Katherine's shoulder before she could speak. "Your daughter managed to talk herself out of the convent you had placed her in. I happened to seize the ship she traveled on. As she has no protector, I have taken up that role myself."

Katherine jumped to her feet. "Father! He has seized *me!* And he keeps me against my will! He wishes me to be . . . to be his mistress!"

Gerald shoved himself to his feet.

Katherine froze, realizing she should have kept silent a bit longer, glancing from one man to the other. They stared at one another like watchful rivals prepared to duel. Eleanor also watched the men, her eyes bright with interest.

Finally Gerald spoke. "How lucky for you, O'Neill, that my wayward daughter chose to run away from the nunnery in France and that I am exiled like this, in such poverty, unable to take action against you."

"Yes."

Katherine cried out. "But Father! Surely you can pay him some small ransom! And talk him out of his intent!"

"Be quiet, girl," Gerald said.

Katherine backed up a step, finding it hard to breathe. But she could not keep quiet, she could not, not when her entire future was at stake. "Father, I must be freed. I cannot stay with the pirate—I wish to wed—surely my uncle can arrange some reasonable sum, and if not, surely you can come to some agreement with the pirate."

Gerald's expression softened slightly and he finally looked at her. "Katie—I have nothing but the clothing on my back and the air that I breathe. I cannot pay the pirate any sum, small or otherwise. And I cannot find a husband for you, not now. No respectable man would have you—none."

She gasped. "But . . ."

"You argue with me?"

Katherine flinched slightly, then squared her shoulders, keeping her head high. "No," she whispered.

Gerald sucked in his breath, trembling now. "I have NOTHING left! All was taken from me. Taken from me

and given over to damned Englishmen. I have nothing, yet
you complain that you have no husband!''

Katherine stared at her father through a haze of sudden tears.

"Desmond has been destroyed," Eleanor added, her
voice shrill. "Your father's ambitious cousin FitzMaurice
was quick to leap into the breach after Affane, to rouse
the other Irish lords, to chase out the English. But dear
God, he burned down all the countryside—and what he
left intact, Sir Henry Sidney then burned and pillaged next!
Today the Irish hide in the bogs and forests, kern and
noble alike, men, women, and children, freezing and starving to death!" Eleanor wiped her eyes. "Desmond is destroyed, your father has lost everything, and you come to
us thinking that we can find you a husband? Our problems
are far too grave to bother with such nonsense."

Katherine was stricken. She told herself that she was as
selfish as her father and stepmother accused her of being.
"I am sorry."

"If only I knew what FitzMaurice does now," Gerald
cried vehemently. "Damn my cousin."

"FitzMaurice was chased into Glen Aherlow by the new
lord president of Munster," Liam said. Everyone stared at
him, Katherine included. "He lay low for the winter, but
I expect him to emerge and renew his battles very soon."

"Yes, spring is a good season for war," Gerald spit.

"FitzMaurice claims to be the earl of Desmond in your
father's place," Eleanor said harshly to Katherine. "And
he is far too clever. Even now, he has the support of the
Pope and Spain. He will not stop until he has stolen Desmond from its rightful lord!"

Katherine was white, her heart pounding painfully. "I
did not know any of this," she whispered. But her regard
slid to Liam O'Neill again. How did he know so much
when he claimed he had no clan, no country, no life but
that at sea?

"Now you do know." Gerald shook in impotent rage.
"You should have stayed in France. I cannot support
you, Katie."

Katherine hugged herself.

"I will support her," Liam said quietly.

Gerald lashed Liam with his angry gaze. "No. I will not have you using my daughter like some common country maid. She is the daughter of two great houses."

Liam smiled slightly. "I am afraid that, in this instance, you cannot stop me."

And it was as if the women in the room had left. Gerald stared only at Liam. "How much like your father are you?"

Liam shrugged with indifference. "I am exactly like him—or so 'tis said."

"I do not think so," Gerald said, smiling grimly again. "I think you are very, very different from Shane O'Neill. Katie being as yet unhurt is proof of that."

"You can think whatever you wish, FitzGerald." Liam shrugged. "But now that I have shown Katherine that she has no choice but to remain with me, she and I will depart."

"No," Katherine whispered, her voice thick with unshed tears. And she stared with undisguised hostility at Liam—the son of the notoriously vicious Shane O'Neill. He had not told her. She should have guessed. Her father was wrong. The pirate was exactly like Shane—she knew that firsthand.

Gerald stated, "I have a proposition for you, O'Neill."

"Indeed?" Liam asked skeptically. "What could you possibly propose that would even remotely interest me?"

Katherine looked from her father to her captor, not liking the sudden new direction of the conversation. Her dread had grown by leaps and bounds.

Gerald did not even glance at Katherine. "How badly do you want her?"

Katherine gasped, certain that she had misheard.

"Badly enough to keep her against her will, and against my better judgment," Liam said calmly.

Gerald paced stiffly to Liam, his eyes bright black flames. "Badly enough to marry her?"

Katherine cried out in horror, but was ignored.

Liam was still but a moment. "What need do I have for a bride?"

"Every man needs a wife. She has no dowry, but I would give her to you with my blessing," Gerald said. "I might be destitute, Desmond gone, but Katherine's blood is noble. The FitzGerald line goes back to the Conqueror himself. And she is like her mother—exactly. And her mother gave the earl of Ormond seven strapping sons before he died. You cannot think to do better. You are the bastard of O'Neill, the son of an Englishwoman. Your clan will never appoint you their lord. Your kin will never accept you. The English hate and fear you." Gerald's black eyes gleamed with fire. "But I will accept you, Liam."

"Father!" Katherine cried, shaking uncontrollably. "No!"

Liam's eyes were slits. "I do not need a wife to give me sons and you know it. Nor do I need sons. As you have correctly pointed out, I am no nobleman. What would they inherit? The pile of rock I call home? My three pirate ships?" He laughed harshly. "I do not wish a wife, Fitz-Gerald. I have never needed a clan. And if she gives me a son, why, then his blood will be blue instead of red."

"One day," Gerald whispered feverishly, "your son could inherit a part of Desmond."

Katherine was hugging herself, telling herself that this was not happening. That this could not be happening.

Liam's smile was mocking. "Your offer lacks substance. Desmond is no more."

And Katherine stared at the pirate's hard, handsome face and hated him more than ever.

For a long, pregnant moment Gerald was silent—a moment in which both men stared into one another's eyes and assessed one another's needs and ambitions. Gerald broke the simmering tension. "Were I still the earl of Desmond, you would take her were she an ugly mule—in the blink of an eye—without a dowry!"

Liam inclined his head. "Probably."

Gerald stared.

"As you can not dissuade me from my goal, my lord, we shall be on our way," Liam said softly.

Katherine began to weep silently. Some small remnant

of her pride kept her from throwing herself at her father's feet, from clinging to his knees like a small child afraid of being abandoned or taken away. His betrayal was like a dagger in her breast.

"I will have your head, O'Neill," FitzGerald finally said. But his tone was mild. And his eyes still gleamed.

"Indeed? I wish you luck in making the effort." Liam turned toward Katherine. "Come. We leave this instant."

Katherine lifted her head and saw through her tears that he was completely unmoved—as determined as ever. But he had expected this. For him, it had been a game, nothing more. She was the fool. For she had expected Gerald to make a sincere effort to outwit her captor—but he had not. He had offered her to him in marriage instead.

Liam's gray gaze met and held hers. His hand closed around hers. She was too numb even to try to shake him off. "Come, Katherine," he said, almost gently, "your cause is lost."

Katherine sucked down a sob.

Gerald stared at them both, his expression impossible to read.

Liam strode to the door, one arm around Katherine, propelling her with his strength. She was determined not to think. It hurt too much.

When they were in the dark hall downstairs Eleanor called out to them from behind, making Liam pause, his arm still around Katherine. She hurried down the stairs and to them. "O'Neill. There is something you should know."

Liam paused. "Be quick, then."

Katherine did not want to hear any other thing that Eleanor might have to say, but despite herself, she lifted her gaze to her stepmother's.

Eleanor smiled. "Although I do not think he will interfere, I cannot be sure. Perhaps he will be enraged—that you have stolen what belongs to him."

Liam was annoyed. "You speak in riddles and I have no time for games. Speak plainly, Lady FitzGerald."

"Aye, then, I shall. I am speaking about Hugh Barry."

At the name of her dead betrothed, Katherine froze.

"What game is this!" she cried. "Hugh is dead, Eleanor. He died at Affane. He died six long years ago."

"No, Katherine," Eleanor said. "Did you not know he survived his wounds? When 'twas time to bury him with the others, it was realized that he still lived. Yet he was close to death, and many weeks went by before the physicians knew he would survive his many wounds. 'Twas a miracle, a gift of God, they said. He lives, Katherine. Hugh Barry lives."

Katherine reeled. Liam caught her. Katherine knew this must be a lie, a horrible, evil, hurtful lie. For if Hugh were alive, he would have sent for her long ago. Yet— Eleanor could not possibly tell such a lie. The floor seemed to be tilting precariously beneath her feet, and her world had become dizzy; she sagged in Liam's arms.

And when the pirate spoke, his voice sounded strange and far away. "Who in hell is Hugh Barry?" he demanded.

Eleanor chuckled. "Katherine's childhood sweetheart— the man she was to wed on her fifteenth birthday." She directed a long look at Liam. "Perhaps you will decide to marry Katherine after all, O'Neill."

5

*H*e had stopped caring about most things long ago, when he had been a small Irish boy at court, an outcast and a bastard, cruelly taunted and teased by the other children. Liam watched Katherine wiping her eyes with the corner of her cloak. He told himself he did not care. He refused to care.

Caring in itself was dangerous, but for him, it might open up old wounds he had long since healed—or long since closed and set aside.

His face impassive, Liam led her toward his blood bay stallion, one arm still around her, supporting her. In her hysterical state, she would not be able to ride by herself.

Suddenly what he was about to do must have registered through Katherine's shock, because she balked. To his surprise, she whirled to face him, speaking through her teeth. "I won't ride with you, O'Neill!"

"You are not fit to ride alone," he countered.

Tears filled her eyes and spilled down her cheeks. "I will not ride with you," she cried again, and she rushed to her own mount, which Macgregor held, and mounted in a flurry of skirts and leg.

"Then you must concentrate on riding," Liam said flatly. Despite himself, his tone softened. "Can you do that, Katherine?"

She glared at him as if *he* had betrayed her love and trust, then yanked her reins free of Macgregor. Liam understood what she intended instantly. As she sawed on the reins, whirling her mount around while viciously kicking the mare's sides with her heels, Liam lunged for the bridle.

He missed. The mare took off. Katherine was galloping through the front gate as Liam jumped into his own saddle with a curse.

Even though her actions irritated him, he could not help but admire her as he quickly drew abreast of her, their mounts' hooves clattering loudly upon the road. Reaching down, he caught her mare's bridle, and both horses slowed from their headlong gallop to an uneven trot. Katherine uttered a strangled, angry cry.

He stared at her. Dawn was breaking behind her and her hair, long since free of its coif, was set aflame by the rising sun. Her beauty held him entranced. Her spirit amazed him. How unusual she was. How she tempted him, even now. His loins throbbed at the thought of what it would be like to mount and then tame such a woman.

Liam urged his stallion up against her gelding, his knee touching hers. "I am not going to allow you to escape, Katherine."

She was pale and furious, and still tearful. "But I can try!"

Not trusting her, Liam took the lead line firmly in hand. With her emotions running so wild, she might very well try to escape him again. He counted on the fact that, later, when she was calm, she would become reasonable, finally recognizing that she had no choice but to remain with him.

Yet a deep sense of guilt he had never felt before nagged at him. For keeping her against her will. No woman had ever resisted him before. He glanced at Katherine as they galloped across the London Bridge, past wagons and carts, drays and mules. He had never tried to seduce a virgin before.

He thought of Hugh Barry. Her betrothed, who yet lived. Savage emotion rose up in Liam, hot and hard. He most certainly was not freeing her so she could return to him.

He had wanted her from the moment he had first seen her—and never had he been so patient in his life. He would take her sooner or later—no matter that Hugh Barry lived. He was her protector now. He alone.

She turned her gaze to his and lifted her chin. Her glare was defiant. A challenge was definitely there. She intended to fight him until the end. Liam's admiration for her grew.

But her challenge was dangerous. She was dangerous. He must somehow pick up the gauntlet she threw at him, yet he could not beat her down as he would a real enemy. He must tame her, seduce her, win her.

For he was not like his father, as Gerald FitzGerald had seen. Shane O'Neill would have already used the girl, mercilessly, and by now would have tired of her and tossed her to his men. Liam knew damn well that he was not like his father at all, despite the fact that the comparison was ofttimes made. Still, damnably, he felt qualms. And Shane O'Neill had never felt a single qualm in his life.

But there was no place for a conscience in his life. Men who survived by wit and will, by sword and cannon, did so because of an utter lack of conscience. His was a life of constant warfare. Victory meant survival. And to the victors went the spoils—and Katherine FitzGerald was another prize in a long line of prizes he had won. But not just any prize—oh no.

Gerald FitzGerald's offer to give Katherine to him in marriage came back to him, as cruelly teasing as those highborn British youths had been when he was a boy at court. Good God. He did not need a wife. He did not need sons. In fact, he was determined to remain childless. And the mockery of his life would end with him. He would not bequeath it—or any anguish—to a son.

Besides, too well, he recalled her horror when Gerald had offered her to him as his bride.

Still, even though he did not need a wife, even though he refused to have children, Liam found the thought of taking Katherine FitzGerald as his bride vastly tempting. It was unthinkable that a man like him might wed with such a woman.

Liam comforted himself with cynicism. How eagerly impotence sought an alliance with power, he thought. Fitz-

Gerald, once a great earl, was now eager to give his daughter in wedlock to Shane O'Neill's son.

Liam wondered what Gerald hoped to gain by making him his son-in-law. Did Gerald hope to use him to escape Southwark as he had tried to use that other sea captain who had turned Judas on him two years ago? Liam doubted it. Only a fool made the same mistake twice. In all likelihood, Gerald sought far more than escape from his prison.

Did he think to harness Liam's control of the seas he sailed? To undo his cousin, FitzMaurice? Liam could easily prey upon those Spanish and French ships who brought the rebel Irish leader his victuals and supplies. But that alone could not help FitzGerald, who was a prisoner in exile, who had lost Desmond forever. That would but weaken FitzMaurice, making him ripe for capture by the queen's men.

What did Gerald hope to gain from an alliance with the man the world had labeled the Master of the Seas?

A possibility began to tease Liam. He straightened in his saddle, shot Katherine another, but sharper, look. There was no rush, he reminded himself. Katherine was his, and should he dare to think the unthinkable, to do the undoable, a mistress could become a wife easily enough.

Despite his intentions to remain as cold as stone, to remain conscienceless, guilt nagged at him. He stole another glance at Katherine. He had her best interests at heart, did he not? Otherwise, she would return to Ireland to beg for bread, no different from the other homeless victims of the wars there. She needed his protection, she needed him. And in time, she would be as pleased with him as his other women had been. He would make sure of it. He would satisfy her in bed, and out of it, he would shower her with more wealth than she had ever seen.

Their gazes collided and held. Her defiance remained strong. Animosity and resentment made her green gaze glitter brilliantly. They were leaving Londontown behind them now, and Liam felt a flaring of pity for his captive that he could not rein in, that he could not control. His heart seemed to lurch with it, the feeling sickening. Too well, he recalled what it was like to have everything taken away from oneself, to be powerless, an innocent, unwilling victim of those in power, in absolute control. As he himself had been on that day sixteen years ago when Shane O'Neill had so abruptly appeared in his life, changing it forever.

Essex, 1555

The boy heard them shouting and he crept silently to the window, crouching below it. He realized that his mother was weeping, and his fear intensified. He lifted his head to peer outside.

He gasped.

Some dozen men sat a dozen horses in the small yard outside their home. They were all big men, wearing shaggy bearskins and old iron shields upon their backs, their heads shaved, huge swords strapped to their sides. Beneath the fur cloaks they all wore coarse woolen tunics, and their legs and feet were bare. The boy stared. He had never seen such strange and savage men before.

"You cannot do this, Shane!" his mother cried.

The boy glanced at his mother. Mary Stanley was a fair woman with fine, delicate features. She was elegant of bearing and dress, but now her gray eyes were wide with fear. The boy cried out as the huge, shaggy-haired stranger facing her raised his arm upward. "Enough, woman!" Shane shouted. And he hit her.

The boy's mother fell to the ground. The sound of the brutal slap resounded in the courtyard.

With a cry, the boy rushed from the house, realizing too late that he had no weapon with which to fight this intruder. "Halt!" he shouted. And he jumped at the stranger.

"God's cock, what is this?" Shane O'Neill was four times bigger than him and swatted at him with little effort. He fell into the dirt beside his mother, who abruptly pulled him into her arms, her face white with fear, tears shimmering in her eyes. But he did not want her protection—

he wanted to protect *her*. He struggled free of her grasp. As he rose to his feet, Shane reached down and grabbed him by the back of his velvet doublet, actually lifting him off his feet.

Shane turned to face his men. "This is my son?" He was incredulous. "A silly English fop?"

Liam ceased struggling, for there was simply no way that he could free himself from this man's hurtful grip. This man, Shane O'Neill, the father he had never met— the man who had raped his mother once, so many years ago, when she had been traveling at sea. Mary had never told him the truth—but he had heard the story many times, for they had talked about him and his mother behind his back when he and Mary had lived at court, first with the Dowager Queen, Catherine Parr, and then with the Princess Elizabeth.

Now the Irish warriors chuckled and grinned at the sight of the boy in the blue doublet and white hose, hanging from their leader's hand.

Disgusted, Shane dropped him so abruptly that he landed on his backside on the hard ground. Hatred welled inside him. Immediately he lurched to his feet. "Don't hurt my mother."

Shane's gaze widened, then he laughed. "I do what I please, boy, and from now on, you do as I please. You're coming with me."

"No!" His mother rose unsteadily to her feet and clutched at Shane's arm desperately, one side of her face swollen and mottled an angry red.

He was frozen.

"The boy comes with me!" Shane roared. "God's teeth, I see now that I am almost too late, that you have turned him into the kind of boy that other men coddle and swive! God's cock! I'll not have my son a puny, piss-drinking Englishman!"

"Lord, no!" His mother fell to her knees, clinging to the hem of Shane's tunic. "Please, Shane, do not do this, please, do not take my son from me. Please, I cannot bear it!"

Shane kicked her away. Before the boy could react and

rush to his mother—or run away from his father—Shane gripped him by one ear. "We're to Tyrone. Aye, from now on you're an O'Neill. You ride with me now, boy. I'll make you a man, a real O'Neill, or I'll kill you in the trying." And he dragged him forward, then lifted him and threw him on a huge brown horse.

He was dazed, in pain, his ear feeling as if it had been torn from his head. But he managed to throw one leg over the other side of the horse. Filled with panic now, and acutely aware of his mother's soft, heartbreaking sobs in the background, he was determined to escape.

"You'd disobey me?" Shane shouted at him, gripping his bony knee, preventing him from slipping off the other side of the horse. One hamlike hand swung out, cuffing him hard on the other side of his head. Sparks exploded in his brain, his stomach heaved. When he regained some of his senses, Shane was mounted behind him and they were cantering away from Stanley House.

"Liam! Liam! Oh, God, Liam!" his mother screamed.

He twisted in the saddle in spite of Shane's unyielding hold. His mother ran after them, stumbling on her skirts, sobbing, hands outstretched. She screamed for him again, and this time tripped and fell in a heap of silk and velvet into the dust.

A sob escaped his breast.

"No son of mine cries. Tears are for women, not men," Shane growled, smacking his head yet again.

He sucked down another sob, swallowing it, and then another, and another, ignoring the pain, both in his heart and his head. His first lesson from his father had been a cruel one. But it was a lesson he learned instantly. And he had never cried again.

London, 1571

"Sir William!"

William Cecil was asleep in his canopied bed at Cecil House in London. His valet had to call his name several times before the secretary stirred. Grunting, he sat up.

"What passes, Horace? Good God, 'tis past the midnight hour!"

"Sir William, a gentleman is waiting in the antechamber. He insists 'tis most urgent and that he must speak with you!"

Cecil groaned and threw the heavy down covers aside, sliding to the floor. His valet helped him don his fur-trimmed velvet robe. Following the valet, who held the taper aloft, Cecil left his bedchamber. His eyes widened and then narrowed when he saw his guest. He turned. "You may leave us, Horace."

The valet obeyed, shutting the heavy walnut door behind him.

Cecil faced his cloaked visitor. "What has happened?"

" 'Twas a most strange dawn at St. Leger House," the stranger began. "When I made my rounds, the guards were waking up. Some gentleman had taken them unawares. But one had just regained his senses in time to hear many voices in the courtyard. One was that of Eleanor FitzGerald. He managed to get to his feet in time to see three riders tearing away toward London Bridge. One of the riders was an uncommonly tall man with fair hair. Of the other two, one was a woman."

"Eleanor FitzGerald—gallivanting about at dawn?" Cecil asked sharply.

"Nay, 'twas a different woman, far taller than Eleanor. Eleanor returned to the house."

Cecil absorbed all of this, his brow furrowed. "A trio of visitors at St. Leger House. What in God's name are FitzGerald and his wife up to now? Who would dare to ally himself—or herself—with FitzGerald?"

Cecil did not expect his agent to respond, and he continued, speaking very much to himself. "FitzGerald has yet to reconcile himself to eternal exile from that wretched land he calls his home. I doubt he ever will. And now this—new players." Cecil faced the spy. "You will instruct your men that St. Leger House is to be watched at all hours. If these visitors return, I must learn their identity."

The agent nodded and left.

Cecil spoke to the empty room, grim. "God's blood! Visitors in the night must mean a conspiracy—and Fitz-Gerald conspires yet again against the queen! But who dares to conspire with the Lame Earl now? Who could be so foolish—or so bold?"

Cecil had grown very thoughtful. He was so sick to death of the Irish problem, a never-ending problem of defiance and rebellion, carried out by half-mad, savage Celts; it was a problem that had to be solved. The queen had to have complete control over Ireland. Otherwise England's enemies would establish a toehold there. And had he not said from the very beginning that it was madness to remove FitzGerald from Ireland? And he had been right. The proof of that was one too-clever lunatic, the leader of the rebels, James FitzMaurice, already supported by France, Spain, and the Pope.

Sir William was determined to learn the identities of the new conspirators. Perhaps, just perhaps, there was an opportunity here—one that might please everyone, one that might solve everything.

The man screamed.

The soldiers were impassive as they watched his body being stretched out upon the rack. When the unholy screams had faded, one stepped forward, in red doublet, pale hose, and a sword that was clearly not ceremonial. The castellan of Tilbury Castle put his face close to the man's. "Come, sailor, surely you can speak now? Why did you and your friend come upon Tilbury Beach? Who did you bring? For whom do you wait? You have a scant minute to tell me what I will learn from you. The next time the wheel turns, your arms will be torn from your body, perhaps your legs as well."

"Please, God have mercy, no!" the sailor sobbed. "I speak, I speak!"

The castellan nodded. "Out with it."

"We—we come from the *Sea Dagger*."

The castellan's eyes widened. "The *Sea Dagger*? Liam O'Neill's ship?"

The sailor made a guttural sound that was obviously affirmative.

"O'Neill is here? At Tilbury?"

"No, your lordship. We're waitin' fer him. To take him back to his ship."

The castellan began to chuckle. He rubbed his hands together in real glee. "God's blood! 'Tis my day of fortune! How pleased the good queen will be when I deliver her the sea's most notorious master!"

Abruptly he turned to the sailor still stretched out upon the rack. "Where did O'Neill go? What mission does he perform?"

The sailor whimpered. "I don't know."

Displeasure crossed the castellan's face and he signaled to the man cranking the wheel of the rack. The sailor screamed. And screamed, and screamed.

They cantered up the road, Tilbury Castle looming ahead of them. Katherine was so tired she could barely stay in the saddle, so tired now she could no longer think. Her body screamed in aching protest, her sore muscles badly abused from the many hours she had spent in the saddle that day. But the sight of the castle, etched against the blue sky, gave her strength. Although she was being taken to her doom—the pirate ship—she was far too exhausted to care about anything other than getting down from her mount as quickly as possible. After she had rested, she would face her future. Until then, she must cling to the knowledge that Hugh was alive. For that knowledge gave her another choice—and it gave her hope.

Liam suddenly stiffened in his saddle; his hand tightened upon his sword. "Mac," he murmured. "Something is amiss."

Macgregor reached for his pistol, and a second later they were set upon by a horde of swordsmen.

A dozen infantrymen erupted from the woods and swooped down upon them. Katherine screamed as swords clashed and sang. Liam did not dismount, driving his horse forward as he thrust and met his first attacker, instantly thrusting past the man's blows to wound him in the chest.

The man went down, blood blossoming on his jerkin. Swiftly Liam slashed yet another assailant, and then another, and then another. His mount screamed shrilly, nicked by a sword, beginning to bleed.

Katherine's terror did not diminish when she realized that she had been boxed in by both Liam and the Scot, as if they were protecting her. Liam parried still, with the same results, slaying or wounding another soldier. Meanwhile Macgregor had tossed his pistol aside, after killing one assailant, and now wielded his sword with the same kind of stunning skill his captain displayed. Katherine clutched her reins, watching in abject fear as Liam and Macgregor fought off their numerous attackers. Already the ground around them was littered with gray doublets. It did not seem possible, surely not, that Liam and Macgregor could actually fight off these troops? Yet it seemed that victory was soon to be theirs.

And then Katherine saw the reinforcements—musketeers. Her heart lurched. The musketeers came charging down the road, cloaks flying, their doublets red. Katherine opened her mouth to warn Liam—too late.

A musket ball whizzed past his head. And then another screamed by. Liam was still engaged in a sword fight with his last two adversaries. Katherine had never imagined that any mortal man could fight so effectively, so lethally, slaying his opponents one after the other. Then a third musket ball pierced Liam's shoulder, leaving a hole in his cloak. Liam grunted, still parrying with one of the last remaining swordsmen. Katherine watched as the hole in his cloak turned red. He had been hit in his left shoulder, on the back. Had it been his right, he would have been lost.

But as it was, his right arm moved with lightning speed, slashing down his last opponent. And suddenly it was over, just minutes after it had begun. For the musketeers had surrounded them, a dozen deadly muskets primed and raised, ready to blow off their heads.

Liam lowered his rapier. So did Macgregor. Both men were panting, sweat streaking their faces. Their hands and arms were covered in blood. Katherine looked at the bloody patch of wool on Liam's back. Her stomach threatened to disgorge itself. Her entire body was shaking.

A man detached himself from the troops, riding forward to face Liam. His red doublet was gay with gold braid and black ribbons. His plumed black hat was set at a severe angle. He held his rapier in a gauntleted hand almost casually. But there was nothing casual about his black eyes and hard expression. "I am Sir Walter Debrays, castellan of Tilbury," he announced. "Lay down your blade, Captain O'Neill. You are my prisoner."

Liam held his gaze for another heartbeat, then laid down his weapon.

They were escorted across the lowered drawbridge, through the raised portcullis and into the second ward. There they were told to dismount. Despite herself, as Katherine obeyed, she was frightened. Although she had no fondness for her captor, she knew that, within days, he would meet his Maker. No pirate would be allowed to live, not even in confinement. Somehow it did not seem right.

But Katherine could not think about that now. She stood between Liam and Macgregor, achingly aware of Liam's silent battle with pain. Debrays shoved between them, pulling Katherine forward. She wore her hood, and he pushed it back off her face. "Who are you?" he demanded.

Katherine did not respond. Of course she should reveal that she was a prisoner. Then she would be freed. But then she would be adding the crime of abduction to that of the many other crimes Liam would be charged with. She hesitated. He deserved punishment, but she did not think he deserved death. After all, he had not raped her. He had captured her, true, but neither he nor his men had harmed her or Juliet.

"She does not answer." Debrays smiled and turned to Liam. "Your doxy is beautiful, O'Neill. But then, they say your women are always astounding jewels."

Liam's expression was impossible to read. He actually appeared bored, despite the fact that he held his injured left arm tightly against his side. "She is not my doxy. She is my prisoner."

Debrays laughed in disbelief. "Were she your prisoner, O'Neill, she would not be looking at you with such concern! Come, they say you are more than clever—but that was exceedingly stupid."

A muscle in Liam's jaw ticked. He finally turned his gray gaze upon Katherine—and she thought she saw a warning there.

Debrays smiled and jerked her against his side. He slid his hand into her cloak and squeezed her breast. Katherine cried out, bucking against him. Liam jumped forward, only to have five rapiers press their sharp, pointed tips into his chest, shredding his shirt. He froze. Debrays lifted a brow, still stroking Katherine's breast, and making a display of it. "Ahh—we are possessive of our toys?"

"She is my prisoner," Liam said harshly, "and I intended to reap a ransom for her. 'Twas our reason for coming afoot on English soil. She is Katherine FitzGerald, Debrays, daughter of the earl of Desmond. I suggest you treat her with the respect she is due."

Debrays faltered.

Katherine wet her lips. It had dawned upon her that Debrays, unlike Liam, would rape her, and enjoy inflicting the abuse, too. She also realized now that Liam was defending her. "I am Gerald and Joan FitzGerald's daughter," she managed to utter. "And I demand you remove your hand from my person."

He removed his hand. He looked at her briefly, at her pale, lovely face. His jaw clenched. "Randolph, take her into the hall and see that she is given a chamber and all else she needs." He turned to face Liam. "You, O'Neill, will adjourn to the dungeons while I await orders from the lord admiral."

A young soldier had come to stand beside Katherine, his gaze inquiring. Katherine ignored him. Liam and Macgregor were grabbed roughly and pushed forward, across the ward. Katherine bit off a cry as she watched them. The back of Liam's cloak was mostly red. She realized that he might very well die from his wound and not from a hangman's noose.

"Lady FitzGerald?"

Katherine met the young soldier's hesitant gaze. Then she whirled to face the castellan. "Sir Walter!" she cried. "You cannot send that man to the dungeon without a physician attending him first."

Debrays raised a brow. "How concerned you are for his welfare, my lady. Perhaps you are not merely his prisoner? Perhaps you are not his prisoner at all?"

Katherine recalled Liam's large, aroused body covering hers, recalled the storm of need and desire she had felt in response. Flushing, she said, "I was abducted on the high seas, sir. As a matter of fact, Captain O'Neill made his demand for ransom not too many hours ago," she lied.

"And the pretty prisoner has begun to hanker after the virile sea captain?" Debrays almost sneered.

"No!"

"Then do not concern yourself with his welfare, *Lady* FitzGerald." Debrays nodded at the young soldier. "Take her to the hall, Randolph."

"Aye, sir." Randolph gripped her elbow and Katherine had no choice but to follow him across the ward and into the main hall. She told herself that she was glad. She was free of her captor at long last. But she kept seeing his bloody back, kept imagining him in some dark, dank dungeon, lying near death.

Katherine was given a small chamber on the floor above the hall, and her own maid to attend her. She bathed but had little appetite. The events of her entire adventure, beginning with her capture at sea by the pirate, kept replaying in her mind. She recalled how her father had offered her in marriage to Liam O'Neill. She thought about the pirate's wound, and wondered if it would fester and kill him.

She passed a restless night. She dreamed of her father, not as a shabby prisoner in St. Leger House, but as the earl of Desmond, presiding over their home, Askeaton. In her dreams, Gerald was bold and ebullient, dressed in all his finery, and her elegant mother, the Countess Joan, still lived. Katherine was surprised when Hugh appeared, a freckle-faced boy trying to steal a kiss. Katherine was happy to oblige him. They kissed and laughed and kissed again. But then Liam materialized, enraged, and pulled them apart. Katherine was no longer a girl, but a full-grown woman, and Hugh had disappeared. When Liam embraced her, his arms dissolved into blood. Katherine screamed. Liam was gone, and her hands dripped red.

Katherine awoke feeling as if she had hardly slept at all. As she was in England, she said a hurried and furtive mass on her knees in her room, having sent her maid away to fetch a small break-fast. Katherine made sure to finish her prayers before the maid returned. While the queen did not really persecute or pursue papists, one and all had to conform outwardly to the new religious ways.

Katherine spent the rest of the morning pacing her small chamber, unable to prevent herself from wondering how Liam fared. She told herself it did not matter if his wound festered and he died, but she did not really mean it.

One of Debrays's men came to her chamber shortly before noon. It was the young soldier, Randolph. "You must come with me, my lady. Please bring your cloak."

Katherine had little choice, and she followed the soldier down the narrow stone stairs. Katherine's heart beat hard and fast. Had Debrays decided to allow her to attend to Liam after all? Or was she being released? The latter did not seem likely, at least not yet.

When she entered the ward, she saw him and faltered. Liam and Macgregor were being escorted by six soldiers from the other side of the ward. Although both men were squinting in the daylight after having been immersed in total darkness for more than twenty-four hours, Liam walked without help. His arm had been bound in a crude sling to his side. As he came closer, she saw that his shirt had been torn up and used as both a sling and a bandage. Beneath his bloodstained cloak, he was naked from the waist up, and the muscles in his stomach and chest rippled as he moved. She also saw that he was somewhat flushed with fever. But she had seen color far higher and far worse. Clearly the pirate had the constitution of an ox.

His gaze met hers. Somehow it was amused and knowing—as if he sensed her concern—and that infuriating gleam made her scowl at him. Liam was far from death. She should have known that a small musket ball was no match for him.

Debrays suddenly said from behind her, in her ear, "How pleased you are, my lady, to see your *captor*."

Katherine stiffened and slowly turned. "I am pleased that he lives, Sir Walter. 'Tis called Christian charity and human kindness, nothing more."

"Mayhap I would like a little of your Christian charity," he leered.

Katherine was rigid. This man knew, or sensed, far too much. But he could not know, could he, that far more than innocent doings had passed between her and Liam? Katherine was aware that she flushed with guilt. She looked forward to the day they quit Tilbury and this dangerous man. "Why have you summoned all of us to the ward?"

Debrays's yellow teeth flashed. "You have been summoned to Whitehall, Lady FitzGerald, the three of you. The queen commands your presence posthaste."

Katherine started. Her glance found Liam's. He did not react to the news that he was to journey to an audience with the queen, to his final prison-place—and to his ultimate death.

6

With the exception of her recent visit to her father in Southwark, Katherine had never been to London before. In fact, up until that horrible day of the Battle of Affane, when she was just thirteen years old, she had never been farther than Cork in the west and Galway in the northeast, except once, when she had accompanied her parents to Dublin. Dublin was the largest city in Ireland, but as it was in the Pale, and controlled by the English lords who resided there, neither the earl of Desmond nor his countess went there very often.

London put Dublin to shame. Unquestionably it was the largest city Katherine had ever seen. And there was so much to see! From the grand Gothic homes of the gentry and nobles lining the banks of the Thames to the dilapidated and ancient thatch-roofed buildings housing brothels, stews, and ordinances in the slums. Soaring cathedrals presided over neighborhoods with narrow, refuse-filled streets and timbered tenements. Thin mules and carters transporting faggots of wood bumped up against splendid coaches and chariots boldly embossed with coats-of-arms and servants in livery that could feed a small family for an entire year. Dark-robed students rubbed shoulders with young artisans, and both turned to gaze, either wistful or hostile, after the lavishly transported noblemen. Beggars of all ages and both sexes chased the extravagant conveyances, and should a lord or lady dare to walk the streets, even escorted, cutpurses and cony-catchers were instantly about their work.

There were markets everywhere. Passing through one, Katherine was agog. The street stalls were teeming with more produce and wares than she had realized existed in all the world, much less in one place. She glimpsed spices and silk from the faraway Orient, Venetian glass, and furs from the forests of Sweden and Norway. There were all sorts of fripperies, hats for the men and gloves with cuffs, fringe and even studs of gems, ribbons of all colors and plumes equally exotic, embroidered pillows and enameled pomanders, and even French caqueteuses—those strange little chairs with narrow, horizontal slabs of wood where a person was expected to place his arms. One vendor sold nothing but pots of cosmetics. Katherine glimpsed milk white powders and several different shades of rouge. Another sold nothing but warming pans—and dear God, they were silver. Other vendors hawked spicy cakes and sweet pasties. Katherine would have dearly loved to wander through the crush of the market square, to eye the wares and watch the gentlemen and women as they browsed and bickered with the merchants, artisans, and farmers for the goods they wished to purchase.

But it was not to be. Not that day. She was a prisoner, no longer of the pirate, but of the queen. She was on her way to a royal audience—on her way, perhaps, to her fate.

The King Street Gate appeared before them. Katherine's heart raced. She glanced at Liam, riding between two of Debrays's men, but he showed no sign of fear, no sign of dismay or dread. She could not believe he had no feelings, and she had to admire his composure. Her own composure was in shreds.

Some two dozen guards, all the queen's men, resplendent in red and gold, met them the moment they had passed through the low, square stone archway of the gate. They traveled down a paved road inside the huge inner ward, the vast Privy Gardens to their right, the shrubs still green, the trees bare, tennis courts and cockpits on their left. On the other side of the gardens were other galleries and various lodgings. Ahead lay the queen's new Banquet

House, the Privy Gallery, and the part of the palace that contained the Great Hall, the Council Chamber, and the Privy Apartments. Far to Katherine's right she could just glimpse the Chapel, and beyond that, she knew, lay the River Thames.

Their mounts were halted. The captain of the Guard, a lean, dark-haired man, dismounted and approached Debrays, who also slid to his feet. They spoke briefly, the captain turning a bright blue gaze first upon Liam, then upon Katherine. He started briefly when their gazes met. A moment later he detached himself from Debrays and moved to Katherine's side. "Sir John Hawke, captain of the Guard," he bowed. "If you would dismount, Lady FitzGerald?"

Katherine slid from her horse and in her fatigue and distress nearly fell into his arms. Hawke righted her instantly. She stepped away, murmuring her thanks, and was suddenly aware of Liam's eyes upon her. She was startled. She had the feeling that he did not care for her being handled so familiarly by another man, even through there had been nothing inappropriate about it.

"Lady FitzGerald?" the captain said politely, his blue eyes holding hers again. "If you will follow me."

Katherine had no choice but to obey, as it had not been a suggestion but a command. She shot another glance at Liam and saw that he brought up the rear, surrounded by numerous guardsmen, as was Macgregor. Debrays also accompanied them with six of his own soldiers. Captain Hawke escorted them into the Gallery, a long, timbered structure, and directly down its vast length. Katherine muffled a gasp. The ceilings were wrought in stone and gold, and the wood wainscot was carved into hundreds of beautiful figurines.

Ahead were a pair of massive closed doors. The group paused and they all waited as a sergeant-at-arms announced their arrival. Katherine's heart beat unsteadily. She could not comprehend how Liam still appeared so calm. She did not have to be told to know that the queen was behind those huge closed doors.

A stream of courtiers and ladies left the Privy Chamber.

Katherine's mouth dropped open. She could not help but stare. She had never seen such finery, such wealth. The men wore silver or gold-buckled leather shoes, fine silk hose in every shade imaginable, and doublets with padded hips and embroidered bodices, the sleeves slashed or beribboned. Fantastic ruffs framed their faces, and almost every male sported a short beard and mustache. They wore numerous heavy gold chains and gem-set rings. More than a few wore black hats with extravagant plumes.

Then Katherine stared at the women. Their dresses were the richest brocades and velvets and silks she had ever seen. Their skirts were huge, held out by Spanish farthingales, making tiny waists seem tinier. Every woman wore bejeweled gold or silver chain belts, from which they hung their keys, a fan, or a looking glass. The bodices of their dresses were low and square, puffed sleeves were slashed. The women's ruffs were almost as fantastic as the men's. The women also wore chains, and extravagant earbobs and rings as well. All wore coifs. The coifs were silk or velvet, embroidered or cut out, and often encrusted with gems and pearls. It was also clear to Katherine that the women all wore cosmetics. Everyone was exceedingly pale, their cheeks glazed with egg whites, their eyebrows plucked, their lips painted red. Some of the women had even painted fine lines upon their very bare bosoms, exposed almost indecently by their low-cut bodices, in order to represent thin veins.

When the stream of courtiers and ladies had passed, Debrays was ushered into the Privy Chamber alone. The doors were pulled closed. Katherine jerked, realizing she had been staring after the parade. She met Liam's gaze, and saw that he was smiling ever so slightly at her open reaction to the dazzling splendor of Queen Elizabeth's court.

Katherine was angry that he might guess just how much of a country mouse she actually was, worse, her own gown was years too old, and even had it been new, she saw now how obviously poor it was, and how out of fashion. She also wore no cosmetics, and would not have even guessed how to start. How dowdy she must appear. A wren among a flock of swans. She turned her face away, her mouth tight.

God's blood! How could he dwell on her, when he was about to meet the queen and would shortly thereafter be thrown into the Tower? Those other women were so fair! Surely one of them had caught his rampant eye—to think otherwise was impossible!

Katherine kept her back to Liam, her shoulders squared. She saw that the doors to the Privy Chamber were still closed. What could Debrays be saying? Was he telling the queen that he doubted Katherine had been Liam's unwilling prisoner? Would the queen believe him? Would she free Katherine, allow her to return home in order to marry Hugh?

Katherine realized her determination to do just that had become fierce. These last six years had been a tremendous loss, she understood that now. She had been in such complete isolation, had missed living six crucial years whilst in the prime of her life. Not only had she not known of her father's fate, or that of Desmond, not only had she been denied husband and children, she had been denied the wondrous modern world.

It was not too late, she told herself vehemently, to make that loss up now. She was not yet old. She would have children, and she would live. Surely after she bore a few babes, she would be able to travel back to this exciting place. She tried to imagine herself with Hugh and small children, laughing and gay, exploring the London market, but as she had not seen him since he was a boy, she could not picture him as a man, and she gave it up.

The doors opened suddenly and Debrays appeared, looking smug. Sudden fear swamped Katherine. Her father was in absolute disgrace, and she herself might fall into that same disgrace within a matter of minutes. To be ordered to her father's side in Southwark was no better than to be returned to the priory at Saint Pierre–Eglise. Katherine resolved to speak with great care. She knew only what common gossip held about the queen. That she was well educated, being able to speak many languages with ease. That she was quick to temper, and often lost it when her subjects crossed her. But that she was also fair. Katherine must pray that justice would rule this day. And she must be prepared to help her own cause, for no one else would.

A portly man appeared in the doorway, framed briefly by the two marble pillars on either side that stretched up to support the high, vaulted ceiling of the paneled hall they waited in. His glance skidded over Liam, Macgregor, and paused briefly on Katherine. "I am Sir William Cecil. Her Majesty will see you now."

Katherine sucked in her breath and stole one last glance at Liam. He wore the slightest smile. Of encouragement? She marched behind Cecil, still feeling Liam's eyes upon her as he followed her, Macgregor in the rear.

Suddenly she stumbled, confronted by the queen of England. Elizabeth sat upon her throne on a dais. She was unmoving, as if carved from stone, and for one moment, Katherine stared—and the queen stared right back.

She was so magnificent that she dominated the incredible room, and Katherine did not even remark the fantastic Holbein mural upon the wall behind Elizabeth—she saw nothing but England's queen.

She wore a purple damask gown encrusted with thousands of gold beads and embroidered with gold thread that showed off her narrow waist advantageously, which was encased in a thick gold girdle studded with rubies and pearls. The low-cut gown revealed an immense amount of ivory bosom, making the Queen appear somewhat voluptuous. A ruby larger than Katherine's thumb winked from her cleavage. The largest ruff Katherine had ever seen, a stiff pinkish white froth, framed her entire head. Her strawberry-gold hair was frizzed and pulled back severely, a dark velvet coif hemmed with multicolored gems pinned there. The queen was thirty-seven years old. Once, she must have been beautiful, and she was still handsome. Her skin was flawless ivory—she wore no egg whites, and her face a perfect oval, while her eyes, although kohled, were bright and keen with intelligence. Her figure was very slim. Had she not possessed her father's longish nose and narrow mouth, she would have been a beauty in spite of her age.

William Cecil coughed.

Katherine realized she gawked like a country maid and she dropped into a curtsy, color flooding her face. When she righted herself, she saw the queen's gaze flickering over Liam O'Neill. It was cool, imperious, yet a spark was there. She turned back to Katherine, who was still hot with shame. "Are you in conspiracy with your father against Us, mistress?"

Katherine gasped, and the whole world seemed to drop out from under her feet. "I—I beg your pardon?"

"You heard. Do you conspire with your father against the Crown of England?"

Katherine gasped again. It had never occurred to her that she would be accused of conspiracy—of treason! "No! Your Majesty—how come you by such an abominable thought?"

Elizabeth's gaze flickered over Katherine from head to toe. "When the Master of the Seas has a predawn appointment with Gerald FitzGerald, the daughter in attendance, I must needs assume the worst."

Katherine gaped, glancing at Liam, who was unperturbed. Indeed, the fool stood negligently, despite his sling, booted stance wide, as if relaxed. Beneath his open cloak, Katherine saw that his bare, broad chest did not heave. Was he not going to speak? To stop this dangerous tack before it went any farther? "Your Highness!" Katherine cried. "The Master of—I mean—Liam O'Neill abducted me on the high seas. He met with my father to ask a ransom—nothing more! I can assure you of that!" Katherine's color was high now, for lying yet again, this time to England's queen.

The queen eyed Katherine. "But why were you present, mistress, if not to plan treason?"

Katherine was white. Her mind raced to find some credible reply. "I begged h-him—I had not seen my father— in six long years!"

Elizabeth studied Katherine without any apparent softening. Then she turned to Liam. "What is true, rogue?"

He smiled. "I did capture a small French trader, never dreaming it held such a prize, Your Majesty. And surely you know the way of the high seas. The booty was mine. All of it. I went to FitzGerald to ask a ransom, nothing more.''

Katherine stared from Liam, who was still wearing a small smile, to the queen, whose mouth remained in a tight, unforgiving line. ''This is a fantastic tale.'' There was warning in her tone.

Liam's smile flashed, more seductive than before. ''The lady can be most persuasive. I saw little harm in her accompanying me to her father.''

The queen stared. ''Is *she* harmed, Liam?''

He inclined his head. ''Hardly.''

Katherine was still terrified, unsure if Liam had defended them against the charges of conspiracy, and she was also in disbelief. What was happening here? It almost seemed as if the queen knew Liam—it almost seemed that she was, just slightly, fond of him. But that could not be. Liam was a pirate. ''Your Majesty, I have not been harmed,'' Katherine said quickly. ''And O'Neill speaks the truth entirely and I beg to be freed.''

Elizabeth turned to Katherine, who, too late, realized she had interrupted their private conversation. One reddish brow lifted. ''You defend this man after all he has done to you?''

Katherine flushed. ''I am a virgin, Your Highness. He left me my virtue. For that I am grateful.''

''How honorable you are,'' the queen murmured to Liam. ''Yet your reputation does not rest on honor—or on a soft heart.'' Then she said to Katherine, ''You defend him. Debrays said you were fond of Liam.''

''No!'' Katherine cried. ''I am not fond of him—not at all!''

Elizabeth stared at her grimly, as if she did not believe a word she spoke.

''He abducted me, prevented me from returning home, made it clear ...'' Katherine broke off. She could not bring herself to speak the entire truth—to reveal that Liam intended to make her his mistress.

''What did this rogue make clear, mistress?'' the queen demanded.

Katherine blanched at her sharp tone.

"Your tongue!" the queen cried. "Find it!"

Katherine was frozen. Her face had drained of all color. She could not speak.

Liam stepped forward and calmly said, "I have asked Mistress FitzGerald to be my mistress. As she has no protector in this world, I will gladly assume that role."

The queen stared at Liam coldly. Her regard flickered but briefly to Katherine. Then she said, "You have not changed, Liam. But your pirate ways are becoming far too daring."

"If I have offended you, then I am truly sorry," Liam said.

"I doubt that!" the queen cried. "So this entire game was only that, a game?" Elizabeth said. "To ask a ransom when no ransom could be paid, to entertain a young girl's whim to see her father—and to take her as your mistress when all was finally done?"

"Does not the entire world know how fond I am of games, Your Majesty?" He bowed his head, a smile playing at the corners of his mouth. "Surely there is no one who would make an objection to such a game? Not Fitz-Gerald, who is in disgrace. Not her brother, who is but two years old. Surely not her stepmother, who wishes no rivals in her home."

Katherine blinked. This was the first she had heard of having a baby brother.

The queen stood. "Knave!" She was clearly furious. "We object! Your games go too far! And this game rings of something more! Insolvent knave!"

Liam jerked. So did Katherine. He said softly, "I would never commit treason against you, Bess."

Katherine gasped, certain that Liam would be thrown into the Tower without further ado for addressing the queen so disrespectfully.

Elizabeth stared only at Liam, her eyes wide, her gaze hard, weighing his words. Liam remained motionless.

"You have gone too far, O'Neill!" she finally said, her bosom heaving. "And We doubt you do not know it. Your arrogance needs be taught a swift and sure lesson. You

cannot plunder where you will, without a care for Us.
FitzGerald may be in disgrace, but the girl is Our subject,
and fresh from a convent, not a prize for a man like you.
You have gone too far—but I pray you have not gone as
far as conspiring with FitzGerald.''

Liam's gaze was lowered, so that Katherine could not
see his eyes.

''Perhaps your ardor will cool whilst you pass time in
the Tower,'' the queen snapped. She signaled two ser-
geants, who leapt forward, each taking one of Liam's
arms. ''And think on *all* your guilty ways, pirate,'' she
added ominously.

Katherine choked off a cry, watching as Liam was led
away.

Later that afternoon, the Privy Chamber was once again
cleared of all the queen's favorites, with the exception of
Sir William Cecil. ''Did you send for Ormond?'' she
asked.

''He shall be here at any moment, Your Highness,''
Cecil replied.

''And the FitzGerald girl?''

''She is asleep in the chamber where she has been confined. Thus far, she has not done anything to give credence
to the conspiracy theory,'' Cecil said.

Elizabeth paced. In doing so, she made a magnificent
figure, and she was aware of it. Like her father, she was
vain. And because she was a woman, her vanity was,
perhaps, greater than his. Not only did she know that she
was the most beautiful and best-dressed woman at court;
she knew no other lady could dance as well—no other
lady had as many admirers. ''I have never heard such
nonsense,'' she finally said, facing Cecil. ''Surely this
FitzGerald girl went to Liam O'Neill, bearing a secret
message from her father. And FitzGerald hates Us, he
would want but one thing—to plan to escape to Ireland
and commit treason.''

''Perhaps,'' Cecil said.

''There is no other explanation for the dawn meeting.
None!'' Elizabeth said fiercely. And finally, her face fell.

"Blast that rogue, Cecil. How could he do this to me? Curse my golden pirate! I do not hear from him in over a year, and now this! How many times have I summoned him to court in all that time?" She paced, not waiting for an answer. "I wonder how many other ships he has plundered, that we do not know about. I wonder if he plunders all the lady travelers, as well! Should I even doubt it?" Her face screwed up. "Ahh, well, he is no sad, lonely little boy now. He thinks to pervert that poor virgin—and mayhap he thinks of treachery against me." Tears suddenly filled Elizabeth's eyes.

"Your Majesty, be careful of reaching the wrong conclusion. O'Neill is very clever, far too clever to be caught at treason in such a fashion, and I doubt all is as it seems."

"What do you say?"

"O'Neill has been so useful to us until now, and I find it hard to believe that such a clever man would risk his future in order to dabble in Irish politics." Cecil's tone was bland; he did not blink.

"He has gotten too bold, too cocksure," Elizabeth said, but less certainly. "He does not think to get caught."

"Perhaps. But while 'tis obvious what FitzGerald would gain from such an alliance, think on what O'Neill would gain."

"FitzGerald would gain all. He could use Liam to escape and return to Munster, so that he could war with his own cousin FitzMaurice to regain control of his kin and his land. There is naught for Liam to gain," Elizabeth said sharply, "except the promise of some future reward, which could not possibly entice Liam into treachery. The only other thing he could gain is the girl. But she is worthless."

"Agreed. The girl is worthless with her father in exile, stripped of land, title, and all power," Cecil said carefully. How different this conversation would be if the girl were still the daughter of a powerful earl. Then Liam O'Neill's purpose would be quite clear.

"So you think O'Neill was merely amusing himself—and truly asking a ransom?"

"I am not sure." Cecil paced the room, pausing to stare

at the life-size figure of Henry VIII painted on the far wall. "We must allow the game to play out, Your Majesty. We must see where the players lead."

"If O'Neill has allied himself with FitzGerald at this time, I like it not. There are problems enough with the papist FitzMaurice." Elizabeth could not repress a shudder. Her head ached now, but whether in response to more Irish problems, or because of how betrayed she felt by Liam, she could not tell. "In God's name, what is keeping Ormond?" she snapped. "He knows FitzGerald as well as anyone; they have lived their entire lives as enemies. He would know if this conspiracy is true."

"I hear a commotion," Cecil said. He moved to the closed doors and opened them just as the earl of Ormond was about to be announced. "Tom! We are eager to speak with you."

The earl of Ormond, known as Black Tom because of his dark complexion and his dark moods, entered the chamber with long, strong strides. A brown, sable-lined cloak waved about broad shoulders—he tossed it back with undisguised irritation. "It is damnably wet out this night," he said, grim. "Not an eve to be riding about Londontown."

"But you have come to Us with all haste, have you not?" Elizabeth said coolly. He had kept her waiting for over an hour. "The cause is grave, dear Tom."

He eyed her, pulling off one heavy glove after another and slapping his hard thighs. "Indeed. Is it true, my cousin, my queen? Have you tossed the Master of the Seas in the tower?"

"Only for a while." Elizabeth spoke slowly, then, so that she might judge his reaction to her next words. "So that he might cool his raging lust for your little half sister, your dear mother Joan's daughter—Katherine FitzGerald."

Ormond started and then he swore.

7

*T*he earl of Ormond finally smiled, grimly. "You would enjoy reminding me of the fact that my mother married that bastard FitzGerald." He did not add what everyone knew, and had, at the time, delighted in—that Joan Butler, countess of Ormond, had married Gerald FitzGerald despite his having been twenty years her junior—and almost the same age as her own eldest son.

Elizabeth was serene. "Have you met your dear half sister, Tom?"

"Once, many years ago," he growled. "And do you think I give a damn about FitzGerald's brat—even if she be my half sister?"

"Oh, come, Tom, surely you do not want to see her innocence despoiled by someone like Liam O'Neill."

Ormond's gaze was flat.

"You really have no feeling for her? Do you know that she looks so much like Joan, although her hair is red, not blond. She is a tall beauty and she carries herself with pride despite her diminished station in life."

"I care as much for her as I do for a country whore."

Elizabeth sighed. "You must know that the girl claims to have been abducted by O'Neill." Ormond did not react. "O'Neill has told us an absurd tale, one I find difficult to believe." Elizabeth told her cousin about the dawn meeting at St. Leger House.

"God's blood!" Ormond cried. "O'Neill and FitzGerald in conspiracy, this must be stopped!"

"I thought that might move you," Elizabeth said, satisfied.

Butler's jaw was tight. "Do you not know what will come about if Shane O'Neill's son is allied with FitzGerald? Within months FitzGerald will escape and return to Ireland. By this time next year, he will undoubtedly be as strong as he ever was."

The queen was grim. She glanced at Cecil, who was sitting in one of the room's two chairs of state. "We have spoken of little else. But William is not convinced of such an alliance."

Ormond inhaled. "Then he is wrong. FitzGerald is damnably clever, and he must have offered his daughter to O'Neill to sway him to his cause."

"But the girl is worthless."

Ormond was exasperated. "Come, coz, not to O'Neill."

"What do you say?" Elizabeth demanded.

Ormond began to pace. "Liam is the bastard of Shane O'Neill—a man who died a traitor, his lands forfeit to the Crown. The pirate is rich, your spies know that, but as no man has ever infiltrated the pile of stone where he abides, no one knows the extent of his treasure stores. He is rich, but for what, for whom? He is without family. Without clan. The Irish distrust him. Yet he is hardly an Englishman. He *is* Irish, cousin. 'Tis Irish blood flowing in his veins, no matter that Mary Stanley birthed him. To marry the FitzGerald girl would give him a family, a clan—a country. The FitzGerald girl would give him respectability, and his sons would have blue blood in their veins." Ormond faced Cecil and Elizabeth. "I know that this is what the pirate wants. All basely born men want to be elevated through marriage and their sons. And I am sure that FitzGerald has sweetened the offer and promised him some future reward as well, undoubtedly the promise being some parcel of Desmond land."

Elizabeth and Cecil exchanged glances. Cecil said, "As you have more to lose than anyone except the queen if FitzGerald regains his place in Ireland, you jump more quickly to conclusions that may not be right, Tom."

Ormond cursed. "Even should FitzGerald return to Desmond, his land is destroyed, many of his kin dead—he will never again wield the kind of power he once had. I will *never* share the rule of Southern Ireland with him!'' His expression was thunderous. ''How my mother could have married such a curse upon the world—I know not,'' he said harshly. He went to Elizabeth, ignoring Cecil, and gripped her hand. ''No alliance must be allowed, my dearest cousin. FitzGerald will use O'Neill's power on the seas most effectively. Not only to escape you. In winter he could starve out his cousin, FitzMaurice. That would please us all, of course, but once FitzMaurice is brought down, he could blockade your own royal ports—starve out your own royal troops. In no time at all you will be faced with Desmond's power and defiance again.'' Tom's dark blue eyes flashed. ''Or, God forbid, the two cousins could unite against us.''

Silence fell across the room. Elizabeth finally sat down. She was grim. For a long time she did not speak, unwilling to believe that Liam O'Neill moved against her. Surely it was not true. As William had said, there was no proof yet. ''Mary Stanley was—is—my friend. When Catherine Parr died, I took her into my home—her and her small son. I pitied them both, mother and child—as everyone did. Most of us tried to hide it, but some did not. They both knew. They both knew they were different, that they were cases of charity.'' She looked up. ''I remember watching Liam playing alone in the gardens at Hatfield House, one early spring day. It was a day not unlike this one. Not yet warm, but not too gray, the sun pale and feeble. He was five or six. He was using a stick as if it were a sword—and so fierce was he, 'twas as if he fought the entire world.'' She sighed. ''He was so alone—so lonely. He was such a quiet boy. He never spoke unless spoken to, he never laughed. And the other children were so cruel to him, taunting him, calling him an Irish bastard to his face.''

''He is no little boy now,'' Ormond said sharply. ''Make no mistake of that. Do not let your old affections interfere with your good judgment, Bess. He is a dangerous man.''

The queen regarded him. "I can not dismiss the past as if it never existed. I do not know that he has committed treason yet. I believe he has some affection for me, too, some gratitude."

"You must not think like this!" Ormond cried. "You must see him as he is! Not his handsome face, but his cold, barren heart!"

Elizabeth looked at her cousin. "Then perhaps I should not favor you, either, dear Tom, as we have a special history as well."

"We are blood," he reminded her. "And our cause is one. I am loyal to you—always."

Elizabeth sighed. "Yes, our cause is one and you I trust," she said, gesturing him to her. When he came she gripped his hand and stroked it. "I know you only seek to protect me." Then she pressed her hands to her temples. "In truth, I do not want to believe that Liam O'Neill is the savage traitor his father was. The very notion is a blow to my heart, to my soul."

"Their rendezvous is proof of their plot against us, against you," Ormond snapped. "Cousin, listen to me now. Keep O'Neill in the Tower. If you do not wish to try him and hang him, then let him rot there. And send the girl to me," Ormond said flatly. "She is my half sister, and who better to be her guardian? I will install her with one of my brothers at Kilkenny Castle and she will be watched carefully."

Elizabeth glanced at Cecil.

Having patiently awaited his turn to speak, knowing that it would come, Cecil said, "O'Neill has not been proved guilty. We have no cause to detain him like a common criminal."

"He is surely guilty of piracy." Black Tom laughed mirthlessly. "I can find you a dozen witnesses to his bloody deeds."

Elizabeth raised her hands, her face pale. "*No.* There will be no charges of piracy."

Ormond was disgusted and he turned away, not seeing the look Elizabeth and Cecil exchanged. Cecil patted her arm. "You are right, Your Majesty, for if we imprison

O'Neill and send the girl to Ormond, we will *never* know if FitzGerald has made a new plot against you. Let him go. Let them both go. I will have my agents watch them. And we will let their actions speak the truth.''

Ormond had turned to face both sovereign and councillor. " 'Twill be a costly, bloody mistake!''

But Elizabeth was nodding. ''Yes, the plan is so simple but so good. Let their actions speak the truth. I see where you lead, Cecil.''

Cecil smiled.

''Yes, We shall release them,'' Elizabeth said. She patted Tom Butler's rigid shoulder. ''And there will be immediate signs to show us if they conspire or not. If they go to Ireland, it adds grave suspicion of guilt.'' She paused. ''And if Liam marries the girl, then we know that Tom was correct—'twould be all the proof of guilt we seek.''

Katherine had just awakened and had barely finished performing her ablutions, when she was summoned again to the queen. It was a new day, but she was far more afraid than she had been the day before. Had the queen decided she had enough evidence with which to charge her formally with conspiracy, or God forbid, treason? And what of Liam O'Neill? What would happen to him now? Katherine told herself she was merely curious, and not at all concerned about the pirate's fate.

Katherine hurried beside the sergeant escorting her, her palms perspiring, out of breath. They did not go to the Presence Chamber, but to the queen's royal apartments. The antechamber was a large withdrawing room with linenfold paneling, molded ceilings, and fresh rushes upon the gleaming oak floors. The queen was with William Cecil yet again, but another man was present as well. Tall and dark, he stared at her with cold black eyes. Even though it had been many years since they had last met, when Katherine had been but nine or ten, she recognized him. He was her half brother—her mother's oldest son from her first marriage. He was her father's worst enemy, Thomas Butler, the earl of Ormond.

''Lady Katherine,'' Elizabeth said, smiling.

Katherine dropped into a curtsy, her heart hammering, wondering what Ormond was doing here—and why the queen was acting so warmly. Straightening, she watched the queen approach. She could not summon up an answering smile. The queen paused in front of her. "You need not be afraid anymore, dear girl," she said gently. "We have determined that your story is true."

Her eyes widened. "You have?" Then, realizing that she sounded as guilty as sin, she blushed. "I mean—thank you, Your Highness." She curtsied again.

But this time the queen lifted her to her feet. Katherine towered above her. "Please forgive Us for Our suspicions, but surely you know that your father has displeased Us so greatly with his treasonous ways that We must be vigilant always."

Wisely Katherine did not answer. She could not tear her gaze from the fond expression in the queen's eyes. Elizabeth smiled. "But fortunately, you take after not Gerald, but your dear, departed mother."

Katherine felt that she was required to speak, so she said, "Y-yes."

"Tom!" It was a command, and Ormond moved forward, still staring at Katherine. "Does she not remind you of your mother, Joan?"

His jaw was tight. "Yes."

Elizabeth nodded. "Your mother was a great and beautiful lady. I knew her well. We were good friends. The first time your father tried Our patience and We were forced to put him in the Tower, why, she came to me directly to intercede for him, greatly distraught. We assured her then that We were only teaching the young, wayward earl a lesson, and indeed, the following year he was freed." Elizabeth sobered.

Katherine heard herself say, "But he arrived home too late. Mother was dead."

Elizabeth's gaze turned sharp. "Yes, your memory serves you well. Yet you were but a child then."

"I was twelve," Katherine said, staring at her feet. How could she have said such a thing, even if it were true? How could she have risked raising the queen's ire again?

"Your Highness, I am sorry—I loved my mother so. I have yet to reconcile myself to her loss."

Elizabeth patted her hand. "We understand. We, too, mourned her passing. Everyone who knew her did. Now—why do you not exchange greetings with your half brother? He is most eager to meet you."

Hesitantly, Katherine looked past the queen and at Thomas Butler. There was nothing eager about his expression, which seemed dark and forbidding. "My lord," she said uneasily. "Good day."

"Lady Katherine . . . Sister dear. The queen is right. You are our mother's image exactly." He did not seem pleased about it.

Katherine thought that one and all lied. Her mother, in her youth and even when she had married Gerald at the age of forty, had been one of the reigning beauties of her time. Katherine knew she could not be as lovely. But she accepted the false praise politely. "You honor me—thank you."

Ormond said nothing more, and silence fell between them.

Elizabeth shot him an annoyed look, then pulled Katherine across the room and indicated for her to sit in a small caqueteuse. Katherine did so gingerly, and so as not to appear a country lass, she put her arms on the wooden slabs, feeling very foolish as she did. The queen sat on a bobbin chair beside her and patted her hand. "You need not worry any more about Liam O'Neill."

Katherine jerked. "He—he is not dead?"

The queen laughed. "No, Katherine, no, he lives. 'Twould take more than a paltry musket ball to down the Master of the Seas."

Katherine couldn't help feeling relieved. She was aware of the queen watching her, closely, so she said, "O'Neill is a pirate—is he not?"

"Of course he is a pirate—how could you ask?"

Katherine hesitated, afraid to plunge into dangerous waters. "You . . . you seem to know him—Your Highness."

The queen laughed. "Indeed I do. When my father married Catherine Parr, I went to live with her and my brother,

Prince Edward. Liam's mother was Mary Stanley—the niece of Catherine's first husband, Edward Borough. She was pregnant, in disgrace, but Catherine took pity upon her and installed her as one of her privy ladies. I saw Liam O'Neill soon after he was born, when he was but a wet, red, squalling newborn babe.''

Katherine gaped.

The queen shrugged. "Even after my father died, I stayed in Catherine's household. She was like a mother to me. Three years later she married Tom Seymour, and still I stayed. So did Mary Stanley and her son. In fact, when Catherine died, Mary came into my household. Liam was four at the time. I recall it well, because 'twas his birthday soon after. She and Liam stayed with me until my sister Mary ascended to the throne.'' Elizabeth's tone was light. Too light as she spoke of Bloody Mary. "Then she requested leave to go to her parents' home in Essex, and because of her firm religious beliefs, I agreed, thinking it far better.''

Katherine's mind was spinning. Liam was hardly a savage pirate—he had been born at court and he had been raised with a prince and princess, by a Dowager Queen. And although half-Irish, he must be Protestant, as his mother had been. She could hardly credit what she had heard. Seeing her expression, Elizabeth smiled. "You appear stupefied.''

"I am. Is O'Neill English or Irish—noble or knave?''

"He is both,'' the queen said flatly, unsmiling now. "Never forget that his father was Shane O'Neill, a savage murderer, the man who raped his mother violently. And Shane claimed him when he was a young boy of ten, wrenching him from his mother's arms—raising him in savagery.''

Katherine stared.

"You are very interested in Liam O'Neill,'' the queen said casually. "He is handsome, is he not?''

Katherine told herself she would not blush, but she recalled his every expression, his slight, amused smile, his seductive tone and his hard, powerful body, aroused, pressing against hers. She flamed.

"You are free now, you know," the queen said when she did not answer.

Katherine cried out and impulsively gripped the Queen's hands. "Your Majesty—thank you!" Abruptly she dropped the pale, cold hands, but the queen took her palms up again, enfolding them in hers.

"We are friends now, Katherine. Remember that. What would you do now?"

Katherine thought of the green rolling meadows near Askeaton, of the forests and hills, of Hugh, and she leaned forward eagerly. "I would go home!"

"To your father in Southwark?"

Too late, Katherine realized her blunder—she no longer had a home in southern Ireland—it had been forfeited to the Crown. "Your Majesty—please forgive me. These past years I was so secluded I did not know of all that had happened to my father. I . . . still think of Munster as home."

Elizabeth murmured a soothing reply, but her glance met Cecil's, then Ormond's.

Katherine saw it, but did not decipher it. She cleared her throat. "I would return to Ireland," she said boldly.

"And what would you do there? Where would you go?"

"To my betrothed."

The Queen stared. "You are betrothed?"

"To Hugh Barry, Lord Barry's heir. I was betrothed to him from the cradle, but after Affane I was sent away. I have waited many years to wed, Your Majesty. I am no girl now, but a woman of eighteen. I wish to wed him, Your Majesty. Immediately."

The queen stared, brows raised. Her gaze darted to Cecil, to Ormond. To Tom she said, "What know you of this?"

He shrugged. "I recall the betrothal. I do not recall the ending of it. I suppose you must send her to Barry—to Ireland." His dark gaze was hooded.

Elizabeth stared at Katherine, making her think that she had done something wrong. Then the queen smiled.

"Well, then, you must be on your way to Ireland, my dear, to your wedding—to Hugh Barry."

Katherine trembled with relief. But once again, she saw the queen exchange knowing glances with her men.

It was late. Soon the church bells would toll the midnight hour. Liam listened as he heard the door to the small chamber he had been confined in being unlocked. It could have been worse. The fact that he was in a veritable chamber with pallet and nightstool indicated that he could extricate himself from royal suspicion. He was not surprised to be summoned now.

A cloaked man opened the door, offering no explanation. Liam did not ask for one. He tossed his bloody cloak about his shoulders, wincing slightly as he did so, and followed the man without a word. They descended the three stories and exited onto the wharf which butted into the river. A small barge awaited them. Liam climbed in, as did the queen's agent. Two oarsmen began to row them upriver to Whitehall.

Although he had been confined in a small, airless space for an entire day, he avoided breathing in the river and night air too deeply. With the advent of warm weather, there was little pleasant about the Thames, even on a cool night. And mentally, he prepared himself for what was to come.

Sometime later he was ushered up the Whitehall Stairs, through the River Gate, and upstairs into the queen's private apartments. When he finally entered her withdrawing room, he saw that she sat, fully dressed in crimson, at her small writing table, penning some note or another. She saw him and attempted a scowl, which soon fell apart, and she smiled.

"Sometimes you are very naughty, Liam."

So the queen had changed her tune. More sure of himself now, Liam sauntered forward, took her hand, and kissed it. His lips caressed her skin. She withdrew, blushing like a virgin—which she reputedly was. "That will not get you anywhere, rogue," she chided.

She was in a playful mood tonight and he was pleased.

Far better that she be playful than suspicious, but now he was suspicious, too. Did Bess play a game, or was her changed mood merely the result of her mercurial nature? He smiled, his eyes twinkling for her. "How pleasingly soft your hands are, Bess," he murmured. He captured one elegant hand again. Everyone knew how vain she was, especially of her beautiful hands. "How soft, how lovely."

She was pleased and could not hide it, and she smacked his wrist lightly and gestured for him to sit. "I must apologize," she said baldly.

Liam remained silent, waiting for her to speak, knowing he must be very careful not to make a false move. He was just barely innocent of the charges of conspiracy, it was only a matter of degree. For he was forming plans. Yet even were he entirely innocent, innocence did not always serve the victims of injustice well. He needed to know if she thought him innocent, or if she played a game of chance with him instead.

"I have witnesses to your plunder of the French ship and your abduction of Katherine FitzGerald," the queen said.

He doubted the veracity of what she said, for it would take some time to locate witnesses, but he did not say so. If this was the basis for her sudden empathy, then she still believed he was teetering on the brink of treason. Elizabeth had *always* been clever.

"I am relieved. But my heart is still sore, Bess. That you would think me a traitor to *you*."

"*My* heart was sore," she retorted, leaning toward him, her eyes searching his face.

He knew then that despite her doubt, she wanted him to be innocent. He took her small hand in his and gripped it too warmly. His fingers kneaded her soft flesh. "I am your friend," he said, low and intimate. "Always."

She allowed him to hold her hand and she pressed against him, her arm to his arm, as if ardent. "I hope so, dearly do I hope so, Liam." Their gazes held, and he was fully aware of the power he exercised over her. Her lips were parted slightly and they trembled; she sighed again. The air coursed with sudden heat. "Liam," she murmured.

His jaw flexed. He gazed into her eyes and saw the yearning there. The queen was gone, and in her place was a woman, a woman he had known his entire life. He sipped an arm around her. "Bess," he repeated, "I am your friend."

And it was true. He would never forget all that she had done for his mother, when he was but a small boy. He would never forget that, even before she became queen, she had been kind to his mother, unlike most of the other ladies at court. But he had never felt desire for his queen. Even though, for a man like him, for any man, it could be advantageous.

She pressed against him, her body quivering noticeably. "Liam, I have missed you. Why have you stayed away so long?"

He smiled gently at her. "My life is hard, Bess. I have no grand palace to lure me to this island; I earn my bread at sea."

She whispered, unsteadily, "That could change."

Liam froze.

Elizabeth began to blush, but she did not drop her gaze.

His pulse pounded now. "Even should you give me a grand palace, that would not make me an Englishman."

"You are half-English."

"Yes." He touched her lower lip with his finger. "And my father was—and will always be—Shane O'Neill."

"But you are not like him." Her stare was bold. "Or are you?"

"No." He held her gaze, knowing that if she gave him one more sign, he would have to kiss her.

She laid one of her palms on his chest, atop his pounding heart. Their gazes locked. "I am sorry for thinking you a conspirator with FitzGerald, but surely you can understand, for the meeting appeared so strange. Now, of course, knowing the truth from my witnesses of Katherine's abduction, I comprehend you were but seeking a ransom. Obviously the girl, beauty that she is, was pleasant company on your trek, and no hindrance." She smiled too warmly, but her gaze dropped from his eyes and moved over every feature of his face—finally lingering on his mouth.

Ah, Bess, he thought, *the tale sounds absurd even from your lips. You do not believe me innocent, although you wish to. And do your ardent glances, filled with longing, mean that you wish to take me as your lover—after all this time?*

Liam had no desire to bed his queen. As far as he knew, despite the rumors about her and Robin Dudley, whom she had made the earl of Leicester, and those about her and her cousin Tom, she was a virgin and intended to remain that way. Still, he was a man, one with experience, and he knew she found him very attractive. This was not their first privy meeting, 'twas not the first time that she had flirted with him, touched him, and cast sidelong glances at him. Yet the signals this night were stronger than ever.

With both Leicester and Ormond, the two men whom she had loved for many years, she was far more openly affectionate—which was why the gossip ran so rampant about them. Leicester often enjoyed the queen's company unattended in daylight hours—much the way Liam did now, at midnight. And sometimes Elizabeth would refer to Tom as her ''black husband,'' causing much speculation that he shared far more than just her company. No one could ever know for certain what passed behind Her Majesty's closed doors. If any man were her lover, most likely it was Leicester, for it had become clear that she favored him over Ormond.

Liam was well aware that becoming the queen's lover would help him politically, now. In the future, it could damage him. Somewhat foolishly he hoped that tonight she would *not* decide to take him to her bed—if she were in such a habit of taking lovers. For no man, he knew, could refuse a queen. He would not be able to refuse her either.

But he did not wish to use her. That was not the way in which he would repay her for all that he owed her.

Elizabeth sat very still, looking at her hands. Then she glanced up at him. Naked desire gleamed in her eyes.

Liam was frozen but a moment, then he acted on instinct. He pulled her close, hoping she would come to her senses. "Bess? Is this truly what you want?"

Her gaze darkened. Her mouth parted. He expected her to mouth the word "yes." Then she cried out incoherently and lunged to her feet, very much like a frightened virgin. Or a Virgin Queen. She paced. Liam took a deep breath, relieved.

"Still," she said, her back to him, her shoulders shaking, "the truth hardly absolves you of your other crimes, Liam." She faced him, as a mother might face a wayward child. "You can not abduct noblewomen and get away scot-free. Even if they are the daughters of defiant, treacherous, disgraced earls. And this one is a virgin, one convent-raised."

"I confess to the error of my ways," he said easily, unrepentant. They both knew it.

"What punishment shall you be forced to pay?"

He rose lazily to his own feet. "Have I not suffered enough? A ball in my shoulder—a night in the Tower?" His tone was soft.

"You have hardly paid for terrorizing poor Katherine."

Liam smiled wickedly. "She has hardly been terrorized."

Elizabeth regarded him, her expression stiffening. "No, I imagine she did not object to your kisses and caresses."

He met her unwavering gaze, no longer smiling. He felt hemmed in by the queen on one side, and Katherine on the other. Was the queen jealous of his interest in Katherine? "If she did not object, it does not condemn her, only me."

"Yes—it condemns you for a lusty rake, one too experienced for his own good," the queen said peevishly.

She was jealous. 'Twas not a good sign for Katherine. 'Twas not a good sign for him. "Would you have me be something less than a man?"

Elizabeth's glance skidded down his body, skimming his groin. "You know I would not." She jerked away. "You cannot have the girl."

Liam was careful not to reveal any dismay. He had not counted on the queen's being jealous of Katherine. "Your

Highness, the French merchant was the fifth I have taken this year.''

She faced him, jaw flexed. "Do not think to bargain with me!'' she cried. "I know damn well how many French vessels you have seized, you pirate! The French ambassador has repeatedly asked me for your head! Catherine de Medici has placed a bounty on it, as well—has even written me directly!''

Liam had to chuckle. "And what, pray tell, did you reply?''

She eyed him. "I replied that, if I could capture the Master of the Seas, he would come to trial, but that so far he has eluded my navy, just as he has eluded everyone else on the high seas.''

Liam grinned.

"Do not become too cocksure! You know well that if another nation captures you, there is naught I can do to free you, jackanapes!''

"Indeed, I am well aware of what fate awaits me should I wind up in a French prison or on the Spanish rack.'' His gaze was hard. "I am ever loyal and you know it, Bess. I have done more for you this year than your whole damned navy. Five French ships, two of which were bound for Scotland, supporting the rebels there, and three Spanish vessels, one a galleon laden with silver plate destined for the Netherlands. Come, I deserve a reward.''

"And you think I will reward you with the girl?''

"She is of no value to anyone now. She has no station, no dowry. I will treat her well. I will not abuse her.'' And the intriguing thought flashed through his mind—that perhaps he might dare to marry her in time. If he could play the game he had just begun—and win it well.

"She is betrothed.''

"That betrothal is ancient, made years ago. I doubt Hugh Barry is expecting to wed her.''

"Nevertheless, it stands, and I have agreed that she shall return to Ireland to marry him.''

Liam's face paled. An instant later he was furious, and he could not contain it. "And my reward?''

Elizabeth grabbed the papers on her desk and thrust

them upon him. "Here! The letters of marque you have
been begging for. Against *all* Spanish vessels, not just
those aiding the papists in Scotland and Ireland and Flan-
ders. What? Are you not satisfied? You are legal now,
Liam. At least, in regard to the Spaniards you so love
to plunder."

Liam held the letters authorizing him to prey upon all
Spanish ships, in effect thwarting any official Spanish
claims against him. In England he could no longer be
prosecuted for plundering Spanish ships, and at sea he
could become more ruthless and more daring than he was
in his dealings with the French. He had no letters of
marque against them, just a careful understanding with
Elizabeth, who hated Catherine de Medici, hated and
feared her, yet was unwilling to aid the French Huguenots
openly as she had once done.

"Are you not pleased? Come, Liam, I cannot believe
you want one particular girl so badly. She is hardly *that*
special."

Liam did. He had thought about little else other than
the beautiful, fiery, intelligent Katherine FitzGerald since
he had captured her. He had wanted her the moment he
had first seen her. He was still livid about having won
a prize, only to have it taken from him. He had been
outmaneuvered. It was a rare event. Truly rare. But if he
kept his head, and waited, then surely he could emerge
the victor as he usually did. Tonight, clearly, was not the
night to press the queen for the other woman.

But how could he emerge triumphant?

He could not abduct Katherine again. Already Elizabeth
suspected him of conspiring with FitzGerald, and he dared
not arouse her suspicions any further. No, he must be
more careful than that, more clever. Elizabeth must be
maneuvered to his side in this cause. But how?

One fact was clear. He could not allow Katherine to
wed Barry.

He bowed his head, contrite. "I am pleased to gain the
letters, Bess. Pleased and grateful. You will not be sorry.
I shall keep the Spaniards under heel, as you wish me
to do."

Elizabeth nodded, but her gaze was sharp.

Liam looked her in the eye. "And you must forgive me. I am a lusty man." He paused significantly. " 'Tis not easy to be a man, to have lust aroused . . . and then denied."

Elizabeth's expression softened. "You are an intriguing man, Liam. A rogue to the very bone—and you know just how enticing it is."

He smiled into her eyes. "And you are an intriguing queen, madam."

She smiled, too. "I have a favor to ask of you. I had intended to make it your punishment, but now . . . 'twould be a boon for me. And—a sign of how I trust you."

He bowed. Inside, he tensed, expectant. "I am at your command."

"You brought her here. I ask you to escort her now to Barry."

Liam quickly hid his surprise—and his pleasure. Inwardly he was triumphant—for now he knew he would win this battle after all. "As you wish, Bess."

Elizabeth smiled, and Liam realized she was just as pleased as he was.

8

*K*atherine took her dinner just before noon the following day with some hundred other courtiers in the Banquet Hall. The room was huge, supported by thirty great "masts," each forty feet high. The canvas walls were painted to look like stone and were festooned with holly, ivy, and flowers garnished with spangles of gold. The ceiling was painted to look like the sky, complete with the sun, stars, and clouds, and from it hung pendants of wicker flounced with exotic fruits. There were ten tiers of seats for spectators, and most of the seats were occupied. The hall also boasted 290 windows.

Dinner was a deafening and wondrous affair. Katherine could barely believe her eyes. She found it difficult to eat, and not because she sat on a bench crammed between two large gentlemen who eagerly introduced themselves as Sir John Campton and Lord Edward Hurry, of Campton Heath and Hurry Manor, respectively. There was just so much to see.

But Katherine soon found herself trying to dissuade the gentlemen from their obvious overtures, which became lecherous when she had, reluctantly, given her name. "Such a fine and beauteous Irish lass," Hurry crooned. "So far from home, my dear?"

Katherine managed a nod, tearing a hunk of warm bread dripping with butter into two pieces, careful not to encourage him. Elbows jammed her from either side. Hurry made another comment but she ignored him. She chewed the

bread, unable to enjoy the sweet, raisiny taste. Her gaze
kept wandering, first to the other courtiers, a resplendent
sight, then to the painted heavens above, and finally to the
animated crowd of spectators seated along the walls, who
kept calling out to the diners below.

She gave up trying to eat. She had no appetite. After
dinner her escort was to arrive, and her journey home
would begin. As interesting as court was, how excited,
how thrilled, she was to be leaving. Soon she would be
at Askeaton, and she could imagine the proud castle with
its round towers and square medieval keep set upon its
island looming above the thick forests surrounding Lough
Shannon. She could hardly wait.

Soon she would be reunited with Hugh. She tried to
envision his surprise. Perhaps he had thought her lost to
God after all these years. She almost laughed aloud at the
thought of herself becoming a nun. Marriage and babies
was what she wanted.

Undoubtedly she was off to a sunny and bright future
as Hugh's wife. Hugh Barry would have turned into a
brave and strong man. His father and cousins had all been
well formed; none had been ugly. And she loved Hugh.
Once she was in his arms, she would forget all about the
golden pirate so aptly called the Master of the Seas.

But Katherine could not imagine lying in Hugh's bed,
in his arms. But surely that was because she had not seen
him in such a long time, and had thought him dead.

Too, once wed, she would try to find a way to free her
father. It was intolerable that he remain an impoverished
prisoner at St. Leger House. The queen was proving herself a kind friend. Katherine decided that she would return
to court to plead her father's cause before the queen, to
convince her of the injustice of his confinement. While
Katherine knew there was no hope of his title or land
being restored to him, at the very least he might be able
to return to Ireland—to Askeaton, where he had been born.

Katherine glanced around the incredible hall once again,
and knew that she would not mind returning, not at all.

Finally Katherine pushed her pewter plate aside, unable
to avoid her misgivings. She had to face the real reason

for her lack of appetite. Although she was thrilled that Hugh was alive, and that she was to marry him, she was frightened, too. She had not seen him in years. What would their reunion be like? What if he no longer wanted her? Why had *he* not sent for her in all these years?

And why did Liam O'Neill's image keep crowding her mind?

"Why do you brood, mistress?" A rich and familiar voice asked.

Katherine stiffened.

Behind her, he bent low, and when next he spoke, his breath licked her ears. "Are you not filled to overflowing with joy now that you can go home?" Liam teased.

Katherine twisted to stare up at him. It was as if she had conjured him out of thin air with her thoughts. "B-but— what do you here!"

He laughed, and suddenly shoved himself between her and Lord Hurry, who scurried to make room for him. Immediately 'twas Liam's rock-hard thigh pressing against hers and then he picked up her hand.

"Good morn, sweetheart," he murmured as if they were alone in a bedchamber, nay, alone in bed.

She snatched her hand away. "You are not in the Tower!"

"No, I am not."

"I do not understand." Her heart was beating quickly. His warm thigh was jammed against hers. She did not dare to move.

"The good queen has seen fit to pardon me for my sinful ways," he laughed. Suddenly his hand was on her leg, squeezing her once.

Katherine swatted it off. "You mean, rogue, that you have used that golden charm of yours to get yourself freed!"

"Mayhap." His gray eyes gleamed.

She huffed. "I am not surprised that even the queen cannot refuse you." She tried to turn her back to him, but twisting that way was so uncomfortable, that she faced her plate instead.

"A compliment from your pretty lips, Katherine? I had never thought to see the day. I shall cherish it."

She was so angry. She stabbed her meat with the knife. "You may cherish whatever you choose, O'Neill."

He smiled. "Ah, then I choose to cherish you."

And before Katherine could respond, he leaned even closer to her, and again his hand crept up her thigh. He whispered, "Why are you angry, dearest? I had thought you would be pleased to see me spared the hangman's noose."

"I am hardly pleased to see you alive and . . . well!" She jammed her elbow into his shoulder and succeeded in dislodging his hand. "I am trying to eat, O'Neill, and even did I wish to converse, I would not choose you as a partner."

"Come, Katherine, confess. You heart is not stone. Not where I am concerned. You were worried about me." He still leaned close, and she could feel his breath against her cheek and throat.

Katherine had had enough. She would never, ever, confess what he wished to hear—even if it were somewhat, and very slightly, true. "You are the very last person I would ever worry about. Now go away!"

Liam laughed. "I'm afraid I cannot do that, darling."

She faced him, her green eyes on fire. "Do you not have affairs of murder and mayhem to attend to, pirate? Or did you stop here to torture me?"

"There is no pressing murder I must commit this day, no," he said easily. "But tomorrow—ah—that is another tale."

"Perhaps I will leave then, if you insist upon staying." Katherine had no chance to move, though, for his hand quickly gripped hers.

He eyed her bosom. "But I can add torture to my agenda this day, Katherine. Sweet, soft, sucking torture."

She flamed. "I know not what inanities you speak."

"I think you lie," he murmured.

She struggled to pull her hand from his so she could leave the table—so she would not have to put up with his mockery anymore, his suggestions and innuendos, or the proximity of his big body.

But he was relaxed and he released her hand—although his fingers managed to stroke hers as he did so. "Katherine, I suggest you finish your dinner. There will be little chance for more refreshment once we leave Whitehall."

Katherine jerked. "What?"

"I do not intend to stop once we leave Whitehall," Liam said. "I wish to be at sea and en route as soon as possible—by nightfall."

Katherine stared, speechless.

He smiled, lazy and predatory, at once. "Did not the queen explain? I am to escort you home."

She could not believe her ears.

"Come, darling, do not look so distraught. I might become insulted."

"Whatever could she be thinking!" Katherine cried. "Surely you jest—or you lie!"

His glance raked her. "I neither jest nor lie, dearheart. The queen wishes for me to atone for my sins, and as 'twas I who interfered with your voyage home, 'tis only just that I should assist you in completing your voyage." He grinned.

"I shall not go with you," Katherine gasped. "You have no intention of escorting me home! You will abduct me. . . ." she faltered, her cheeks red.

He laughed. "And what else is it you think I shall do?"

She gripped the table, about to leap to her feet. The urge to flee was instinctive.

He clamped his large hand upon one of hers, more forcefully this time, so that she could not move. "Katherine, I will take you to Hugh. I am no fool to arouse the queen's ire—and suspicions—again by repeating abduction. But . . ." His eyes turned to smoke. And he shrugged.

Katherine's heart beat wildly. Dare she believe him? That he would take her home—that he did not intend to defy the queen by abducting her a second time? She was stunned; she could hardly think. She supposed she must believe him. Liam would be an utter fool to anger Elizabeth after obtaining a pardon. Katherine felt a touch of bitter jealousy. Surely the queen had been prettily seduced to have agreed to such madness—to have pardoned a damnable pirate and charged him with escorting her home. Katherine looked into his gaze. She did not doubt that he would continue to attempt to seduce her.

She promised herself that he would not succeed.

Katherine cleared her throat. "The queen approves of my marriage to Hugh."

Liam did not respond.

"If you trespass upon what belongs to Hugh, you will also arouse her ire."

Still he made no comment, watching her steadily with silver eyes.

"So you are thwarted, O'Neill."

Finally he began to smile. Katherine grew uneasy. He did not look like a man who had been denied his prize. "Am I truly thwarted, Katherine?" he asked.

She was wary, refusing to reply. Their gazes clashed, held.

Instinct warned her the time had come to leave the table. She almost jumped to her feet. Too late. His hand gripped her chin, anchoring it in place. Her knees buckled and she sat again. And then he pulled her face forward and his mouth claimed hers.

Katherine's hands came up and she pressed his shoulders, to push him away. It was futile. Worse, with thumb and forefinger he exerted a subtle pressure and her jaws opened. Instantly his tongue swept deep into her mouth. And with that invasion came another kind. Molten heat pooled in Katherine's body, condensing between her thighs.

She gasped into his mouth. His tongue moved more disturbingly. Katherine's body shook. As his kiss continued, she grew dazed. She fought the languor stealing over her body and managed to punch his shoulder. He growled his response and continued kissing her, this time forcing his tongue around hers.

Katherine managed to make a sound, but it was raw and only partly a protest. Somehow her fists had uncurled, and she held his shoulders.

He tore his mouth from hers, unsmiling, eyes ablaze. Wide-eyed, Katherine stared at him, absolutely breathless.

Lusty male cheers and hoots sounded amidst female giggles and whispers. Then the hall was filled with thunderous applause, and the spectators began to cheer them. Katherine started, came to her senses, glanced wildly around. It seemed that a hundred men leered at her, that a hundred women cast covetous glances at Liam. She jumped to her feet. This time he let her go, rising as well, one hand under her elbow. "If I am thwarted, then what, pray tell, was that?"

Katherine met his potent gaze, and feared her virtue would soon be lost.

Somehow, the stakes had changed. Yet she knew not what game they played. She knew only that she was still the prize—and that he was bent upon claiming her.

A few hours later, Katherine was aboard the *Sea Dagger,* which was racing toward the sea. She had hardly spared Juliet a thought in the preceding days, but now she was glad to see her friend, and the two girls embraced warmly. Juliet's stay upon the pirate ship had been uneventful, but Katherine had plenty to impart, and she told Juliet all that had occurred since Liam had taken her to see her father. Juliet listened, wide-eyed.

"What happens now?" Juliet finally asked.

"We are on the way to Cornwall, so that you may be returned home," Katherine responded. "And then O'Neill shall escort me to Hugh Barry."

Juliet took Katherine's hand. "Why are you so grim?"

Her face pale, Katherine looked straight into her friend's eyes. "Because I am afraid of what the pirate intends for me this night."

Guy held open the door to his master's cabin and Liam entered, carrying a heavy tray. It was well past twilight. Lanterns had been lit, and the cabin was warmly aglow. He set the tray down on the dining table, looking for the girls. His eyes widened, then narrowed, when he saw that Juliet lay on the bed, with Katherine attending her, sitting by her side. What game was this? Was this how Katherine thought to thwart him? He was too annoyed to be very amused.

"Anything else you be needing, sir?" Guy asked.

Liam turned, looking fondly at the orphan he'd found wandering about the harbor at Cherbourg two years ago. "No," Liam said. "Get some rest, lad. You deserve it for a day well done."

Guy suddenly smiled, unable to hide his pleasure at those simple words of praise, and it lit up his entire face. He turned to go.

"No dicing and no tables," Liam called after him.

Guy threw Liam a glance, flushing. "No, sir, Captain."

As Guy closed the cabin door, Liam faced the two girls. Juliet moaned.

He sighed. He should have known. That fate would intervene—or that Katherine would take it upon herself to forestall him.

Liam strolled over to the bed. He was aware of Katherine's avoiding his eyes, of how she sat very still and very erect. He himself was somewhat erect as well. He had been cherishing his thoughts of the night to come. A night he had intended to spend in his bed with Katherine, seducing her, pleasuring her.

"I see Juliet is ill," he remarked.

Katherine finally looked up. "'Tis her stomach. She has terrible pains. I am afraid to leave her."

"Will she moan all night, I wonder?"

"I do not know," Katherine said tersely.

Liam reached down and touched Juliet's forehead. She did not open her eyes. Her cheeks were red—but that could be from the use of rouge. "She is not feverish."

"No."

"I suppose you wish to attend her?" Katherine nodded so eagerly he almost laughed. He sighed. "Katherine, tomorrow Juliet leaves this ship. And it will be just you and I for the remainder of our trip."

She paled.

He bent closer, so that he could have easily kissed her

small nose had he wished. "You merely delay the inevitable," he said softly.

Katherine's brows rose, but she remained mute.

Liam turned abruptly, deciding to give her a reprieve—just in case the dark-haired girl was really ill. He exited the cabin, leaving the tray of food.

The next morning, when he returned, every single morsel was gone.

Thurlstone Manor, Cornwall

"Juliet! Have you been harmed?"

Juliet's uncle was not a particularly kind or caring man, but those were the first words he uttered upon seeing her. She managed to smile at him, somewhat tearfully, and her tears were from the joy she felt at finally being home. "I have had an adventure, Uncle," she said rather timidly. He had always managed to intimidate her.

" 'Tis hardly what I would call an adventure," he said sternly. "But you are back, and you appear sound." Hixley faced Liam O'Neill grimly. The pirate had brought Juliet home, and had calmly explained how he had seized her ship at sea, and then been instructed by the queen to return Juliet to Thurlstone immediately. "And I hope that you, Captain, shall understand why I will not invite you to dine with us."

Liam shrugged, his face devoid of any expression. "I have no wish to dine with you, Sir Richard, for I have a ship to return to." He bowed then at Juliet, the gesture grand and sweeping, as any courtier might. Then he spun on his heel and strode for the door.

Juliet started, then raced after him. "Captain! Captain O'Neill!"

He paused, turning slightly to face her, raising one slashing golden-brown brow.

"Please, take good care of Katherine, and see that she, too, rests unharmed," Juliet pleaded.

His gaze held hers but for a moment. "I shall take good

care of her," he finally said, "I promise you that." And then he was gone.

Juliet stared after him anxiously.

"Come with me, Juliet," Richard said. "I wish to speak with you."

She turned, unable to smile. Her uncle was of average height, but quite portly. His face was pleasant to look upon, but his brown eyes were stern and unforgiving. Her father had appointed him the guardian of his estates just before his death, after he had become ill. Juliet's mother had died many years before that. She and Hixley were not related by blood; he had become her uncle when he had married her aunt. He had his own wealthy estate farther north from Thurlstone Manor, on the edge of the Atlantic. Juliet knew that the guardianship had forced him to divide his time between Thurlstone and his own home and his wife and children.

Juliet's anxiety grew. She guessed what he wished to discuss—but it would not be a discussion. "Uncle, I have only just returned, and I am hungry and tired, as well as quite dirty. Perhaps we might speak later this evening?"

"We are having guests this evening," Richard said flatly.

Juliet had no choice, and she followed him through the manor. Thurlstone was a medieval manor, but it was a rich one, thanks to the vast deposits of iron ore that had been discovered by her grandfather and had been mined so assiduously ever since. Brilliantly colored tapestries covered all of the walls. Coats-of-arms hung high above them, boasting the black Stratheclyde dragon upon a gold ribbon and a field of red. Medieval weapons, which had been in the family for generations, also graced the walls. Crossed swords, a mace and dagger, and several ceremonial spears. Stratheclyde pennants hung from the timbered ceiling.

They entered a long brick gallery which had been added onto the original manor before Juliet's father died. Richard faced one of the glass windows, while Juliet sat down on a bench.

"You know, of course, why I summoned you home."

Juliet nodded, feeling miserable even though she knew that she should be thrilled.

He faced her, but seemed to look right through her. "I know you are still a bit young for marriage, but I am growing old, Juliet, and it is difficult for me to administer two estates properly."

Juliet resolved to be gracious, to say nothing. Instead she quavered, "But I will not be sixteen until June."

He shrugged dismissively. "I have drawn up a list of candidates for your hand, men from good families, and I intend to arrange a betrothal by your next birthday." He looked at her directly. "These suitors will wish to meet you."

Juliet could not restrain her lower lip from trembling. These suitors wished to meet her. She was not completely naive. They wished to determine that she was no skinny hag, nor any fat cow. While she, she had no desire at all to meet them.

"You do not appear pleased, Juliet."

She knew she should thank her uncle for all of his efforts. She said, in a low whisper, "I'm only fifteen. Other women do not wed until they are eighteen."

"I must find someone to manage Thurlstone," Richard said sharply.

She gazed into his eyes. "What . . . what if I do not like him?"

Richard stared at her, shocked.

She flushed and looked down at her lap.

"This is nonsense," Richard admonished. "If you start crying, Juliet, I shall send you to your room as I would a small child."

Juliet said nothing. She did not cry.

Richard continued. "In truth, the list of suitors is not a long one. I have decided upon three prospects after interviewing ten times that number."

Three prospects. She would only be paraded before three men. She was not relieved. Juliet was finally beginning to realize how imminent this was. By June, she would be affianced. Oh, God. To a man she did not know, did not want—did not love.

Juliet realized that she was on her feet. Somehow she forced the words from her lips. "Thank you, Uncle. I appreciate all that you have done."

And when she was finally alone, in her bedchamber, she lay down, holding her pillow, dreaming of love—and wondering why it was too much to ask for.

Juliet was gone now. Katherine hugged herself, standing at the porthole in Liam's cabin, watching the sun sinking lower and lower, a fiery red ball, over what had been the tip of Cornwall. The ship continued to speed northeast toward the coast of Ireland.

They were in the Atlantic Ocean. It was far rougher than the Channel or the seas off the Cornish coast. Katherine stood with her legs braced far apart, one shoulder against the wall, as the ship lurched through the waves, pushed by strong and favorable winds. Already the sun hung low upon the horizon, which was turning ink-dark. How was she going to avoid Liam O'Neill this night?

Katherine had no answer. She kept recalling his kiss in the queen's dining hall. And her knees grew weak, her blood grew hot.

Katherine rubbed her face against the smooth, wooden wall. She thought about the kiss. She shivered. She thought about his hands—his dangerous hands.

She thought about Hugh. The man she was on her way to rejoin. The man she would marry. Oh, God. There was no place in her mind for Liam O'Neill. Damn him. For being so golden, so virile.

She froze as she heard the bolt being lifted on the door and she half turned. It was only the boy, Guy.

He carried her supper inside. "The captain says to tell you to go ahead and eat alone. He'll be down later."

Katherine stared at Guy. "How much later?"

Guy shrugged and left.

Katherine regarded the tray. She could smell fried fish and fresh bread, but she had no appetite. She turned again to the porthole. The sun was gone. The sea was black now, as was the sky, and there was no way of discerning where one ended and the other began.

Katherine stood there, trying not to think. It was impossible. She knew what was going to happen. She watched the stars blink. She watched the moon appear. It was full. Dread warred with anticipation.

Yet she knew that she must fight him. She must fight him and win.

She turned and walked to the table and poured herself not a glass of ale, which was what women usually drank, but a glass of French wine. She sipped it quickly, hoping it would steady her nerves. It did not seem to have any effect.

It was not until Liam appeared in the doorway, a small light in his hand, that she realized she stood in complete darkness. She stiffened, she stared.

He smiled at her, then closed the door carefully. He moved across the cabin, in no apparent rush. He met her gaze again. Her heart fluttered wildly. There was no mistaking his intentions. None.

His gaze slid over her, then the table, but he said nothing in response to the fact that she had not touched the tray of food, except for the goblet of wine which sat half-empty upon the table. He walked away from her, to the bed. She watched him set the taper in the small nook in the headboard designed for that purpose and cover it with an open glass dome. He closed the door to the nook, securing the light. And he faced her. "Come, Katherine."

"What?"

"Come." He stood with his booted legs apart, his hands on his hips. The candlelight flickered over him. Katherine decided that the bulge in his breeches was more notable than usual. "Come to bed."

"I am n-not sleeping with you."

His smile flashed, impossibly confident, impossibly seductive. "This bed is large enough to share."

"You do not think about a simple sharing of the bed!" she cried.

"I will not force you to do anything you do not wish," he said, silken and soft.

The sound Katherine made was strangled.

"Katherine, come."

Katherine hesitated, and then she rushed for the door, which she knew was unlocked. He caught her before she had even crossed the room, murmuring softly in her ear as he pulled her up against his very hard body. "I want you, Katherine."

She froze. He stood behind her, his arms locked around her waist, his massive manhood pushing against the cleft of her buttocks, his lips against her neck. "I want to pleasure you, Katherine," he said softly, and then he lifted her into his arms and carried her to the bed.

9

*L*iam deposited Katherine in the center of the bed, coming down on top of her. For one instant he stared into her eyes, and in that instant, Katherine felt every inch of him, from her chest to her toes. His hips pressed hers, and his manhood pulsed strongly against her sex.

It all flashed through her mind with lightning speed. The convent and her flight from it, the violent capture of the French trader on which she had escaped, and Liam surveying it all from the forecastle as if it were his kingdom. And Hugh. Hugh, who waited for her, to give her his name, his home, and his children.

"Katherine, sweet," Liam said roughly, his thumb stroking over her cheek. His hand was shaking.

Katherine stared into his smoky eyes and was almost mesmerized by the desire she saw there. How potent, how powerful, it was. But she was not totally ensnared. She had a shred of sanity left. Her hands were free, and she raised them with the intention of clawing him, or forcing him to release her. But Liam caught her wrists before she could touch him, wrenching them up over her head so abruptly that pain shot up her arms into her shoulders. He stilled her bucking by pinning her legs with his own powerful thighs. "Cease!" he commanded. "Damnation, woman, I am not going to hurt you!"

"You lie!" Katherine cried. She thought of his kiss, his hands, and her body shuddered beneath his. "You are going to ruin me—rape me!"

He was grim. "I have no intention of raping you. Not now, not ever. So cease fighting me."

"I do not believe you," she spit. "You are the son of Shane O'Neill!"

"How tired I am of being reminded of that unfortunate fact," he said sharply.

"Then you should behave like a gentleman." Katherine tried to buck again and failed. "He raped your mother, did he not? Poor Mary Stanley!"

His nostrils flared, his eyes darkened even more, but his tone was conversational. "I am not my father, Katherine. Never forget it. And now"—his smile did not reach his eyes—"I shall prove it." He bent his head to kiss her.

Katherine jerked her face to the side so that his mouth landed against her cheek, where it played very softly. His kisses were feather-light. She panted, "I belong to Hugh!"

"After this night, you will know that there is only one man for you—and it is not Hugh Barry." He still held her wrists above her head, but with one hand. With the other he turned her face to his and covered her lips.

Katherine bucked frantically, but she only succeeded in pushing up against his erection, so she stilled. This time he had not forced her jaws apart, so she refused to open her mouth. But he did not seem intent upon hurrying. His lips brushed hers. Tears formed in the corners of her tightly closed eyes. Already he was unleashing a storm of desire within her body—as she had known he would.

When he paused, murmuring, "Bend to me, darling," Katherine jerked her face aside.

Panting, she said, "The queen approves of my betrothal to Hugh!"

His gray eyes gleamed. "Bess has been known to change her mind."

Katherine wished that he would shift his body so that she would not have to be so aware of every throbbing inch of him. "She will be furious with you if you really do this!"

He smiled at her, bent, and with his tongue, tested the tight seam of her lips. Katherine's clenched mouth eased slightly but she managed to swallow a choked, mewling sound.

"Do not worry about Bess," he murmured, his tongue flicking first one corner of her mouth and then the other. He paused, met her eyes, said huskily, "I can manage Bess."

Katherine stiffened in shock. As he spoke, he had begun to rotate his hips, very languidly, and very gently—all the while watching her eyes. She choked then, for the effect was to push his rock-hard sex back and forth against her soft, swollen loins. Katherine finally gasped, arching up beneath him—to meet him.

He laughed and claimed her mouth with his, stroking inside with his tongue. Katherine knew she was about to succumb to him. Against her will, her own hips were lifting restlessly, eagerly, against his. Her body was on fire. She had one determined thought. To spread her already open legs wider still and take every inch of him inside her.

Hugh. She must remember Hugh. Shane O'Neill. She must remember who this man's father was—and who and what this man himself was. A savage pirate, a murderer. She must not give Liam O'Neill her virtue. Her entire future was at stake.

Katherine seized the thought—and bit down on his tongue.

He howled in pain-filled rage, leaping up. Katherine cried out, too late realizing that she had gone too far. But he had been withdrawing his tongue when she had bitten, fortunately for him, and she did not see any blood at the corners of his mouth.

He stood beside the bed now, enraged, one hand on his mouth. Katherine realized that she was free, and she scrambled to sit up, backing as far from him as she could.

"Wench!" he finally spit out, and she saw a fleck of red. "Damnable wench!" His face turned harsh and grim.

Katherine knew she was in dire jeopardy, and she cried out. "No! I am sorry!"

But he leaned toward her, grabbed her arm and jerked her to the center of the bed, then pushed her down on her back. Before Katherine could jump up, he tied her wrist to the near poster of the bed with one of the red-and-gold cords that had tied the bed-curtains back. "Damnable wench!" he said on a long breath. Now he jerked up her other arm, ignoring her wild struggles. "You almost bit my tongue in half—damnation!"

"You forced me to do it!" Katherine gasped, straining at her bonds. "I was only defending myself!"

He tied her ankles to the posters at the bottom of the bed as well, then lanced her with a dark, dire look. "You are lucky, Katherine, 'tis but a scratch." Suddenly the corners of his mouth lifted very slightly. "Had you dismembered me, one day, you would have sorely regretted it."

Her temper flared; she forgot her bonds. "I should have bitten you harder!"

His eyes widened. "You seek to provoke me now?"

Instantly Katherine realized the folly of indulging her anger. "No! No! Please untie me. Please." She had never been more vulnerable or exposed in her life, and it had been insanity to forget her predicament even for a moment. But it was not fear that caused her pulse to thunder in her ears.

He did not answer. His eyes had turned a startling silver and as he smiled slightly, his dagger appeared in his hand. "Punishment," he said softly.

Katherine pulled against her bonds. They were not so tight that she was completely immobilized, and she found she could move somewhat.

He strode to her and hooked the center of the neckline of her gown with the dagger. Katherine began to comprehend his intentions and she froze in shock. He slid the dagger slowly through the faded blue silk, down between her breasts. Katherine watched the blade and whimpered. Her ribbon-edged shift was revealed. The knife moved down her torso, down her stomach, and between her legs. Katherine did not move a muscle, did not breathe. He slashed then quickly down to her toes. He had cut her gown in half. But she had not felt the knife, not even once.

"Stop," Katherine said hoarsely. Her breasts were heaving, and every breath she took so laboriously parted her cut gown even more.

He eyed the expanse of her linen-bound breasts, stared at her protruding nipples. His gaze moved to hers, and then he hooked the tip of his knife in the shift. Katherine tensed. Still looking into her eyes, he began to move the knife between her breasts.

Katherine gasped, watching as a swath of ivory skin was revealed as her underclothes were sliced in half. Cool air followed in the wake of his dagger. Very carefully, very slowly, he slid the knife down her torso and stomach and between her legs. A moment later he had sliced her petticoats in two.

Katherine was panting. All that was left intact upon her was her open, crotchless drawers. His gaze lifted to hers. It glittered wildly, but his face was formed into harsh lines. Katherine could not look away, nor could she breathe.

He hooked the tip of the dagger in the center of the lace-trimmed waistband, revealing her navel. Katherine stared at the glinting knife. She could not tear her gaze from the silver blade as it began to shred the fine lawn material, moving down her belly, revealing the nest of auburn hair as it paused between her thighs. Just barely she could feel the cool blade between her legs.

His gaze lifted abruptly. Silver smoke. Katherine made another sound, wet her dry lips nervously. Every nerve ending she had seemed to be swollen, throbbing madly.

His jaw flexed. He then quickly slashed a line down the inside of each leg. He sheathed the knife, and met her wide, unblinking gaze.

Then he reached down and pushed open the two halves of her dress and shift, revealing first her full, heaving breasts, then her slender rib cage, the nest of dark auburn curls at the juncture of her thighs, and then the long length of her pale legs.

Katherine sucked in her breath. It had become feverishly hot in the cabin, making it difficult to breathe. She opened her mouth to tell him to stop, but only wound up tossing her head from one side to the other. Her whole body undulated as her head moved.

"You are beautiful, Katherine," he said hoarsely, sitting beside her. His hand swept over one breast and Katherine gasped. Her nipple was already taut, but it seemed to swell as his palm caressed it. She had never dreamed that a man's hand would feel this way against her naked skin. "You wear your gowns too tight, hiding the bounty you are blessed with." He rolled her nipple, caught her eye. "You like that, Katherine?"

Katherine shook her head no.

He laughed, sudden and abrupt. "Then you are either a liar, or a fool." His gaze moved to her other nipple, which he plucked gently. "I know you are no fool, sweetheart."

Katherine stared, torn between dismay and desire, as he bent and flicked his tongue over her nipples, one by one. She was lost. Her eyes closed and she moaned, long and low, earthily.

He murmured an endearment and began to suckle her. Katherine began to writhe. The more he laved and teased her, the more he sucked, the more anguished her aching sex became. Katherine gasped, cried out, twisting beneath him. She was shocked when her hands came free of her bonds. She did not dwell upon the realization that, somehow, he had cut her free. Instead she gripped his head, moaning, pressing him closer to her breasts.

But he dragged his head down. Katherine cried out. He kissed her belly, her navel. Katherine had wrapped her long legs around him, and she pumped her hips toward him furiously. But she stilled when his hand cupped her sex.

She was panting. He was still nibbling her belly, but his fingers were separating the thick, wet folds of her flesh. Katherine gasped as he rubbed her there, crying out as his thumb stroked inside their folds, then flickered over her clitoris.

She moaned and thrashed. Dimly she was aware that his kisses were becoming dangerous, for as he played with her sex his head moved lower and lower. She froze when his mouth brushed the thatch of pubic hair. She did not move as his lips kissed the inside of her thigh, his face brushing the cleft he had been just toying with.

He kissed the cleft.

Katherine gasped his name.

He parted her and kissed her again, languidly. Katherine moved. She pumped against him. Holding her open, he stroked her with his expert tongue. Katherine cried out. And cried out and cried out, as a huge and terrible wave of anguish built and became pleasure which crested and finally crashed over her.

She sagged into the bed. Ecstasy faded, pleasure ebbed. Katherine became aware of the feel of his silken hair in her hands—which she clenched tightly. She became aware of the feel of his scratchy cheek, pressed against her inner thigh. She became aware of his fingers, which still fluttered over her sex.

In one stunning moment, she realized what she had done. As she had predicted, her body had welcomed him eagerly. Although he was a bloody pirate and the son of the notorious rapist Shane O'Neill, although she was betrothed to another, she had welcomed him, had been on fire for him—and as he had said, he had not had to rape her.

Nor would he have to. He need only use that cunning tongue of his, and within moments she would be begging for his cock.

Katherine twisted onto her side with a sob, only to realize her legs were still tied to the bed. She subsided onto her back, covering her face with her hands, telling herself that she would not weep now in shame in front of him.

"Katherine?"

It was no use. Katherine sobbed into her hands.

Liam raised his head from her leg. She felt him looking at her. "Why in God's name do you weep?" he asked harshly.

She dropped her hands and gazed at him with murderous fury. "Are you pleased? Pleased? That you have proved just how manly you are—and just what a whore I am?"

His eyes widened.

"Do you what you will," she said, choking a fist

against her mouth. "Damn you, God damn you, how I hate you, O'Neill! How I hate myself."

He stared at her. "You are not a whore, Katherine. We both know that," he said harshly.

Katherine covered her face with her hands. Waiting for him to touch her. But he did not.

"Don't cry, Katherine."

Katherine heard him but ignored him. She was struggling to control her hysteria—and her sudden, complete hatred for this man, who had seduced her so easily.

She heard him cursing savagely, and then he cut her legs free. Instantly Katherine rolled away from him, sitting up with her back to him. Maybe he would, miraculously, leave her alone now. She doubted it.

Silence filled the room. Suddenly he touched her shoulder from behind. Katherine froze.

"You are not a whore," he repeated. "Don't do this to yourself. What we did is the most natural act between a man and a woman, Katherine. Especially with the kind of desire we share."

Katherine whirled. "We do not share desire!" she shouted, knowing full well that she lied.

His expression was restrained, yet clearly skeptical.

Katherine wished that she had not turned to face him. Especially after uttering such a blatant lie. She found herself staring. His gray eyes glittered. A trickle of perspiration teased his temple. His nostrils were slightly flared; his breathing was hardly steady. Cords stood out in his strong neck. Katherine saw his pulse beating there, thick and strong and steady.

His shirt was damp with sweat and completely unlaced, revealing his muscular chest, and much of his flat belly. She knew she should not look any lower, but her glance slipped just once—and once was enough.

He was a stunning man, as powerful of body as he was of mind and will, and he was still heavily aroused.

He had been watching her, following her gaze. "That's right. I still want you, Katherine. I still need you."

She wanted to plug her ears. Even his words had power—even his words were seductive. "But I don't want you." His glance skewered her and Katherine had the grace to blush. Before he could point out the obvious fact that she had just wanted him very much, she said, "My body may want you, but I want Hugh."

His jaw tightened. Unpleasantly, he said, "You thought him dead for six years. Do you try to tell me that you have remained faithful in your heart and mind for all that time to a man you supposed dead?"

She had hardly even thought of him in all those years, not after the first few months of mourning, but she nodded. "I love him. He is my betrothed; soon we will be wed."

Liam smiled. It was a very dangerous smile. "Really?"

Katherine tensed. "Yes."

Suddenly he moved closer, towering over her. "I don't think so," he said.

He couldn't possibly know her most secret fears—that Hugh had long since forgotten about her and had no intention of marrying her. "You think wrongly," she whispered. It was hard to get the words out.

"Do I?" His lips curled. Their gazes locked. A silent moment crackled and sizzled between them. "We will find out soon enough, Katherine, won't we—whether your lover truly wants you?"

"Yes," Katherine managed, gripping the coverlet.

Liam stood very still. "And when he casts you aside— will you come to me freely, then?"

She inhaled. The sound was loud and sharp, cutting the air like a whip.

"Will you?" he demanded, his eyes blazing. "Then will you come to me freely?"

"No."

He stared for the space of a single heartbeat, then wheeled and strode away. As he slammed the door hard behind him, Katherine collapsed on the bed in a heap. And it was a very long time before she even thought of sleep.

10

*L*iam prowled the night-dark deck of his ship. The wind was strong and steady now, a fine sailing wind, and it whipped his face, his body. He paused at the bow, in a circle of mellow moonlight, allowing sharp slivers of icy water to spray his face.

His jaw was tight. He was rigid, tension delineated in every line of his body. He felt as tightly strung as an archer's well-prepared crossbow.

Her weeping, her curses, her accusations, echoed in his ears.

He was not like Shane O'Neill. Goddammit, he was no murderer, no rapist. He plundered for the queen, never without her implicit approval. His targets were always political. Few men died in those battles, far less than in most wars. It was his standard practice to free the crews of the ships he seized, while he took the booty, keeping it or disposing of it as he saw fit. And he had never raped any woman—and he never would.

Liam shook. He had been with many women. Many. Some had been, like Katherine, innocent victims, captured by him at sea in consequence of his piracy. But he had never attempted to seduce any woman who was without some experience, or who had not given him a sign that she was interested.

Until Katherine.

Liam had decided to seduce Katherine in spite of her lack of experience, in spite of her obvious unwillingness.

He knew that he should stay away from her, because of her unwillingness, because of her inexperience. But he could not.

She was an unusual woman—an extraordinary woman, a woman much like her infamous mother, Joan Butler FitzGerald. Her pride, her defiance, her independence, it did not repel him. To the contrary. Knowing her somewhat now, he wanted her more than ever. Other women paled in comparison to Katherine.

But Liam did not want to be like his father. Taking where he was not wanted, as he willed. And Katherine was determined to resist him. Liam knew he could seduce her and bring her to the point where she begged for him to go inside her. But now he suspected she would hate him even more if he did such a thing.

It occurred to him that a forced seduction might be close enough to rape to make him very much Shane O'Neill's son.

Liam gripped the wet, wooden railing of his ship. What in hell should he do?

A moral man would release her to Hugh Barry. Liam knew he was not moral enough to be that kind of man.

He was furious. He was furious with himself, for wanting her so obsessively. He was furious with her, for pushing him past his limits, for showing him just how much like his father he really was. And he was ashamed.

For acting like a beast, becoming a savage beast, in front of Lady Katherine FitzGerald—an animal no different than his father.

Katherine stood at the porthole in Liam's cabin. Her eyes widened. She saw land. She saw, quite distinctly, the wild Irish coast.

A day had passed, during which time she had sewn her poor abused gown together. Already washed and dressed, now she hurried from the cabin, flying up the narrow stairs. Out of breath and mindless of it, she crossed the deck to the rail. She smiled, staring at her homeland, which she had not seen in six long years. Her smile widened as she watched the pale strip of beach at the base of cliffs growing broader as they approached. She threw back her head and laughed exultantly.

"Good morning, Katherine."

Her laughter died and she turned to face Liam. She had not seen him since the night before last, when he had almost succeeded in seducing her completely. He was unsmiling, but so was she. His gaze moved swiftly over her face, pausing on her mouth, then it slipped briefly to her breasts. There was no doubt about what he was thinking. Katherine felt her color rising. Her own gaze had inspected him as thoroughly; she had been helpless to prevent it. If only that horrible, intimate night had not happened. "Good morning," she managed, turning away from him to face the coast, trying to ignore his proximity.

She had been hoping that he would no longer have any effect upon her.

"You are so pleased to see me," he murmured. "I had hoped that a brief separation might make you somewhat fonder of me?"

Katherine stared straight ahead. "I am fond of one man—and he is not you."

"Ah, yes, your long-lost lover. Or should I refer to him as long dead?"

She turned, her gaze fierce. "I would prefer that you do not speak of him at all."

"But that is impossible." His gray gaze held hers. "As I am consumed with jealousy at the mere thought of you with Hugh."

Katherine could not move.

His tone lowered. "But surely you know that, Katherine." It was a husky caress.

Her pulse had quickened. "I know only that you are a conscienceless rogue, one as adept at seduction as you are at mayhem and murder."

He smiled lazily. "I spill my heart to you and you toss it back in my face. You are cruel, Katherine."

"You spill naught but nonsense," she cried. She wanted to leave the railing now, to leave him, but sensed that he would stop her if she tried.

"I have passed two miserable nights."

Her pulse thundered. She could imagine why he had not slept well. She could imagine him tossing and turning, burning with forbidden heat until dawn—just as she had done. "I . . . I do not care," she finally said.

His only answer was another lazy smile, one both superior and knowing.

He guessed. He guessed that she had slept as badly as he—and for exactly the same reasons. Her cheeks hot, Katherine gazed at the shore. "I am surprised that I do not see any landmarks which I recognize." In fact, she did not recollect such sheer cliffs at all near the mouth of the Shannon estuary.

"You are familiar with Cork?" He crossed his arms and leaned on the railing beside her.

"Cork!" she cried, spinning toward him. "We approach Cork? We do not go to Askeaton?"

"We shall put in at Cork and ride for Barrymore. 'Tis the seat of the Barrys, is it not?"

She gaped at him. "B-but, I thought we would go home first!"

"Why?" he studied her face. "You love Hugh, do you not? Surely your first thought is to rush into his arms. Askeaton is fifty miles from here."

Dismay crushed her. "But by sea we could be there by nightfall, could we not?"

"I was instructed to escort you to Hugh Barry," he said firmly, his jaw flexing. "By the queen herself."

Katherine choked and faced the coastline again. Now she saw that they sped toward the bay. There was an English garrison at Cork. It was an English town. "You will be fired upon the moment they sight you," she said, somewhat fearfully.

"No, I don't think so," he said, glancing upward.

She turned and saw that he was flying the queen's flag. "Will they not think it a trap?"

"Mayhap." He shrugged. "I have sealed letters from Her Majesty for Lord President Perrot. Instructing him of my mission." His cool gray eyes found and held hers.

Katherine forced her disappointment aside. It did not matter. Surely she would be able to visit Askeaton soon.

It was better that they go directly to Hugh. And as Barrymore was not far from Cork, soon she would be with Hugh—who was the answer to all of her dreams.

Sir John Perrot arrived shortly after they had docked and he boarded the ship with a large escort of armed men. He was a very fat man, with flaming red hair and a long beard of an equally brilliant color. He wore his scarlet doublet open, as he could not close it over his huge girth. Yet he was no comical figure. He had been appointed lord president of Munster last December by the queen. His orders were to crush the rebels, who sought to drive the English settlers out, and who were thus far succeeding. His orders were to catch the leader of the traitors, James FitzMaurice. He was a determined man, a renowned soldier, but well past his prime. 'Twas widely held that he was the bastard son of King Henry VIII.

Liam awaited him and his troops at the head of the gangplank, standing casually, but wearing his rapier. The two men came face-to-face and a few words were exchanged. Liam handed the lord president a letter bearing the royal seal. Perrot tore it open abruptly, then proceeded to read it for many long minutes. Finally he looked up at Liam and frowned. They spoke again. Liam turned and beckoned Katherine forward.

Katherine had been standing beside one of the masts with Macgregor, watching the interchange. Her heart had been thundering. Now she was relieved. She had been unable to prevent herself from thinking that Liam would be arrested almost on sight, not just for being a pirate, but for being an Irish pirate, a far graver offense.

Perrot glanced at Katherine somewhat rudely. He noticed the seam running down the front of her gown. He did not bow or kiss her hand. He said, "So you're FitzGerald's girl. I hear he pines away for Desmond, eh?"

Katherine tensed. "My father misses *his* land, yes."

Perrot smiled. "Desmond land belongs to FitzGerald no more, girl, and we both know it. So you are to marry Barry's heir? I have heard it said that he is secretly supporting that papist lunatic, FitzMaurice."

Katherine said stiffly, "I would not know." Then she felt Liam take her elbow, quite firmly—warningly.

"You can give him a message from me. I will capture FitzMaurice and present his head to the queen. The day he stood outside the walls of Cork and pronounced Her Majesty a bastard and a heretic was the day his fate was sealed. To think he seeks to overthrow the Crown! He is mad—and he will rue his ways. You tell Barry that his head will join the papist's on a pike if he dares to ride against me. I will crush these rebels. Every last one. Mark my words."

Katherine ignored the pressure of Liam's hand, which was so tight now that pain shot up her arm. "No Englishman can crush all of Ireland," she said fiercely. " 'Twould be an impossible feat."

Perrot's face turned red.

Liam jerked her against his side. "Do not heed her, Lord Perrot. She is overwrought with bridal nerves, and other womanly ailments," he said smoothly. "She knows not of what she speaks."

Katherine felt like kicking him in the shin. She glared at him, but he ignored her.

"When might we get our traveling papers?" he asked.

Perrot faced Katherine. "If you think to entice your betrothed farther into treason, think again. I have no qualms about placing your head alongside those of all other traitors, Mistress FitzGerald."

Liam's fingers dug into her arm. "She is but convent-bred, Sir John. She knows nothing of the world, of men, or of men's ways." He smiled slyly. "She will do naught but entice her husband into bed, I assure you of that."

Perrot's gaze flickered over the front of her dress. "And a good romp it will be, I warrant. But you already know that, eh, O'Neill?" He laughed a little.

Liam smiled, too.

Katherine seethed.

Perrot shot Katherine another glance and turned, calling over his shoulder, "You will have your papers within the hour, Captain. But know this. If the queen did not command my aid, I would deny you this mission." He strode down the gangplank, his huge weight making the wood groan. At the other end he snapped to his soldiers, "No one is to leave this ship unless they carry orders from me!"

Liam and Katherine watched as he was assisted onto his horse and thundered away with his cavalcade. When he was gone, she jerked away from Liam, rubbing her arm. "Spineless worm!"

Liam's eyes narrowed. "Do you slander him—or me?"

"You!" she cried. "You are no red-blooded Irishman, but a blue-blooded Brit—aye, you have proved yourself this day!"

"I have heard that before," Liam said, his jaw tight, his eyes blazing. "And you, dear Katherine, are a total fool to bait the most powerful man in Ireland."

"Powerful, bah!" she spit. "My father was powerful— he is but a fat, long-tongued toad! I suppose you enjoyed your comradely male exchange?"

Liam towered over her. "Without traveling papers, we go nowhere, mistress, nowhere."

"Traveling papers? Why do we need such papers?" she shot.

"Lord Perrot has enacted many new laws since his appointment—all designed to make life miserable for the Irish. One disallows travel. That is, no one is allowed to travel anywhere without papers sealed by him. And that includes us."

Katherine stared. "Why—that is intolerable!"

"No more intolerable than the outlawing of bards and poets, of native dress and glibs," Liam said.

Katherine was aghast. "He has outlawed rhyme and harp?"

"Among many other things."

"He is a pig!" Katherine cried.

"Actually, he is a distinguished and capable soldier. And he is lord president now, appointed by the queen. Although we enjoy the queen's blessings now, he could decide to detain us anyway. Especially after the treasonous way you spoke. He has the power of life and death over both of us, Katherine, and I suggest you do not forget it." Liam strode away.

Katherine watched him go, pale, no longer fuming.

*   *   *

Cork was an important trading town, and had been so since medieval times. Narrow cobbled streets ran this way and that. Single- and double-storied homes, stuccoed and timbered and partially made of stone, crowded against one another. Ofttimes shops were below, where craftsmen and artisans plied their trade, where bakers formed their fresh-made loaves and pies. A crumbling old Norman church lay in the shadow of a soaring cathedral that had been completed during the reign of Henry VIII. The walled castle and the garrison within it were adjacent to the harbor, and the entire town was walled as well.

It was but two summers earlier that Cork had been besieged by FitzMaurice and the rebels. The seige had not lasted long, for the rebels had retreated when news of Sir Henry Sidney's arrival had reached them. Sir Henry had relieved Cork with both victual and troops, but FitzMaurice had already been declared a traitor to the Crown, not for laying waste to the countryside, not for killing whatever English settlers he could find, but for denouncing the queen as a heretic publicly before the city walls.

As Katherine, Liam, and Macgregor now rode through the town's northern gate, she was appalled. Once upon a time the countryside surrounding Cork had been lush meadows, dotted with sheep and cows, and fertile farmland, planted with rye and oats. Thick forests had fringed the farms and crept over the hillsides. Now all was changed.

The land had been devastated by war. The meadows and farms were burned and barren. The forests were sparse, blackened sycamore amongst the few lonely surviving pine. Piles of rubble that had once been stone cottages marked each passing farm. "Oh dear God," Katherine said. "What has happened? Damn the English! Damn them!"

Liam sent her a grave glance. "Unfortunately, your cousin FitzMaurice did as much of the damage as Sir Henry Sidney. He was determined to drive off the settlers, even if it meant destroying the land. He managed to do both. Then, of course, the queen sent Sir Henry Sidney after him. And Sidney, chasing FitzMaurice west, left a similar trail of destruction in his wake. If this war continues, all of southern Ireland will be, for all purposes, useless and dead.''

Katherine could not speak. Horrible images assailed her, of the thick, nearly impenetrable forests outside Askeaton Castle burned and blackened, of the meadows turned grassless and charcoal gray. She swerved her mount toward Liam so sharply that their knees knocked. ''Askeaton?''

His glance softened. ''I do not know if any of the fighting was near your home, Katherine. Most of it was between Cork in the east and Limerick in the west, between Tralee and Kilmallock.''

''Limerick!'' she cried. There was a royal garrison at Limerick—and it was only twenty miles north of Askeaton, also on Lough Shannon. ''Oh, God, I must go home.''

Liam's glance slid over her. ''That will be Barry's decision, will it not?''

She stared at him, unable to look away. It did not seem real—that she was on her way to Barrymore and would be there shortly. She swallowed. ''Yes. That will be Hugh's decision.''

They were not far from Barrymore.

Liam's hands trembled on his reins, making his mount nervous. His instincts were urging him to throw all caution to the winds. He could imagine abducting Katherine even now, and riding hell-bent for Cork and the *Sea Dagger*. Once at sea he could not be caught. Once at Earic Island, she would be his until he commanded otherwise. No man would dare assault his island fortress, and Katherine had no protector even if one were insane enough to dare and fail.

Liam knew that he must be far more subtle, and far more clever now than before. A second abduction was the last resort. He preferred not to try the queen's temper another time. Inadvertently he had aroused her suspicions, which he now wished to allay.

It was a miserable game he played. And in order for Liam to win, in order for him to survive, he must stay in the queen's good graces. With the stroke of a pen he could be deemed a traitor, his letters of marque canceled, a bounty placed upon his head. Liam did not relish the idea of being chased across the seas by men like Drake and Hawkins. He did not relish standing completely alone, although he was not so foolish nor so romantic as to think he really had a country or a queen.

How ironic, though, his recent behavior must appear. He had plundered a politically insignificant French vessel, and Liam expected those advising Elizabeth soon to realize this fact, and to wonder at where that single act was leading him. No one could suspect the truth. Not yet. And if anyone were clever enough to suspect it, there would be no proof, merely speculation.

Liam knew he must be cautious, patient, and circumspect. That he had to be more clever than ever before, if he were to outwit all the players in this particular game, if he were to win. Because if he decided to take Katherine to wife—and he was indeed finding her father's marriage offer more and more intriguing—he must pick up the reins of her father's fight, and then he would be moving into the very jaws of conspiracy.

No, a second abduction was probably unnecessary in any case. Liam was certain Barry was not interested in marrying an impoverished and untitled woman.

Yet Liam could not be absolutely sure. Katherine was an extraordinary woman, and Barry might lose his head and forget all about her current circumstances. No matter what happened, he could not allow them to marry. He could not allow Hugh Barry or any other man to possess Katherine. Her fate had been decided long ago, when he had first laid eyes upon her. And he, Liam O'Neill, was her fate, one way or another.

Castle Barry rose out of the forest's treetops, standing on a small, cleared hillside somewhat above them. Liam ground down his jaw, fighting a jealousy and possessiveness he had never felt before. He glanced at Katherine. Her cheeks were flushed with anticipation; her eyes sparkled. He could imagine her running into Barry's arms. He could imagine Barry's lusty kiss—and Katherine's own

eager response. Liam reminded himself to go slowly, but
surely. This was one battle he must not lose.

Katherine interrupted his thoughts. "Thank God there
was no war here," she said in an unsteady tone.

They rode up the road now toward the castle's barbican,
its outermost entrance, and rumbled over the lowered
drawbridge. Iron gates were down, but no watchman appeared to inquire after them. Liam rode forward and found
a bell cord and rang the watchtower's bell.

The bell tolled loudly, breaking the silence of the Irish
countryside, scattering pigeons from the walk above. Barrymore had been built in medieval times, no uncommon
thing, and the square stone keep dominated the fortress,
although other buildings had been added to it over the
centuries. Yet there was no brick, nor glass, in evidence
anywhere. The inner ward was dried mud, not cobbled
stone. There was no sign of modern civilization; it was as
if they had traveled back through time, into a world of
mailed knights and tunic-clad damsels. The castle appeared
to be deserted, adding to the illusion, and Liam almost
expected to see the ghosts of these long-dead knights appearing in the courtyard.

Katherine looked at Liam. " 'Tis most strange. Is there
no one home?"

"It does not appear so," Liam said, pleased that Hugh
Barry was not in residence. "We shall inquire in the village," he said. He nodded and began to wheel his rangy
horse around, Katherine and Macgregor following, when
one and all became aware of a contingent of riders approaching swiftly from the west across the flats. The group
broke into a gallop, having spotted the trio at Barrymore's
front gates. Liam grabbed Katherine's reins from her and
urged their mounts across the drawbridge and to the road,
where, should a fight erupt, they had room to maneuver
and flee. Macgregor stayed on Katherine's other side. He
had his hand upon his pistol. Liam opened his cloak, so
that he might access his rapier should the need arise.

"Who is it?" Katherine cried in fear. "Surely you do
not think to fight a dozen armed men?"

Liam did not answer, watching as the riders thundered

up the road toward them. He heard Katherine gasp, and she clutched his arm. His heart seemed to sink, for he could guess who these Irishmen were. And clearly they were Irish, for all were clad in native gray mantles, many were mounted upon smaller, locally bred horses, and some of the men sported the outlawed glibs—the forelock of hair worn hanging low to hide their features. " 'Tis your betrothed?'' he asked.

She nodded, beaming.

Liam looked at the man who was her intended, despising him on sight. He was far younger than Liam himself, closer to Katherine's age, and like her, he was red-haired and fair. In fact, Hugh Barry was an attractive man, far more so than average. His features were rugged but pleasing, his eyes Kerry blue. Liam gripped his rapier. Perhaps the beast in him would win this day after all.

Hugh drew his horse to an abrupt, rearing halt. "I am Lord Barry,'' he declared, his gaze on Liam, not Katherine. "Declare yourself as friend or foe.''

Liam gripped the smooth, well-worn hilt of his blade. How his hand itched to do battle now. Barry was but a pup, a brave and battle-hardened one—Liam both sensed and saw that. Yet he was a pup and Liam could kill him in a matter of seconds. If he allowed the beast in his breast to run free.

He dropped his hand. "Liam O'Neill,'' he began, smiling unpleasantly, but he was cut off.

"Hugh!'' Katherine cried in a husky voice. "Oh, God, Hugh!'' Tears spilled down her cheeks.

Liam saw, and froze.

Hugh turned to face her, perplexed.

"I truly th-thought you d-dead,'' she cried.

Comprehension—and shock—transformed his expression. "Katherine? Katherine FitzGerald?''

She nodded, unmoving, unbreathing, eyes wide.

"Good God!'' he cried. "Katie! Little Katie!'' And then he laughed, showing strong white teeth, and a moment later he had ridden over to her and had swept her off her mount and onto his stallion and into his arms.

11

*K*atherine was so surprised that she clung tightly to Hugh, seated sideways on his lap, his horse moving restlessly beneath them.

"Katie FitzGerald!" he cried again, his arms tight around her. Smiling widely, he lightly kissed her mouth. Their gazes met and held. It was then that his smile died, that he stared at her, his brow creasing.

Katherine smiled up at him uncertainly, but her heart was pounding in relief because she had thought, God, she had thought, that he would be dismayed to see her—that he would send her away.

Still staring, no longer smiling, Hugh slid to the ground, Katherine still in his arms, and he slowly slipped her to her feet. His hands held her waist lightly and he frowned, his gaze moving over her features one by one. "God, Katie, I cannot recognize you. 'Tis a beauteous woman you've become."

Katherine managed a choked sound, that was only partly a laugh.

"Aye, beauteous," he said, his tone lower now and husky.

Katherine wet her lips. She was so nervous, and somewhat confused. This was Hugh, not a strange man, who held her so intimately, who would soon be her husband. Hugh. Not a stranger. But she had not seen him in six years. "And you," she managed. " 'Tis a fine man you've become—no scrawny boy."

"Yes," he murmured, his hands pulling her closer until her hips bumped his. "I am no boy now, Katherine, begging for a kiss and not knowing how to go about it properly."

Katherine sensed his intentions and she stiffened. "'Twas very sweet," she began.

"But not sweet enough," he said, dipping his head.

Katherine's body stiffened as his mouth covered hers. Her instinct was to push him away.

Yet he was her betrothed and her frantic mind commanded her to be still, to accept his kiss, to bond with him now as she must do. His lips were insistent and firm. He wanted her to open her mouth—Liam had taught her about that. Liam. Oh, God. Liam who was watching even now.

Katherine did not want to resist Hugh, yet she could not relax. Especially not with Liam watching them. But Hugh would soon be her husband—she must kiss him back.

Gripping his shoulders, Katherine began to kiss Hugh with determination and passion—for this was Hugh, the man she loved.

Finally the kiss was over. Hugh stared at her, eyes wide and dazed. Katherine backed a step away from him, her heart hammering, telling herself that Hugh's kiss had been a wondrous thing. And she would *not* compare his kiss to Liam's.

"Sweet Mary," Hugh said, a gasp. "What a fine woman you've become."

Katherine colored, aware of his men chortling behind him, aware of Liam, who did not move and did not make a sound. She dared to look over her shoulder, and glimpsed raw fury in his eyes. Katherine started. Had he been telling the truth when he'd told her that he was jealous of the mere idea of her with Hugh?

But when he sauntered forward, abreast of Katherine, his gaze was shuttered. "I am Katherine's escort, Lord Barry. Might we adjourn inside? We have only arrived at Cork this day, and have ridden long and hard to arrive here before dusk. Lady FitzGerald is much fatigued, and nigh ill with hunger, as well.'' His smile flashed, cold and brittle.

Katherine was neither tired nor hungry, but she was relieved by Liam's request. But why had he referred to her by a title that no longer belonged to her? It was as if he were reminding Hugh of the demands of propriety.

Hugh came to life. "How remiss of me. I was so stunned to find Katie here—and such a woman, at that.'' His glance slid over her far too boldly. "Come, we shall take supper in the hall.''

As an old man and a young boy had appeared and now winched up the portcullis, Katherine tried not to look at Liam, watching Hugh. She told herself that she was very lucky that he was pleased to see her, that he desired her, that he wished to bed her. Her fears that he had forgotten all about her in the past six years as her own family had were clearly untrue.

Hugh moved to her and took her hand, tucking it into his arm. "You must stay beside me, Katie,'' he said, his tone intimate, his grin crooked. He patted her hand and they entered Castle Barry, Hugh's home, which would soon be her home too.

At Barrymore the great hall in the original keep was still used as a dining hall, and they entered it directly. It was hardly furnished. Old rushes were upon the floors. The walls were bare. A few old servants had appeared to light tapers. Soon wood trenchers of breads and cheeses and cold meats were brought forth with beer and ale and set upon the long trestle table. Hugh's dozen retainers quickly took their places.

Katherine wondered if her memory served her correctly. For she recalled visiting this hall as a child, when the walls had been hung with bright tapestries, when graceful oak sideboards had stood against the walls, when the trenchers had been silver, and fine glass goblets from London had been used and the tables had been laid with silver knives and spoons. She recalled the room as being sweet-smelling, not foul. She recalled many well-dressed servants, and a banquet fit for a wealthy lord, if not a king.

Hugh saw her wandering gaze. He looked grim as he seated her at the head of the table beside him. "We have lost everything in the past few years, Katie," he said. "I have had to sell off all the furnishings, and most of the great Barry horses. My men have all joined FitzMaurice, except for the few you see seated below you. I cannot keep many servants, for I can not feed them. But 'tis not just the clan Barry who have suffered. All the great clans have suffered here in the south, as well. I try to tell myself that I am pleased that Castle Barry remains standing, and in my own hands, but 'tis not enough."

"I am sorry, Hugh," Katherine whispered. "We saw signs of war everywhere. 'Tis ghastly."

He nodded, pulling a trencher forward and spearing meat, which he placed upon her plate. Katherine was aware of Liam taking a seat on the bench just below her on her left, and she stiffened. His knee, beneath the table, touched her.

Quickly she faced Hugh. "Your vassals have joined my cousin FitzMaurice?"

Hugh nodded soberly.

Katherine gripped her eating dagger. "My stepmother says he styles himself the earl of Desmond."

Hugh eyed her. "I have heard that said, as well. But when I met the man, he called himself the captain of Desmond, nothing else. And surely you know that your own father appointed him as such after being imprisoned by the queen? Someone had to manage the Desmond lands."

Katherine had not known that. "Does he think to usurp Desmond from my father?"

Hugh took her hand. "Katie, dearest one, Desmond does not belong to your father anymore. When his lands were forfeit, many Englishmen settled upon them. Hundreds. Many of those planters are now dead, for FitzMaurice burned them out. Others he caught and hung. Others he chased to the English cities on the coast, where they begged refuge. Most of the Irish have quit our land. Only a few have dared to stay to fight for their holdings. Thanks to FitzMaurice."

She stared at him. "You speak as if he is a great hero."

"He is a great soldier, Katie, and he alone has held together the many clans in order to oppose the English. Even Ormond's brothers joined us in our battle for a while. Sir Henry Sidney could not capture him—and neither will Sir John Perrot." Hugh spit out Perrot's name.

"And you, Hugh? Does FitzMaurice hold you, too?" Katherine trembled. "Do you ride with the usurper?"

"How bold you are still, just like the Katie I once knew." Hugh refused to answer, patting her hand. "Enough of such grim news. In truth, tales of war do not suit a lady's lovely ears. We have yet to speak of each other, and I have yet to speak with the man you are traveling with." Hugh glanced past Katherine at Liam.

Katherine did not respond, thinking the worst—that Hugh did secretly support FitzMaurice, her father's cousin and enemy, a man determined to usurp FitzGerald's patrimony.

Liam lounged upon the bench indolently. "And of what would you like to speak?"

Hugh stared. "Your name. Liam O' Neill. Surely there can not be two men sharing the same notorious name?"

"I doubt it."

Hugh's eyes gleamed. "Are you telling me that the Master of the Seas sits at my own table?"

Liam nodded, pouring beer into his goblet.

Hugh folded his arms. "And how, pray tell, did you come to escort Katie to me?"

Liam's own dagger appeared in his hand. It was a fighting dagger, twice as long and three times as slim as the knives laid upon the table with which guests were to dine. He used it to spear a piece of meat, laying it upon his plate and flicking it in two. No blade could be more sharp. No blade could move more swiftly, for the silver glinted in a blur. "I captured her upon the seas."

Hugh rose to his feet.

Liam also stood, smiling.

Katherine no longer dwelled upon the probability that Hugh Barry, whom she would wed, was allied with her father's enemy. She jumped up as well, planting herself between the two men. "Hugh! Please! 'Tis not what you are thinking! We have come from the queen."

Hugh did not look at Katherine. "Oh really?"

Liam's smile did not waver, and he brushed Katherine aside, putting her behind him. "The queen herself."

Hugh's nostrils flared. Liam's eyes glittered. Katherine realized her error too late. If Hugh were secretly allied with FitzMaurice, then he was an enemy of the Crown—and the queen. As Liam had come from the queen, that would make him his enemy, too. Then, almost hysterically, Katherine realized that Hugh was also *her* enemy—because he was allied with FitzMaurice against her father. Yet they were to wed.

"You know, it does not surprise me that you have business with the queen. After all, your blood is tainted; your blood is half-English," Hugh said vehemently. "And you were raised at court amongst English princesses and princes by heretic Protestant tutors."

"True." Liam made no attempt to defend himself.

Katherine stepped abreast of him. "But his father was as Irish as you or I, Hugh. He is half-Irish."

"His father was a murderer, if my memory serves me correctly," Hugh said.

Liam smiled coldly. " 'Twould be beneficial for you to think on that fact. For 'tis often claimed I am just like him."

Katherine grabbed Hugh's arm, forcing him to look at her. "Hugh, the queen pardoned Liam for his crimes, and ordered him to bring me to you. That is all. He does not have any other business with her—he is a pirate—I know that firsthand!"

"You defend him?" Hugh was shocked. "You defend this half-English bastard? You defend Shane O'Neill's son? A bloody pirate who has murdered and plundered across all the high seas? Who has loyalty to no one—not even his own clan?"

Katherine hesitated. On one hand, she recalled the charred and broken decks of the small French trader which Liam O'Neill had plundered, and she could still hear the moaning of the men who had been wounded, but he hadn't murdered anyone. He'd let the French crew go after he'd taken what he wanted. And he hadn't harmed Juliet. Then she thought about how Liam had ruthlessly tied her down to his bed, cutting her clothes off of her with his knife. But . . . he had left her with the last thing of value to her, her virtue. Katherine knew that he could have continued his seduction that night, but he'd stopped when she'd begun to cry. Softly, she said, "He brought me to you without harm, Hugh."

Hugh stared at her face, then at her dress. "Who tore your dress, Katie?"

Katherine did not hesitate now. "I have been in France these past years, you know," she said quickly, never taking her eyes from his. "I ran away from the convent where my stepmother sent me after Affane. I was trying to find a berth home. A sailor on the docks there did this."

Hugh cupped her cheek. "Poor Katie."

Katherine closed her eyes, so he would not see her lie. For a moment her face rested upon his hand.

"Yes, poor Katherine," Liam said, his tone ice. "How touching your concern is, Lord Barry."

Katherine jerked away from Hugh, glanced at Liam, saw the silver light in his eyes again. He *was* angry, but he had no right to be angry with her. She had just saved his miserable neck. For Hugh would have killed him for cutting her dress off of her without asking for any other details. Then Katherine knew that that was not so. Hugh would have tried to kill him, but Liam would have undoubtedly been the victor in any contest between the two men. And Katherine knew instinctively that Liam would have enjoyed destroying Hugh. She shivered.

Hugh faced only Katherine. "You have had a time of it, I know. Being sent to France, your father imprisoned and dispossessed, now this." He touched her arm, stroking her sleeve. "Come, eat. You need your sustenance." He ignored Liam.

Katherine nodded, relieved that the tension had passed, and sat as he did, turning her attention to her plate. She was acutely aware of Liam finally sitting down as well.

She sighed deeply, in relief. She did not want to see either man's blood spilled upon Hugh's stone floors.

Katherine had no real interest in cold meat, and she finally took up a piece of cheese and some stale bread. She was aware of both men eating now on either side of her with ravenous gusto. She stole a glance at Hugh.

He really had become a handsome man. His nose was a bit broad, but it suited his square jaw and round face, his mouth was well shaped, his eyes were a brilliant blue, and his hair was redder than her own. She should be pleased. Every woman yearned for a handsome husband. She herself had, recently, yearned for a husband both handsome and lusty. Hugh was both. She should be ecstatic. She told herself that she *was* ecstatic.

She made sure not to look at Liam. God's blood. She did not want to compare the two men. She would not. Yet Liam's image filled her mind. Golden, harsh, striking. He was the sun, and beside him any man, even Hugh, was but a distant, winking star.

Katherine shut off her thoughts abruptly. And concentrated on eating.

Hugh had finished eating and he faced her, smiling and replete. His hand covered hers, his fingers stroking her knuckles. Katherine saw the amorous light in his eyes and felt some trepidation. "So you have been convent-reared," he remarked, his gaze drifting to the edge of her bodice.

Since Katherine had done a fairly good job of repairing her dress, her voluptuous bosom was crushed flat, still, his regard unnerved her. "Yes."

" 'Twas a waste, Katie."

Katherine shifted in her seat. What did Hugh mean?

Hugh smiled, his manner friendly. "The Katie I knew was always barefoot and running wild out of doors. I remember you as a child in long braids, climbing trees. I can not imagine you confined to a nunnery, with a needle in your hand, working embroidery."

"I have become a fine seamstress, so a man might say the years were well spent."

He laughed. "A talent every woman should acquire, no doubt." His gaze was warm. "I remember how your mother despaired of your ever learning such a womanly art. I recall your father laughing it off. Gerald was always amused by your boyish ways.''

Katherine smiled, recalling, as Hugh did, Joan Fitz-Gerald's fond dismay whenever she had seen her daughter rushing off, barefoot and disheveled, and more often than not in a farm lad's hose and jerkin. Now she also remembered how her father had laughed about it. He had been secretly proud of her ability to climb trees and ride as well as any boy. Katherine beamed at Hugh.

Liam set his goblet down quite loudly, then proceeded to fill it with beer.

Hugh enfolded her hand in his. "But Katie, there is one thing I do not understand. Did I hear correctly? That the queen ordered O'Neill to escort you to me?"

Katherine nodded. " 'Twas most generous of her, Hugh. I was afraid she would send me to my father's side in St. Leger House.''

"Well," Hugh said, "I am most pleased that you are here, and you may reside with me indefinitely, but why would she send you here instead of to your father or your uncle?''

Katherine froze.

"Katie?"

She had been aware of the fact that Liam watched them like a hawk, unwavering and even predatory. She had to glance at him now. His gaze was cold, narrowed and watchful. She turned to Hugh. "Wh-where else would she send me, Hugh? We-we are betrothed. 'Twas only right that she send me to you.''

Hugh still held her hand, but he was obviously stunned.

"Hugh?" Katherine said hesitantly.

He released her hand. "Katherine! What in God's name has ever given you the idea that we are yet betrothed?''

Katherine gripped the table. "We were betrothed in the cradle. Co-correct me if I am wrong. That betrothal was never broken.''

Hugh stared at her with open dismay.

Katherine's heart beat wildly.

He recovered, taking both of her hands in his. "Katherine, I do not know how to speak of this."

Katherine told herself to breathe. She told herself it would be all right.

"The betrothal between our fathers was for my marriage to the earl of Desmond's daughter. In fact, three times the contracts alluded to you as Desmond's daughter. Only once was your birthname given."

"I do not understand."

His jaw flexed. His gaze dipped to her mouth, to her breasts. "God's blood, you are so lovely, but . . . you are not Desmond's daughter. The earl is no more. The betrothal ceased to exist the day the earl of Desmond ceased to exist. Do you understand now?"

Katherine was on her feet. "My father's lands were forfeit to the crown, his title taken from him. But *I* still exist, Hugh."

Hugh also stood. "Katherine, I took it to the brehern. The judges agreed, as your name was used but once, that the betrothal was a contract betwixt myself and the earl's daughter—not betwixt myself and Katherine FitzGerald."

She gasped.

"The judges have decided it, Katherine. 'Twas decided shortly after your father's trial."

She was stunned, but deep inside herself she had known something had to be amiss, for he had not sent her word or ordered her home in all the years that she had been gone. Now it made sense. The earl of Desmond's daughter no longer existed. Hugh Barry would not marry Katherine FitzGerald—Mistress Nobody. Her chin lifted although tears formed in her eyes. "And who brought it to the brehern, Hugh?"

He hesitated. "I did. Of course, I did. Katie—no matter how beautiful you are, I cannot marry you. You have no dowry, no name, nothing. Surely you understand that?"

She managed to keep the tears from falling.

"Besides, I have been betrothed for three years now to the earl of Thomond's daughter. This spring she will be fifteen and we shall be wed."

Katherine could not help but make a noise. She sucked in her breath, squared her shoulders. "I do not care."

"Katie." He took her arm. "Let us talk privately."

"No."

"Please."

Katherine really did not care what he had to say, for he had made himself clear, he would only marry a noble-man's daughter, one whose rank was appropriate, one who was not as impoverished as she. She was aware of Liam rising to stand beside her. "Katherine is tired, Barry. Your privy discussion can wait."

"I think not," Hugh said flatly.

Instantly Katherine became aware of the tension that sizzled anew between the two men. It had only been re-pressed. They hated each other and wanted an excuse to leap at one another. She could feel the air crackling be-tween them. "All right," she said, moving to Hugh. Any-thing to avoid a fight—and to end this horrid evening.

Hugh smiled, taking her arm. He guided her across the hall and up the narrow stairs. Katherine felt Liam watching them, thought she could feel his seething hostility, but did not care. Although Hugh had frightened her because he was a stranger after all the years that had passed, he had been her childhood sweetheart once, he had been her dear friend. His rejection was brutal. The betrayal cut through flesh and bone to her very soul. As she had secretly feared, he did not want her, had forgotten her, had chosen another. All she could wonder was—*what will become of me now?*

And Liam's golden image filled her mind.

Hugh closed the door to a small chamber on the floor above, which boasted naught but rushes and a small bed. "You can sleep here this night, Katie," he said.

She shrugged, having moved away from him to stand in the center of the room. Her back was to him.

He moved up behind her. "Katherine, I am sorry you did not know, and that you came all this way thinking to marry me."

She said nothing. She had regained her composure and

she turned to face him. For the first time, she realized that she was just slightly taller than he.

"But I am also glad, because you are the most beautiful woman I have yet to behold, and had you not come, we might never have seen one another again."

"It matters not," she said tersely.

"Oh, it matters." Hugh touched her cheek. Katherine flinched. "I am your friend, Katie. If you think on it, you will realize that you have nowhere to go. If you return to London, there is only your father's prison, St. Leger House. Askeaton has been abandoned, and you will be a penniless burden upon your uncle and kin, for their circumstances are far graver than mine. They lost everything when your father lost Desmond. I would not be surprised that they should send you back to France—except that they can not afford your passage, nor your pension to a nunnery."

Katherine's skin began to prickle with unease—and fear. "They will not turn me away. Surely they can feed me, and we have other castles, other homes."

"Castlemaine, Shanid, Newcastle, and Castleisland, to mention but a few of your father's holdings, have all been abandoned. In fact, Castlemaine houses the queen's troops." Katherine gasped in horror. "Your kin still holds Dingle, as far as I know, but 'tis a small tower, and much overcrowded now," Hugh said, watching her. "They will not have a place for you there."

"I do not believe you!"

"I would not lie to you, Katie," Hugh said, not unkindly.

Katherine worried the folds of her gown. Somehow she had never dreamed all would be lost—all except for Dingle and perhaps a few very small, very old keeps.

"They can not keep you," Hugh said. "Do you wish to be married off to a sheep farmer? To a kern?"

She stared at him, shook her head no.

"You can stay here," Hugh said.

Katherine met his bold gaze and wanted to weep. What offer was this?

"Why do you look so surprised? Do you think I would abandon you just because of my troth to another?"

"You offer me a home?" she asked, confused.

He smiled. "'Aye, I do. A home, with a strong roof over your head, food upon the table, and a good, warm bed."

Katherine stared at him and saw the heat in his eyes. It was becoming difficult to breathe. "Are you saying that I will have my own bed—or your bed?"

He laughed at that. "You always were clever, Katie. My bed. You would share my bed. I could not keep my hands off of you if you lived here under my roof, darling. You are beautiful. I want you. You are the stuff a man dreams of. How sorry I am that your father was dispossessed."

Katherine clenched her fists. "What a fine friend you are, Hugh."

"Why are you angry? You are no child, not anymore. It was O'Neill was it not, who tore your dress?"

She paled.

"I knew it! And you were a virgin, weren't you—after having been in the nunnery?" He was red with anger now.

She found her tongue. "I am still a maid, Hugh."

His eyes widened. "Then I am very pleased—and O'Neill is a fool. So, Katie? What do you say? Will you stay with me?"

She fought for words. "I cannot believe what you speak," she said bitterly. "I cannot believe what my own ears have heard."

"'Tis no insult," he said quickly, "I am hardly the first man to take a mistress, and we are friends, longtime friends, and you will not be unhappy."

She was close to weeping. But she would not cry—not over him. "Once I loved you," she said, "but no more." She dashed past him and rushed down the stairs.

Perhaps she hated him now. She could not recall being this hurt, not ever. The steps were narrow and so smooth from centuries of use that she stumbled and slipped. But Liam was pacing at their foot and he caught her there.

For a moment Katherine embraced him, reflexively, regaining her balance. She looked into his gray eyes and saw not his anger, nor his worry, but only recalled that here was another male who wished to use her for his bedsport—for his pleasure. Furiously she pushed at him. He released her.

"What did he want?" he demanded.

Katherine spit, "What all you men want, of course!" Her eyes flashed, even filled with tears. "He wanted me to stay here at Barrymore and warm his bed," she said bitterly. "I am not good enough to be his wife, but I would make a fine whore!" She darted past him, but only managed a single step, for Liam's arm shot out and he caught her, whirling her violently around.

"And what did you say?" Liam asked, his face close to hers, his eyes brilliant with fire.

She twisted against him. "I should have told him to go to hell! Now I tell you, O'Neill—go to hell and leave me alone. Both of you—leave me alone!" She broke free of him and ran across the hall and outside into the raw, blustery night.

There, against the castle wall, cloakless and cold, she wept. Soon her tears were shed. But the cold remained, wrapping icy tentacles around her empty heart.

12

*L*iam stared after Katherine. Despite the fact that he had just won a major victory—by Hugh's default—and he was most definitely pleased with Hugh's rejection of Katherine, he was concerned for her. But he did not chase after her. The impulse was there, but he resisted it.

Katherine held him in no higher regard than she now held Hugh, and maybe she liked him even less. Once she had loved Hugh, their history together was long and intimate, a shared history no man could undo; perhaps, despite his rejection, which was purely political, she still cherished him. He and Katherine, on the other hand, shared no past, and shared few memories—and those were only memories of her abduction and the moments she had unwillingly passed in his bed.

Liam heard Hugh coming down the stairs and he turned. He had been right. Hugh had rejected Katherine. Although he would not have done so if he had been in Hugh's place, Hugh had acted as any nobleman would. Landed lords did not marry penniless beggars, 'twas as simple as that.

Hugh's gaze met and held his. Liam stared back. He understood the other man exactly. Hugh would not marry Katherine, not in her current circumstances, but he was determined to take her as his mistress. They had a great deal in common.

As two mighty elk might lock horns, their gazes fused for many moments, hostile and determined. The challenge was clear and accepted by both men. Only one of them would succeed in winning Katherine. Liam turned and walked back to the dining table. Hugh followed and refilled both their mugs with bitter beer.

"So, O'Neill, was Katie right—or wrong? Do you traffic with the queen or not?" Hugh asked.

Liam sipped the beer. How he preferred hearty red French wine. "And what concern is it to you?"

"I am not pleased to entertain an Englishman in my home."

"Then think of me as Irish."

Hugh stared. "I would like to think of you as Irish, but I am wary of making such a judgment."

Liam merely smiled, waiting to see where Hugh would lead, but already he guessed his course.

Hugh asked, "Are you a heretic?"

Liam smiled, not pleasantly. "I am a Protestant."

"Then you do follow your *Protestant* queen."

Liam noted that Hugh did not dare label Elizabeth a heretic as other papists did. "I follow the winds of fortune."

Hugh now smiled. "So you are loyal neither to God nor queen."

Liam smiled again. His eyes gleamed. "And do you wish to offer me a great fortune, Lord Barry?"

Barry smiled. " 'Tis not every day that the Master of the Seas comes calling at my home. Would I not take advantage, I would be the greatest fool."

"I have not yet judged you fool or wizard," Liam said easily. "Perhaps your offer will tip the scales."

Barry stared. "This country is at war."

"As all children know."

"The Spanish saw the Irish people through the last winter. 'Twas bitterly cold. Without their supplies, many more would have died than the hundreds who did."

Liam drummed his fingers upon the table. "Do you think to move me with pity? I have no pity—not for anyone."

Hugh snorted. "So 'tis said. 'Tis said you prey without mercy upon the many nations who sail the high seas. That no one can escape you if you determine to set chase. 'Tis well-known, also, that you seem to prefer Spanish booty to all other prizes.''

Liam's gaze was hooded. He shrugged. ''You mistake me. Treasure is treasure, and I care not who the holder of it is.''

Barry leaned forward. ''We can use you, O'Neill.''

''We?''

Barry's jaw clenched. ''FitzMaurice and the other great lords who fight to rid our land of the English—of the queen.''

''You ask me to throw my lot in with a bunch of papist traitors?'' Liam asked calmly, one brow lifted.

''You are already a traitor, O'Neill. I am amazed the queen pardoned you your bloody crimes. I cannot guess what you offered to attain her pardon. But should you wind up in the Tower again, we both know that most likely you will swing from a gibbet.''

''I quake.''

''You have naught to lose and much to gain by joining us.''

Liam's mouth curled. ''I see much to lose and little to gain, Barry.''

''Do you not have an ounce of sympathy for your native land?''

''But I am *English*, remember?''

Barry flushed. ''Shane O'Neill fought the Crown until the day of his murder. No man fought the Crown harder or more bravely than he. He hated the English—he hated the queen.''

''As you said earlier this evening, he was a murderer, not a hero. And he was also a rapist, and a savage,'' Liam said coldly.

Barry lifted his brows. ''I beg your pardon. We had never met.''

''Then you are lucky,'' Liam said flatly. ''You will not move me with pleas related to my father. I do not give a damn who he fought—or why.''

''I can arrange a meeting with FitzMaurice for the day after the morrow, if you but agree to it,'' Barry said, leaning forward, his face set with determination. ''I have failed to persuade you to our cause, but he is most fervent, and he has swayed others less interested than you.''

Liam rose to his feet. "He could be the devil, Barry, offering me immortality, but that would not persuade me to the cause of popery and treason.''

Barry also stood. "Christ—you are godly!''

Liam's smile was thin. "I've no wish to endear myself to papists and fanatics who think naught of burning men, women, and children at the stake.'' He pushed vivid memories aside, memories that were far more than visual, his ears filling with a woman's horrible, unforgettable screams, his nostrils filling with the scent of her burning flesh.

"There have been no burnings in Ireland!''

"Not yet. But FitzMaurice has hanged boys as well as men, has allowed women and children to starve—all in the name of God.'' Liam eyes blazed. "Find someone else to play your game of treason, Barry. I will not meet FitzMaurice—unless it is to give him over to the queen.''

Barry stared furiously as Liam stalked across the hall to a pallet Macgregor had laid out. "I do not believe you,'' he finally called. "I do not believe you are loyal to the queen. I believe you can be bought, my friend.''

Liam turned the pallet with his booted toe so one side butted up against the wall. He smiled. "You are right in that. I can be bought. But only when the price justifies the risk—and you can not afford my price in this happenstance.''

Barry sat back down, reaching for more beer. Liam settled upon his pallet, wondering if he had heard the last of this, and doubting it.

But as he lay in the growing darkness, he thought about how the Crown feared and despised FitzMaurice, who was a far greater threat than FitzGerald had ever been, and how they despaired of ever capturing him and ending this rebellion. Queen Elizabeth would be a very grateful monarch, should FitzMaurice be forced to surrender. Should FitzMaurice be captured. In fact, Liam imagined that the man who brought FitzMaurice down would be able to name his own reward—no matter what it should be. And FitzMaurice was the enemy of Katherine's father.

Yet should the papist be caught soon, that hardly affected FitzGerald, who would remain an impoverished prisoner at St. Leger House—unless some other circumstance occurred, precipitating his restoration as Desmond's earl and his return to Ireland. Liam wondered just what that circumstance might be.

And he also wondered if he dared play a dangerous and deadly game, if he dared to become the broker of power in southern Ireland? Excitement swept through him. As Liam fell asleep, his mind was spinning out incredible possibilities, and he sensed that, despite his recent avowals, he would soon become involved in the papist rebellion against the Crown—one way or the other.

Katherine lay curled into a ball on her pallet in utter blackness. Swallowing her tears, she wondered what would she do now? She had left the nunnery so that she might be wed. She had left the nunnery not knowing of her father's circumstances, not knowing that he had neither the means nor the will to arrange a marriage for her. And, of course, her uncles and cousins and all FitzGerald vassals had lost everything when Gerald had been convicted of treason, as their lands were held from him. Hugh had been right when he said that she would be a burden upon her kinsmen should she go to them. He had been right when he said that she had nowhere to go. What he had not said was that she also had no one to turn to, no one.

Except for Liam O'Neill. But he was the cause of most of her problems; he could never be the solution.

A sudden chill entered the small, cold chamber.

Katherine slept in all of her clothes, her fur-lined cloak and the blanket she had found upon the bed, but she shivered, wondering at the draft. Then she tensed, hearing the soft rustle of clothing. Her heart banged wildly in a sudden rush of fear.

"Katie?" Hugh gripped her shoulders gently.

Katherine gasped, rolling over to face him, now on her

back. He had set a small taper upon the floor as he knelt at her side. He smiled at her.

Katherine sat up, her palm splayed upon her breast. "Hugh! What do you here? You have frightened me! I thought I was about to be murdered in my bed!"

He chuckled softly, then suddenly his hand was on her cheek. Katherine went still. His thumb rubbed her full lower lip. "I did not come to murder you, Katie. I've come to woo you to my cause."

She understood. She had been a fool not to comprehend his intentions immediately. She saw the hot lust in his eyes too clearly now. "Get out."

He laughed, his hand sliding to her shoulder and suddenly gripping her hard. "No, not yet."

She struggled to free herself. "Get out!"

"I will not hurt you—at least, 'twill only hurt a bit at first. I've had other virgins, Katie, I am a man who knows what he does." He pushed her onto her back, shoved his knee between hers, and mounted her.

Katherine screamed, bucking wildly, trying to strike him.

He cut off her shrill cry with his mouth, caught both of her wrists in one hand, then quickly dragged her skirts up to her waist and spread her thighs with his. Katherine fought harder, aware that he was fully aroused, terrified now. He fumbled with his hose, freeing his manhood, which flicked her belly. Katherine panted and grunted and tried to heave him off. He tore his mouth from hers. "Dammit, Katie, we are friends! Relax!" he snapped. "You will enjoy this!"

"We are not friends," she gasped, panting heavily. Then she leaned forward and bit his forearm with all of her might.

He grunted and smacked her hard across the face. Pain crashed over Katherine and she lay still, stunned, stars exploding in the night, vaguely aware of his fingers groping the dry virgin flesh between her thighs. She knew that she must move, but her limbs felt weighted and lifeless. Her mind began to function, panic flooded her. She was about to be raped. She twisted ... and suddenly Hugh's body was lifted from her.

It was a blur. Hugh flying across the room and slamming headfirst into the wall. Katherine's vision cleared and she saw Liam yank Hugh to his feet and send his fist into his face with a mighty crack. Hugh grunted, crumbling, but Liam hoisted him up again, and this time sent his fist into the man's abdomen. The breath whooshed out of Hugh. A moment later he lay in a battered heap upon the floor.

Liam's dagger appeared in his hand. He rolled Hugh, who was groaning and only partly conscious, with his bare foot onto his back. He turned to Katherine. "Command it and I will kill him. Or castrate him if you prefer."

Katherine jerked her skirts down, staring. Her heart still beat wildly and uncontrollably. She was shaking. She felt close to vomiting. "N-no."

He straightened, the dagger disappeared. He looked at her.

Katherine sagged against the wall. Then she turned and leaned across the bed and retched.

Liam retrieved the chamber pot from the corner of the room and held it beneath her. Katherine's heaves were dry. He put the pot aside and laid a hand upon her back. She shook wildly. "Katherine," he said harshly.

She leaned back, covering her face with her hands, telling herself she would not cry. But it was too much. She had known Hugh since birth. How could he try to rape her?

"Katherine." Liam's tone was sharp. He sat beside her on the narrow bed, not touching her. "Are you hurt?"

She sucked in her sobs and her breath. She managed to shake her head once, negatively.

He took her hands and pulled them from her face, holding them. "Did he hurt you?" he asked again.

Blinking back the flood of tears, Katherine moved her head again. "N-no."

She saw Liam's jaw flex in the candlelight. He hesitated, their gazes locked. Then he lifted his hand and very gently he touched her face. His thumb stroked her jaw.

Katherine stared into his solemn gray gaze and could not move.

Then his eyes chilled. He turned her head to one side. "He hit you."

Katherine nodded, holding herself in check very firmly. Because she was an instant away from rushing headlong into this man's embrace.

His temple pulsing visibly, Liam studied the side of her face where Hugh had hit her. She was aware now of how her cheek throbbed and ached. She winced when he touched her jaw. Liam released her, standing.

"I think I will kill him after all," he said.

"No!" Katherine grabbed his wrist. It was then that Katherine saw how bloody his hand was. She dropped his palm. Their gazes met again. "I . . . please. Enough. Enough has been done this night!"

Liam regarded her for a long, assessing moment. Finally he nodded. "You are a very brave woman, Katherine. Brave and unusual. Most women would be in hysterics by now." His gaze searched hers.

"I am . . . in hysterics." She could not look away from him.

He smiled slightly, and it was as if the sun had just cast aside black, threatening clouds. "You are hardly hysterical." Then he sobered. "I do not blame Hugh for wanting you so badly," he said, staring at her. "I only blame him for his lack of finesse." Liam walked to the door, which was ajar. "I will have Lord Barry removed to his own bed. As there is no bolt on the door to your room, I shall move my pallet to the floor in the hall here. However, Barry is not going to wake again this night to torment you."

"I know," Katherine said unevenly. "Liam. Thank you."

He froze, her use of his given name seeming to resound between them. How intimate it seemed. He finally moved, bellowing to wake the dead. Shortly after, Hugh was carried from the chamber by two of his men, and Katherine lay unsleeping, knowing that Liam also lay outside her door, as sleepless as she.

*   *   *

They left soon after sunrise. The mild weather of the past few days had disappeared and the morning was damp and wet, a fine drizzle misting them. Hugh Barry did not see them off. He remained abed, apparently nursing his wounds, as well as his pride.

Katherine cantered alongside Liam, Macgregor on her right, trying to forget about all that Hugh had said and done—trying not to think of how Liam had rescued her. At times she wondered if she had dreamed most of the events of the past night. Not the near rape, which was so horrid and real that she knew she would never forget it, but Liam's kind, gentle touch. He had been concerned for her. She had been certain of it then, and was almost certain of it now.

Except that this morn, he said not a word to her. Once, briefly, he had looked at her bruised face, but then he had turned away. Katherine knew she was a horrendous sight. A looking glass had told her that. The right side of her face was swollen and turning purple. Katherine found that she yearned for some sign from him that last night's concern had been genuine, but she did not receive any.

They slowed their mounts to cross a stream. Katherine thought that this was as good a time as any to bring up the issue which haunted her—where she would now go. As their horses picked their way across the rocky bed, Katherine hesitated, unsure of how to address him after he had rescued her so gallantly last night. His given name was on the tip of her tongue, but it seemed far too intimate to use today. "O'Neill?"

Their horses lunged onto the opposite bank. Liam glanced at her. "Are we returning to the *Sea Dagger*?" she asked nervously.

"Yes."

Her pulse rioted. Did he think that she was his prisoner, now that Hugh had refused her? She was afraid to ask the next question, but had no choice. She must learn his intentions. "Where are you taking me?"

His gray gaze was piercing. For a moment, Katherine thought he would not respond. "We must speak, Katherine. But not now." He no longer looked at her. "We will speak when we get back to my ship."

But Katherine could not wait. " 'Tis my future you wish to discuss?" she cried.

"Aye."

"Then we must discuss it now!"

"There are starving outlaws everywhere, looking for prey such as ourselves. This is not the time." Abruptly he spurred his mount into a canter. Katherine's mare immediately followed. Filled with anxiety, she allowed the animal to have its head.

By noon they had reached the walled town and were admitted through the northern gate. They continued through the narrow streets at a brisk pace. Soon the harbor was in view, Cork Castle and the British garrison to the left. Many masted schooners and smaller barges and fishing vessels bobbed at anchor. The *Sea Dagger* rode the swells of the bay in its very midst, also at anchor, black and sleek, her many white sails puffing in the breeze, appearing every inch a pirate ship, appearing, too, as if she yearned to be set free to race the wind and ride the sea.

Katherine glanced at Liam, watching his face soften as he regarded his ship. She could not blame him for being proud of it. The ship might be a pirate's weapon, but she was a beautiful and stirring sight. It occurred to Katherine that the ship and its owner somehow suited one another perfectly. "Will we be allowed to leave?"

They had stopped at the edge of a dock. Katherine saw that a rowboat was being lowered to fetch them. "No one would be able to stop me if they tried," Liam said as one might state a fact.

"But—Sir John Perrot?"

He glanced at her. "I believe he will wish to converse with me before we go. However, as I have nothing to say to him, I do not think I will do him the courtesy of remaining here awaiting his permission to depart." He smiled. "Such a rude man deserves rude behavior—does he not?"

Katherine could not smile back. She had little doubt that Perrot would be furious when he discovered the *Sea*

Dagger gone. "You like this," she said suddenly. It was an accusation as well as a stunning comprehension.

He quirked a brow.

"You like danger. You like the challenge to leave before Perrot should know and order you to stay. You enjoy danger!"

He laughed. "I had never quite thought about it, but perhaps you are right." He slid to his feet. "Boy!"

A dock rat came running.

Liam handed the small, ragged boy some pennies. "Take these horses back to the livery."

The coins had disappeared. "Aye, aye, sir." Then, "Be you the pirate captain?" The urchin was wide-eyed. In his dirty face those eyes were huge and blue.

"That I am," Liam said, and then he scowled quite ferociously. "Now off with you before I decide to take your pretty little arse with me!"

The boy grabbed all three pairs of reins and began to run, the huge horses trotting after him.

Katherine looked at Liam archly. "Did you enjoy scaring him?"

Liam grinned. The effect was dazzling. "He was expecting a big, bad pirate. The least I could do was oblige him."

Katherine smiled back.

His own smile faded and he stared at her before abruptly turning away to face the bay. Katherine gazed at his broad, cloaked shoulders. Last night he had been concerned about her—she was almost certain of it. But today, he was as careless of her as a stranger. Why? She could not comprehend it. She could not comprehend him.

But why should she even want to? He was a pirate, and she must remember that. A pirate and Shane O'Neill's son.

Once the *Sea Dagger* was racing through the bay and heading toward the open sea, Liam relinquished the helm to his first mate and stepped off the forecastle. He stood at the prow, watching the iron gray water speeding toward him. It was icy cold, but he enjoyed the sea spray upon his face. How the *Sea Dagger* loved to run. But she had been designed for racing, for she was quick and light and lean. When they hit the open sea, he would let her sails out and let her race the wind. But race to where?

Liam knew he was running out of time. He had to approach Katherine with his offer soon. As it was, she was awaiting him in order to discuss her future.

He was afraid. It was astounding. He knew no fear when a battle approached, merely an icy and frozen calm, an acute sharpening of mind and wit. But now, he was afraid of a woman—afraid of a woman's rejection.

Katherine had refused Hugh, her childhood sweetheart. Liam was rigid with tension. He would be a fool to think that she would accept him, an infamous pirate, the son of a murderer, as her protector instead. His offer would have to be far better, far more than all that he had thus far offered her.

And still, he sensed that it would not be enough. Too well, he recalled Katherine FitzGerald's pride—and her scorn. But . . . had not something changed between them last night?

Liam was afraid to think so, afraid to hope so, but his blood beat hard with the very notion, with his hope.

Yet still he was afraid to approach her. He hung back at the ship's railing, reluctant to turn and go. His pulse raced, his heart quickened. His mind told him that he was a damned fool. To dare to reach above himself, for a prize worthy of a far different man, a far better man. But his heart dared to be contradictory.

Finally Liam turned and crossed the ship, to go below, to confront Katherine, to ask her to be his wife.

Katherine stood at the open porthole, unable really to enjoy the cool touch of the sea breeze upon her face, waiting for Liam. She watched the wooded northern shore of the bay recede as they raced toward the sea. She wondered anxiously about what he wished to speak to her—and, as anxiously, she wondered what the future would hold for her now.

"Katherine? I would speak with you."

At the sound of Liam's voice, her pulse rioted and her shoulders stiffened. Slowly, she turned.

He closed the cabin door behind him, his expression impossible to read. He stared at her, making her uneasy. She thought about what Hugh had tried to do last night, and how Liam had stopped him. She thought about Liam's purple-canopied bed, on the other side of the cabin; she thought about the red-and-gold cords. "Where are you taking me?"

Liam approached her then paused when a few feet yet separated them. "Katherine, I am unwilling to let you go."

She froze.

His gaze roamed over her face before meeting her eyes. "There is much I can give you, you know."

She did not say a word, her pulse running wild, knowing what would come next. She had no wish to be confronted with another illicit proposition. She had no wish to be tempted, even a little bit, by this man. She began to shake her head no.

He spoke quickly, then. "I saw you that day when we rode through Smithfield Market." He smiled slightly, his gaze deadly earnest. "I saw how you looked so eagerly at the clothing and the goods. I saw the delight crossing your face time and again; I saw how, when we left, you turned to look back, how you appeared as wistful as a child who has left her very first fair."

Katherine's eyes were riveted upon his handsome face. In spite of her anger and her dismay, she recalled, far too well, the incredible wealth of merchandise she had seen at the market—too well she recalled the splendor and extravagance of the queen's courtiers and ladies. All of the baubles she would never have, never know.

"I can give you every trinket you have ever dreamed of—and all you have never dreamed of, as well. I am not a man to brag, but this time, I will condescend to boast. I am richer than some kings, Katherine. You wish for sable and mink? Or ermine and lynx?" he shrugged. "You can have them all. You are a woman meant to enjoy beautiful things. You are a woman meant to be cherished, treasured, and pampered like any queen." He eyed her old, mended, ugly gown. "You should be clothed in silks and velvets, in ribbons and lace. You should be gowned in the splendor and wealth of royalty, Katherine. You should wear diamonds on your ears and rubies at your waist, and if you so desire it, sapphires and emeralds in your hair. Or is your preference more demure? Then it shall be pearls and gold. There are no limits, Katherine. You need but ask, and it shall be yours."

He offered her incredible riches so that she might become his whore. Katherine shook with anger. She shook with hurt. Even while, deep inside herself, a secret part of her filled with yearning. Just last night he had rescued her from Hugh. Last night he had not been a pirate, last night he had been a hero, a kind and caring one.

"Hugh was a fool and a clod," Liam said. "And impoverished, as well. I know I am not noble, but I would never hurt you. Surely I have proved that."

He had proved that, but his offer made it clear that he was little different from Hugh after all. "I refused Hugh his abominable offer. And I refuse you," she said harshly. "I will be no man's mistress."

Liam stared at her, his gaze as gray as the ocean, and as fathomless. "Katherine, I am not asking you to be my mistress, I am asking you to be my wife."

Katherine did not comprehend him at first. Surely she had dreamed his words!

"I am asking you to be my wife," he repeated, and now she saw that a vein throbbed visibly in his temple.

Shock washed over her in huge waves. She could not move, could not speak.

Grimly, he said, "My home is far to the north; 'tis an impenetrable island. We would be safe there from all those who might think to thwart us, though, in truth, I think the scandal of our marriage would soon die down. Have you not said, repeatedly, how much you wish to wed? Have you not said how much you wish a husband, a home of your own? Although I do not use it, on the island there is a brand-new brick manor house, as fine as any in England. If you do not like it, I will tear it down and build you something else." He hesitated. He stared at her, his eyes dark, charcoal gray. "Your father wishes this union. It would be helpful to him. I would be helpful to him."

She began to breathe again—but laboriously. Her breasts heaved. Her fists were clenched at her sides. Suddenly she fought temptation—and there was so much of it. "Oh, God," she whispered, agonized. He was offering her his name. *His name.* He was offering her marriage.

His tone was harsh. "You should think very carefully, Katherine, on my proposal. You are an intelligent woman. You will not have another marriage offer like this. You will have offers from farmers or men of similar station, perhaps, but you could never be a farmer's wife. Do you need some time to think about it?" He did not smile. He had not smiled even once at her. "I understand that you must be greatly surprised."

To say that Katherine was greatly surprised was a vast understatement. "Why?"

He blinked.

"Why, Liam? Why do you wish to marry me now?"

His jaw tensed. "I have thought about it carefully, ever since your father's offer. I want you, but I will not force you. I want you to come to me willingly."

"I see." Tears finally spilled down her cheeks, and she brushed them impatiently aside.

"Take all the time that you need," he said, turning to leave.

"No," Katherine said, sadly. "I do not need time to consider marriage to you."

He froze.

"I cannot marry you, Liam. I am sorry. I cannot marry a pirate." She hugged herself, trembling. "My father may be destitute, but Katherine FitzGerald has not changed. I am nobly born. I could never wed a pirate. And it matters not that my father wants this union for his politics."

He was rigid, as unmoving as if carved from stone. His face, however, was carved in lines that suggested pain.

"I am sorry," Katherine whispered.

"You are not thinking clearly," Liam finally said. "You are still overwrought from last night. I will go."

"No," Katherine said, wiping more tears away with her knuckles.

His jaw flexed. "You have no other choices now, Katherine. My offer is the best that you shall receive. I ask you to be my wife. Other men—*noble* men like Hugh—will only ask you to be their whore."

He was right. Katherine turned away, filled with her own pain.

"Perhaps a good night's sleep and some reflection will make you change your mind." She heard him turn and walk to the door.

"I am not changing my mind. Oh, God!" She sagged against the wall, perilously close to weeping.

He said, "My offer stands. Think of all that I can give you, Katherine. Perhaps it will overcome your contempt for my origins, and for what I am." He walked out.

Katherine sank to the floor. Did she ask for more than any other woman asked for? How had the world conspired to rob her of her due? She was a noblewoman. The daughter of an earl. But her life was reduced to receiving shameful propositions from noblemen like Hugh and marriage proposals from pirates. Katherine hugged her knees to her chest. Knowing that Liam O'Neill was right. That Katherine FitzGerald had no real choices left, and that she was not going to receive a better offer of marriage—not from anyone.

But she could never marry Shane O'Neill's son. Not ever. Not even if she really wanted to.

13

*K*atherine quickly realized that she had one other choice.

Dusk was falling. She hurried from the cabin, not surprised to find the door unbolted this time. On the deck above she wrapped her cloak around her more snugly, glancing about for Liam. He was once again at the ship's helm. Her pulse began to pound. She hurried forward, and with some difficulty, began to climb the ladder to the forecastle where he stood.

He noticed her at once. "Wait, Katherine." He left the helm with another seaman and hurried to her, bent, and with seemingly limitless strength, hoisted her up. Katherine steadied herself by gripping him, then quickly dropped her hands. The feeling of his hard muscles lingered. "I would have a word with you, Liam."

His eyes flashed. "You have reconsidered my proposal?"

She had not mistaken the eagerness in his husky tone. "No. I have not reconsidered—I cannot—will not—marry you."

He flinched.

"I do have one other choice," she continued, determined to ignore his disappointment, which he failed to hide. He was watching her very closely. "I wish to go to the queen," she said.

One tawny brow lifted. "And you will throw yourself upon her mercy?"

"Yes!" she cried. "Better to be at her mercy than that of men like Hugh and you and oh-so fickle Fate!"

"And if she decides to send you to your father? Or back to the convent?"

Katherine lifted her chin. "Then so be it." But she had no intention of being sent into a lonely exile in Southwark, or an equally lonely existence in a nunnery. She was prepared to beg for her future if need be.

His mouth twisted. "So I am the greatest of all evils."

She stiffened. She had not said that. "Do you deny who and what you are?"

His expression was mocking. "How could I even try?"

His words disturbed her. He disturbed her. "You are a pirate, O'Neill, and we both know it," she said angrily. She was not going to feel any sympathy for this man. She must not. "Will you take me to London? Or am I your prisoner now, regardless of my refusal?"

"Katherine, if you were but my prisoner, and if I were naught but a pirate, I would have taken your lovely body against your will—with or without rape."

Katherine said nothing, knowing better than to refute him.

"But there are degrees of bestiality, it seems," he said. His smile sardonic, he shrugged. "However, this beast, who has not hurt you, nay, who has even rescued you from abuse at the hands of your dear and noble friend Hugh, will accede to your wishes."

She did not move.

"You wish to go to the queen and beg for her help? Mayhap you are right. Mayhap she will decide to intervene, even arrange a marriage for you." His eyes glittered. "Mayhap, in all of England, there is some gentleman who will not care that you are destitute, that you are Irish, that you are Catholic, and that you have lost your name."

"I am hoping so," she managed huskily.

His gaze held hers, cold and angry. "You will never give up, will you?"

"No."

"That makes you exactly like your father." Liam turned his back on her and shouted out an order. Men began to scramble up masts, and slowly, the boat began to come around. Katherine watched him return to the helm. Telling herself that she was only being just to herself—and that it did not matter if she were unfair to him. He was a pirate, he was Shane O'Neill's son. He had chosen the life he now lived—while she had not chosen hers at all.

And although she was doing what was right, when the ship finally sailed south, she could not help but feel trepidation. There were no guarantees. Queen Elizabeth had been kind to her once, but at their first meeting she had accused her of conspiracy and treason. Whether she would be kind to her this third time they met was a matter of great speculation indeed. Katherine knew she might very well be sent to Southwark, to reside there as a prisoner with her father for the rest of her life.

And the thought teased her—perhaps the pirate's offer would then be a better thing.

Two days later they sailed up the Thames toward White-hall. Katherine could not help but be astonished that Liam would bring his pirate ship right to the queen's palace. True, he had been pardoned, and charged with escorting her to Ireland, but it seemed incredibly bold given who and what he was. Needless to say, by the time they reached the palace, word of their arrival had preceded them, and they were met by one of the queen's men, who informed them that Her Majesty would see them posthaste.

As it was not yet dinnertime, the queen had not yet descended to the Presence Chamber. But they were required to wait for almost an hour outside the doors of her private apartments, where she still dressed. Katherine rehearsed her plea. With every passing moment she grew more anxious and more afraid. Liam appeared bored.

The queen's door opened and a tall, dark, handsome man appeared. Katherine had to look twice. Other than Liam, he was by far the most splendid male she had ever laid eyes upon. He saw her and also looked again, then smiled and bowed. His smile faded when he discovered Liam, and a moment later he was gone.

Katherine stared after him. "Who was that?"

Liam eyed her. "Robert Dudley, the earl of Leicester."

Katherine had heard all of the stories about him. Rumors that the queen was going to marry Dudley had abounded in the first few years of her reign—until she had offered him to her cousin and rival, Mary Queen of Scots. Mary had refused the man reputed to be her cousin's lover and swain, and Dudley himself had been furious—but then Elizabeth had entitled him with Leicester, raising him up to a rank suitable to marriage with royalty—and some said that his being offered to Mary had been a ruse to begin with, in order that Elizabeth might elevate and ennoble him so she could marry him herself. But still, years later, the marriage had not come about.

It was clear, though, that from the first, Elizabeth had favored Dudley, that she was enamored of him, and she spent many moments alone with him—or so the gossips said. When they had first met, Dudley had been married to Amy Robsart, forestalling the possibility of marriage, but a few years later she had fallen down the stairs and broken her neck. The courts had deemed her death an accident, but many said that Dudley was behind it, hoping to free himself so that he could marry the queen—and still others said that the queen herself had planned the murder with him. In any case, Amy's untimely death had made it impossible for them to wed, for to do so would raise the accusation of murder.

Katherine had never paid attention to the gossip, which had reached her in the nunnery in France, as the doings of royalty interested everyone, everywhere, and most especially ladies isolated in a convent. Now, staring after Dudley, she could well imagine that the queen was in love with him. But murder? Having met Elizabeth but twice, nevertheless she felt strongly that it could not be possible.

"You are still staring, Katherine, although he is but long gone," Liam said coldly.

Katherine jerked and flushed.

Liam turned away, his anger obvious. Katherine knew it was small of her to be pleased with his obvious jealousy. After all, she did not want him, not in any way—not his jealousy, nor his lust, nor his love, should a man like that be capable of such a romantic emotion, which this man in all likelihood was not.

A moment later a lady appeared and ushered them both inside the antechamber. Elizabeth was not present yet, so they stood waiting silently. Finally she appeared from within her bedchamber. Through the open doorway, Katherine could see into the room, which was very dark, having but one window. Yet through the glass Katherine could see the Thames, where many colorful barges passed amidst a flock of floating swans and one small naval vessel. Even now, in tribute to the queen, the galleon was firing a round of cannon.

Katherine could not help but stare into the queen's most private chamber a moment more. The ceiling was entirely gilt. But Katherine gazed at the large bed. How striking it was, composed of woods of many different colors, with quilts of silk and velvet, embroidered in both silver and gold. Indian silks hung down from the bed's far side.

The queen had been alone in her bedchamber. Katherine wondered if she had met Leicester in there unchaperoned. If so, knowing men now as she did, she was quite certain that more than mere words had been exchanged.

"Katherine?" The queen smiled, coming forward, her hands outstretched. "Sweet Katherine!" She embraced her, still not looking at Liam. Her cheeks were flushed, and her eyes glowed. "Although I am greatly surprised to see you, how pleased I am, too."

Katherine almost fainted with relief, and found herself beaming at the queen. "'Tis wonderous to be back at court, Your Majesty," she said, meaning it. In fact, the moment she had seen London's many towers and rooftops from the river, her pulse had quickened in excitement.

"And have you brought your betrothed with you? Lord Barry? Or are you Lady Barry now, dear?"

Katherine's face fell.

The queen regarded her, then finally glanced at Liam. "Is aught amiss?"

Liam bowed. "Your Majesty."

The queen flushed slightly. "Liam, pray tell, what has passed?"

"Lord Barry is otherwise betrothed, Your Majesty."

Elizabeth's eyes widened slightly and she regarded Katherine. "So the betrothal was broken after all? But your family did not know of it?"

Katherine explained how Hugh had taken the contract to the Irish judges, the brehern, to decide the validity of their troth once Gerald had been convicted of treason and dispossessed.

"You poor dear," the queen said, patting her hand. "So you have been to Ireland on a wild-goose chase, and now you return to court."

Liam eyed Elizabeth.

The queen faced him. "And how benevolent of you, Liam, to bring the child back to London. I presume she means to go to her father? Or has she already told him the sad tidings?"

"Katherine has yet to speak with FitzGerald," Liam said quietly.

The queen's brows were arched and she said nothing.

Katherine realized she had been holding her breath. She let it out. "Your Majesty, might I speak?"

"Please do," Elizabeth smiled.

Katherine gripped her own hands nervously. "Hugh deemed me unworthy to be his wife, as I am no longer an earl's daughter. My father, untitled now and dispossessed, is also destitute. I know all that. But . . . my dreams have not changed. I have not changed."

Elizabeth cocked her head. "Pray continue."

Katherine stepped forward. "I only want a woman's due, Your Majesty. A home, a husband, and children of my own. How I yearn for those three simple things. How I have always yearned for them! Katherine FitzGerald has not changed, she has not, and my dreams remain as strong as ever. I dared much in leaving the convent, because to remain there unwed, homeless, and childless was no better than dying a slow and terrible death. Your Majesty, I throw myself upon your mercy and your generous spirit. I know I offer nothing now but myself, and without land or dowry, a woman's worth is so little. Too, I am somewhat long in the tooth, but as you can see, I am passing

fair, and more importantly, I am strong and well made
and I am certain I can yet bear some two or three or even
four children. Please. You did as you thought right when
you took Desmond from my father. I am his daughter—
must I share his fate? And did you not say that you were
Joan's good friend? In her memory, perhaps, you would
act. Please. Would you not find me some simple, yet gentle, man? I understand that he would not be terribly noble,
nor would he be rich, that in all likelihood he would be
a widower, with children, perhaps. I love children. I would
raise another woman's children as I would raise my own.
Please, Your Majesty.'' Katherine clasped her hands to
her breast as she would in prayer, and silently she did beg
God to move the queen to her cause. But as she had said
all that there was to say, she did not move, her gaze glued
upon the queen, anxiously awaiting her reply.

Elizabeth stared at her, intent and unsmiling.

Liam stared at her as well, his regard piercing, his expression strained.

Finally Elizabeth moved and took Katherine's two
hands in her own, clasping them tightly. ''Your plea was
most eloquent, Katherine.''

Katherine swallowed, but her heart soared with hope.

''I will think on the matter,'' the queen said.

Katherine stiffened, having expected an immediate
answer.

The queen dropped her hands. ''Now, I have matters of
state to attend to.'' She began to move past them and
paused. ''Katherine, you will remain here at court until I
have decided this matter. One of my ladies will show you
to a chamber. Liam, I will wish a word with you later, do
not leave.'' And with that, she swept out, her golden,
pearl-studded skirts rustling about her.

Katherine turned away from the queen and met Liam's
searing gaze. She did not care if he was angry, or dismayed. Her chin lifted and she stared at him with a hauteur
she did not feel.

''God's blood,'' he finally cursed. ''You are far too
bright for your own good.'' And his hands curled about
her wrists.

"What?" Katherine cried, too late.

For he was pulling her into his arms. With one powerful arm behind her back he held her pressed against his chest, with his other hand he tilted her face up to his. "Too bright, and too damned beautiful. I still want to make you my wife, Katherine."

Katherine's eyes widened and she began to protest. Liam cut it off effectively with his mouth, which was hard and hungry. Katherine stilled. Although she had come to court to find a husband, this might very well be their farewell. She really did not want to fight him. Not now. His lips sucked on hers and opened hers. A moment later her hands curled about his shoulders as he thrust his tongue into her mouth. He thrust deeper still, bending her backward over his arm. Katherine gave in. As she had wanted to do for so long now. She kissed him back.

Wildly. Her mouth pulled at his, sucked his, and her teeth caught his. In a frenzy their tongues sparred. Her fingernails dug into his arms.

Katherine realized that she was being lowered to the floor. Liam dropped to his knees. Although she reclined against him, supported by his arm, he continued to kiss her wet and open-mouthed and she kissed him back as feverishly. Katherine's fingers slid inside the loosely laced front of his shirt. Touching him was like touching silk-sheathed stone that lived and breathed. She panted into his hot mouth. Her hand slid down his belly. Frantic and feeling, exploring. Liam gasped.

And neither one of them saw the man standing in the doorway, watching them. William Cecil's first reaction was to cough and clear his throat, to alert the lovers to his presence—to break them up. But he had thought long and hard these past few days on the coil that the triangle of FitzMaurice, FitzGerald, and O'Neill represented. Long and hard had he thought on how strange it was that O'Neill had seized such an insignificant French vessel—one politically valueless—unless one counted Katherine FitzGerald's possible—future—worth. Staring, witnessing Liam's lust now firsthand, he suspected that Ormond was right. And finally his thoughts congealed. He closed the chamber door quietly, turned, and walked back through the antechamber. He stopped a passing servant. "Leave the work in the queen's apartments for later," he instructed her.

And her eyes flickered to the closed door. Comprehension showed in her gaze. She curtsied, and turned away.

And as Cecil moved down the hall, he thought, *Is Liam O'Neill yet friend, or foe? How far will he go in his alliance with FitzGerald?* For Cecil was certain that the alliance existed. And finally he wondered if there was some way to use the girl to control him. Or did Katherine FitzGerald already control him in a way as old as time?

The queen smiled at Leicester, who stood beside her where she sat upon her throne. "I am pleased you are here, Robin," she said archly.

He smiled at her, patting her hand with great familiarity. "Your concerns are my concerns, Your Majesty. Always—you know that."

Elizabeth was pleased, and she faced her cousin, Ormond, who scowled at them both, and Cecil, who was impassive. "I have just received a missive from Sir John Perrot," she stated. "He claims that the FitzGerald girl is as Irish as any rebel, akin with her father, and not to be trusted. He had O'Neill and the girl followed. They went to Castle Barry, nothing more. They but stayed the single night. There was nothing overtly suspicious to report, except for the fact that O'Neill departed Cork in great haste, without awaiting his papers, and, of course, the fact that Katherine is not to wed Barry. But as we know, O'Neill brought the girl directly to Us—and that is not an act of conspiracy."

It was brilliant, Cecil thought, just as Liam O'Neill was brilliant, but he did not say so.

Ormond growled. " 'Twas a ruse from the start. She never went to Munster to wed with Barry, but to relay information from her father. Your Majesty, FitzGerald is up to his old tricks again—only this time he has enlisted the Master of the Seas to his rebel cause!"

Leicester was annoyed. He gave Ormond a quelling

glance. "There is no proof, Butler, that O'Neill conspires with FitzGerald. Your hysteria leads you astray."

"Oh, it does? And what do you suggest?" Ormond demanded of Dudley, dark with anger. "To release a traitor into our midst?"

Leicester stared coldly at his chief rival for the queen's affection. Since FitzGerald had been removed from southern Ireland, no lord there was as powerful as Ormond. "FitzGerald is hardly the traitor that his cousin is, Tom. We would all be better off should he regain his lands and oust the damnable papist."

"Enough!" Elizabeth snapped before Ormond could retort. "I thought we'd finished this business three years ago when 'twas decided to try FitzGerald for treason. I have no wish to go backward now. I want to go forward." Elizabeth looked at Cecil. "What say you, Sir William? Does my golden pirate conspire against me?"

Her secretary said, "While evidence is growing, there are other possible explanations for O'Neill's conduct. I can not conclude that there is a conspiracy against you, Your Majesty. Not yet." His face was impassive, giving no clue to his innermost thoughts—and the conclusions he'd recently reached. It was not his method to bother the queen with matters she did not need to know.

"He is obviously involved in conspiracy," Tom Butler almost shouted. "Dear God, has not one of you your wits about you? Why else would O'Neill bring the girl to her father? And if FitzGerald is gathering allies, the south will be at war for many more years! Do you wish to have both FitzMaurice *and* FitzGerald running wild in southern Ireland?" he demanded of the queen.

"You know I do not," she cried.

Leicester's glance found Cecil's and rested there. Although they were hardly friends, both jealous of the other's influence with the queen, from time to time they allied themselves in a cause. This was one of those times. After but a moment, Cecil looked away.

Leicester took Elizabeth's hand. "Surely O'Neill is smitten with the girl's beauty. He may be a foul pirate, but he is a man. And he is renowned for his conquests—

remember the Dowager Countess Marian?'' Leicester was
pleased to see Elizabeth flinch. ''As always the pirate
seeks but two things, gold and the satisfaction of his lust.''

''You still support FitzGerald,'' Ormond accused.

''Must you both be at daggers always?'' Elizabeth cried.
She wrung her hands, flushed with distress. ''One thing is
clear, though. Perrot claims the girl is not to be trusted,
that she is fiercely loyal to FitzGerald and her kin. I would
trust Sir John's judgment. But whether she is a conduit or
not . . .'' Elizabeth trailed off. ''I think not. No, Liam
would not do this to me.''

Instantly Ormond snapped, ''Bess! She is a conduit! Do
not be fooled! Give her over to me as a ward and all this
conspiracy will be ended!''

Leicester's eyes narrowed. ''Do you have sudden broth-
erly feelings for your long-lost sister, Tom? Or do you
have other, more manly, ones?'' he sneered.

Ormond ignored him and stepped closer to the queen.
''Dearest cousin, let me take care of her. I am her half
brother and there would be nothing strange if you were to
give her over to my protection. I will send her to my
brothers in Kilkenny where she shall be watched closely.
She will not be able to make contact with her father, I
can assure you of that.''

''She asked me to marry her off,'' Elizabeth said. ''Her
plea was most eloquent. She made a most convincing case
that her only desire is to be gently wed. If she speaks
truthfully, there could not possibly be a conspiracy between her father and Liam O'Neill.''

'' 'Twas theatrics,'' Ormond inserted.

''She is a clever lass, her plea showed that,'' Elizabeth
murmured. ''God knows, her mother was most intelligent,
and FitzGerald is sly as a fox.''

Cecil spoke up. ''I advise we leave her be. I, too, think
she is innocent. And if not, then let her work her business
of treason *if* that is the case. FitzGerald is but a prisoner,
Your Majesty, and as such, can do little harm. If she is
guilty, the girl will lead us to any hornet's nest that ex-
ists.'' Cecil hardly blinked. He was counting on O'Neill

to be far too clever to be caught just yet at the deadly game he now played.

Ormond groaned. Leicester stared at Cecil, unspeaking, and Cecil calmly met his gaze. Although Cecil did not care for Leicester, this time he knew they understood one another and were allied. Leicester for self-serving reasons, as he despised Ormond. Cecil because he wished to protect his country and his queen.

"You could," Leicester said casually, "marry her to someone close to you, someone loyal, someone who would be able to spy upon her—and control her or use her if need be."

Elizabeth twisted to stare directly at him. She did not smile. "If I had but two of you, Robin, I could marry her off to one of you." Her gaze was diamond hard.

He smiled, white teeth flashing against his swarthy skin. "As I am but one man, 'twould break my heart, Elizabeth, were you to give me any bride."

Elizabeth's gaze was sharp upon his features. Finally she softened. "We have decided," she announced. "We will combine all of the ideas aired here. The girl will remain unwed for now, for if we do decide to marry her off, it must be with great thought. She shall remain with Us here at court." Elizabeth smiled. "As one of Our privy ladies. And We will give her some degree of freedom, allow her to visit her father, in the hope that We can uncover this hornet's nest. And to make sure that We do not miss a single trick, We will give her a tiring woman of her own—who will spy upon her every movement and report back to Us each day."

Everyone smiled. It was agreed. Katherine would become the queen's lady-in-waiting in the hope that she would lead them to a nest of conspiracy and treason.

14

*L*iam was summoned to the queen, not at midnight, as he had been summoned before, but the following morning well before the noon meal. He had not expected a nocturnal audience. Not after seeing Leicester leaving the queen's bedchamber after what had obviously been a private—and friendly—interview. Leicester was clearly back in the queen's favor.

Liam was relieved.

Elizabeth greeted him in her withdrawing room, magnificently dressed, two of her ladies in attendance. The ladies were both married noblewomen, nevertheless, they simpered and smiled at Liam, blushing prettily, trying to hold his eye. He ignored their flirtacious efforts and Elizabeth shooed them away, scowling. She closed the door firmly and they were alone.

She smiled at him, but it was restrained. " 'Twas most generous of you, Liam, to escort poor Katherine back to Londontown," she said, withdrawing a sealed letter from her sleeve. "How distraught she must have been after such a fiasco with Hugh Barry." Her gaze swept over him, more than thoroughly.

He smiled at her briefly, then sobered. "Katherine was not pleased."

"But she is a strong woman, and much like Joan. Already moving forward, hoping that I will be generously disposed toward her and make her a good marriage."

Liam tensed. "And will you be generous toward her, Bess?"

Elizabeth held his gaze. "Mayhap. You appear somewhat disturbed by the thought."

He shrugged, unable to find a retort.

The queen stared. "Is she still unblemished—or have you lived up to your pirate's reputation?"

"She is yet undamaged, Bess."

Elizabeth arched her brow. "So your reputation is but a tall tale?"

His smile reappeared. And with it, the faintest of dimples. "The tallest of tales."

Elizabeth understood. "Rogue!" Elizabeth's own bantering ceased. "If she is yet a virgin, I imagine 'tis not through lack of effort on your part."

"Did you not warn me to keep my lust in hand?"

"Yes, I did. But since when do you listen to me, Liam?"

"You are my queen. I am your ever-humble and obedient servant." He inclined his head.

Elizabeth snorted. "Undoubtedly the girl resisted you, having far more common sense than I had thought her capable of. But then, as her plea did show, she is unusually intelligent. I was quite moved by her eloquence."

"So you will honor her plea?"

"I have yet to decide what to do with her, but she is not for the likes of you in any case. You cannot have her, Liam." Elizabeth stared at him unwaveringly.

He regarded her back as steadily. But within his chest, his heart sank. Her jealousy was hardly hidden, and it seethed about her, snakelike and venomous. He would have to find a way to bring Elizabeth to his cause.

"I would never allow a marriage betwixt you, as much for reasons politic as for reasons social. Do you comprehend me?" she said.

Liam chose his words carefully. "I never said I wished to marry the lady in question."

"And you shall not—nor shall you use her as men are wont to do with unprotected women." Elizabeth held his eye. "We protect her now. We demand that you cease your pursuit of her.'' Elizabeth paused, and her tone softened. ''Perhaps in time I will find some gentleman for her to wed. 'Twill be no easy task in any case, but far harder if she is well used and carries your child.''

''So her plea *was* successful.'' He could not keep the anger from his tone.

Elizabeth's regard was sharp. ''I told you, I have not decided what to do with her. Her father was a traitor and a rascal, but I did love Joan FitzGerald dearly. 'Tis because of Joan that I am disposed somewhat favorably toward Katherine—thus I have decided to have Katherine attend me.''

Liam's eyes widened but he managed to hold in a sigh of relief. ''Katherine will not be unhappy. I think court life will suit her for a time.''

''I do agree.'' Elizabeth handed him the sealed letter.

Liam did not break the seal. He regarded her, a question in his eyes, as finally they came to the business at hand.

''Another letter of marque.'' She smiled. ''You shall be most pleased, I am sure.''

''And upon whom does the *Sea Dagger* now prey with the Crown's approval?''

''You shall pursue any who dare to trade with, or support, in any way or manner, the rebels led by FitzMaurice.''

Liam said nothing. No hint of emotion crossed his face or showed in his cool gray eyes. No sign of agreement—or defiance.

''And you shall prey upon any who dare to support any *others* who rebel against my authority in Ireland,'' she said as firmly.

Liam nodded, slipping the letter of marque into a pocket in his cloak. Any others—such as Gerald FitzGerald. So the game has truly begun, he thought. He had made the opening move by abducting Katherine, then followed with a second play by taking her to her father. The queen's counterpoint was far more precise—and far more challenging.

''Are you not pleased?'' she asked, somewhat archly.

''I am very pleased,'' he murmured. Indeed, despite the

fact that the odds were against him, and that the stakes were so high, his blood raced with the eagerness and excitement displayed by highly bred horses held in check at the starting line before a championship race. He had decided his course. Not only must he have Katherine as his wife, her father must be restored to his title and lands. So recently, when he had been accused of conspiracy and treason, the charges had been false. Should such an accusation be leveled at him again, they would be valid. He must proceed with care—as all traitors must.

"Good," Elizabeth said. She plucked his sleeve. "I am trying to think of a suitable manner in which to reward you for all that you have so far done in my behalf," she said softly, gazing into his eyes. "I depend upon you, Liam. You are my very own golden pirate."

"I shall be grateful, Bess, for any small reward, or even none."

"Every man wants some reward. Do not be afraid to come forth with a petition, Liam. I will entertain it gladly."

Liam bowed his head. When the time came, he would most definitely remind Elizabeth of this moment. "Thank you, Bess."

"You are welcome." Elizabeth smiled. "You have permission to leave, Liam."

He turned to go.

She grabbed his hand. "I look forward to when next we meet," she said suddenly.

He only hesitated a heartbeat. He squeezed her hand and bent and brushed his mouth to her cheek. "And I." A moment later he was gone.

Elizabeth stared after him, the royal facade gone. In her eyes were a young girl's wistful dreams.

"The queen has chosen me to be your servant," the girl said. She was small and slight and very fair and quite pretty. Her name was Helen.

Katherine was still reeling with shock. The queen had informed her earlier that she was not just to remain at court, but to be one of her privy ladies. Katherine was more than thrilled. She had not even thought to ask for such an honor—and an honor it was. She had not thought such an honor could be bestowed upon her, an Irish traitor's daughter. Only yesterday she had been at a loss, with nowhere to go, with no future. Now she had a place to stay, a purpose in staying. It was not marriage, but it was second best, and if the truth be known, Katherine would not mind being one of the queen's ladies for a good while. How fascinating life at court would be!

"Helen," Katherine said, facing the petite girl, "perhaps you can start your service to me by having a bath brought up, as I have not had a chance to bathe in days. And I have no clean clothes. Could you find me something to wear while my own things are laundered and dried?" She began to worry about her nonexistent wardrobe. Privy ladies were fabulously dressed. She had naught but a single, torn gown.

"I think so," Helen said, smiling.

"Good." Katherine stiffened as Helen turned to go. Liam O'Neill stood watching them in the open doorway of her small room.

Her heart lurched wildly. He hadn't left yet. She thought of the way he had kissed her yesterday in the queen's apartments. He had introduced her to desire and it stormed her now, fierce and unyielding. With it came shame.

Oh how well she recalled her own irredeemable behavior. Not only had she encouraged his kiss, and kissed him back as wildly, and she had touched the naked skin of his chest and stomach with appalling boldness. In fact, she dared not imagine what would have happened had Liam not regained his senses and recalled that they were in the queen's chamber! She bit her lip, wishing somewhat desperately that he would go away—but hardly meaning it.

Liam stared at her, grave and unsmiling. He did not look even once at Helen, who scurried away. "I have come to say fare-thee-well."

Katherine turned her back on him, her thoughts muddled, already breathless. She reminded herself that he was a pirate, a pardoned pirate but a pirate nonetheless, and that she had no business enjoying his kisses or desiring him at all. None. Not unless she became his wife—which was out of the question. "I thought you already gone," she managed to sound callous.

"Can you not show that you care, even if only a little?" Liam asked sharply.

Katherine did not turn to face him, and she refused to answer—telling herself that she did not care. A silence filled the room. Katherine strained to hear what he was doing, if he moved, recalling his marriage proposal on the ship. She was mad, surely, even to think of it. Or to have this strange aching inside her breast.

Suddenly his hands settled on her shoulders. "When will you give in to me?" He had come up behind her and she had not even heard him.

Katherine jerked away. "Don't touch me!"

His eyes glittered. "You are not afraid of me, Katherine. You are afraid of what I do to you—you are afraid of the passion in your own breast—you are afraid of the woman inside yourself."

She refused to consider his words. "No. I am afraid of you—nothing more."

He laughed then, amused. "What a liar you have become. You were not afraid of me yesterday in the queen's bedchamber."

She turned red. "I lost my mind, obviously."

"Obviously." His eyes gleamed. He reached for her again, pulling her to him. Ignoring the stiffening of her body. "But I like your madness, Katherine. Do you not wish to send me off to sea with a proper good-bye?"

Katherine's pulse raced. He was leaving, and this time it was reality. She was dismayed. It was ridiculous for her to be distressed, but there it was, impossible to deny. What if he died? He lived by the sword. His business was plunder and piracy, murder and mayhem. Oh, God. That she was even thinking of his safety was appalling, and made even worse by the fact that some brazen little witch inside her had given her the idea that another, parting kiss would not really hurt—because he was leaving—and she might never see him again.

And did she not owe him some gratitude for all that he had done so far for her?

"What thoughts speed about in that clever brain of yours?" Liam asked.

Katherine tried to tell herself that she would not kiss him. It was wrong, and that was that. Yet her body began to shake. "Wh-where do you go?"

"I go off to plunder Spaniards," he said with a slight smile and a spark in his eye. "The queen has given me letters of marque."

Katherine gasped. Suddenly it all made sense. He was not a pirate but a privateer—with letters of marque from the Crown. "I should have guessed! You could have told me! Knave!"

"And would that have made a difference? I had no letters authorizing me to seize the French trader you sailed upon." His gray gaze snared hers.

She remembered the smell of gunpowder and smoke, the broken and charred deck, the wounded men, and she shivered. "No."

He touched her chin with one strong forefinger. "You seem sad, Katherine. Sad that it does not make a difference. I will never be a fancy courtier, nor will I ever be a nobleman."

"I am well aware of that," she said. And that was why she would not marry him. That was why she could not ever marry him.

"You are so green," he said roughly. "Katherine— beware of all that goes on here. Beware of the intrigue, petty and otherwise. Do not trust anyone. Beware of men like Leicester—and mostly, beware of him."

Katherine stared into Liam's dark, flashing eyes. "I can take care of myself."

He laughed then. "Yes, you can, and 'tis most extraordinary." He sobered. "Leicester will try to have your skirts up before the week is out."

She started.

"I will kill him if he takes what is mine," Liam told her.

Katherine gasped and tried to pull away from him but

his grip tightened on both of her shoulders, his eyes smoldering. He shook her once. "You can deny it all you want, but *you are mine*. Call it passion, call it obsession, call it whatever pleases you, but you run hot and wild in my blood, Katherine—I cannot give you up."

She shook her head, her fingers fisted in his shirt, unable to speak, her heart hammering hard enough to leave her breathless.

He ignored her slight gesture of negation. "Mark my words. When the time is ripe, I will return for you, Katherine. This I vow."

She found her tongue. "No." She struggled against him. "You arrogant jackanapes!" But a secret part of herself was thrilled—to be wanted so fiercely by this man.

He made a deep, raw sound and swept her up against his hard, aroused body. Instantly Katherine went still, agonizingly aware of his massive manhood.

"Better," he said, eyeing her trembling lips. "Much, much better." He touched her cheekbone, pushed back strands of stray hair. Then he bent and, very leisurely, he plied her lips with his.

It could be their last kiss, no matter what he claimed, and Katherine could not forget that. Dear God, she could not resist him now! Liam pushed her against the wall and soon she found herself riding his powerful thigh the way the wanton in her breast yearned to ride him. Katherine dug her nails into his nape as he pushed her square neckline down, uncovering her bare breasts. His hands molded her. Katherine tore her mouth from his, head thrown back, neck arched, moaning with pleasure. Liam cupped her and bent and licked each taut nipple, all the while rocking his thigh against her sex. Every motion brought his pulsing phallus into contact with her throbbing loins. Katherine buried her face against his neck, whimpering. As swiftly as a striking snake, Liam slipped his hand beneath her skirt. He touched her wet, swollen lips through her crotchless linen drawers. Katherine convulsed, moaning. Liam continued to stroke her until she sagged against him, begging, "Don't! No more!"

He held her.

She clung to him, her sanity returning, afraid to lift her head and meet his mocking eyes.

"Kate," he said harshly. "Sweet, priceless Kate." He pushed her back against the wall and tilted up her chin. Katherine had no choice but to meet his smoking gaze. "You are mine. Mine. Remember that when the nights are long and lonely—or when Leicester and his kind come panting after you." He turned and strode to the door, then paused. "I am coming back. And when I do, I am coming for you."

Shortly after Liam had left, a servant brought Katherine a large, linen-wrapped bundle. Katherine had just dressed. She was still weak from the passionate encounter with Liam, and feeling somewhat bereft. She told herself that it was nonsense. That she was glad he was gone.

Now she stared at the manservant, who held the large parcel in his hands. "What is this?"

"A gift from Liam O'Neill," the servant said.

Katherine's pulse raced. She told herself she must send the man and the gift away, but instead she said, "You may put it on the bed."

When the servant had left, Katherine closed and bolted the door. Then she rushed to her bed, tearing open the inexpensive, colorless wrapping. She pulled out a brilliant turquoise gown, embroidered in silver thread. She discovered two more gowns, just as beautiful. Of course he had included ruffs, coifs, underskirts, and undergarments. Katherine laid the clothing carefully aside.

"Damn you, Liam," she whispered hoarsely. She blinked back a tear, then hugged the turquoise gown to her breast. She buried her face in the soft silk. His parting words echoed in her mind. *You are mine. Mine. Mine . . .*

She inhaled, still clutching the gown, until she realized that she would wrinkle it. Promptly she stood and laid it flat. What did he mean by this act?

Was it charity, generosity, or both? Or did he seek to entice her toward him, knowing as he did how she secretly yearned for such finery? Or did he merely think to prove his point: that she was his; therefore, he would clothe her as other men did their wives? Did he still think to make her his wife?

If so, he thought erroneously. Katherine looked longingly at the pile of clothes, knowing she could not wear them.

Not because people would speculate about how she had come to be dressed in such a noble and expensive fashion, but because she sensed her weakness, sensed she could be seduced by him—even from afar.

Katherine looked down at the gown she was wearing, which Helen had procured for her. Her dismay tripled. It was a plain brown velvet. Once it had probably been quite pretty, but it had been well worn. The cuffs of the sleeves were faded and tearing, and the scalloped hem of the skirt was frayed. Katherine sighed, then quickly, before she might stop herself, she jerked a beautiful ruff from the pile of gowns on the bed. Her hands shaking, she fixed it to her gown, watching herself in the small looking glass above the room's single table. It improved the gown enormously. And she would not dwell on who had given it to her.

Katherine unbolted the door. "Helen?"

The maid appeared. "Mistress?"

"Please fold the garments on the bed and put them away neatly, as I will not be wearing them." Her voice was not quite steady.

Helen nodded. Then, "Mistress, the earl of Ormond is below in the gallery. He wishes a word with you."

Katherine froze.

"Do you wish me to tell him you are otherwise occupied?" Helen asked quite shrewdly.

Katherine's heart beat again. "No, no," she said. And as she went downstairs to meet with him, she told herself that it was foolish to be afraid. She was one of the queen's ladies now and although Ormand was her father's age-old enemy, he was also her half brother, and surely he would not hurt her, not in any way, not now.

Katherine hesitated before entering the Stone Gallery on the floor below. The weather was not inclement, and through the windows facing west she could see ladies and gentlemen strolling on the walks of the Privy Gardens outside. A multitude of other windows on the hall's opposite side looked out on the River Thames, where fishermen and barges jostled for space, and on the banks, where carriages passed one another and numerous pedestrians. Many other courtiers and noblewomen ambled up and down the long hall inside, or were clustered in small groups, conversing.

Katherine saw Ormond at the same time that the earl espied her. She did not move as he detached himself from a group of gentlemen and strode to her. He appeared as he had the last time they had met, a tall, dark, and imposing man clad in dark, almost funereal clothes. He was not smiling. Katherine tried to still her racing heart yet again by reminding herself that they were related.

He took her arm. "I wish to speak with you, Katherine," he said, moving her back the way she had come.

Katherine was stiff, but she tried to relax. "What passes, my lord?"

Still no smile. "I wish to know my sister somewhat."

Katherine was uneasy. She recalled Liam's warning not to trust anyone at court. "You have a sudden fondness for long-lost sisters?" she said, striving for a light tone.

They began to stroll down the length of the gallery behind another couple. He still held her arm. "I think that I do."

Katherine met his dark gaze. She finally freed herself from his grasp. He wanted something from her, but she could not sense what.

"Are you happy, Katherine? To be honored with the queen's appointment as one of her ladies?"

"Yes, I am." Katherine smiled. "I am very honored, in truth. Although . . ."

"Although what?"

"Although I still pray that she will eventually heed my plea."

"Your plea?"

She met his regard. "My plea to marry."

"Ahh. So you do not pine for Hugh Barry."

Katherine tensed. "My lord, Hugh was my betrothed for many years, and I was happy. When I thought he died at Affane, I was aggrieved—and 'twas my grief, in part, that caused me to be sent to the sisters in France. Returning to Southwark, I was overjoyed to learn that Hugh lived." She paused, coming to a standstill in front of a portrait of King Henry VII.

"But?" Ormond stood slightly behind her.

Katherine glanced back at him. "I was also aggrieved to learn the brehern had judged our betrothal invalid. But I saw a side of Hugh I had not suspected to exist before." Her jaw firmed. "Let me just say that I am glad we are not to be wed after all."

"What did he do?" Ormond asked.

To her dismay, tears filled her eyes as she recalled his violent attempt to rape her. She shook her head.

Ormond stared. "What did he do, Katherine?"

She met her half brother's shadowy gaze. "He was . . . he was not a gentleman, but then, I am no gentlewoman anymore."

Ormond's stare was unwavering. "I am sorry," he finally said. "It cannot be easy, I suppose, to lose all that one once had."

She turned to face him, unsure of whether he commiserated with her plight or not. "If you are sorry, my lord, then perhaps you will be moved to help me somewhat."

A muscle ticked in his jaw. He did not respond.

Katherine grew wary. This man was an enigma. "Am I asking too much? From my own half brother?"

"I sense you have hardly begun to make your request," Ormond declared.

"I am sorry to have even mentioned it. I beg your pardon." Katherine started to turn away. "I do not need your help after all, it seems." She knew now that he did not care for her at all.

But his hand restrained her. He turned her to face him again. "You are very much like our mother," he said softly.

Katherine started.

"And I am not remarking the physical resemblance,

which is great.'' He was grim. ''Joan knew not when to hold her tongue. She was always forthright. Forthright, determined, and intelligent.''

''Is this praise?''

''Perhaps. If you aspire to being the woman she was.'' His tone was suddenly bitter.

''Of course I wish to be like her,'' Katherine could not help but cry.

''Do you?'' He was darkly mocking. ''Do you even know of what you speak? Joan was strong and clever, but she created the greatest scandal of her time when she began her affair with your father.''

Katherine was resentful. ''She is dead and you slander their love.''

''Love?'' He laughed. ''Your father was a boy when Joan began to think of marrying him, shortly after my father died. Indeed, to stop *that*, she was married off posthaste to Sir Bryan. As soon as Sir Bryan became ill, our mother began to ride about the countryside with your father—who was but eighteen, and younger than I. Joan was twenty years his senior. I could go nowhere without hearing of their affair. She accompanied him openly everywhere—hunting all across Munster, joining him at the Galway fair, even residing for a time as a guest at Askeaton. 'Twas scandalous—the height of disrespect, not just to the dying Sir Bryan, but to herself, the countess of Ormond, and to me and my brothers.''

Katherine had always known of the vast disparity in age between her parents, but had never thought much of it—many widowed women remarried younger men. But now she felt Tom Butler's pain. ''How difficult it must have been for you,'' she whispered. And she could not help being somewhat shocked by her mother's indiscreet behavior—yet proud, too, of her iron will and refusal to bend to the dictates of society.

His glance was sharp. '' 'Twas more than difficult. The feud between Ormond and Desmond went back generations, and for my mother to behave with the Desmond heir in such a fashion was a direct affront to me and mine—it was—it is—unforgivable.''

Katherine's chin rose. "She loved Gerald greatly, despite his age. 'Twas a marriage made for love."

"Aye, she loved him," Ormond said darkly. "And that, too, is unforgivable."

Katherine felt for Tom Butler then, seeing into his very soul. "She loved you, too," Katherine cried. "I remember as a little girl when my father took his army to meet yours. I remember my mother weeping in fear for *your* safety! I remember that she disobeyed my father and rode after him as he rode to make war on *you*."

"Yes." Ormond's face softened. "For thirteen days she rode back and forth betwixt husband and son, betwixt our two great armies, which lay crouched like hounds prepared to pounce and fight. The soldiers on both sides began to call her the Angel of Peace. And she begged first him then me, repeatedly—morning, noon, and night—to cease our fight. She was tireless." He glanced out of the window. "She was an Angel of Peace."

"And?" Katherine hardly breathed.

Ormond smiled faintly. "I cannot remember which of us heeded her first. But in the end there was no battle; both armies, led by husband and son, turned around and went home."

Tears glistened in Katherine's eyes. "Joan was a *great* lady."

"She was formidable, clever, and headstrong. Too headstrong. She did not care about the scandal attached to her and Gerald; indeed, she laughed about it." Ormond eyed her.

Katherine hugged herself, uneasy. She thought of Liam now—and her own passionate nature where he was concerned. Now she knew that her dark side came not just from her father, but from her mother as well.

But surely she was not like Joan in all respects. Katherine could not imagine laughing at any scandal that might arise in regard to her and the pirate, Liam O'Neill. A scandal would horrify her; she would die of the shame.

"Did he abuse you?" Ormond asked abruptly.

Katherine knew he also thought of Liam, but she feigned ignorance. "Who?"

"The pirate, O'Neill. Talk is all over town. A hundred ladies and gentlemen saw him kiss you in the Banquet Hall before he bore you off to Ireland. Now another rumor flies about, that someone saw you alone with him in the queen's private rooms, in a compromising, nay, scandalous position."

Katherine flushed scarlet. Oh, God. Someone had seen her on the floor in Liam's arms? But who?

"Are you more like Joan than I thought?"

"No!" she cried, suddenly furious. "I am not eager to court scandal! I do not laugh at hearing these rumors! I want nothing from the pirate, nothing but for him to leave me alone! I am determined to marry a decent, God-fearing man. 'Tis most important to me!"

Ormond's gaze was penetrating. "And what does your father wish for you?"

"I do not know," Katherine replied truthfully. She could not help but be somewhat bitter. "I have not seen him since that night O'Neill took me to him. I doubt he knows that Hugh has betrayed me. I . . . doubt he cares. He is overwhelmed with his losses and his confinement."

Ormond said nothing, but his gaze was unblinking.

"My lord," Katherine said earnestly, "I am past eighteen. Although I am pleased, nay, thrilled, with the queen's appointment, time hardly favors me. By now, most women have had several babes, and if a few more years go by, I will be past my prime childbearing years." Suddenly her gaze was beseeching and locked with his. "Could you not help me, sir? You are the queen's cousin. Could you not sway her to my cause? I do not expect much, just a gentleman who is decent of nature."

Ormond stared at his sister. She was much like Joan, and it was almost painful. But she was not Joan. His sister had no power. She had been stripped of her name and possessions. She had naught but her beauty—which men like Hugh Barry and Liam O'Neill preyed upon eagerly. Despite his overwhelming interest in protecting Ormond's power he did not particularly care for the thought of Katherine being used by either man. Although he had no use for a sister, nor any care for one, they had shared the same mother.

He reminded himself that she could not be as innocent or as sincere as she sounded and appeared. She had every reason to conspire with her father to regain what had been lost, and if she were like Joan, she would use her beauty to ensnare a powerful man like Liam O'Neill as a determined ally.

And as this was the case, her wish to wed must be a clever, treacherous ruse.

Given Liam O'Neill's interest in her, it was best to remove her completely from his grasp. And what better way to do so than with a husband of her own? "Aye," he said abruptly. "I will take up your cause, Katherine."

She gasped, then clapped her hands with girlish glee. "Thank you, my lord brother!"

Ormond managed a smile. He turned away in case she might think to embrace him. He was determined now to find her a husband, and was not daunted at the prospect of having to persuade the queen. Yet he found himself deeply confused. Katherine's joy seemed both childish and sincere—so sincere. Yet it could not be real. It could not.

Katherine FitzGerald had to be a conspirator, and he was determined to prove it.

15

"**K**atherine," Lady Hastings whispered, "Have you heard? Is it true?"

Katherine stood in the withdrawing room with the six other privy ladies in a cluster as they waited for the queen to emerge from her bedchamber. Also in the antechamber were dozens of noblemen: earls, barons, and knights, all royal officials or royal favorites, including her half brother, the earl of Ormond, and the earl of Leicester, Lord Robert Dudley, the Master of the Horse. Also present were some two dozen scarlet-clad Gentlemen Pensioners, the queen's personal bodyguard.

Katherine knew that the other ladies had quieted to hear her reply. Likewise, she felt Leicester's eyes upon her—as she so often did. She feigned ignorance of the subject. "I beg your pardon, Lady Hastings, but of what do you speak?"

Anne Hastings tittered and raised her fan, her eyes glowing. "Come, Katherine, you know of what I speak. The entire court has been abuzz with the news all week! Could it be true? Could Liam O'Neill have left the queen and but a day later set upon one of King Philip's money ships?"

Katherine's pulse pounded. The court had deemed her an expert on Liam O'Neill. Ormond had not spoken falsely when he said that the entire world knew of Liam's manhandling of her. Even before the rumor of his latest daring escapade had begun to run rampant, the ladies had bom-

barded her with less than discreet questions about him. It
had quickly become clear to Katherine that several of the
queen's ladies, all of whom were married, and were of
high and important rank, not to mention very beautiful,
were quite interested in the pirate in a way that they should
not be. All week she had tried to pretend that she did not
know him very well and that he had not kissed her in the
most improper manner, both publicly and privately.

Liam O'Neill was the talk of the court. For not a day
after he'd left Whitehall, he had set upon a Spanish galleon
bound for the Netherlands. And it had not been just any
Spanish galleon that he'd attacked, but one laden with
silver plate and gold bullion, sent by King Philip of Spain
to finance the duke of Alva in his campaign against the
Protestant rebels there. Although the *Sea Dagger* was but
half the size of the Spanish vessel, and equipped with half
the cannon, Liam had attacked.

Rumors of his astounding victory had been reaching the
court all week. But one and all wondered if it were true.
Katherine wondered, too. Could the much smaller pirate
ship possibly defeat a Spanish man-of-war? It hardly
seemed possible. In fact, the reverse was far more likely.
Katherine grew cold all over when she thought of Liam
defeated by the Spanish, bound and manacled and sent to
a prison in Spain. She tried to reassure herself by telling
herself that if any man was a survivor, it was Liam
O'Neill.

But what if he were dead?

"Katherine?" Lady Hastings said again, more loudly.
"Could your pirate have been so bold and so daring?"

Katherine turned red. She met Leicester's brazen gaze.
She knew he had heard their every word. Quickly she
faced Anne. "He is not my pirate, Lady Hastings. I must
protest such language!"

Anne laid her Oriental fan with its ivory handles upon
Katherine's arm. "If he is not yours," she whispered,
"you are a fool—and I will gladly take him!"

Katherine could only stare in shock. And she was saved
from making a reply, for the queen appeared, followed by
her four ladies of the bedchamber.

Katherine muffled a gasp. Not a day went by that she did not reel at the queen's magnificence. Today she wore naught but white. Her white silk gown was beaded with pearls and embroidered with silver thread. Her pale silver underskirts were heavily embroidered in a lighter shade, and she wore gold, pearls, and rubies at her waist, around her throat, and dangling from her ears. Her ruff was huge and fantastical, and every little point bore a tiny, glowing pearl. As she emerged, a small crown of state upon her head, those she looked at quickly dropped to their knees. When she graced Katherine with a smile, Katherine knelt as well, her heart pounding.

The queen moved forward. The noblemen, all magnificently dressed and bejeweled, preceded her as she left her apartments. Behind the barons, earls, and knights of the Garter was the lord chancellor, bearing the seals of state in a red silk bag. On his either side were two liveried gentlemen attendants, one carrying the royal scepter, the other the sword of state in a red scabbard.

The queen followed them. She was surrounded by her Gentlemen Pensioners, her personal bodyguard, all noblemen of the highest rank and from the finest families, carrying gilt battle-axes. Her four maids of honor came next, then the ladies of her bedchamber. Katherine and the other six ladies of the Privy Chamber followed last.

They proceeded through the Presence Chamber into the hall, where many courtiers and petitioners awaited. One and all knelt as the queen passed by. In the antechapel she paused so that several petitions might be presented to her, which she received with a gracious smile. Several people, perhaps new to court, perhaps not, cried "God save thee, Queen Elizabeth!" Elizabeth smiled again, murmuring "I thank thee, my dear people." She then followed her noblemen into the chapel for the morning mass. As Katherine knelt for the service in one of the last pews, she finally answered Anne Hastings's question to herself.

Of course she believed the rumors. Liam would be so daring, and so bold, as to attack one of King Philip's ships laden with gold. Of course it was true. He was probably laughing about the matter even now—if he were still free, if he were still alive.

And then she found herself praying for the pirate's welfare, and asking God to speed him to safety.

Later that day Katherine rode across London Bridge surrounded by a dozen of the Queen's Guard. What a sight they made. Every yeoman wore a brilliant livery of scarlet, a golden rose embroidered upon its back. Each man carried a gilded halberd, its handle clothed in red velvet, and each rode the finest horseflesh, decked in silver-studded tack. Katherine herself was a dowdy wren in comparison to such splendor, clad as she was in the borrowed brown velvet and her old gray cloak. But it did not matter. What mattered was that the queen had given her permission to visit her father, as long as it did not interfere with her duties, and as long as she alerted Her Majesty to the fact of the outing. How kind the queen had become. And she had even instructed her to take her maid, Helen, to wait upon her during her family reunion.

Katherine knew that she should feel like a queen herself, to be escorted in such a manner to her father. But she did not. She was filled with anxiety instead.

She had been at court for several weeks, yet had not gone to see her father even once. Their last reunion had been so painful. Katherine had avoided recalling Gerald's attempts to foist her off on Liam O'Neill. Now recollections of that horrible time filled her mind, no matter how much she wished to forget it. Katherine became resolved. Today she and Gerald would converse in a natural manner, as a long-separated father and daughter should. Despite his betrayal, Katherine still loved her father.

The gates of St. Leger House were open at this time of day and, as the small cavalcade clattered into the cobbled courtyard, Eleanor soon appeared on the front step, wideeyed. She espied Katherine instantly. Katherine smiled at her but did not dismount.

The captain of the Guard, Sir John Hawke, had been kind enough to escort her to her father himself. He slipped from his blood bay gelding and strode to Katherine, who sat one of the palfreys from the royal stable. He made a dashing figure in his red uniform, the epitome of a soldier and a gentleman. He held her a moment longer than was necessary when helping her to dismount, and Katherine was aware of it. Liam had made her aware of all the innuendos of desire that passed from a man to a woman.

Sir John seemed to be a suitor. Ever since she had begun to attend the queen, it had been clear that he, amongst many other gentlemen, found her very desirable. Sir John came from a fine family, and although the fami ly's fortunes were dwindling, should Katherine catch such a man 'twould be the ultimate match. He was handsome and pleasant and very noble, and she had heard naught but good about his character and family. Yet he did not keep her awake at night. Katherine wished it were he of whom she dreamed. Unfortunately, Liam O'Neill haunted her from afar.

Sir John bowed to her. "Mistress FitzGerald, take your time. I will await you no matter the length of your stay."

She could not help flirting. She had been so long in a convent amongst women, and now, even clad in ugly brown velvet, she felt young, female, and free. She touched his arm lightly and fluttered her lashes as she had seen Anne Hastings and the other ladies do. "Thank you, sir. You are too kind."

His eyes sparkled.

Katherine turned, to meet her grim-faced stepmother. "We heard you were there, one of the queen's ladies," Eleanor said angrily. "Are you a traitor to your father, then, Katherine?"

Katherine's smile faded. "I am no traitor to my father!"

"No? You have become one of them—how clear that is!" Eleanor turned her back on her and marched into the house.

Katherine did not move. Although she had not expected a warm or friendly greeting from Eleanor, neither had she expected to be accused of betraying her very own father. And was Eleanor right? She had been enjoying herself immensely these past weeks, overwhelmed with the goings-on of the court and the queen and those closest to her. Did that make her disloyal to her own father?

Katherine realized that Sir John had come to stand beside her. She did not want him to fathom how distressed she was, so she flashed a too-bright smile and hurried on into the house.

Gerald stood leaning upon a cane in the dimly lit dining hall. He was unsmiling. His gaze searched her face as she came forward. Katherine was afraid that he would also call her a traitor.

But he did not. "So the queen has taken you into her protection, Katie? That is good."

Katherine almost swooned with relief. Instead she gripped his arm, wanting to embrace him. "You are not angry, Father?" She was aware of Helen coming into the room, carrying a basket that contained some refreshments from the queen.

"Not at all." Gerald seemed about to say more, but then he spotted her servant. "Who'd you bring with you, Katie?"

Katherine half turned. "The queen gave me a maid, Father."

Gerald nodded, then guided Katherine to the table. "I heard that Barry decided to break the troth."

Katherine sat down, then watched her father maneuver himself painfully onto the bench. "Yes." She heard the catch in her throat. "Hugh never cared for me. He only wanted an earl's daughter and the expected dowry."

Gerald patted her back. " 'Tis the way of men and you should know it. Tell me about Desmond." He leaned toward her, at once eager and impatient.

Katherine saddened even more. Images of the charred land around Cork and Castle Barry swept through her mind. "Oh, Father. There has been so much war."

Eleanor burst from the kitchens with a serving woman, carrying a wood trencher herself, the servant bearing ale and mugs. "Aye, and all is burned to the ground, it is. Isn't that right, Katherine?" She smacked the trencher of bread and cheeses down.

"Much is destroyed," Katherine agreed.

"Askeaton?"

"I do not know. I was not allowed to go home. Liam told me the castle has been abandoned—that many of our holdings have been abandoned. 'Tis true?"

Gerald nodded.

"So it is Liam now?" Eleanor asked.

Katherine flushed.

Gerald shot Eleanor a dark glance. "And FitzMaurice? Have you heard aught of my conniving cousin? I am surprised he has not taken up residence in Askeaton himself!" Gerald's fists were clenched.

Eleanor also jumped to her feet. "Have you heard that he styles himself the earl of Desmond?" she asked Katherine. She did not wait for her stepdaughter to reply. "I tell you, he is after your father's land and his title, and if he raises himself high enough—he will force the queen to give him all that was once ours! While we are reduced to begging, myself reduced to serving the table like any common cupbearer!"

Katherine's heart was wrenched in two. "I am glad the betrothal is broken," she told her father fiercely. "How could I marry Barry when he consorts with FitzMaurice against you?"

"You are a good lass, Katherine," Gerald said, but he was agonized. Abruptly he stood, leaning on his cane. "I am not hungry," he announced. "I do need air. Katie, walk with me."

As Katherine had already eaten with the other ladies, dining on the queen's leftovers—which were designed to feed her household—she got to her feet. As they left the hall, Helen followed. Gerald turned and waved her away. "No need," he said, his tone friendly. "Can you not help my wife in the kitchens, mistress?"

Helen nodded and turned to help Eleanor clear the table.

Outside, it was chill but sunny. Katherine and her father walked arm and arm in the courtyard, Gerald leaning upon his daughter. Katherine was aware of Sir John and the other soldiers guarding the front gate, pretending not to watch them. Gerald paused. "We cannot trust anyone, Katie," he said.

Katherine looked at him. "Surely you do not have spies in your own house?"

" 'Tis not my house, 'tis St. Leger's," he said. "But Cecil has spies everywhere—you can be certain of that."

Katherine was dismayed. Gerald's next words distressed her even further. "Do not trust anyone," he said sternly, "not even that pretty little maid."

She gasped. "Why, Father! That is ridiculous! The queen herself appointed her to attend me! 'Twas most thoughtful."

"Listen, daughter, and listen well. Do not trust *anyone*."

Katherine grew uneasy. She nodded. She wondered if her father walked outside with her because of Cecil's spies—or because of her maid. But the thought was too chilling. Surely Elizabeth had not planted a spy upon her—surely not.

"Tell me about O'Neill."

Katherine's unease grew. "You wish to talk of the pirate?"

"He is quite the man," Gerald remarked, regarding her.

Katherine felt her cheeks heat. "He is a pirate," she said grimly. And she prayed Gerald would find another topic upon which to converse. Surely he did not still think the unthinkable. Katherine was glad that he did not know about Liam's proposal of marriage to her.

Gerald took her hand. "You are in a position to help me, sweetheart. And I need your help desperately. Will you aid your poor, exiled father?"

Her heart thundered. "How can I help you?"

"You are installed at court—it could not be better. Befriend the queen. Woo her gently, very gently, to our side. Once she loved Joan. She loved Joan greatly and it aided me time after time. If she comes to love you, and I am sure she will, we might be able to win my release. I can regain Desmond, Katie, if I am returned to Ireland. Once home, the lords will join me—and so will the people."

She looked at her father, who stood tall now, oblivious to his pain, his dark eyes burning with the fervor and the excitement she remembered seeing so often as a child. He did not ask too much. The queen had unfairly deprived him of his home, his rank, and his land, and Katherine knew she must help him regain all that he had lost. He was her father. But . . . she felt that even to contemplate doing as he asked was somehow wrong. For already she loved the queen. The queen who had been nothing but kind and generous to her. It did not feel right to use her friendship, to use her love, for any cause—not even this justifiable one.

Gerald took her arm. "And we must play O'Neill as carefully, nay, far more carefully, than Bess."

Katherine had stopped breathing. "Wh-what?"

"He lusts for you. A man lusting for a woman is a powerful thing. Such a man is easily led. I need him, Katie. He is the Master of the Seas. If I am returned to Ireland, how easily he could aid me! And even now, if he were allied with us—how easily he could thwart FitzMaurice, who relies upon the Spanish, the French, and the Scots for his victuals and supplies. Yes, we must have O'Neill at our side."

"What are you asking me to do?" Katherine asked fearfully.

"Lead him on a merry chase. Do not allow him his way with you, girl. Too often men grow bored with the spoils, 'tis the hunt they enjoy. Let him hunt. Lead him on. Bring him to our side. If his lust grows great enough, I might be able to entice him right to the church's altar. 'Tis my grand desire, Katherine, to see you wed to him."

Katherine choked. She had thought this horrific subject dead. Oh God. 'Twas hardly dead—and now she began to understand the jeopardy she was in. "Father—he is a pirate," she managed thickly. "I did not understand before—I do not understand now. I am your *daughter*. How could you suggest this alliance—again?"

"Because I have no other allies," Gerald cried. "And if I must gain but one, then let him be greatly powerful. And he is the key to my future and my freedom, Katie. He is the key to your future and your freedom, as well."

"He commits murder—and mayhem—he is a thief— ignobly born—the son of a murderer, the son of a rapist— he is conscienceless!" And she refused to think of that

other side of him, the one that was hardly vicious,
hardly ignoble.

Gerald faced her, his jaw clenched tight. "O'Neill wants
you badly. He is playing right into our hands! 'Tis a kind
act of Fate, my dear—an act we must seize to our advantage. You must do as I instruct you to."

Katherine looked away, sick at heart and shaken. "I
wish to marry honorably," she whispered. "I want what
is my due."

"You will never be honorable, not until I have Desmond again," Gerald snapped. "Barry did not want you
for a reason. All men of consequence will share his view.
You have no choice, Katie—I am not giving you a choice
in this matter."

Somehow Katherine squared her shoulders. Somehow
she lifted her chin. A tear spilled from the corner of one
of her eyes. "I cannot," she said. There was a lump in
her chest and it hurt terribly. "I cannot do this."

"You will do it," Gerald said sharply. "Because you
are my daughter, Katherine FitzGerald, and you are loyal
to me before anyone else—even before yourself."

Katherine tried to pull away.

"Katie." His tone softened. "You are the only one who
can help me now, do you not see that? You have the
power now to breathe life back into my dead soul. Katie?
You *must* help me."

Katherine stared, torn, wiping away her tears. And although she knew that she had little choice in this matter,
not if she were to remain loyal to her father, she did not
speak up, she did not tell her father that Liam O'Neill had
already proposed marriage to her, and that in all likelihood, he would do so again if she gave him the least
encouragement. Stubbornly, defiantly, her dreams of the
future would not die. And they did not include Liam
O'Neill. They did not.

16

*T*he queen loved masques. The current masque told the story of the five daughters of the African river god Niger, and the cast included slaves and sultans, princes and princesses, nymphs, mermaids, sea dragons, and numerous other fanciful monsters.

For this particular masque, the queen had ordered the entire court to attend in some form of costume. Elizabeth's courtiers had obeyed, and Katherine was astounded to see all manner of dress, everything from ancient Greek goddesses scandalously draped in gossamer silk to tribal kings sporting garlands of flowers and fruits as their crowns. Katherine herself had no funds with which to buy the materials necessary for a costume, but Helen had procured a splendid red satin mask, one beaded and beribboned. She wore it with her tired brown velvet gown.

The pageant had ended sometime after midnight, the queen flushed with pleasure, standing up to applaud the cast of players. And the court had begun carousing in earnest then—the festive revelers growing progressively more animated and inebriated as dawn crept upon them.

Flutists, harpers, drummers, and viol players were performing a lively Irish jig now. A single bagpiper joined them. Despite her perpetual despair over the never-ending resistance of the Irish lords to her authority, the jig was the queen's favorite tune for dancing. Katherine clapped her hands in delight when the wild jig began. Her feet would not keep still. How she wished to dance.

Leicester partnered the queen. He was dressed as Julius Caesar, wearing naught but a white toga, which left one broad shoulder and part of his hard chest bare, a big leather belt and a huge, ancient sword. Upon his head he wore a crown that bore a remarkable resemblance to one of real gold. Katherine watched them, smiling, admiring not the queen, who was an excellent dancer, but the earl himself, whose white teeth flashed, whose strong bare legs never missed a beat.

Then, in the press of the crowd, someone gripped her elbow from behind. "Come, Mistress FitzGerald, teach me your native dance."

Katherine turned to look into the vivid blue eyes of John Hawke. Like herself, he had forgone a costume, but he was resplendent in his crimson uniform and pale hose and a demimask. "How could I refuse," she cried, "when my blood is singing and my feet are itching to perform this dance?"

He grinned at her and proved himself a bit of a liar, for as he whirled her on the dance floor, it became clear that he had danced a jig at least a few times before. But he was not Irish. No one at court was Irish, with the exception of the earl of Ormond, who had already left the festivities, proving himself as dour as his demeanor so often seemed. Katherine knew she could outjig even the queen, and she set about to do so.

Her knees flew so high that her brown velvet skirts and cream-colored underskirts flew up to twirl about her thighs, revealing her long curved calves and her knees. Katherine was wearing her own pale, plain hose, but earlier that day, for some nonsensical reason, just as she had taken to wearing the ruff which had been amongst the clothing given to her by Liam, she had sorted through his gift again, this time choosing a pair of purple garters. They hardly matched her white stockings, her underskirts, or her gown, much less the red satin mask, but Katherine did not care. Laughing, she jigged harder, and higher. She whirled and whirled and stomped and stomped. Sir John was laughing too, gripping her hands tightly, imitating her every movement, determined to keep up with her and to dance as hard as she. They were enjoying themselves immensely, and they exchanged wide grins. She saw, also, how his glance strayed to her smooth, gartered thighs, and how he watched her heaving bosom, the neckline of her dress creeping lower and lower. Katherine did not care. She was having more fun than she had ever had. She felt beautiful, alive. When the jig was over. Katherine collapsed against him, and into his arms.

"God's blood," he gasped into her ear, his arms tightening around her. "No one can dance a jig like you!"

She pressed away from him and he let her go. "I hope not! What kind of Irishwoman would I be if a bunch of English lords and ladies could outdance me?"

"That sounds almost treasonous," a deep voice murmured from behind her.

Katherine twisted to face the earl of Leicester. Sir John dropped his hands from her arms.

"Would you dance with me?" he asked, smiling pleasantly—but his eyes were smoldering.

Instantly Katherine looked about for the queen. Elizabeth danced with another of her favorites. "I do not know this dance," she said nervously. She did not have to be very wise to know that the queen would not like her dancing with Robert Dudley. She was often very jealous of him. Recently she had set down two of her ladies, both sisters, Francis Howard and Lady Douglas Sheffield, a widow, for being so obviously in love with him.

Leicester took her elbow. "I will teach you."

Katherine was alarmed, and she looked to John Hawke for support. He was scowling, but then Anne Hastings came up beside him, and a moment later she was coaxing the captain onto the dance floor and clinging far too closely to him while she was about it. Katherine found herself being led in the steps of a far more sedate dance, her hand in the earl's. Her heart was speeding, but not from exertion. She met his dark regard again.

He smiled at her, then glanced at her bosom. Although low-cut immodest gowns were fashionable, Katherine, having more to display than most, had never followed the mode. Her pulse quickened even more as his gaze skimmed her bare flesh.

A memory flashed through her mind: of herself, twisting upon a bed, her hands bound with red-and-gold cords, while Liam O'Neill sucked and then teased her nipples with his tongue.

"That dress does not do you justice, my dear," Leicester remarked.

"I am well aware of that," Katherine said somewhat tartly. She recalled Liam's warning, as well, that Leicester would seek to get beneath her skirts within a sennight. Three weeks had passed since she had come to court, not one, and ofttimes when he came to visit the queen his unwavering regard had settled upon her, however briefly. But they had never conversed or been alone—until now.

"You deserve the finest silks and velvets, the finest emeralds and pearls."

Katherine missed a step. "And you would give them to me?"

His gaze darkened, moved to her lips, which she had daringly rouged. "Aye, I would. Katherine, these past few weeks, you have run the other way every time you saw me coming. You have no reason to be scared of me, my dear. I do not seek to hurt you."

"No?" Her tone was dry. "Then what do you seek, my lord?"

His handsome face tightened. "Barring matrimony, I wish to befriend you, and I am certain that you know it."

She did. Like Hugh Barry, he wished to make her his whore. Katherine tried to pull away from him, but his grip was steel and she could not. She glared at him. He no longer smiled. "Katherine, you misunderstand. God—I am the earl of Leicester now, one of the richest, most powerful men in this realm. I would marry you, my dear, in the blink of an eye, for I need not a dowry, but a warm, willing wife and healthy sons. I sense you would be far more than willing, and 'tis obvious you are made for bearing sons. But I cannot marry." His tone was not bitter, merely resigned. "I cannot marry any woman. One day, God willing . . ." he glanced toward the queen, and Kath-

erine knew he thought of becoming England's king, but
he did not speak of it. "Come. We must talk in private.
This cannot wait another day."

Katherine was appalled as he put his arm around her
and thrust her into the crowd. She flung a glance over her
shoulder and saw Elizabeth staring after them. Her heart
flipped in fear. She dug in her heels as a wayward child
might do, but Leicester was big and strong and not about
to be deterred. He propelled her forward, practically carrying her through the animated, raucous crowd. A moment
later they were in an empty hall, and then he had pushed
her into an empty alcove. He pushed her mask up atop her
coif, and gripped her arms, holding her so closely that her
knees bumped his.

"Do not say no," he said hoarsely, pressing one fingertip to her lips. "Katherine, I am your father's friend."

Katherine's protest died.

"I'm the one who opposed Ormond when he brought
your father to the queen as his prisoner after Affane. Butler
wanted your father stripped of his lands and titles even
then. I'm the one who fought for your father in the ensuing
years—and even fought against the very idea of a trial
for treason."

Katherine stared into Leicester's eyes, breathless and
afraid. But her mind was racing. Leicester was very powerful—he had the queen's ear. He could champion Gerald's
cause yet again if he had a reason. She began to shake
her head slowly in a frightened negation.

"Do not say no yet," he said, his eyes gleaming. "I
would take you to Kenilworth. Where you would lack for
nothing, Katherine. But we would have to be discreet."

"Discreet!" she gasped, trying once more to pull away
from him and failing. "You do not understand the meaning of that word," she panted. "The queen saw us leaving
together! She will dismiss me from my position this very
night!" But she was shaking, feeling very much cornered
and trapped.

Leicester was silent for a moment. "Mayhap that is for
the best," he finally said. " 'Tis not a good thing for us,
your being here at court with her."

Katherine was incredulous. "There is no us! And I do not wish to fall from the queen's good grace—dear God— I do not!"

"You dissemble," he told her, abruptly pulling her up against him. Katherine stiffened. She had been aware of the heavy, thrusting bulge of his loins on several occasions; more than once since she had come to court she had noticed his manliness, but those prior times she had chosen to ignore it, thinking, as some of the other ladies did, that he wore a codpiece. He certainly did not wear a codpiece now, or any other thing, under his Roman toga. His phallus, unrestrained by his wool garment, rubbed against the well-worn velvet covering her belly. "I have seen how you look at me," he whispered, pressing her into the wall. "Do you think I am a foolish boy, to make such a mistake?"

Katherine choked. "Do not do this, my lord," she begged. He did not repulse her. Like Sir John, he was a fine, virile man, and she could not be immune to him, not like this, when his hard body pulsed against hers. But it was a mere shadow of the kind of desire aroused in her by Liam O'Neill and she was acutely aware of the difference.

He studied her drawn expression, then bent his head. Katherine turned her face quickly away, and instead of plundering her mouth, his lips plied the delicate skin of her throat. She tried to push him off. One of his hands slipped into her bodice, his thumb flicking her nipple, which instantly grew taut.

Finally, because he too knew they could be discovered with grave consequences, he ceased his manhandling of her and she darted away from him. She stared at him, wide-eyed, flushed, and truly afraid.

"You will enjoy it, Katherine," he told her.

She wanted to tell him that she would not, because there would be no liaison between them. Yet he was, as he had said, one of the most powerful men in the realm. If anyone could help her father, it was the earl of Leicester. Katherine knew that Leicester was a far more powerful ally than Liam O'Neill.

"I will not take no for your answer," he whispered, his breath stroking her cheek.

And Katherine knew that he would force her into his bed whether she wished it or not. And should he do so, should it even be rape, she would have no recourse at all—because the queen would blame her, not him. But if she were clever, she would use him the way Gerald had asked her to use Liam. Muffling a cry, she turned and fled—not back to the dining hall, but to the stairs and her own small chamber on the upper floor. Never had she felt so adrift upon stormy seas that could only be navigated by one far more astute than she.

With but a single taper casting a dim, dancing light, Katherine hung up her beautiful mask and plain dress on a bedside hook. She wondered where Helen was, whose duty it was to help her prepare for bed. Undoubtedly she was involved in the festivities as well, not having expected her mistress to retire so early. Katherine could not blame her.

It was a damnable task, unlacing the farthingale herself, but she managed, trying not to think about Leicester and what might become of her should he seek to finish what he had begun this night. She placed the whalebone corset on the room's single trunk, slipping off her chemise and then her linen drawers. Sitting, she slid off her shoes, then rolled down her stockings, one by one.

The undersides of her breasts were red from where the whalebones had dug into them, the price one paid for wearing a small corset in order to flatten oneself, and she began to massage herself gently. It was a nightly ritual. Once, at the convent, it had been innocent. Then, she had ignored the sweet tightening of her nipples, caused by her own fingers, and the pulse of pleasure shafting her loins. Now it was impossible to ignore the stirrings of desire. Molding her breasts, Katherine thought about how Leicester had touched her. He was the kind of man a woman— any woman—dreamed of marrying, at once powerful and rich, both virile and handsome. But Leicester was not available, not as a husband, not to her, not to anyone. He belonged to the queen and everyone knew it.

Katherine whimpered a little. She crushed her breasts just once, wishing it were Liam O'Neill, a man no woman dreamed of marrying, who had touched her tonight as Leicester had. Her hands stilled. Her nipples pointed over her fingers, red, rosy, and so erect that they hurt. It was impossible to ignore the feverish heat that throbbed between her thighs, a heat so strong that it made Katherine moan.

"Of whom are you thinking, Sir John Hawke, Robin Dudley—or me?"

Katherine shot to her feet with a gasp.

Liam stood in the open doorway of her room, leaning against the door. Her eyes were wide—because, for a single instant, she had not recognized him.

He was dressed as a blackamoor. He wore loose white breeches, a wide purple sash, and his own sword—which she now recognized. His broad chest and powerful torso were bare—and the color of dark oak. He had also stained his arms, neck, and face, even his hair, while wearing a red turban to complete the disguise. His gray eyes appeared remarkably silver in contrast to his dark skin.

Then she realized what he had seen—and what he was seeing now—and she felt her cheeks flame.

He smiled with no mirth, entered the room, and kicked the door closed, tossing the turban aside. The muscles in his chest and torso rippled and flexed as he turned to her. His gaze skimmed her pale curves, lingering on her heaving breasts and jutting nipples—and then on the area between her thighs. He pushed himself off of the door.

"How long were you standing there!" she cried.

He stalked toward her. His smile was not pleasant; he briefly touched his hugely swollen loins. "Long enough to have enjoyed a very good show, one far better than that staged below."

Katherine stared at him. He had been spying upon her. She was as furious now as she was embarrassed.

Turning her back on him, she whipped the blanket from the bed. As she frantically wrapped it around herself she heard him coming toward her. Katherine faced him just as he tore the blanket from her and hurled it across the room. He gripped her arms. "You have not answered me."

Her chin lifted, despite her sudden fear. She was panting, acutely aware of being naked and in his arms. Her nipples brushed the soft hair of his chest. "I owe you nothing, knave."

He growled. "I saw you tonight, cock-teasing first Hawke, then Dudley!"

She hissed and struggled, hoping to free herself and strike him, hard. He only laughed at her and gripped one of her buttocks in one palm. She froze. He pulled her against his own rock-hard, silk-sheathed loins. Katherine choked on thundering, demanding, feverish desire.

He laughed again. To make matters worse, his splayed fingertips inched lower, from the curve of her buttock to the joining of her thighs. Katherine gasped when he began to tease her virgin's canal.

His jaw flexed so hard it looked as if it might snap. His gray eyes blazed. "You are ready to come! Who were you thinking about!"

"Leicester!" she shouted, lying, knowing it would enrage him.

He thrust her hard away from him and she fell across the bed. "Damn you! I knew it!"

Katherine lifted herself to her hands and knees, panting. "He offers me more than you," she gasped throatily, knowing she was goading him, but unable to stop herself. She knew what was going to happen, and she wanted it— fiercely. For her sanity had fled the moment he had revealed himself to her.

Liam towered over her. "What does he offer you? What, Katherine?" he roared. "Other than his big cock?"

She knelt on her haunches, aware of his gaze darting to her swinging breasts. "Kenilworth." It was an exaggeration, hardly the truth.

Liam stared, laughed once. "You are a fool. The queen will behead you if you become his wife. Behead you and take from him all that she has given him. Do you understand me, Katherine?''

She eyed him defiantly. "You are just jealous because he can give me more than you. Because he is noble and worthy, while you are naught but a pirate, naught but Shanc O'Neill's son."

His nostrils flared. "Can he give you more?" He jerked her hand forward, grinding her palm against his loins. Katherine gasped at the huge, throbbing feel of him. " 'Tis said he is a big cocksman—but then, so am I. Do you wish to compare us, Katherine—before making your decision?''

Katherine moaned, incapable of speech, the muscles knotting so painfully in her thighs, high up inside, that finally she cried out. Liam pushed her onto her back and she fell willingly, knees open. Their gazes met. Katherine was well aware of being shameless. She was well aware that she was about to lose her dearly cherished virginity. Somehow, this night, she no longer cared.

Liam grabbed her knees quite hurtfully, forcing her legs farther apart. "You push me too far," he ground out, staring at her. Abruptly he reached down and thrust his forefinger deep into her, until he was stopped by the membrane that branded her an innocent. Katherine gasped, his name on the tip of her tongue, arching up against him. He did not move now. Katherine began to moan unashamedly, thrashing from side to side.

"So Leicester did not get to you yet." Suddenly he palmed her hard. "Nor will he, Katherine. Do you understand me?''

She blinked up at him, realizing what he had just done. "You bastard!" she shrieked, sitting up and trying to yank his hand from her. But he was unmovable. "You—you think to examine me? Like some physician? Damn you!''

" 'Tis becoming harder and harder to believe that you are convent-reared,'' he taunted. He suddenly slid two fingers inside her and Katherine inhaled, going motionless.

"Lie down," he ordered, "and we shall finish this now. Not that Leicester will care if you are not a virgin. But I'll be damned if he will take what I have marked as mine!''

Although Katherine wanted nothing—*nothing*—more

than to have Liam's huge penis, stiff and hard, inside of her, his words infuriated her. She rose up on her knees, her fists banging hard upon his chest. He caught her wrists, laughing at her, which only enraged her more.

"I do not belong to you," she hissed. "I belong to myself, and one day, to my husband."

Liam laughed with real amusement then, jerking her forward so that she was in his embrace. "Darling," he murmured, his tone seductive now, "I hate to tell you this, but no other man will marry you after we are through." A moment later his mouth covered hers, forcing her lips open with sheer, male domination.

He had thrown ice water upon her, not dousing her desire, but forcing reality to intrude upon her. She wanted this abominable, despicable man. She wanted him to thrust inside her, to plow her as a stallion does a mare. God, she did. But she truly did not want to be a whore, not his, not Leicester's, not anybody's. She wanted to be a wife. She wanted a husband, a home, and her own babies—and she had yearned for these things for many years, far longer than she had yearned for Liam's powerful body and his burning touch. She tore her mouth from his. "Stop," she said, tears welling up in her eyes.

He held her face in his hands, panting roughly. "No more games," he rasped.

"No," she wept, turning her face away. "Oh, God, what is happening to me?" She choked on her sobs. She no longer knew herself. The woman who had emerged this night was a total stranger. How could she want him so much?

"God's cock," he cursed, gripping her chin and turning her to face him. "Now you decide to play the virgin? Now?!"

She gazed into his blazing silver eyes. Then, helplessly, she looked at his perfectly shaped mouth. "I cannot," she whispered hoarsely, her gaze pleading when it met his again. "Oh, God, I am so wicked, Liam—I want you. *I want you*. But I cannot give you my virtue, I cannot."

He stared at her, his mouth twisted and downturned, in

both disbelief and disappointment. "These games can kill a man," he finally said, harsh and rough.

Katherine swallowed. "I am dying, too," she whispered.

Their gazes collided. Something sizzled and flared upon the impact. Katherine's eyes widened when he pushed her down, onto her back. She started to protest—even as her thighs opened. He murmured, "Hush," touching her mouth with one of his fingers. Katherine closed her eyes and nipped it, trusting him.

Liam bent over her, kissing the sides of her face softly. Then he growled, the sound impatient, and an instant later his tongue was deep inside, rapacious and plundering. His hand stroked between her legs, his thumb between the heavy, throbbing folds of her sex. Katherine cried out. A moment later she felt his tongue there. Her desire exploded, and she wept and keened at once.

Liam lay beside her, pulling her into his arms. He gave her no respite. Katherine was still dazed when he took her hand and molded it around his naked penis. Her eyes flew open and she gasped. Liam gripped her tightly, making her stroke his huge, hard, slickly swollen length. Katherine's eyes widened in fascination, her pulse beginning to pound. She looked from his face, strained and rigid, to his manhood. She had dreamed of touching him before. This was reality—and far better than any dream. Without thought, her grip tightening, Katherine bent and kissed the ripe, plumlike tip. Liam gasped and arched off of the bed. She pulled his hand from hers and stroked him somewhat awkwardly, until his own hand guided hers, showing her what to do. Within moments Liam cried out.

Katherine went into his arms, atop him, whimpering. He hugged her once, hard, and whispered, " 'Tis all right. I will take care of you again, love."

Neither one of them saw Helen standing in the corner of the room.

17

"*M*istress? Please, you must awaken."

Katherine sighed. She was in bed, her face buried in her pillow, and she was snug and warm beneath blankets and furs. She did not want to awaken, not yet—she was so tired she could hardly move. Indeed, she felt drugged. Helen called her again. Katherine rolled away from her maid and, in a single blinding instant, recalled the night before.

She stopped breathing. Liam. Oh, God, Liam had come to her room, and they had made love, in a manner of speaking—oh, yes. It had been wicked and wonderful and she was still a virgin, quite miraculously. She began to smile. She wriggled her toes, contracted her muscles, thinking of how he had loved her not once but twice— and the second time so endlessly, so thoroughly, so perfectly, she had finally had to beg him to cease. Her cheeks were hot.

Katherine stared at the stone wall while, on the other side of the room, Helen moved about. He was gone now. She had fallen asleep sometime before dawn and had been unaware of his leaving. Realizing that he was gone made her feel bereft. When would she see him again?

Her soft smile faded, and so, too, did her joy. She was mad, mad to be sad over his departure, mad to be remembering their heated encounter in such a dreamy, wistful way. She was mad. He was a notorious pirate. She was a

noblewoman. She'd had no right to do the unspeakable
things that she had. No right—none.

Katherine did not move, frozen now with dismay. How
wrong she was. She'd had every right to play the whore,
she now recalled. Her father had so recently asked her to
take on that very role.

Katherine closed her eyes. Although Gerald would have
approved of what she had done, she could not be pleased
with her own behavior. She was ashamed. Especially as
she did not want to play Gerald's game, did not want to
become O'Neill's wife. Yet she had played the whore
well, far better than her father would have ever asked her
to. Her true nature was far darker, far less genteel, than
Katherine had ever dreamed.

Perhaps men looked at her and discerned her sensual
nature. Perhaps they all saw through her, Katherine
thought miserably. Was that why Hugh Barry and the earl
of Leicester, two very noble men, wished to make her a
mistress instead of a wife? Could a man look at her and
see that forbidden passion stirred in her veins?

How ironic it was. Hugh Barry and the earl of Leicester
wanted her to be their whore, but Liam O'Neill wanted
her to be his wife.

Katherine hugged her pillow. Perhaps Gerald would succeed in marrying her off to O'Neill. It was certainly becoming more possible, as a result of her recent behavior,
and the fact that she could not seem to resist the pirate's
embraces. But Katherine, although well aware of her duty
to her father, had been hoping that Liam would not return
to court, that he would leave her alone, disappear from
her life, so she might resolve her own future in a satisfac-
tory manner. But it seemed now that Gerald might actually
get his way one day.

But would it be so terrible?

Instantly Katherine was horrified with her wayward
thoughts.

"The queen wishes to speak with you, mistress," Helen
said, cutting into her disturbing thoughts. "Really, you are
a slugabed this morn."

Katherine sat bolt upright, the covers dropping to her

waist, oblivious of the fact that she had slept without her
nightgown. The queen! "God's wounds! What time is it?
Why did you not wake me sooner?" Katherine had not
slept more than a few hours, but she leapt from the bed,
as naked as the day she was born.

" 'Tis almost eight, and the queen wishes to speak with
you before the mass. I did not wake you because you
appeared near dead, so tired were you from last night's
excesses."

Katherine froze, meeting Helen's wide blue eyes. But
Helen only smiled sweetly at her, her gaze innocent of
any hidden meaning. Of course she could not know. Of
course she only referred to the celebrations that had taken
place in the hall below. Despite the scent of man and
woman which wafted from the bed, despite the fact that
Katherine had slept without her nightclothes.

"Hurry, mistress, you must not annoy the queen."
Helen was holding out Katherine's undergarment. Katherine needed a bath, but would not have a chance until the
evening and she nodded. Damnation, she thought, at once
uneasy and irritable. She stepped into her linen drawers.
"The queen wishes to speak with me? Whatever for?"

Helen shrugged, helping her with her chemise and farthingale. "I do not know, mistress. She sent Lady Anne
to summon you. I told the lady that you would be forthcoming immediately."

Katherine was ready to jump into her dress now. She
was supposed to be at the queen's side at a quarter to
eight, as were all her ladies, even though it was the ladies
of the bedchamber who helped the queen to awaken and
dress. She rushed into her dress, then froze, espying a
parcel wrapped in red silk and tied with a red ribbon
on the coffer at the foot of the bed. "What is that?"
she murmured.

Helen shrugged, handing her the parcel. "I know not.
It was here this morning when I came to awaken you."

It could only be from Liam. Katherine glanced at Helen,
but the maid's gaze was blank as she fetched Katherine's
coif from the table. Her heart pounding, Katherine took

the gift and tore it open. Her eyes widened. "Why—what is this? How beautiful it is!"

She and Helen stared at the fragile web of white fabric, which was sewn in intricate patterns, so intricate, in fact, that in places mere threads seemed to hold the material together. "I have never seen anything like this before," Katherine cried in real delight.

"I have," Helen said, her tone hushed. " 'Tis Spanish lace."

Katherine looked at the airy, white material. "Spanish lace," she murmured, envisioning it as cuffs on the sleeves of her gown or frothing at the neckline of her dress. " 'Tis wonderous and beautiful at once."

"Aye," Helen said as reverently. "Even the queen has yet to obtain this stuff. The Spanish ambassador has taken to wearing this *lace* recently," Helen said. "Everyone remarked it. The ladies will be green with envy when they learn you have this."

Katherine sat down on the bed, her gown yet unbuttoned, unfolding the fabric. A small sealed missive fell out. Katherine's pulse rioted and she pulled the seal apart. There were but two single scrawled words upon the parchment—*Enjoy, Liam.*

Katherine held the paper to her breast, thinking about the mad passion they had shared last night. It was wrong. Despite her father's instructions. But what was truly unbelievable, was her behavior, not his. And even now, her body warmed from thinking of him.

Katherine crumpled the parchment, standing abruptly. On the room's single table was the flint used to light the tapers and oil lamps. She struck it and set the note aflame. When it began to burn, she dropped it into the pewter bowl containing her wash water.

Katherine stood, took a deep breath, and shoved her thoughts aside. The queen was waiting. "Helen, I must hurry, please button my gown and help me with my hair."

As Helen obeyed, Katherine stared at the folded white lace. Helen finished with her gown and quickly combed and pinned up her hair. Finally she was coiffed, and Helen went and opened the door for her.

But Katherine did not follow. Instead, she picked up a small, old-fashioned ivory-handled dagger, one meant to be worn on her girdle as decoration rather than to be used for eating, and she cut off a long, narrow strip of the material. Facing a looking glass above the table, she tucked the lace into her bodice, so it peeked over the neckline of her gown. Then she turned and moved past Helen, her stride quickening as she went to meet the queen.

Katherine's heart sank when the queen glowered at her and ordered everyone out of the antechamber. In a flash, Katherine recalled Leicester dancing with her, then forcing her from the dining hall and into a secluded alcove so he could proposition her. Her face grew hot. Her stomach churned with fear and dread. "Come here," the queen snapped when they were alone.

Katherine approached, feeling faint.

"Have you become a wanton, Mistress FitzGerald?"

Her eyes widened. "I . . . I beg your pardon?"

"Is not the attention of a single male enough?"

Katherine swallowed. "Your Majesty, I am not quite sure . . ."

"I saw you with Lord Robert last night!" The queen was standing and in a rage.

"We . . . only danced," Katherine cringed.

"So it was to dance that he took you from Our presence?"

Katherine could not respond, recalling Leicester's mouth upon her throat, his hands within her bodice. "I do n-not want his attentions, Your Majesty," she said, her voice shaking.

"No? Is it Sir John Hawke, then, that you prefer—or Liam O'Neill?"

Katherine felt faint. "I . . . what . . ."

"Did the pirate visit you last night or not?" the queen demanded.

Katherine inhaled. How could the queen know? *Helen.* Helen must have seen them. Her father had been right—

Helen was a spy. Somehow, she managed to lift her chin high. "Yes."

The queen's brows rose. "So you confess to a clandestine meeting in your chamber?"

Katherine nodded.

The queen's hand smacked sharply across Katherine's cheek. Katherine cried out in pain, for the queen wore numerous rings, and one of them had grazed her. She dared not retreat, however, or even touch her throbbing, scratched cheek. "How dare you carry on like a strumpet in Our court!"

Katherine said nothing, tears filling her eyes. But she would not cry. This was the price one paid for sinful, wanton behavior.

"Your mother would be ashamed of you," Elizabeth said. "And at least *she* had the sense to cavort with the heir to an earldom!"

Katherine bowed her head. There was not a single word she could speak in her own defense.

"Do you really think to marry, girl—or to be a slut?" When Katherine did not answer, the queen barked, "Well?"

Katherine looked up. "I w-want to marry."

"So Ormond says." The queen stared at her, less furious now. "We took you in because We loved your mother, and We feel somewhat responsible for you. Ormond has apparently decided to champion your cause, as well. He has petitioned Us to allow you to marry despite your father's disgrace. We have been thinking on it, but now . . . We do not know."

Katherine was frozen with horror. Suddenly it seemed that she might gain all that she dreamed of—and she dared not lose the chance she wished for now. "Your Majesty . . ."

"Silence! How can We find you a decent husband if you have not a whit of value left—if you have not even your chastity—if you carry another man's child?"

Katherine licked her lips. "I do not c-carry his ch-child."

"Liam O'Neill is an expert cocksman. Do not tell me he is impotent! Do not dissemble now!"

"I do not lie!" Katherine cried, wringing her hands.

"He spared me my virtue, I vow it on all that is holy! Oh, God, I am sorry, I am so sorry!"

The queen stared at her assessingly. "Get down on your knees and beg Our forgiveness."

Katherine obeyed. "Please, Your Majesty, forgive me— I beg your pardon most humbly."

The queen's tone softened. "Rise, Katherine, and wipe the tears from your eyes."

Katherine got to her feet.

"You must proceed with caution. You are very beautiful, and many men will chase after you with little or no provocation. You must remain strong, you must not yield. Not even to a handsome rogue like Liam O'Neill." Her gaze darkened. Katherine knew she thought of Leicester.

"You are right," Katherine said, clenching folds of her dress. "I have made a grave mistake."

"Perhaps court life does not suit you," the queen said reflectively.

Dismay flooded Katherine. The queen was going to send her away—and she could not be blamed for doing so.

"We think that today you will not attend Us. Go to your chamber and ponder upon the past—and the future. Meantime, We will think on what should be done with you."

Katherine had been dismissed. Consumed with dread, feeling more trapped with every passing moment, she left the antechamber. Outside the queen's ladies, advisors, Gentlemen Pensioners, and assorted noblemen awaited Elizabeth. Katherine did not look at anyone as she pushed through the crowd. Until someone touched her arm, forcing her to glance up. Her gaze met Leicester's. A question was in his eyes.

With a small cry, Katherine tore free of him and ran down the hall.

No way out, she thought incoherently. There did not seem to be any way out of her terrible dilemma, caught as she was in a web formed by so many men, one consisting of their secret intrigues and powerful ambitions.

Katherine was subdued when she came down to supper, finally allowed from the confinement of her room. As she took her seat at the dining table in the Banquet Hall, she had the feeling that most of the court knew that she was in disgrace. She prayed it were not so. She prayed that, if anyone knew anything, it was that she was in disgrace for sharing a few minutes alone with Leicester. Should the world know that she had entertained Liam O'Neill in her chamber last night, she was ruined, no matter that she was still chaste.

But the stares which were turned her way were not snide or lewd or wolverine, merely pitying. Katherine hesitated, unsure of where to sit and whom to sit with. Anne Hastings smiled at her, waving her over. When Katherine approached, she stood and put her arm around her. "You poor dear! Do not fret overly, Katherine," she whispered. "You are not the first that Leicester has eyed and that the queen has reprimanded so sharply. She is but protecting the man she thinks she owns."

Katherine felt hot relief as she sat down beside Anne on the crowded bench. "But she does own him, does she not?"

Anne shrugged. "She has made him, enriched and ennobled him, but he is manly enough to one day do as he wishes. He must eventually marry again if he wants a legitimate heir."

Katherine bit her lip. She would not tell Anne that Leicester had hardly suggested marriage. She twisted to face the dark-haired lady. "Anne? What else do they say about me?"

Anne cast a sidelong look upon her. "Not much, in truth." She wiped her mouth with her sleeve. "Well, there is a strange rumor going about—that your pirate attended last night's festivities."

Katherine froze.

" 'Tis not true, is it?"

"I know not," Katherine managed to lie.

"Hmm. Surely had he appeared, one and all would have remarked him. A man like that could not possibly be missed, even in disguise." Anne picked up a chicken leg and began to nibble upon it.

Katherine felt more relief. If that was the extent of the current rumor about Liam O'Neill, then her reputation was safe. But in that moment she realized that she had come dangerously close to ruining her life. So dangerously close. It must never happen again. Katherine was astute enough to know that if it did, she would be a hairbreadth away from marriage to the pirate, and she was not ready yet to give up all of her dreams, despite what her father asked of her.

Surely there was some way to help Gerald, some way which did not involve her becoming Leicester's leman, or becoming O'Neill's wife.

Katherine thought about the earl of Ormond. It seemed that her half brother was her champion after all, urging the queen to find a suitable marriage for her. Another irony struck Katherine. Of all the men here at court, somehow her father's greatest enemy was proving to be her best ally. Perhaps Ormond would succeed—taking the matter of her future out of her own hands entirely.

"She has confessed. She was with Liam O'Neill last night."

Ormond flushed. "The next time I see him, I shall kill him."

The queen was not looking at him, but at Leicester, who stared at her, frozen by her words. Elizabeth smiled at him, far too sweetly. "Is something amiss, dear Robin?"

Dudley came to life, his expression relaxing, a smile forming upon his dark, handsome countenance. "The pirate has great gall, to come uninvited to your court, and to sneak into a lady's room."

"Perhaps she invited him," the queen remarked, staring at Leicester. "He is a glorious man. Why, all my ladies are moved to swoon when he comes into the room."

Leicester's smile disappeared. It was a well-known fact that he prided himself on both his appearance and the fact that many women coveted him. "I doubt Mistress FitzGerald would invite any man into her room for such a purpose."

"Ahh—you know her well, then?"

Leicester's jaw flexed. "You know I do not know her! We but shared a dance!"

"And mayhap, afterwards, a kiss?"

Leicester's eyes blazed. In that moment Elizabeth was afraid, despite the fact that she was queen and he but her subject, for she sensed she had pushed him too far. She did not move when Leicester strode to her, towering over her. Her pulse quickened now in a purely feminine reaction to his proximity and his power. "I am a man, Bess, as you damn well know," he ground out, so low that only she could hear, "and if I steal a kiss from her, why do you care?" His eyes were twin black fires. "You know I would not hunt elsewhere should you give me what I want."

Elizabeth trembled. In that moment she wished they were alone. She knew that if this were a private discussion, Dudley would sweep her into his arms, whether she wanted it or no. 'Twas what she liked best about him—and what she liked least. For the woman in her was joyous, the monarch enraged.

Elizabeth stared at him. As always, she could not decide what his smooth words really meant. Did he speak of her body, which she had thus far successfully denied him—or her throne? "I shall deny you as I will, Robin," she finally said, "and you, of course, can kiss where you will."

Leicester continued to gaze at her, refusing to back down. Elizabeth grew afraid. Perhaps she *was* pushing Dudley too far. She smiled then, widely, and touched his hand below his ruffled cuff. "Forgive me, dearheart, for being overbearing, as we women are wont to be."

He relaxed. "Let me come to you tonight, Bess."

Her gaze flickered away from him. "I shall consider it."

He gripped her hand, preventing her from turning away. "I am coming, Bess," he warned.

Elizabeth's heart beat too hard. She had not entertained Dudley in private for many weeks now. Finally she nodded, and as she turned away, she saw satisfaction gleaming in his eyes. She could not help but anticipate the evening ahead.

Elizabeth faced Ormond. "You have won this day. I agree with you, Tom. We must find her a husband, and quickly."

Ormond's face brightened in surprise, while Leicester, beside her, stiffened. Yet Dudley dared not speak now and Elizabeth knew it. It was at this moment that Cecil stepped forward. "You have changed your mind, Your Majesty? From what was previously agreed?"

"Yes," Elizabeth said firmly. She had most definitely changed her mind. It was not unusual, for those who knew her comprehended that she could blow first east, then west, without so much as a backward glance. Now Elizabeth decided to tell her most trusted advisors some of the truth—but not all of it. "I am not convinced that she is a conspirator. I know her somewhat now, and I believe she is far too naive to be involved in any treasonous plot with either her father or O'Neill. However, it would not surprise me if both of those too-clever men were thinking to use her in their games. I wish to remove her as a pawn from their play—before any play is begun."

William Cecil said naught. Yet he was aware that serious play had already begun. He had gleaned startling information from his own spies several days ago. The *Sea Dagger* had been spotted at anchor in Dingle Bay, which was close to Askeaton. The bay was also used by the papist FitzMaurice. As FitzGerald resided at Southwark, Cecil thought that the *Sea Dagger*'s use of Dingle Bay signified the beginning of a far more dangerous game, one O'Neill was clearly waging in deadly earnest. And Cecil was intrigued. How clever the pirate was. If he dared as Cecil thought he did.

And Cecil said naught, for the pirate must be allowed full rein.

Elizabeth raised her hands, gaining everyone's attention. "I want the girl married to one loyal to me," she stated. "If she is married, her value to Liam becomes naught—and to her father, even less."

Ormond smiled in grim satisfaction. "Do you have some loyal vassal in mind?"

Elizabeth nodded, not adding what was the most compelling factor of all in her decision to marry off Katherine FitzGerald. It had nothing to do with conspiracy and treason. It had everything to do with passion.

The girl was far too beautiful, and far too seductive, to remain at court, a constant provocation to Elizabeth's favorite men. The queen could not allow the girl to ensnare Leicester, nor did she care for the fact that Liam O'Neill appeared besotted with her. In fact, even dear, beloved Tom seemed to be bending toward her. Elizabeth had sensed a change in him for some time now. No, having Katherine at court was a grave mistake. How foolish Elizabeth had been to be so kind as to allow her to remain in the first place.

Elizabeth imagined Katherine ensconced in Cornwall on a country estate, heavily pregnant, with children at her skirts, and she could not help but smile. Neither Leicester, O'Neill nor Black Tom would find her very attractive then.

"In fact, I have already spoken with the bridegroom." Her smile widened. "Although John Hawke was seeking to do far better than to marry a penniless Catholic Irishwoman, I shall provide her with a small but rich estate in Kent as a dowry." Elizabeth's smile was serene. "Sir John has agreed. The wedding date shall be April 15, but four weeks hence. Now all I must do is to inform the girl that her future has been decided." Elizabeth added, "Undoubtedly she shall be most pleased at achieving her heart's desire."

And Cecil wondered what the pirate's next move would be.

18

"*K*atherine!"

Katherine turned, having left the dining hall. John Hawke strode toward her. "Might we speak?"

She looked up at his handsome face, noting the sparkle in his eyes. She could not help but smile back at him. "You appear well pleased, sirrah," she said playfully, touching his strong arm. "What good tidings do you bear?"

His blue eyes held hers. "Let us walk in the gallery," he said. A moment later her hand was securely entwined with his arm.

Katherine glanced at him and found him watching her intently as they strolled through the hall. "You are truly in a fine humor, sir. It does me good to see a soul so gladdened—but by what?"

"You are an impatient wench," he said, lowering his tone intimately. "Are you impatient in all things, dear Katherine?"

Katherine's smile faded. Something was afoot. John Hawke was far more amorous than usual, and she guessed his words to bear a sexual meaning. That last she did not like. Until now, John had been nothing but proper and gallant, unlike Leicester—unlike Liam. She did not wish to see him turn into a cocky rogue. She pulled her hand from his arm as they entered the long gallery, which was empty, for most of the court still dined in the Banquet Hall.

"Have I upset you?" he asked, instantly concerned.

She paused and faced him. "I am not sure."

He touched the side of her face very briefly. "Katherine, I did not intend to distress you." He paused. "I have great news."

"Which is?"

He no longer smiled. His gaze bored into hers. "The queen wishes us to marry, and I have agreed—if you will but have me."

Katherine gasped. She was stunned. An image of Liam flashed through her mind. Liam, golden-haired and gray-eyed, his beautiful face strained with passion, as he rose up over her, his hard, powerful body throbbing against hers. She forced the image aside. It was no easy task. She blinked, and saw the dark-haired man standing before her, his face so grave, his blue eyes sober.

"You have turned white. I thought you held me in some esteem."

Katherine fought to clear her head. "I do! 'Tis that I am surprised!"

"Will you marry me, Katherine?" Hawke asked.

Katherine stared at him. At Sir John Hawke, the captain of the Guard, a fine and noble man. Her dreams could come true. Her dreams of having a handsome, noble husband, a home of her own, and many sweet children. If she would but say yes.

Again she thought of Liam. Anger filled her; she forced his image aside. She thought of her father, imprisoned and in disgrace, stripped of all that he had once had, who was depending upon her to lead the pirate to their cause. But she did not wish to marry Liam, she did not!

"You do not wish to wed?" John asked tightly.

Ignoring any and all consequences, Katherine seized his arm. "No! I do wish to wed!" She wet her lips. "I will marry you, Sir John."

His eyes brightened and he grinned. Then he gripped her shoulders. Katherine tensed, knowing full well that he intended to kiss her. His long-lashed eyes had turned a stormy shade of blue. His strong jaw flexed. Katherine did not move.

"You are a beautiful woman, Katherine, and I am very

pleased that you shall be my wife," he said huskily. He hesitated. "Surely you have been kissed before?"

Katherine flushed. "Yes," she whispered unsteadily. It was suddenly dawning upon her. All that she had done. She had been kissed last night, and held and caressed, and far, far more. Oh God. By another man. But today, today she was affianced. And she felt sullied and unworthy of Sir John because of what she had done.

Thank God Sir John did not know—would never know.

"I do not mind," John Hawke said harshly. "I am hardly a fool. I am sure you have had many ardent admirers." Still he did not kiss her.

Katherine wet her lips again. She would not make a confession, she must not—yet neither would she lie. Dear God, she would have this man as her husband soon, and she must not begin their marriage with lies—or with whorish infidelities. "I have had a few admirers," she whispered, managing a small smile. "But now I shall know to chase them away if they dare to pursue me another time."

He did not smile, but his eyes gleamed. "No one will dare to pursue you now, Katherine. Do you not know my reputation? There are few finer swordsmen in all of England. We are trothed. We are to be wed in four weeks. No one—not even that pirate, O'Neill, will dare to touch what is mine."

Katherine tried to imagine John Hawke and Liam O'Neill clashing—fighting. It was a horrifying thought. One man would surely die from the encounter—if they did not kill each other. Then her thoughts were diverted, for Hawke was pulling her to him, lowering his mouth to hers.

She held his broad shoulders uncertainly as his mouth moved softly on hers. His kiss was gentle, without demand. Without the fervor she had expected. Katherine was relieved. She was in no mood for kissing now. But her relief vanished in the next instant. His mouth swiftly firmed. His lips became insistent, urging hers to part. Like the other men who had pursued her, this man was an expert at seduction. Yet Katherine could not obey his summons. She whimpered a little, not in desire, but in dismay.

He mistook her and pressed her against the wall. Katherine allowed him to suck on her lips, and then on her throat, telling herself that she must not push him away, acutely aware of his large, heated loins pressing hers. She reminded herself that he was handsome, noble, and kind. Yet her body remained indifferent.

Oh why could she not feel the passion for him that she had felt just last night for Liam O'Neill?

He finally tore his mouth from her throat. Katherine forced herself to meet his gaze, reassuring herself that, in time, she would adjust to him, that she would seek his embrace as she had sought Liam's the night before. But guilt consumed her. She thought she saw confusion in his eyes, confusion and disappointment.

But then he smiled and put his arm around her, and she knew she had misread him.

They would be married in London at St. Paul's Cathedral. The queen and her entire court would attend the nupitals, but afterward the bride and groom would ride to Barby Hall, the estate dowered Katherine by Elizabeth, where they would spend their wedding night. Preparations for the wedding began immediately. In the interim, Katherine was given leave to adjourn to Sir John's ancestral home in Cornwall, so that she might meet his father and acquaint herself with her future duties as mistress of his estate.

Katherine was happy. Soon she would be a married woman, and not just any married woman, but the wife of a knight who would undoubtedly rise through the ranks in Elizabeth's administration as he grew older. One day he might become a knight of the Garter, or even a privy councilor. Elizabeth often rewarded those loyal to her by ennobling them and enriching them as she had done with Leicester. Why, just last month Sir William Cecil had been made a peer, and as Lord Burghley was now lord treasurer of the realm—one of England's most powerful men.

Katherine was happy. This was what every woman dreamed of—marriage and security, a fine, noble man and an ancient home. Not pirates who stole into dark chambers

in the middle of the night with wicked, amoral intent—
not pirates who swooped down on innocent traders, plundering and committing mayhem, seizing innocent women.
Not in the interest of assuaging their lustful natures, giving
scarcely a thought to their hapless victims.

Katherine knew that she was very lucky—the luckiest
lady alive, no doubt.

She had not seen her father, either, not since the betrothal had been made and announced. She had ignored
Gerald's summons, which had come almost immediately
after she had accepted John's proposal. She also had ignored her own conscience, refusing to think of how she
disobeyed her father. But when it became too strong, too
insistent, and too intrusive, she decided that being an English gentleman's wife might very well aid her and Gerald.
For in time she would discuss her father's predicament
with her new husband, and in time, he would begin to
address the issue with the queen. Katherine knew that Elizabeth was very fond of John Hawke— he was one of her
favorites after Leicester and Ormond. Surely the queen
would listen to Sir John when the day came that he
pleaded for her father's return to Ireland.

They left for Cornwall immediately. Katherine advo-
cated their hasty departure, feeling some urgency, eager
to escape London. Both to thwart Gerald and Eleanor,
either one of whom might dare to chase her down at court,
and to thwart Liam—who was so bold that he might very
well attempt another midnight rendezvous—this time with
catastrophic consequences.

Meanwhile, night after night, she lay awake, impossibly
restless, thinking not of her betrothed, but of the damned
pirate.

John's father, Sir Henry Hawke, was a somewhat portly,
handsome man, who greeted them before they had even
dismounted. Katherine knew from his grim expression that
he was not pleased with the alliance. She could guess all
the reasons he was against her. She was Irish. Her father
was the queen's prisoner, and in disgrace. And although
she kept her faith secretly, as all true believers were required to do, everyone guessed that she was Catholic.

She and John had discussed the matter of the religious upbringing of their children, to no avail. He was staunchly Protestant, could not abide popery. Katherine could not imagine worshiping without the vestments, or by reading in English from the Book of Common Prayer. They dropped the topic before they began to argue, agreeing to discuss it another time.

Although Sir Henry Hawke was not pleased with her, having undoubtedly hoped that his handsome son would snare a titled heiress, he was not rude or unkind, and eventually he began to thaw. On their second day at Hawkehurst, Katherine made a startling discovery. She and Hawke were astride two Cornish ponies, out upon the moors, enjoying a mild and sunny March day. He began to tell her about the guests who would attend a fête given by his father in their honor, one where she would meet the local lords and ladies. Katherine was stunned to learn that Hawke's closest neighbor was Lord Hixley of Thurlstone Manor. Juliet, as it turned out, was her neighbor!

"John, my dear friend from the convent where I spent the last few years is Juliet Stratheclyde, Thurlstone's heiress and Lord Hixley's ward."

Hawke regarded her. "Stratheclyde died some years back, and I seem to recall there being a daughter, although I did not know she had been sent to a convent."

Katherine spurred her pony to his. "John! Let us go visit Thurlstone. Oh, please!"

John smiled at her. "You are very beautiful, Katherine, when your eyes shine like that. Come, let us go calling."

They waited in the great hall, admiring the rich tapestries, the silver plate, and the cushioned chairs. Juliet was out riding, Lord Hixley inspecting his mines. But the steward was eager to send a stableboy after her. John and Katherine chatted while they waited.

And then Katherine heard soft, running footsteps. She turned, smiling, as Juliet burst into the hall. She had never looked more lovely, her dark, waist-length hair unbound, her cheeks flushed from the outdoors, her eyes glowing.

She wore a damask emerald gown that accentuated her striking coloring. "Katherine! Oh, Katherine!"

The two girls hugged and rocked each other in their arms. Finally, laughing, they pulled apart. "You were a raving beauty before, but this wild clime suits you, Juliet, you are even more lovely!"

"Katherine, you are too sweet! And you are no hag, let me assure you of that. What are you doing here?" Juliet's gaze moved past Katherine and settled upon Hawke. Her smile faded. She stared at him, her cheeks slowly turning pink.

Katherine smiled to herself when she realized that Juliet could not take her eyes off of her handsome fiancé. She turned to introduce John. As she spoke her smile wavered. Hawke stared at Juliet with the same startled intensity with which Juliet stared at him. Katherine had finished speaking, and a sudden silence filled the room—one filled with unmistakable tension.

Hawke came to life. His expression stiffly formal, he finally bowed. "Lady Stratheclyde," he murmured. "How pleased I am to make your acquaintance." His glance, which had been locked with Juliet's, now slipped from her eyes down to her toes, briefly but discernibly—in an unmistakably male manner.

Katherine no longer smiled.

Juliet did not seem to know what to say. Nervously, she glanced once at Katherine, then her eyes returned to John. "Sir John, let me . . . let me congratulate you . . . you and Katherine . . . on your wonderful good fortune."

Hawke's jaw had become incredibly tight. He nodded, and then turned to gaze out of one of the room's beautiful, multipaned windows. Katherine was dismayed. Surely she was mistaken. Surely the air did not crack and sizzle between them—surely not!

As if to make up for her recent lapse, Juliet forced a smile and began to chatter away, her tone too bright. "Katherine, I am so happy for you," she said breathlessly. "How happy you must be! When and where will the nuptials take place? How long will you remain at

Hawkehurst?'' Her smile flashed. ''When will you return?''

Katherine kept one eye on John, who had turned his back on them now and was studying a tapestry of William the Conqueror at Hastings. She sensed that he was listening to their every word. ''We shall wed on the fifteenth of April in London. And we remain at Hawkehurst but another two nights.''

Juliet's face fell. ''Then I will not see you again, will I?'' she said, sounding like her old self.

''Are you not coming to the fête being given in my and John's honor?'' Katherine asked.

''I don't think so,'' Juliet said.

''Weren't you invited?'' Katherine asked.

Juliet hesitated. ''I was, of course, but . . . my uncle prefers that I do not attend.''

''But why?''

Juliet did not answer. ''Katherine, I was truly hoping that we might pass some time together before you left. I wish you were staying longer.''

Katherine took her hand. ''Perhaps we can walk in the garden?'' She turned to her fiancé. ''John, would you mind if Juliet and I spent a few moments together?''

For the first time in minutes, he faced them. His glance strayed to Juliet, lingering upon her delicate heart-shaped face. ''Katherine, we must not delay. My father has invited several guests to meet you at dinner. 'Tis almost noon, now.''

''I know. Please?''

He softened, nodding. ''Be quick,'' he said.

Juliet took Katherine's hand, giving Hawke a grateful look. The two girls hurried outside and into the garden. Beneath a cherry tree they paused. ''Juliet—is something bothering you?''

Juliet looked at Katherine, suddenly miserable. ''How lucky you are,'' she whispered. ''To be marrying a man like Sir John.''

Katherine froze, imagining that Juliet was about to confess her sudden attraction to John Hawke.

''My uncle intends for me to be betrothed by my sixteenth birthday, which is but six weeks away. He has narrowed down the possible candidates for my hand to three men. Oh, God! Lord Carey is three times my age, although still of a fine figure—but he has already had two wives and six children. Ralph Benston is a skinny pimply-faced *boy* who cannot keep his hands to himself. And the third suitor, Simon Hunt, he is actually very kind, but he is hugely fat. I hate them all!'' Juliet cried.

"Oh, Juliet," Katherine said, relieved that her fears were at least not being voiced aloud. But she sympathized with Juliet, greatly, and she did not know what to say. A lady did not marry for love, but good matches were possible. "Can you discuss this with Hixley? Can he not select a husband for you of whom you also approve?"

" 'Tis impossible.'' Juliet said. "He doesn't care at all how I feel. He is leaning toward Lord Carey, who is so terribly frightening. I do not know what to do; how can I marry a complete stranger, who only wants Thurlstone, and live as this man's wife for the rest of my life?''

Katherine took her hand. "You are very beautiful, Juliet. I am sure all three men want you as much as Thurlstone."

Juliet colored. "That is horrible, too! Could you take a man you did not love into your bed, let him touch you, kiss you?'' She shook.

Katherine instantly felt guilty, thinking of Liam O'Neill. She was spared having to make a reply, because Juliet said bitterly, "But you do not have this kind of problem. You are marrying a handsome, noble man. How I envy you, Katherine.'' She looked away, flushing. "How lucky you are,'' she whispered.

"Yes, I *am* lucky," Katherine returned, still feeling guilty—and now her heart lurched hard.

Shortly afterward, she and John left for Hawkehurst, Juliet waving good-bye, her color far too high, a smile fixed upon her lips—her gaze following Hawke. Katherine waved back, but Hawke did not. To the contrary, he seemed determined to ignore Juliet, staring straight ahead out at the moors. But once again, his cheeks were flushed, and Katherine thought that his gaze was troubled.

I am wrong, Katherine thought, suddenly dejected. *Lightning did not flare white-hot between them. Of course, Juliet would find him handsome, every woman does. But he is to be my husband. I am to be his wife. He does not find her attractive—it is I he loves.*

And to make matters even worse, Liam O'Neill dared to intrude yet again, and in her mind's eye he was smiling—and his smile was mocking.

19

Gerald sat in the dark hall of St. Leger House alone. He was cursing his own daughter.

She had disobeyed him, betrayed him. She had not heeded him at all. She had not enticed and entrapped Liam O'Neill, Gerald's last, desperate hope. No, the queen had betrothed her to a damnable Englishman instead, and not just any Englishman, but one unquestionably loyal to the Crown, Sir John Hawke, the captain of her Guard. Did Katherine not understand that, with every day he spent in forced exile in Southwark, he was breathing his last dying breaths? He could not live like this, impoverished, impotent, and in exile, he could not. How could she have done this! And to ignore his summons, by damn!

He could not help thinking that she was every bit as headstrong as her mother had been. Suddenly he felt an intense longing for his first wife, Joan. Although she had been thirty-six to his sixteen when they had first met, their passion had known no bounds. Joan had still been stunningly beautiful, somehow far more beautiful than pretty girls half her age. And in bed . . . Gerald sighed. She'd had tricks of which he'd never dreamed. Her passion had been as willful as she.

But she had been fiercely loyal to him, despite the fact that her son was the earl of Ormond and her husband's enemy. Joan had *never* betrayed him. She had been loyal to him, and she had loved him, until the day she died.

It was one of the great regrets of his life that she had

died alone at Askeaton, without him, while he was in the Tower, a prisoner of the queen. But that had been seven achingly long years ago.

"Gerald? Why do you sit in the dark?" his wife asked, bustling into the room.

Gerald blinked as Eleanor lit candles until the cold, barely furbished hall was ablaze. In some ways she reminded him of Joan. She was very beautiful and very clever—and headstrong as well. A good helpmate, as Joan had been. "I am brooding, what do you think?" he said.

"Well, there is nothing you can do," she said bitterly, reading his thoughts exactly. "You should disown that treacherous daughter of yours, aye, you should!"

Gerald would never disown Katie. She was disloyal and she deserved a beating, but she was his only daughter and his only child from those few years with Joan. "Disown her?" He laughed, as bitter as Eleanor. "I own nothing now—how can I disown her?"

"She and John Hawke have returned to London this day. If you do not go to speak with her, I shall," Eleanor stated, her eyes blazing.

Gerald eyed Eleanor. "I want no discord between the two of you," he stated. "Besides, this matter is not over yet—not until the church bells are ringing."

Eleanor blinked at him. "What are you thinking, my lord?"

Gerald smiled then. "Bring me a quill, lady. And we shall need a messenger, one firmly loyal to us."

Eleanor returned with quill, inkhorn, and parchment, excitement flickering in her blue eyes. "What do you do, dearest?"

Gerald thought a moment, then began to write. "I do not misjudge men. I am informing the pirate of what happens. If anyone is clever enough—or bold enough—to undo what has been done, 'tis Liam O'Neill." He smiled at his wife. "There is just enough time, I think, for the missive to find him—and for him to right things gone awry."

Earic Island, the Atlantic Ocean

The wind was bitterly cold. It was winter's last gasp and it howled across the barren island, which was not much more than a huge outcropping of rock and stone, although at its southern end a forest of firs braved the wilds, the winds, and the sea. Its beaches were but narrow strips of sand, littered with boulders, butting up against soaring cliffs. The surf was violent, even in summer, a never-ending collision of water upon rock and land. On the island's northernmost side was a deep harbor, its mouth narrow and guarded with twin towers and cannon. In the harbor the *Sea Dagger* and several other O'Neill ships, all designed for swiftness and battle, bobbed at anchor.

There was a small village near the docks, where the seamen lived and the shipbuilders worked. There, too, were a few wives and a few children and a few whores. There was a blacksmith, a butcher, a baker and miller, a carpenter, and one merchant who sold all manner of goods, as well as several alehouses.

From the village a narrow path twisted up through the cliffs to Liam's fortress. At the very top, upon a bed of granite, sat the medieval castle. A drawbridge opened across a deep gorge, and one had to pass through a portcullis and barbican in order to enter the high stone walls. Square guard towers with ancient arrow slits dominated the four corners of the fortress. Inside there was a three-storied tower holding a great hall and several other chambers. The fortress had been used by some exiled lord or other pirates in another time. But it had been added onto recently, and a large brick manor abutted the square keep, with windows of glass, not hide. The manor house was gabled, with a steep, tiled roof and five tall chimneys.

Liam had built the house because he hated the loneliness of the ancient keep, which to him seemed dark and haunted. He was not afraid of ghosts, but he had thought that a newer, brighter home would alleviate the feelings of isolation that assailed him whenever he resided on the island. Yet the manor, despite all of its gleaming woodwork and rich upholstery, could not entice him inside. Once, he had tried to live there. To his horror, it had been a far more lonely experience than dwelling in the medieval stone tower.

Liam sat at the heavy, scarred trestle table, alone. Macgregor sat by the fire on a stool, playing a soft tune on bagpipes. The boy, Guy, crouched at Macgregor's knees, firelight playing over his thin, rapt face. The music was meant to soothe, yet Liam had never been more restless. The days passed slowly, with gaping emptiness. How in God's name would he endure even another day here if he felt as though he could jump out of his very own skin? He had never hated being island-bound because of the harsh winters before.

Carefully Liam unfolded the letter again. It was from his mother, Mary Stanley, and had been dated two weeks earlier. Although he always visited her when some affair brought him upon England's soil, this last time he had not. In fact, he had not seen her in a half a year, making him a very poor excuse for a son.

"My dear son, Liam," she wrote, *"As always, you are foremost upon my mind. I trust that all is well with you, that God keeps you safe and out of harm's way. My dear, please guard yourself well. Remember, I could not bear it should aught happen to you.*

"I have heard the latest gossip and in truth, because of our many conversations, I was not that surprised. I should have guessed that this would happen one day. But to abduct the Lady Katherine FitzGerald at sea, as if you were but an evil pirate—and a man like your father?

"Dearest Liam, I know you are not like Shane, that you could never be evil and cruel like him. But 'tis said that Katherine greatly resembles her mother, once both countess of Ormond and Desmond. Well do I remember Joan. She was far more than beautiful, she was strong and intelligent, unusually so. If her daughter resembles her greatly, I fear a great clash of wills betwixt you. Dear Liam, have a care with this girl. Her value to you will far exceed that which is political.

"And remember, too, that Joan was kind to us both when you were but a babe in swaddling. Of all the ladies I met then, in those sad but somehow joyous days (you having been the joy), she was one of the few who were not cruel, who befriended me. I know you would not harm her daughter, Liam, not apurpose. And I understand why you would seize her as you did. Just be temperate, my dear, if you wish to win her, as I suspect you do.

"Hope stirs alongside the love in my breast."

Liam had read her letter perhaps ten times. And he was ashamed. It was not often that he reflected upon the path of his life with regret, for only fools dwelled on what could not be changed. And although Mary had never openly condemned him for his pirate ways, Liam knew that she secretly wished that he might one day transform himself into a noble and pure English gentleman. Her wishes were impossible, fanciful dreams. He could not undo the fact of who and what his father had been, and undoubtedly Katherine would never forget it. His having been born outside both the English and Irish worlds had forced him to the high seas. Mary knew this as well as he.

Liam folded the letter very carefully and placed it in a small coffer, the kind ladies favored for their jewels, which he then locked. The key he wore on his belt. The coffer he picked up and placed on a sideboard.

Liam began to pace. At least in the past he had but to deal with himself when confronted with the emptiness of his life on the island. He could handle that. But now . . . now he saw a flame-haired seductress everywhere he went and everywhere he looked. Even his mother wrote of her.

He recalled Katherine's adamant rejection of his marriage proposal; his face turned red. Both anger and humiliation flooded him. He knew he was too proud to beg her to change her mind, or even to try to change her opinion of him.

Liam faced the fire, reining in his hot emotions with an iron hand. Katherine was now at court, and in this interim, 'twas not a bad place for her to be. The game was moving along now, although no end was yet in sight. But there would be an ending. Liam wondered, though, if he would take Katherine as his wife against her will when that ending came. Knowing her as he did now, he did not think he could do such a thing. Yet neither could he let her go, especially not to another man. A curse slipped from his lips, breaking the silence of the stone-walled hall.

He paused in his pacing, realizing that Macgregor had ceased playing the pipes, and that both he and the boy watched him. Liam forced a smile for the boy's benefit. Guy got to his feet. "Captain, sir, is there aught you need?" His anxious gaze was riveted upon Liam's.

I need a red-haired wench whose lust matches mine, Liam thought. "No, Guy."

Guy hesitated.

"Sit down and listen to Macgregor play," Liam said, his tone far too gentle to be a command.

Guy relaxed and obeyed and Macgregor said, "Someone comes."

Liam had heard the faint tolling of the watchtower bell as well. In winter, the only bell that could be heard was from the tower, because of the shrieking winds. A moment later one of his men entered, his cheeks ruddy from the cold, a cloaked visitor with him. "Captain, sir. 'Tis a messenger for you that has just arrived."

Liam stared as the messenger took off his hood and gloves, shivering. Undoubtedly he had come to the island aboard the monthly supply ship which Liam dispatched to Belfast. Liam did not recognize the man. He nodded for him to sit, and turned slightly.

His steward had materialized, saw Liam's look, and hurried out to return with hot, spiced wine and other refreshments. Liam said to his own man, "Jackie, go into the kitchen and warm yourself and if you have not eaten, nourish yourself with hot food."

The red-cheeked man nodded, disappearing in the steward's wake.

Liam sat down on the bench across from the messenger. Macgregor had begun to play again, but very softly, and Guy had turned away to face the Scot. Quietly Liam asked, "Who sends you?"

"Gerald FitzGerald."

Liam tensed. The man pulled a sealed parchment from under his cloak, handing it to him. Liam hesitated, then stood, moving to the fire. Trying not to display his blazing curiosity, he slowly opened the letter. A moment later, as he read, his eyes widened—and his face turned white with shock.

Katherine FitzGerald was betrothed to Sir John Hawke, and would be wed at St. Paul's on the fifteenth day of April. The Queen had even dowered her with a small but fine estate in Kent.

Liam began to turn red. Fury overwhelmed him. "What goddamned day is this?" he roared.

Macgregor laid the pipes aside. " 'Tis the thirtieth of March," he said.

Liam fought for control. But he could not stop the rage that boiled in his veins as he imagined Katherine in another man's arms, as another man's wife. He shook with it. But when he spoke, his voice was ice-cold. "We go to London," he said calmly, his tone belying the fact that the beast within him had been set free. "Immediately."

But the snowstorm delayed their departure. For twelve full days.

London, April 15, 1571

The church bells tolled.

The great bells of St. Paul's Cathedral rang and rang and rang yet again. The street before the cathedral was highly congested. Queued in the avenue were the numerous coaches and chariots that awaited the noblemen and noblewomen attending the nuptials inside. Dozens of mounted, liveried outriders milled about as well. And hundreds of Londoners lined the sidewalks outside the soaring cathedral, yeomen and gentry alike. A wedding of the nobility was a great event, and curious they were to see the couple who had just married.

The bride and groom finally appeared. The crowd espied the groom first and burst into applause—some of the women swooning. Sir John Hawke wore his scarlet-and-gold uniform, his great ceremonial sword, high black boots, and a plumed hat. Murmurs began, turning to rapid, hushed whispers. The bride was a vision as lovely as the groom was dashing. Her pearl-seeded white velvet gown drew the envy of many a maid, especially as it revealed the bride's ideal form. But it was her face that drew actual gasps, from both men and women alike, because it was so utterly lovely, oval shaped with high cheekbones and full lips. It was her face that made the men envy the groom and think lecherous thoughts.

They threw seeds at the couple, wishing them a fertile and fruitful union. It was not until the couple had ascended into a waiting coach, drawn by two matched white horses, that one and all remarked that neither the bride nor groom had been smiling. How very strange that was.

The fire leapt in the granite hearth, warming up the linenfold, wood-paneled master bedroom at Barby Hall. Fresh, sweet rushes were strewn about the oak floors. A four-poster bed, not canopied but massive nevertheless, stood in the chamber's center, covered with blue-and-gold velvet and furs. The coverings had been turned aside.

Katherine's heart was beating wildly. The exhaustion she had felt after the strain and stress of the wedding and the celebration at Richmond Palace was gone. Now she was nervous. Now she was John Hawke's wife. Oh, God. Katherine closed her eyes as Helen helped her out of her dress and undergarments.

She thought of her father, who had refused to attend her wedding, sending her a private missive instead, one filled with an icy cold reprimand. She thought of the golden pirate, even though she did not want to think of him at all. Now, on her wedding night, she recalled his searing kisses, which she should have never enjoyed.

Her heart beat like a drum. *What had she done?* The thought crept unwanted into her mind. It angered Katherine. It was too late, she told herself sternly, for doubts or misgivings. After all, she was almost certain that she loved John Hawke.

And she was happy, she was. This was all that she had dreamed of, all that she wanted—life was finally giving her due: respectability and gentility, and soon, she prayed, her first baby.

Katherine inhaled, going to the fire to warm her cold hands before it. She was married; it was for the best. And tonight was her wedding night. She would welcome her husband with open arms. Thank God she had a lusty nature. In all probability, she would enjoy herself—or so she hoped.

Helen had unpinned Katherine's wild red hair and it flowed to her waist. "There, mistress, you are lovely. Sir John will be most enamored this night."

Katherine thought of John, who had not smiled at her even once all day. Had he been afflicted with nerves, as most grooms were? Or with doubt? Suddenly she thought of Juliet, who would soon be forced to wed a stranger. Juliet had attended the wedding with her uncle, and Katherine had seen the way she'd regarded John. An inane thought occurred to Katherine—that Juliet should be standing in her place right now, Juliet should be John Hawke's bride, awaiting him on their wedding night.

Katherine began to shake, aghast with such thoughts. *Everything will be fine,* she told herself, inhaling hard, beginning to perspire—*once we spend this night together.*

And even if everything were not all right, it did not matter. She was John's wife, both under law and with God's sanction—until death parted them.

Helen left. Katherine was alone. She went to the fire again, hoping to warm her nearly naked body, clad as she was in a completely sheer wisp of ivory silk that revealed every single curve she possessed. A gown meant to entice. Katherine wished she had chosen a more modest gown now. Then she reminded herself that she wanted a baby—therefore, she must entice her new husband to her bed.

She heard them coming up the stairs. Katherine froze. John's family and closest retainers had accompanied them to Barby for more festivities. Her heart began to pound. Katherine stared at the door, listening to John's comrades shouting at him, offering him lewd advice and knowing encouragement. Katherine shuddered. Some primitive instinct urged her to run to the bed and hide there, but she knew such an impulse was foolish, and she would not give in to it.

The door was opened and John appeared, and before he shut it, Katherine glimpsed some dozen inebriated men behind him—men who stared at her and shouted even more ribald comments upon seeing her. Katherine blanched, folding her arms over her breasts, unable to move now. John's eyes widened the instant that he saw her. A moment later he turned, swore savagely, and slammed the bedroom door closed behind him in the faces of his drunken, lecherous friends.

He faced her, unmoving. He wore but hose and a tunic that was mostly unlaced. His eyes were glittering now, a look Katherine recognized well.

Katherine began to blush even though she was his wife. John continued to stare. She managed a small smile, and despite how chilled she now felt, dropped her arms to her sides. She met John's gaze again, saw that he gazed at her breasts, saw his glance sweeping lower, to the joining of her thighs. A wild thought ran through her mind—he will not be thinking about Juliet this night.

And she was appalled with herself. "John," she began, "would you like some wine?"

Before he could respond there was a great crashing noise from downstairs. John had begun to walk toward her and he froze. From below, a man screamed. An instant later swords began to clash and clang violently, the sounds unmistakable.

And the sounds grew louder, footsteps sounding as men rushed up the stairs.

John whirled, cursing—for he was without shoes, mostly undressed, and swordless. He ran for the door, throwing it open.

Katherine did not move, stunned.

And Liam O'Neill burst into the room.

Rapier in hand, its tip bloodied, his gaze skewered Katherine. A split second later he had the sharp point piercing the thin skin of John's throat. John backed up to the wall.

Katherine clapped her hand to her mouth, shocked. Liam smiled savagely at her for an instant.

He said, "I take it my arrival is timely?"

Katherine gaped.

Hawke was furious. "I am going to kill you for this."

"How?" Liam laughed at him. "Your few vassals are a pathetic excuse for protection, and are even now in bonds. Your rapier lies downstairs, broken by me myself. But if you wish to meet your death, why then, come. I will gladly send you on your way."

John growled and jerked against the rapier, which cut into his skin. Blood welled from his throat.

"No!" Katherine screamed, rushing forward to stop them.

Liam glanced at her dispassionately, then said, "Take her, Mac."

Macgregor stood in the doorway. Katherine had not even been aware of his presence until then. When he moved forward, toward her, she cried out—but had nowhere to run. The Scot caught her in a bearlike embrace.

Other men entered the room. Liam gave a sharp command and John's arms were pulled roughly behind his back and he was locked into steel manacles. Liam sheathed his rapier and gripped John's arm and jerked him forward to the bed. One of his men tossed another set of irons to him, which he caught. He manacled Hawke's ankle to the foot of one of the bedposts.

Hawke was panting, flushed with rage. "You will never get away with this."

Liam had been smiling, as if he enjoyed every single moment of his foul play, but now he faced Hawke, the smile gone, his eyes a silver blaze. "Tonight I will take her virtue as I should have done a month ago at Whitehall."

Hawke jerked against his manacle. "You are as good as dead. I will hunt you down and kill you. You *are* dead."

"She is mine. She has always been mine." Liam turned and, understanding him, Macgregor released Katherine.

Katherine realized now what was happening. Instinct commanded her. She rushed forward to the door. It was both useless and foolish, as O'Neill's men blocked the way. Katherine screamed as they blocked her path, but no one touched her. Katherine tried to shove between two henchmen, but it was like trying to part a stone wall.

Then Liam caught her by her hair from behind, stopping her in her tracks abruptly. She gasped in pain. Then like a wild, untamed mare, she stood panting but fully alert and tensed to leap away, as he slowly wound her hair around his wrist, keeping the tension taught as he approached her. When his face was close to hers, he smiled.

Katherine comprehended his every intent—and she would have launched herself at him in a furious attack, except that if she did so she would rip her own hair from her head because of the way he held her. So she did not move, her gaze wide and locked with his.

Abruptly he released her hair and threw her over his shoulder, striding out of the room. Katherine began to writhe. He smacked her bottom once, hard. It hurt and she stilled, tears filling her eyes. Looking up as she dangled upon his back, she met John Hawke's furious gaze one last time. Katherine wished she could reassure him. She saw that he was not just mad with fury over Liam's abduction, but mad with worry for her, too.

And then Liam was rushing down the stairs and out of the house, Katherine bumping hurtfully upon his shoulder. He dumped her onto her feet. A cloak was thrown around her, he stuffed a gag in her mouth and tossed her onto a huge, dancing gray stallion. An instant later he was mounted behind her, his arm around her like a steel brace, and they were galloping away.

"I told you once before," he rasped in her ear, "that I would come for you when the time was ripe."

Katherine glared at him, her eyes filled with tears and wild, desperate fury.

II

THE BRIDE

20

Katherine had no choice but to hang on to the pommel of the saddle as Liam rode his stallion away from Barby Hall at a breakneck pace. He sat behind her, gripping her firmly, his body one with the horse. They thundered down the dark road, his men following, galloping toward the sea. The night was black, cold and moonless. It was impossible to see. But the huge horse raced flat out, head low, ears back, blowing hard. Liam pushed him savagely. Katherine watched the black road filled with shadows rushing at them, wondering if they would all die this night.

She was coming out of her shock now. Anger was roiling in her veins. But the gag prevented her from speaking, from shrieking, and there was no escaping Liam's grip.

Liam urged his mount off the road. Katherine made a choked sound when she saw the steep, narrow path he intended them to take. Her grip tightened on the saddle even as Liam's grip tightened upon her. Katherine wanted to curse at him, certain they would both break their necks now. The horse began to slide down the precarious descent on its haunches. Far below, Katherine could hear the drumbeat of the sea.

The horse slipped, stumbled, slid. Liam growled, cursed, and spurred the beast on. Tears streamed from Katherine's eyes. The animal finally plunged into the sandy ground of the beach, hopping like a crow. A moment later Liam was on his feet, pulling her off the horse. His men came to milling halts beside them. Katherine found it hard to stand in her exhaustion. She stumbled but Liam caught her.

Katherine turned her furious gaze upon him and swung both fists at his face. She managed to graze his cheek, but the punch did not seem to affect him, for his response was merely to grab both her wrists and jerk her once, a command to be still. He whispered orders to his men. More tears filled Katherine's eyes. In her mind she cursed him again and again. Her shock was gone and she comprehended exactly what had happened—she had been abducted from her wedding bed!

Katherine saw the men approaching them. Like ghosts, they materialized from the sea. Behind their dark, barely formed shapes, she saw the shadows they dragged, shadows that she soon understood to be some half dozen boats.

Katherine sagged against Liam in despair. She thought she could just glimpse the *Sea Dagger*'s huge sails, unfurled and flaccid, gleaming almost silver against the night. She was not going to be able to escape. In a few more minutes she would be on his vessel, and God only knew when he would decide to set her free.

And by then it would be too late.

Liam lifted her off her feet. Instinctively Katherine tried to push away from him, looking frantically back over her shoulder for any sign of pursuit, praying that, miraculously, she would see John emerging from the top of the cliffs. But nothing moved up there, nothing but the wind-driven trees. And moments later she was being heaved into the longboat.

But she could not give in; she could not. Knowing full well that her efforts were undoubtedly futile, as Liam climbed in, Katherine leapt up, intent on making one final attempt to escape.

And because she knew this would be the last time, the last chance, Katherine moved with incredible speed and an iron will. She was halfway over the side of the small boat when Liam realized what she intended. He lunged for her. Katherine felt the shock of the icy cold water as she plunged into the surf, but did not pause. Liam shouted at her, reaching for her, but only succeeded in grabbing her cloak. The wool spun off of her, leaving her more naked than not. Katherine did not care. She was too determined, and too incensed, to feel the bitter cold.

She ran toward the shore, tearing at the gag, but the knot was too tight. She heard him splashing behind her. She heard him coming closer and closer, and finally felt his boot clip her heel. Katherine dared to look backward. She saw a determination on his face that was far greater than her own. His expression was so fierce it was frightening, and in that moment Katherine knew her fate was forever sealed. That stunning knowledge sped her as nothing else could. But Liam caught her hand anyway, whipped her backward. Katherine fell against him, fighting wildly. And then they were both tumbling into the freezing cold sea.

For an instant she was free. She lunged to her feet but Liam wrestled her into his arms from behind, and a moment later she was again being tossed over his shoulder. Katherine pummeled his back mindlessly. He ignored her blows. "You have nowhere to run to, Katherine," he told her, plowing his way through the rolling surf back to the bobbing longboat. "From this moment on, you belong to me."

And Katherine was blinded by an intense feeling of hatred.

The longboat pulled alongside the pirate ship. Katherine sat shaking on the small slab seat, clutching the wool cloak to her cold body, the gag having been removed by Liam. He stood in front of her, reaching for the rope ladder. He turned to her, held out his hand.

Katherine's glare was murderous. She did not take his hand. Instead, determined to defy him, even if it meant leaping to her death, she looked down at the black midnight sea. Could she do it?

The waters would mean the end of all her dreams. But she would have succeeded in escaping Liam O'Neill.

He cursed and pulled her to her feet. "You fool," he rasped as he swung her a third time over his shoulder. Katherine realized what he intended at the same moment she realized that she had no wish to die. "Put me down," she shouted, twisting, "before we both die!"

"Keep fighting and we will get wet, but we will not die, Katherine," Liam answered calmly.

She stilled mutinously. Hanging as she did, upside down, she was faced with the ominous black sea, which was far too close to her for comfort. She gripped his back, her heart moving into her throat, hating being afraid now, when she wished to fight. But with infinite ease, Liam climbed the ladder rapidly. He handed Katherine up to one of the many seamen waiting on the deck for them. Katherine was dropped to her feet. She began to breathe again.

Liam climbed over the rail and took her arm. Her gaze shot to his as she tried to yank herself free of his grip—to no avail. He propelled her forward. Katherine stumbled because of the rapid pace he set. She wished she could think of some truly horrible curse words. A moment later he was pushing her down the narrow stairs and into his cabin.

Refusing to look at her captor, Katherine stood panting in its center as he lit one taper after another. Her gaze darted to the bed. Oh, God.

Liam approached. Katherine turned slowly to face him, wary and alert. His face grave now, he reached for her soaking-wet cloak. Katherine jerked out of his reach and backed away from him, her eyes blazing. "Damn you to hell!"

He crossed his arms and regarded her without any expression. Surely she had imagined the concern she had just witnessed.

"You have ruined me!" Katherine cried. "I will never recover from this act—not ever!"

A twisted smile formed upon his features. "You will recover, Katherine; in fact, I am certain that your recovery will be quite rapid."

Katherine clutched her cloak, which was very wet, to her body, too furious to be cold anymore. "You think to seduce me with your body? Not this time!"

"No?" He walked toward her. Katherine stiffened but did not move, and he towered over her. "What makes this time any different from the last time we lay together—or the first?''

Katherine refused to remember the night of the masque at court, when he had pleasured her with his mouth and she had pleasured him with her hands. She refused to think of the first time, when he had kissed and caressed her, or the second time, when she had been bound to his bed, when he had cut off her clothes with his dagger. She would not remember any of those times—that was the past. ''Because this time you have destroyed my dreams!'' she shouted.

His eyes glittered. Katherine felt a frisson of fear and she tensed. ''Do you love Hawke?'' he asked, his tone conversational and completely at odds with the light in his eyes.

Knowing it would infuriate him, wanting to enrage him, wanting to best him, Katherine spit, ''Yes!''

''Perhaps you are a whore after all,'' he said harshly. ''For I thought it was Leicester you loved.''

How his words hurt. Katherine was stricken by them; she turned stark white. She was shuddering now, not just because she was so icy cold, but because he was right, she was a whore. For despite it all, she knew what was going to happen in that bed, and she knew she was going to like every single moment of his attentions—even though she was now another man's wife.

''Katherine . . .'' Liam stared at her, his chest heaving.

She looked away, then felt him touch her. Katherine fled to the other side of the room. ''Don't touch me!'' she cried hysterically. Panic was replacing her anger, and she was finally aware of how bone-tired she was. How would she find the strength to resist him—to resist her own sinful nature? She told herself that she must not enjoy his love-making—at all costs. She whispered, ''Please set me free. Please let me go back to John. Please don't do this to me.''

Liam stared at her, his jaw rigid. For a long moment he did not speak. Then he said, reluctantly, ''I cannot.''

''What do you mean, you cannot?'' Katherine heard the hysteria in her tone. ''Of course you can free me! Of course you can send me back to John! You are king here, and can do as you will!''

His mouth curved without mirth. ''Yes, I am king here—king of the pirates, the wind, and the sea. Everything you now see, I command.'' His gaze was sharp. ''And you, Katherine, you I also command.''

''You do not command me!'' she almost sobbed.

''No?'' One brow rose.

''Do you like your infamy?'' she asked bitterly. ''That is it, is it not? You like being lawless, answerable to no one other than yourself!'' An idea seized her, a way of manipulating him. ''You like being Shane O'Neill's son.''

His nostrils flared with anger. *''I hate being his son.''*

And Katherine moved to him, gripping his wrist—then wished that she had not touched him. She removed her palm from his hard, tense forearm. ''Then pretend you are not his son,'' she cried softly. ''Play the gentleman, Liam—and release me.''

He inhaled sharply. His gaze locked with hers. ''You ask too much.''

Katherine stared into his glittering gray eyes. He acted rational, spoke in a conversational tone, but what she saw was his lust. In the brief silence which followed she realized that she had lost. Panic surged forth again, and she glanced at the door—her only means of escape.

His jaw flexing, Liam turned and locked the door, pocketing the key. When he faced her again, he said, ''You are cold.''

Katherine realized that she was not just frozen in her soaking cloak, but shivering as well. She shook her head in a ridiculous denial, her eyes fixed upon him—awaiting his next move.

He moved toward her; she leapt away. He murmured, ''I intend to be patient with you this night, Katherine. If you wish to be wooed, so be it. Tonight is not a night for cords or knives.''

Katherine gasped, his words drumming up those old memories she wished to avoid, as she stood beside the teakwood bookcase.

Liam smiled slightly at her, the way he might at a frightened child. Katherine pressed back against the bookcase. But her eyes darted toward the bed, just once. She must flee—but flee where?

"I cannot live without you, Katherine," he said, his gaze holding hers, taking another step toward her. He did not smile; his tone dropped, becoming soft and cajoling. "I cannot function. You are in my mind at the most inappropriate times. My lust is making me lose all sanity."

Her nipples hurt her now, hard and pointed and chafed by the wet wool of her cloak. She was holding her breath, and she expelled it all at once, helplessly glancing down at him.

He smiled slightly. "For you, Katherine. My loins are hard and close to bursting for you." He paused beside her, so that they stood almost cheek to cheek. "You are wet, cold." He touched a strand of her wet, tangled hair, one that curled against her cheek.

A frisson of fiery sensation sparked from his fingertip to her skin and raced through her entire body. Katherine jerked. "No!" She ran from him to the door. She wrenched at it uselessly.

Liam watched her and sighed, using great willpower to curb his impatience. His body wished to explode, sorely needed release, but he must not give in to his lust. Not now, not yet. He wondered if she understood that he spoke the truth. He faced her, waiting for her to calm herself.

She had her back plastered to the door and she stared at him wildly. "I want to return to John," she whispered hoarsely.

His temper sizzled and threatened to make him lose all control. He reined it in, hard. "I am not returning you to John. I, at least, am honest. I want you. I will have you. I will have you willing and warm before the hour is through."

"No." He saw that she was still shivering.

"And you are freezing," he said, matter-of-factly. He turned from her and went to the armoire, opening it. He pulled out a thick towel that was cotton on one side, silk on the other. Casually he said, not looking at her, "Come here, Katherine."

Trembling, she shook her head.

Liam took another towel for her hair. "Do you wish to catch your death?"

Katherine stared at him as if she could not look away. Her lips were parted slightly, her cheeks flushed. No longer, he thought, just from anger, but also from anticipation of where he led.

"Come," he murmured, his gaze boring hers.

She did not move.

Smiling slightly, seductively, he repeated, *"Come."*

She moved toward him, slowly, as if bewitched.

He handed her a towel.

Katherine took it. As she did so, her cloak fell open. Liam glimpsed her large, taut nipples, ruby-colored, beneath the silk gown she wore, which was plastered to her and entirely sheer. Knowing he could not control the shaking of his hands, or the size of his loins, he slowly reached for her. Katherine had not moved. Liam unpinned her cloak. It dropped to the floor.

Still Katherine did not move. She did not even appear to breathe.

He saw every lovely inch of her. "You are soaking wet," he said thickly, reaching for her gown.

Her wide eyes met his. "Stop," she whispered, rawly.

Liam did not answer. He gripped the wet silk and slowly slid it upward on her body. Baring her long legs, the lush mound of her femininity, her curved hips. Their gazes clashed, held. Liam uncovered her breasts, and then he pulled the gown over her head and tossed it aside. A small, soft sound escaped Katherine.

Determined not to pounce upon her, not to show his barely containable eagerness, Liam turned away to take up the other towel. He faced her, his lips set in a small, encouraging smile, murmuring soothing words. Katherine's breasts heaved, begging to be touched. Liam gently wrapped the towel around her shoulders, the cotton side against her skin, then began to rub her firm flesh dry. Just touching the muscles there swelled him even more.

"You are an incredible woman," he murmured. He moved to stand behind her, his hands sliding the towel down her arms. Katherine was frozen, but her breathing was heavy.

"Everything about you entices me—excites me," he said low, kneading her strong yet slim arms.

He paused, looking down at her over her shoulder, at her voluptuous breasts. Katherine was shaking, although he knew she was no longer cold. "Your breasts are beautiful, wet and gleaming like this," he said.

She made a slight, strangled sound.

He reversed the towel and pulled the silk side over her breasts, drying them at first briskly, then slowly. He watched the hard peaks engorge. Katherine began to sway. Liam's hands splayed, cupped her. "I love your breasts," he said thickly, kneading them.

"Oh, God," she gasped as his thumbs finally grazed her nipples.

"You are shaking," he murmured in her ear, well aware that his breath was hot and erotic. "You are so cold, Kate." He rubbed the towel over her belly languidly. Katherine shuddered, whimpered. And as he did so, for the very first time, he allowed his phallus to brush the cleft between her buttocks. Although he wore his breeches, he was so large that the fabric was strained to the breaking point, and Katherine inhaled loudly.

"I am going to make you very, very warm," he whispered against her neck, watching his hand on the towel as he pushed it lower and lower still. "I love looking at you, Kate."

Katherine stood as straight as an arrow, but he heard her swallow. He pushed the silk between her thighs and rubbed it back and forth. Katherine's trembling had become uncontrollable.

"Spread your thighs," he ordered, "so I can dry all of you."

Katherine moaned, obeying him.

Liam molded the silk over her sex, used it to separate and explore her folds, and finally, his own body shuddering, he thrust his thumb up against the silken towel and began to manipulate her clitoris. Katherine sagged against him. Katherine cried out, and he felt her convulsing against his hand.

He caught her with one arm, dropping the towel and pushing her forward and down onto her stomach on the bed. His thumb found her again. She gasped, thrashing, exploding.

Still fondling her, nearly mindless now, Liam ripped open his breeches. Gripping her buttocks, he thrust the huge, bulbous tip of his penis into her. Katherine, her shudders fading, tensed. And Liam cried out, completely blinded by the tight, hot feeling of her as her muscles clamped around him.

Pausing was the most difficult act of his entire life, but he stilled. The cords on his neck standing out, sweat trickling down his face and chest, he bent and kissed her cheek. Katherine whimpered. Her bottom shifted beneath him. There was no mistaking her meaning. His cry savage, he grasped her buttocks and thrust home.

Katherine cried out as he drove himself through her virgin's membrane. Liam could not stop again. He drove into her again and again, knowing he had never attained such pleasure before, knowing he never would again. Katherine arched beneath him. She was wet, slick now, and his frenzy grew. His hand slid beneath her, cupping her sex, and he slammed into her, thrusting home. Katherine gripped his hand, pushing his fingers into her, her nails cutting his skin, writhing beneath him, bucking beneath him. Liam thrust one last time, deeper, harder. And when his seed began to erupt, he cried her name. Not once, but many, many times.

And afterward, when the convulsions finally ceased, he found himself standing beside the bed, looking down at Katherine, who lay flat on her belly, and he saw his palms gripping her buttocks, which were red and welted, and he saw the blood on her thighs, and he stared—unable to believe what he had done.

Katherine felt him slip from her. She screwed her eyes tightly closed, still unable to breathe. Come back, her mind said desperately. Liam—come back!

But he moved away from her. She felt him standing over her, staring down at her. Katherine inhaled, hoping to steady her ragged breathing, gripping the covers of the bed, trying to control the red-hot fever in her body. But she throbbed without relief. Perhaps if she did not move, if she lay still and open and wet, he would return to her, impale her yet again.

But he did not.

She swallowed, dry. It had happened so quickly. His huge, heated entry, her explosion, his explosion. She needed to feel him again. Not once or twice, but thrusting endlessly, deeply . . . oh, God, she did.

Katherine choked on her moan. She rolled into a ball. On her side, she finally looked up at him.

How magnificent he was. He stood fully clothed, his lean jaw hard and tight, his gray gaze wild, his blond hair damp and disheveled, staring down at her as if he had never seen her before. Katherine grew uneasy. She sat up, pulling a pillow forward to cover her nakedness. She stared back, into his stormy eyes.

"Did I hurt you?" he asked harshly.

For one heartbeat, Katherine could not understand why he was asking such an absurd question. She had been weeping with her pleasure. And never had she dreamed he would feel so good inside of her.

"Did I hurt you?" he repeated. His right temple throbbed visibly.

This time Katherine understood. Her pulse was finally beginning to subside. But not the ache between her thighs—for just looking at him made it worse. She inhaled, hugging the pillow hard. Realizing that it was done. Finally, it was done. He had taken her virtue, and somehow, it was a relief. Had she not been secretly anticipating this very moment for a long time?

Katherine grew still. Her pulse picked up its beat. She did not care for the loss of her virtue, but . . . 'twas the last thing of value she possessed.

And she was married to John Hawke.

Katherine froze. Not too many hours ago, she had stood beside John, exchanging vows. Yet now, she sat naked on the pirate's bed, her body pulsing with uncontrollable passion, feverish for another man.

In her mind she could see Hawke now, manacled to their wedding bed, his expression furious.

Sickening dismay beginning to wash over her, drowning her, Katherine shifted slightly and looked down at the coverlet. At the blood. At her blood.

She had lost her virtue. She was another man's wife— but Liam had taken her virtue. And she had given it willingly. Wished to give it to him yet again.

"Katherine?" he asked.

Her gaze snapped to his. What she had done was unbelievable. "Get away from me!" she cried.

He flinched. "I didn't mean to hurt you, Katherine."

She skidded backward on her rump, away from him, until her back hit the bed's headboard, still hugging the pillow. "Oh, God! Get away from me!"

"I am sorry," he said, agonized. "I didn't mean . . . I lost control. . . . I am sorry."

Katherine did not hear him. Her mind was in a daze. But she managed to comprehend the final truth. She had lost far more than her virtue. She had lost her dreams— every single last one of them.

21

Whitehall

*Q*ueen Elizabeth had turned white.

John Hawke stood before her, flushed with rage, his hand gripping the hilt of his sheathed sword. Although fully dressed in his crimson uniform, somehow he appeared disheveled. "I beg you, Your Majesty, to aid me in recovering my bride," he said.

Slowly Elizabeth rose from her throne. Her stunned gaze met Cecil's. "I cannot believe this tale."

Cecil moved to Hawke and put a hand on the man's trembling shoulder. "Your anger will lead you astray."

Hawke's smile was menacing. "You are wrong, my lord. It will lead me exactly where I wish to go, and aid me in killing the pirate bastard when I find him."

Elizabeth turned away from both men, her pulse thundering in her ears. Jealousy consumed her. She had thought to keep them apart. But even now, her golden pirate spent himself on the Irish girl. Defying her and her will.

Hanging was too good for him.

She trembled with rage, facing Cecil. "I demand he be brought to me to answer for his insolence!"

"I will gladly bring him to you," Hawke said.

Elizabeth regained some of her senses. She stared at Cecil. "Does O'Neill dabble in treason? Or is he moved by animal lust?" She became breathless, fearing the worst.

" 'Tis too soon to tell," Cecil said calmly.

Then Elizabeth thought of the girl. Her anger doubled, tripled. "She enticed him, she did, just as she has enticed Robin and Tom," she spit. "And to think that I took her into my court, rising her up far beyond what she was due. This is her fault as much as his! Perhaps they even planned this deceit together!"

"Your Majesty," Hawke interjected, "Katherine was no willing participant in her abduction. I was there, I saw her every action. She was distraught, nay, stunned, by the pirate's actions."

Cecil stepped forward as well. He spoke softly. "Mayhap you judge her too harshly, Your Majesty. 'Tis likely she is an innocent victim yet again, and but a pawn of the powerful pirate."

"I think not," Elizabeth said sharply. "I know not! Nor do I know why you defend her, William, unless she has seduced you, too!"

Cecil said nothing.

The Queen turned to Hawke. "I married her to you so you might control her," she snapped, now furious with him.

Hawke bent his head in obeisance.

Elizabeth faced Cecil. "Now what!?" she demanded. "Now what will we do?"

"There is naught we can do," Cecil said calmly.

"Naught do do?" Elizabeth cried.

Hawke rushed forward. "Undoubtedly he has taken her to his island home far to the north. Your Majesty, I beg you, give me just three ships and one hundred troops and I will not just storm his island, I will destroy it—and him."

Elizabeth was ready to agree. How she wanted to agree. But some innate caution stopped her—or was it affection for the amoral rogue? For she imagined beautiful Liam O'Neill skewered by Hawke's sword and she hesitated. Then her good sense told her that Hawke could not defeat Liam O'Neill in a fight. Not hand to hand, not in a full battle. Anger filled her again. She doubted Hawke could even capture him.

However, no man was as powerful as a man moved by

vengeance. If anyone could capture the damned pirate, 'twas John Hawke. She said sharply, "Is it not said that the island is completely defensible?"

Cecil nodded. "Those are the reports."

Hawke snapped, "No place, and no man, is completely defensible."

Cecil laid his palm on Hawke's broad back. "There is no sense in storming that fortress for the sake of a woman, John. It cannot be taken, not without great loss and expense to us."

Hawke was incredulous. "Good God!" he shouted. "Even now that bastard is using her—hurting her!"

Elizabeth turned away, thinking of the reports she'd had of Katherine. She had been more than eager the few times she had been espied in O'Neill's embrace. Elizabeth could imagine her now, with him, clutching his broad back, accepting his wet, lusty kiss. Accepting all of him.

"I am sorry," Cecil told Hawke.

Hawke rushed to confront his queen. He got down on one knee. "Your Majesty, I beg this boon of you. I must go after him! And if you do not wish to help me free Katherine, think on the fact that I will bring you Liam O'Neill's traitorous head!"

Elizabeth looked into his burning eyes. "I am also sorry, John," she said softly. "But Lord Burghley is right. I can not sacrifice men and ships for one woman—no matter how I wish to have that rascal's head." She did not add that she did not have the money to pay for such a venture, not unless she took it from far more pressing matters.

Hawke rose, his face set in an expression of angry disbelief. Without another word, without waiting for permission to leave, he turned on his heel and strode from the room. Elizabeth stared after him, sighing. Then she cursed Liam O'Neill. And finally, facing Cecil, tears appeared in her eyes. "How could he do this to me?"

Cecil took her hand. "My dear Elizabeth, the pirate knows he cannot have you. He is a man. Men must spend their lust somewhere and you surely know it. He is very fond of you, Bess."

"Bah!" Elizabeth said, but she prayed Cecil was right. "What do you think he will do next?" The question burned. "Will he try to marry her?"

Cecil regarded her. "Unfortunately the Pope will not recognize Katherine's marriage to Hawke, as it is outside the Catholic faith, and it would be easy for O'Neill to marry her in the papist fashion."

Elizabeth paled even as she clenched her fists. "And the Pope would undoubtedly marry them himself," she cried, "just to thwart me!"

"At the very least, he would give them his blessing," Cecil agreed. Last year the queen had been excommunicated; it had been the Pope's means of supporting the Catholic faction in Scotland. "Liam, though, is firmly Protestant."

"His father was Catholic. That rogue could switch his faith easily enough, if he thinks to gain from such a maneuver." Elizabeth paced, wide-eyed. "If he marries her, dear God, then that is proof of his conspiracy with Fitz-Gerald, all the proof we need." She wheeled to face Cecil. "I will not allow John Hawke to divorce her, even if Liam weds her himself!"

William inclined his head.

"So what do we do?" the queen asked.

"We wait," Cecil said. "We wait and see." But Cecil already knew what not to expect. O'Neill was far too clever to move so swiftly, to tip his hand. What Cecil did *not* know was what *to* expect.

Hawke ignored the stares he received as he strode through the palace. Some pitying, others snide. A few men, jealous of his growing influence and power, snickered at him openly. Hawke ignored them too, for otherwise he might very well skewer someone, so angry was he. And his queen would then throw *him* in the Tower.

"Sir John?"

Hawke missed a stride. His heart skipped a beat. Against his will, his steps slowed.

"Sir John?" she called again.

He stopped, tensing, to face the petite form of the lady

Juliet. And then, seeing her, he forgot his own anguish and anger. She had been crying. Her lovely complexion was blotched from her weeping, her eyes and nose were red. "Lady Stratheclyde," he said, bowing abruptly.

She pressed a wadded-up kerchief to her nose, and when she spoke, her words came in a rush. "I just want you to know that I am sorry, so sorry."

He stared at her.

"And . . . I am so worried about Katherine!" Tears spilled down Juliet's cheeks.

Hawke felt a strangely tender urge to touch her, hold her, but he ignored it. "Your concern is admirable," he said rather harshly.

"What will happen now?"

Hawke stared at her, but this time it was not Juliet he saw, but his beautiful bride—in the arms of Liam O'Neill. And every time he saw them in his mind's eye, together and entwined, it was not a rape he saw. God's blood! O'Neill was a handsome rogue, with a rogue's reputation. Despite the fact that he was Shane O'Neill's son, Hawke knew he was no rapist. Hawke shook. Even now, undoubtedly, they were in bed. But was Katherine resisting him? He might never know. There was always the possibility that she could succeed in thwarting him.

"My lord?" Juliet said uncertainly.

Hawke jerked his attention back to her. Despite her recent tears, he could not help but remark how utterly lovely she was. "Nothing will happen now," he said bluntly. "Her majesty has denied me troops and ships, and I have not the means to storm the damned island where he lives without her aid."

Juliet gasped.

Hawke half bowed again. "Thank you for your concern," he said, turning from her. But she touched his hand, halting him in his tracks. Hawke was acutely aware of her touch. Slowly he faced her.

"If it makes you feel better," she said, blushing now, although he knew not why, "I am certain O'Neill will never hurt her. He may be a pirate, but he is also a gentleman. I have heard about his father. He is not a man like that. Not at all.''

Hawke's expression did not change. "If he will not hurt her, then why are you so worried about her?''

Juliet's color increased, and she could not meet his gaze. Nor could she answer.

And dismay filled him. Juliet was Katherine's friend. What did she hide? Hawke did not have to be a wizard to guess. For he had heard the gossip too. The gossip about O'Neill and Katherine. Perhaps Katherine had confessed to Juliet some small thing about him—about them. No, O'Neill would not hurt her. Despair finally claimed him. And even if Katherine tried to remain faithful to him, O'Neill would woo her until he won her.

Katherine was awakened by the sound of a sharp knocking upon her door. She sat up, groggy, not having been able to sleep until well past midnight. Her mind cleared and she looked at the bed in which she had slept alone. It was her second night on the pirate ship—and she had not seen her captor since their one, single passionate encounter soon after they had first boarded.

She swung her legs over the side of the bed and straightened her clothes, which she had slept in. Ultimately she had been forced to wear a dress which she had found in one of the trunks in his cabin; undoubtedly it had belonged to one of his mistresses. She had donned a gold silk with a leaf design and encrusted with tiny glass beads. Katherine glanced at her reflection as she passed the looking glass. Miraculously, she did not look tired. Although her hair was unbound and her head uncoiffed, in fact, she looked quite elegant, even beautiful.

Katherine opened the door, well aware that she would not find Liam on the other side, for he would hardly condescend to knock. The ship boy, Guy, greeted her. "The captain says you can come up on deck, my lady.''

Katherine glanced over her shoulder toward the porthole, and saw dusky light bathing the dark ocean. "It is but dawn,'' she said.

"Aye, not even, but we are putting into Earic Island," Guy said solemnly. "Will you come up?"

Katherine stared at Guy. "Earic Island?"

" 'Tis the captain's home."

But she had already guessed that, yet the confirmation made her heart sink. As she followed the boy out of the cabin, she tried to fathom why he dwelled in a place named Earic Island. Certainly he had not coined the name. For "Earic" was the Gaelic term for blood money—the money a murderer paid to the family of the man he had killed. Blood money was an ancient practice—one that condoned murder and legitimized it.

It was a cool morning, and she had no cloak. Shivering slightly now, she paused on deck. She saw Liam instantly. He stood on the forecastle, gazing out toward the rising, bloodred sun. He was cloakless, wearing naught but his linen shirt and his breeches and his thigh-high boots. He was bathed in the warm, glowing sunrise. The orange light turned his hair a fiery shade of gold. His profile was spectacular. It took her breath away.

Katherine wanted to ignore the ache rising so rapidly within her.

She looked away from him, miserable, despairing. Since he had left the cabin—and her—the first night, she had not been able to do anything other than to think of him and his body and his touch. Her thoughts were shameless; she was shameless.

But he did not want her as much as she wanted him. Otherwise he would have come to her last night—or even sooner, during the day.

Katherine closed her eyes briefly, flooded with deeper despair. She had no choice now but to recognize fully the extent of her passion for him, a man she despised, a man she could never respect, a man who had chosen murder and robbery for his trade. She could not resist him, and worse, she wanted him, passionately. And now she was his prisoner. He would use her when the urge took him, and she would enjoy it, even though she was married to another man. He would use her when he chose, as he chose, and her defiance would be a sham, a facade. Until he tired of her and freed her.

But then, of course, she would have nowhere to go. No man would want a pirate's whore. Hawke would divorce her. There would be no other marriage for her. No marriage, no children. Katherine supposed that she would be able to join her father in his prison in Southwark. Or would he reject her, too?

Katherine bit her lip, thinking about how, once, Liam had asked her to be his wife. Yet somehow it had come to this, instead, with her his whore, his toy.

"This is where I live," Liam said from behind her.

Katherine jumped, not having heard him approach. She found herself ensnared in his dark, brooding gray gaze. With difficulty she looked away, but not before she had noticed the growth of beard on his jaw, and the full, chiseled set of his mouth.

Acutely aware of how close he stood beside her, aware that, if she shifted slightly, her skirts would brush his thigh, Katherine clasped her hands together, to keep them from shaking. "Earic Island. Guy told me." She was careful not to look at him, but she found it hard to breathe normally. Memories of the other night haunted her. "I hope you did not choose the island's name?"

"I did."

She started, her gaze flying to his. "Why?"

He shrugged. "Is it not obvious? My living comes from spilling blood—yet I have never paid a single penny of blood money to anyone."

Katherine inhaled. And she saw sadness in his eyes— but surely it was an illusion, caused by the play of shadows and light cast by the dawn. She turned to face the bloodred sun, was almost blinded by it. She squinted, determined to see the island.

And she was disappointed. It was a pile of soaring rocks, shrouded in the morning mist, bathed in the eerie tangerine light. It seemed naught but a pirate's lair. It did not seem capable of sustaining any form of life. Katherine was about to say so when she spotted the old stone castle carved onto one side of the island, high up on a rock mountain. "Does grass grow there? Are there trees?"

"On the southern end there is a forest filled with game." He added, "But hunting is not allowed."

She turned her head sharply, their gazes colliding.

"I will not allow the game to be depleted. All victuals are brought in by ship from Belfast."

"Why do you live here?" Katherine asked. "In such a forsaken place?"

He did not look at her. "Where would you have me live?"

For the briefest of moments, Katherine had forgotten who and what he was. There was nothing more to say, and she turned toward the orange sun—and the rock island rising up out of the swirling mists and the cool gray sea.

Katherine paused on the threshold of the great hall. Liam spoke to his steward, and she saw other servants, both male and female, hovering at the hall's other end, in the entrance that undoubtedly led outside to the kitchen. The hall was cold, dark, and clearly very old. She had been given a cloak before they disembarked, and she clutched it to her, glancing around.

She did not know what she had expected, but she had not expected this dank, dismal place. Although she had been raised at Askeaton, which was also a medieval manor, it had been luxuriously furnished; it had been bright and cheerful. Katherine could not understand why this was his home. The cabin on his ship had boasted every luxury, from the fine wood paneling on the walls to the silver-plated nightstool, but this, this huge room was nearly bare.

A manservant had stoked up the fire in the large hearth. Katherine moved to stand beside it. Other than the ancient trestle table, the benches, the two chairs, and the scarred sideboard, there were no other furnishings in the room, just a single, faded tapestry. The wind moaned incessantly, as the castle was perched atop the island. And Katherine could feel a draft. She could not imagine anyone spending a full winter here. She wondered if this place ever saw the summer, ever saw the sun.

She was aware of Liam coming to stand behind her. "I will show you to our chamber, upstairs."

Her mind protested his use of the word "our." "You've gotten what you wanted. Why do you not set me free now and be done with it?"

He stared into her eyes, then at her trembling mouth. "I have hardly gotten what I want from you, Katherine." Abruptly he turned and strode away.

Tingles raced up her spine. Katherine finally followed him, torn, at once reluctant and curious. She couldn't decipher the meaning of his last words. He had her virtue. What more could there be?

Despite herself, she imagined endless, torrid nights of shared passion.

On the third story there were but two other chambers. Clearly no additions had been made to the castle in the centuries since it had been built. Liam pushed open a heavy and scarred oak door and then ducked to enter the lord's chamber. Katherine was greeted by a large, but plain bed, covered with furs, neither postered nor canopied. Hides covered the windows, and the room was exceedingly dark. Liam lit a taper. Katherine's dismay increased. He had at least twenty beautiful rugs on the floor of his cabin, and although she was used to rushes, in the past two days she had grown accustomed to the feel of wool beneath her feet. Why did he not have a single rug in here? Why was there no table, no chair? There was naught but a single chest at the foot of the bed, one nightstool, and the oversize fireplace. From his ship's cabin she had surmised that he liked to read, but she saw not a single tome anywhere in the room.

"I prefer your ship," Katherine said abruptly. Somehow this room—this castle—made her angry.

Liam glanced at her, setting down the taper. "So do I." He went to the fire and struck flint to kindling, then shoved the burning twigs under thick, dry logs. A fire blazed to life beneath his capable hands.

She watched his broad back. His shirt was the finest

linen, and she could see his every muscle delineated beneath it as he moved. He still knelt, and her gaze traveled lower, to his hard, powerful buttocks. She turned away abruptly. "When will you tire of me?" Her voice sounded unnatural, even to her own ears.

"I will never tire of you, Kate."

Katherine whirled to face him, gasping. Her eyes were wide; his stare was hard, brilliant, holding hers. Tension had tightened the muscles in his face—and it seethed in the room between them. What kind of declaration was this?

With another piercing, potent look, a look filled with a promise Katherine was afraid to understand, Liam strode from the chamber. Katherine stared after him until she realized that she was very much alone, the solid oak door closed behind him.

Exhausted, she sank down upon the bed. She was trembling. Surely he had not been sincere. But Katherine recalled his eyes, his expression, his stance, and thought that he had meant his every word.

And John Hawke's angry image rushed into her mind.

If only she could escape. She must escape.

She had seen the small village nestled below the castle, by the harbor. He had explained that his men lived there, with their wives and families. From what Katherine had glimpsed, the small village had seemed little different from any other village. The houses had been stone, the roofs thatched, but bright, gay flowers had been planted in many a yard, and she had even seen red English roses climbing one wooden fence. She had also noticed a steeple with a pale golden cross at its apex, a strange and surprising sight, considering that these were not godly men.

Katherine licked her dry lips, wondering if she dared to enter the village alone. She thought about the sleepy village, so innocent in its appearance, and she thought about Liam's men. She had lived amongst the pirates on the *Sea Dagger* these past two days, and those few other days during the winter when he had first abducted her. She could not recall having seen a single sign of debauchery or disrespect in all the time she had been aboard his ship.

In fact, the opposite seemed to be true. Liam O'Neill seemed to generate the utmost respect—his men scurried to obey him without thought or protest. And Katherine had never seen or heard the whip. How did he command such an unruly lot, then?

Katherine had no answer. She had but one burning question now. If she wandered into the village, could she find, or buy, an ally to aid and abet her in an escape? Excitement swept over her.

"What are you thinking, Katherine? Do you pine for Hawke?"

Katherine jumped to her feet. "You keep sneaking up on me!"

His smile was wry and brief. "No. I do not sneak about in my own home. It is you who is overly distracted."

Katherine realized that he held a small coffer in his hands. It was the kind of pretty box in which a lady kept her jewels or gloves. She lifted her gaze to his, unable to hide her curiosity.

He seemed hesitant. Then, swiftly, as if making up his mind, he came to her and sat beside her, thrusting the box into her hands. " 'Tis for you."

She was at once loath to accept it—and eager to inspect it. Katherine tried to clear her confused head. "What is it?"

"A gift."

She shoved the box back at him, pride besting her female curiosity. "I do not want it."

His jaw flexed. "Why not?"

"I am not a willing whore, to be paid with your trinkets."

His nostrils flared. "It is you who keeps using that most distasteful term, not I."

She stood, her hands on her hips. "It does not matter what word I use, facts are facts. You have made me your whore, and I refuse to be paid for your use of me."

He also stood. "I was not trying to pay you for lying with me, Katherine."

"Then you thought to compensate me for my virtue." She blinked back tears, as sad as she was angry. He could say whatever he liked, but the truth was the truth. He sought to pay her for the hours she had warmed his bed. How small—and cheap—she felt.

"No." He shook is head vehemently. "I want to give you beautiful things, Katherine. I have wealth to share with you. I want to share it with you. Why do you refuse me?"

"I cannot be bought. And you are trying to buy me!" she accused.

Suddenly he gripped her chin, forcing her to face him, immobilizing her. "Why do you not let me ease my conscience," he cried.

She tried to pull away, and only succeeded because he let her go. "You have no conscience. Had you a conscience, you would not murder innocent men—and abduct innocent women."

"How right you are." Quick as the blink of an eye, he pulled her up against him.

"I will not whore for you again," Katherine cried, at that moment meaning it. She was furious to be his prisoner, and even more furious with herself, for how eager, and feverish, her body was. She had to control herself before this went any farther.

"You have never whored for me," he said, his mouth close to hers, his gray gaze blazing. "And you never will." Settling his hand in the hank of hair at her nape, he pulled her head back. "I want far more from you than the use of your body, Katherine."

And Katherine stiffened, prepared to fight him.

22

*K*atherine dug her nails into his shoulders, trying to push him away. Because he held her hair in his fist like a rope, high up on her nape, close to her scalp, she could not turn her face away from him. His lips were demanding. Katherine refused to open, despite the feverish excitement exploding in her body. She was agonizingly aware of how hot and hard and huge he was against her own swollen sex.

Liam jerked on her head once, angry because she was not yielding, and pushed her up against the wall. Pinned there, Katherine felt the last of her resistance ebbing away. Somehow, she kept her mouth closed. He finally nipped the corner of her lips and ducked lower, tearing down her bodice as he did so. His mouth claimed her nipple and Katherine cried out. No longer trying to push him away.

He laughed then, against her breast, the sound husky and raw with triumph and excitement. Katherine held him close, gasping as he tugged and sucked, using his teeth so skillfully. When he pressed on her shoulders, urging her to the floor, Katherine did not resist. Instead, his name escaped her lips.

Her bodice was down around her waist, torn. Now Liam pushed up her skirts and ripped off her drawers with both hands. Katherine could not stand the anticipation, not for another instant. Her hands found his breeches, brushing the massive bulge there, fumbling with the tiny shell buttons. Liam laughed again, thrust her hand away, and freed his huge phallus. Katherine moaned at the sight of him straining for her. Unable to resist, she touched him, a long, caressing stroke upon his velvety flesh.

"No more games," Liam said harshly. "Do you understand me, Katherine?"

She whimpered, in acquiescence.

Liam thrust all the way into her. Katherine bucked, meeting him as savagely as he took her. Their cries sounded in unison, their breaths mingled, as he plunged into her repeatedly. Katherine's explosion came very, very quickly.

Dazed, shuddering still, Katherine felt him withdraw his hardness from her. She protested. He hushed her, lying atop her fully, panting and shaking, kissing her ear, her neck. Katherine moaned and, despite the return of partial sanity, she was hardly replete. "Liam," she whispered, stroking his back. Using her nails, letting him know what she wanted yet again.

"You are insatiable," he muttered thickly, "but then, so am I."

He eased his bulk into her again, this time slowly. Katherine shifted restlessly, wanting so much more. But he only smiled at her, his eyes silver, gleaming. His withdrawal was long and so slow it was painful. Katherine hissed at him.

He laughed, bent to nip her nipple, and began to rub the ripe to bursting head of his penis against the folds of her sex. Katherine jerked, crying out, but not in protest, only in need for far more.

"We have hardly had the chance to explore each other, Kate," Liam murmured, rubbing back and forth so languidly that Katherine thought she might die. And then she did. She gripped him, convulsing. Her sudden release took them both by surprise.

Liam hugged her, panting, still stiff and throbbing between her legs. "Greedy bitch," he whispered in her ear. "I can feel that you still want more."

"Oh, God," Katherine whimpered, "I do. I want you inside me. Every single inch of you."

He laughed, the sound arrogant. "You cannot take every inch of me, treasure."

Her gaze grew dark and defiant, wicked and challenging. "No?"

His smile was as sly. "I think not." He raised up on
his hands and knees. Katherine looked at what he displayed. She met his glittering, arrogant gaze. Bold as a
snake, she reached for him and gripped him. Liam threw
back his head, sliding into her hand, moaning now. The
veins stood out on his neck, his biceps rippled and flexed.
Katherine's pulse quickened. She now controlled his
power, it now belonged to her, and she had never felt
more triumphant—or more female.

Liam thrust into her palm, his temples throbbing, his
phallus pulsing, his eyes still closed. Katherine heard herself laugh softly. Two could truly enjoy this game. But
her laughter had hardly died when Liam rose up over
her, breaking her grip swiftly. Stunning her once again,
controlling her once again, he rubbed himself against first
one taut nipple, then another. Katherine lay still, watching,
panting, refusing to beg and plead with him. He was so
red and so swollen, larger now, that she thought he might
very well explode there between her breasts.

"Do you like being so wicked, Kate?"

She nodded, unable to speak.

"Hold your breasts for me, push them together," he
commanded.

Katherine obeyed.

Liam thrust harder, faster. Katherine began to whimper,
to wriggle her hips. Her loins were afire. And finally she
did what she had refused to do until then—she begged.
"Liam, please, oh, God, please!"

With a deep, guttural cry, he thrust between her legs, a
place now slick with her body's secretions, slick and pulsing. Katherine wrapped her long legs around his waist,
begging him for more, begging him to go deeper, harder.
Liam complied, plundering without mercy. Their bodies
made slapping, sucking sounds. Katherine wept as her
peak neared. When she began to keen, Liam jerked away
from her, collapsing on the bed, shuddering with his
own release.

Katherine came out of her sensual daze slowly. She

shifted, her bare leg brushing his breech-clad one. Liam lay upon his stomach, unmoving, but his face was turned to hers, his eyes closed, his dark golden lashes fanlike upon his striking face. She blinked, confusion rising. Why ever had he done such a thing? Why had he pulled out of her, in such a manner, at such a time?

His lashes lifted, their gazes met. He did not smile. "I am undone."

Katherine stared, breathless all over again. Why did he have to say such things? He was an experienced lover, he had had many women. Did he tell each and every one of them such things? She imagined that flattery was second nature to such a man.

He rolled onto his side, his gaze sweeping over her bare breasts. Katherine began to reach for her torn bodice, but he stilled her hand. "You have nothing to hide. You are lovely, by far the loveliest woman I have ever seen."

"Don't."

He sat up. "But it is the truth."

Her glance slipped over him; his breeches were open. Her eyes met his, and she watched him strip off his shirt. The muscles in his shoulders, arms and chest rippled as he moved. Anticipation lanced her. His smile was intimate, for her alone.

"Why did you do that? Why did you . . ." She hesitated, beginning to blush.

"Why did I finish in such a manner?" His smile was gone. He was very sober. "I was incapable of control the first time we lay together. And although it was very difficult this time, I did not want to spill my seed inside of you, Katherine." His jaw seemed tense.

She was amazed. "You protect me from bearing a bastard?"

He rose gracefully to his feet, paced across the room. When he spoke, it was to the stone wall. "I am not so cruel, to bring my bastards into the world." He glanced at her. "I do not want children. I will not have children. I will not bequeath them this life."

Katherine stared at him, suddenly aching for him.

*   *   *

Katherine could not move, nor did she want to. But the fire had long since died, the moon had risen and set, and from the light within the chamber, she knew it was a new day and close to dinnertime.

Her limbs were sore, as was every part of her body, but it was a fantastic soreness. She would never blush again. Had she and Liam not done every possible sexual act that could be done by a man and a woman? She had lost count of the times he had made love to her. Katherine was smiling. She stretched like a cat, sighed at how wonderful it felt, stretched again, and finally sat up.

She was alone. Liam had last made love to her in the full light of morning, and before she had fallen asleep afterward, she had been aware of him rising. She wondered what business compelled him to leave their bed after such a day and such a night. Feeling sated and replete, yet somehow still eager, and amazingly, anticipating the night that would soon come, Katherine pushed the bed covers aside. She was stark naked. She looked down at her breasts, surprised to see red marks on them, then she touched herself, a small pleased caress, and finally she slipped from the bed. Her heart was singing.

Katherine tried to rein in her joy. She was a fallen woman, a pirate's whore, and her mood should be dark and despairing. She sobered slightly, looking around the bare, dismal chamber. She did not want to dwell on what could not be changed, she thought fiercely. She did not want to dwell on what made her sad—on her abduction and her current predicament. She wanted to think only of Liam's incredible and powerful lovemaking.

Then she became still, her heart heavy, thinking of the fact that he refused to spill his seed inside of her. She was relieved, of course. She had no wish to bear his bastard. But . . . there was something terribly sad about a man so determined not to have children.

She shoved such thoughts aside. Her wandering eye spotted the small coffer he had tried to give her yesterday morning. With a jolt she realized that they had stayed abed for more than twenty-four hours. She glanced at the disheveled mattress. It did not seem possible—but it was.

Katherine saw her clothes, strewn about the floor. She reached for her drawers, but they were torn in two, and she tossed them aside. The gold dress she picked up and laid carefully on the bed. The bodice was torn—how well she remembered his tearing it—and she would have to mend it. It was far too beautiful to be left in such disrepair.

Her gaze turned back to the small, enameled box.

Don't, she told herself. But she was unable to stop thinking about his "gift."

"I don't want your gifts, Liam O'Neill," she cried.

Sadness had replaced all of her joy. Katherine sat down on the bed, pulling a fur about her naked body, angry now, staring fixedly at the box. A box she hated because it represented what she had become—what she now was. Angry tears filled her eyes. Somehow she had thought to fool herself and ignore the facts of her life.

Abruptly Katherine stood, dropping the fur, and stalked to the coffer. A small brass key was fitted in the lock and she turned it. The lid popped open. Katherine gasped.

A magnificent necklace met her eyes. Five strands of rubies, each stone set in gold, with diamonds winking about the rim of each gem. The "gift" was no trinket. It was jewelry fit for a princess, but not a whore. Katherine could not believe her eyes. And she could not understand it—or him.

Entranced, she picked up the necklace. It was very heavy, almost too heavy to wear. Wearing it would not, could not, be comfortable. But then, she would never know, would she? Because she would never wear his "gift."

Katherine bit her lip, holding the necklace up to her throat while turning to stare into the looking glass above the chest. But at the sight that greeted her, she dropped the rubies as if they had burned her.

For she had seen a tall, naked woman, one whose wild red hair hung loose and unbound, one whose mouth was swollen and bruised, one whose eyes gleamed with irrepressible excitement, wearing a priceless necklace above her naked, quivering breasts. In the looking glass she had not seen Katherine FitzGerald, the daughter of an earl.

She had seen an expensively paid courtesan—she had seen a whore.

Katherine left the necklace lying on the floor where she had dropped it. Her heart beating very hard and very fast now, she pulled on her shift and petticoats. Unfortunately, she had no other clothes of her own; she had no choice but to wear the torn dress. As she had no comb, Katherine raked her hair with her fingertips, but it hardly helped. Finally she bent and retrieved the necklace, replacing it in the coffer, which she locked. Then, holding the dress together at the neckline, she hurried from the room and down the stairs.

Liam was standing at the fireplace, lost in thought. Guy sat on the floor not far from his feet, playing with a big wolfhound pup. Macgregor sat at the trestle table, engrossed in a book. A book? Katherine had not realized that he, too, could read.

Liam's distant expression turned into a warm smile as he turned toward her. On the bottom of the stairs, Katherine froze. His smile grew fixed as he met her stare, then disappeared. His glance lowered to the coffer she held in her hand.

A sadness so intense it defied description swept Katherine's being. She looked at Liam, at his proud, handsome face, at his big, powerful form, and into his unreadable gray eyes. She thought of the past day. How foolish she had been to wake up so pleased and dreamy-eyed. They had not indulged in lovemaking. Oh, no. It had been nothing more than fornication, no, worse, purely hedonistic sex.

And even if it had been lovemaking, that could not change Liam O'Neill into a man he would never become. He was Shane O'Neill's son, no rapist like his father, perhaps not an overly violent man, but an amoral pirate nonetheless.

"Good day, Katherine," he said levelly. His gaze searched her face. "We are about to sit down to dinner." His glance lingered on her bodice where it was torn and where she held it up. "I have ordered the chest of clothes brought up from my ship. It should be here at any moment. We will wait for you to change before we dine.''

Her heart was in shreds. And it had nothing to do with changing her ripped gown. Katherine moved toward him and handed him the box. "I cannot take this."

His expression unfathomable, he nodded.

"I do not want any gifts from you."

"Very well. That is your decision to make." His tone was without inflection.

Katherine wanted to weep. She turned her back on him, somewhat blindly, to face the table where they would dine. She had awaked ravenous; now she had no appetite. She was in serious danger, but she refused to identify the exact nature of that danger. She knew but one thing. She must escape. No matter how it hurt her to do so.

Several days later, Katherine sat on the floor with Guy, dicing. She was pleased to see him smile and even cry with glee when he bested her, for he was, in general, such a solemn boy. They were wagering twigs and stones, although Guy, the rascal, had wanted to wager actual coin. Now he clapped his hands, flushed with pleasure, having won again. Katherine smiled at him. "I cannot best you, Guy. I think I must concede defeat."

Guy grinned at her, then, seeing someone behind her, his smile brightened even more. Katherine twisted and saw Liam watching them, a strange expression upon his face. Her heart immediately picked up a wild beat. She was very aware of the late hour—and what would soon happen in their chamber upstairs.

For Liam slept with her every night, and their bouts of passion often lasted until dawn. Sometimes, incredibly, he came to her in the middle of the day as well. Katherine had never refused him. She had never wanted to.

Their glances locked, understanding sizzling between them. Katherine felt her cheeks grow hot as she turned to face Guy. She felt Liam approach, felt his body's warmth and magnetism as he stood behind her, over her. His hand brushed her shoulder. "Did you learn to dice in the convent, Kate?"

Katherine laughed, nervously. "Of course not. I learned dicing from my father and my uncle."

He stepped forward and knelt beside her, his gaze warm, stroking over her face. "Your mother did not object?"

Katherine grinned. "She did not know."

He laughed, the sound rich and easy.

Katherine stared at his beautiful face.

Liam's gaze turned to Guy. "I hope you are not taking the lady for all she is worth," he said seriously.

Guy flushed. "No sir, Captain."

Liam reached out and mussed the boy's hair. "Gentlemen let ladies win." He rose, gave Katherine a sharp glance, and moved away. Katherine watched him as he walked to the stairs, her pulse rioting. But when she turned back to Guy, trying to act naturally, she saw the question in his eyes, and how eagerly he was poised to play. Her ready smile faded. The boy was so starved for affection, both hers and Liam's. And although she wanted nothing more than to run up the stairs, she patted his small hand. "Well, do we play or no?" she asked cheerfully.

Guy's gaze flew to hers, and then he grinned. "Aye, lady, we play. But do I really have to let you win?"

Katherine could not sleep. She looked at Liam, who lay upon his back, breathing deeply, his body still sheened with sweat from their wild lovemaking. Katherine's heart clenched. Carefully, so as not to wake him, she sat up.

June had come to the island, and although the days were warm and summerlike, the nights were still quite cool. Katherine pulled the covers up over her bare breasts, her pulse refusing to quiet. Earlier that evening, during their light supper repast, Liam had told her that he was leaving on the morrow.

Katherine had reacted foolishly, asking him where he was going. He had gazed at her with impenetrable eyes, and told her it served no purpose for her to know.

Katherine felt moisture gathering in her eyes. She wiped it away, angry with herself for forgetting, even for an instant, that her lover was a pirate. Of course, he did have letters of marque; clearly he also preyed upon the queen's enemies. Katherine knew that it was simplistic to label Liam naught but a pirate, for his piracy was a part of a very clever and dangerous political game. He was as much a privateer, making him some strange hybrid creation of the two. When he plundered and pillaged the high seas, he did so very, very carefully.

Liam was leaving. He was going pirating or privateering, and that meant that she would finally have a chance to escape.

Katherine looked down at him. The fire still blazed, and warm orange light bathed the room, making it easy to see his beautiful features. Her heart hurt. All the more reason to leave, now, before it was he who ordered her away, as he would surely do one day. Katherine was afraid that she would refuse such a command instead of following it, refuse it and drop to her knees, begging him not to cast her aside in favor of some new, younger mistress.

Oh, God! Katherine hugged herself, the tears spilling now. She did not love him, that was impossible, but he had enslaved her with his sex and his power and his charisma. He had enslaved her, that was all, but slaves could escape their masters, and she must escape him.

Tomorrow he would leave. After he was gone, she would go to the village with the coffer containing the ruby-and-gold necklace. Surely, for such a prize, someone would help her leave the island—and leave him.

23

*K*atherine trudged up the steep, stony path toward the castle, returning from her trek to the village below. She carried a plain gray mantle over her arm, the mantle she had worn to disguise her identity despite the fact of the day's being seasonable and warm. Liam had left that dawn. Katherine had escaped the castle soon thereafter, running out through the castle gates behind a small wagon, pretending to be a serving maid because the servants were free to come and go as they pleased.

Above her, the sun was bright, the sky aqua blue and puffed with fluffy white clouds. Yet she did not feel half as cheerful as she should on such a day, after attaining her goal. For she had found a seaman who, upon receipt of the coffer containing the fabulous necklace, had agreed to help her escape.

Katherine watched a hawk soaring above the castle and she told herself that she was happy. Yes, she was very happy, as happy as a lark, because, in a few days, when the supply ship from Belfast arrived, the sailor would contact her. And when it left to return to northern Ireland, she would be stowed away upon it.

And hopefully Liam would not have returned from his pirating, making her escape all that much easier.

She would escape—and never see him again.

Katherine was furious with her feelings. Furious with the incipient tears, furious to be so torn, and over a damned pirate at that.

She had to leave before she did the unthinkable—before she fell in love with him.

And she must stop thinking of what her reception would be when she finally reached England. For she had decided that she must return to Hawke, who was still legally her husband.

Her heart beat faster now, for her imagination ran wild, and she could see herself facing him, facing the court, then facing the queen. But they would not know. They could not know. That when in Liam's arms she was far more willing and eager and lascivious than the highest-paid, most-experienced courtesan.

And what about her father? Katherine had not spared him even a single thought since her abduction. Yet now she wondered how he would receive her. Perhaps Gerald would be filled with fatherly rage over her abduction and abuse. Or perhaps he would berate her for having failed to obey him fully, for becoming the pirate's whore and not his wife.

"Katherine!"

Katherine stumbled and came to a halt, relieved to be diverted from her thoughts. Guy ran through the raised portcullis, flying down the path toward her. Macgregor followed, more slowly.

Katherine forced a bright smile. "Hello, Guy!" She waved.

Guy skidded to a halt. "Where have you been? We have been looking all over for you!"

Careful to avoid Macgregor's gaze, Katherine ruffled Guy's thick, dark hair. "I felt lonely with Liam gone," she lied. "I decided to take a walk."

"You should have asked me to come with you," Guy protested. "The captain told me it was my duty to protect you from harm."

"Lady Katherine," Macgregor said, "please ask for my escort the next time you wish to leave the castle walls."

Katherine's jaw tightened, and she flashed him a dark glance. "Do you think I intend to escape?"

He stared at her, not answering.

Katherine regretted her words. "There is no way for

me to escape and you know it," she said. "But I refuse to be jailed inside that miserable pile of stone." She shoved past the big man, Guy on her heels.

"Katherine?"

"What is it, Guy?"

"You are not happy here?"

She softened. It suddenly occurred to her that Guy would suffer when she left. Perhaps it had been a mistake to befriend him. But she loved children, and Guy was no exception. She chose her words with care. "Guy, I am not unhappy here. But I have friends and family elsewhere. My stay here is only temporary."

He stared at her, tears welling in his eyes. "I understand. I thought you were different from the others, that you would stay. But like the others, sooner or later you will leave."

Katherine could not move. She had lost her breath. *The others.* How many others had there been? She did not want to know. She had to know. She said, "Yes, I am no different from the others." And she turned away, so he would not see the single tear that crept down her cheek.

Bored and restless, acutely aware of Liam's absence, at once praying that he would return before the supply ship from Belfast arrived, and praying that he would not, Katherine wandered over to the brick manor house. Guy trailed behind her. It was another warm summer day, and Katherine had been picking primroses—flowers she had discovered growing wild on the path outside the barbican.

Now she raised herself up on her toes, holding the wildflowers in one hand, and she tried to peer through a glass window. But the curtains were drawn. She turned to face Guy. "Liam mentioned this house once. Clearly this is a new home. Why does Liam not live here, instead of in that drafty, decrepit castle?"

Guy shrugged. "I have been with the captain more than two years, and he has always lived in the keep. But he built this house, Katherine."

Katherine gasped. Why would Liam go to the effort and

expense of building this pleasing home, and then leave it vacant? "Have you been inside?"

"I have never been inside, not even once. He keeps it locked."

Sending Guy a conspiratorial glance, Katherine hurried to the front of the house. As Guy had said, the two large front doors, both weathered wood but beautifully paneled and engraved, were locked.

"What do you think to do?" Guy asked curiously.

She grinned at him, her eyes twinkling. "Explore."

Guy's eyes widened, and then he grinned, as well. "Perhaps the steward has the keys. But he will not give them to me. And the captain might be angry when he finds out what we have done."

"Leave O'Neill to me." Katherine thought but a moment. "I do not think the steward will give them to me, either, but . . ." Her smile flashed again. "I can try!"

Laughing together they turned, and came face-to-face with Macgregor. His face was carved into granite planes, as usual, but Katherine saw some kind of indecipherable gleam in his brown eyes. "Are you in need of aid, Lady Katherine?" he asked politely.

Since coming to the island, Katherine had changed her opinion of the big, bald, brutish-looking man. She had thought him an illiterate mercenary, but whenever he spoke to her, his words were polite and precise, indicating a level of education above the average. He also was fond of reading. And he did not play just the bagpipes with great skill, but the flute and fiddle as well. No, this big, oxlike man was not at all as he seemed. And the few times he found it necessary to speak with her, he always addressed her with respect, as if she were an earl's daughter—or Liam's wife.

"I wish to go inside," Katherine said imperiously.

"No one goes inside the captain's house."

"Why not?"

He shrugged. " 'Tis not my affair to ask."

"Who has the key?"

"Undoubtedly the captain."

"And the steward?"

Macgregor sighed. "He will not be happy when he learns you have gone inside."

Katherine's smile faded. Liam would not care that she had trespassed into his manor house—because he would be so furious over her escape. Briefly, a sadness she did not want to feel claimed her. Already she ached over their parting.

And Macgregor misunderstood. "There, my lady, do not fret. I will get you the keys—but you shall have to explain to the captain what you are about."

Katherine cried out.

Beside her, Guy stood frozen, his eyes wide.

Katherine could not believe her eyes. She stared at the dusty parquet floors. Even at court she had not seen such precise workmanship. She stared at the paneled walls, surmising the wood to be rich mahogany. These carpenters had known their craft—they could not have come from the village below. She moved through the entrance hall. Staring first at one rich, brilliantly colored tapestry, and then at equally lovely oil paintings in gilded frames. She paused on the threshold of the dining hall.

That room was paneled in dark oak. The table was round, a long, paler version of the same wood, set on a heavy, intricately carved pedestal that boasted gargoyles. Upholstered chairs of state stood around it. And on the oak floors were red-and-gold Persian rugs.

Katherine looked at the two huge sideboards, at the dull silver tureens and vases, then up at the dust-covered gold chandelier. Inhaling, she ran into the next room. This chamber was smaller, but as richly furnished. Paintings hung on the walls. Heavy damask draperies covered the windows. Chairs and stools abounded. A bookcase graced one entire wall, the wood shelves crammed with tomes. And a huge desk, somehow balanced on delicate legs, the feet gold hooves, dominated the room.

Katherine sank down on the nearest chair. For some absurd reason, tears filled her eyes.

"Are you all right, lady?" Guy asked her in a whisper.

She blinked at him. "I do not understand that man."

Guy said nothing, looking in awe around them again.

Katherine also looked around, more tears filling her eyes. "I do not understand him," she said, more fiercely. "He plays pirate, but he is really a gentleman. He plays savage, but he is literate and wise. He calls that dank castle his home—when right next door there is a home that would please any prince—and any princess."

Guy sat down on a wooden stool, the seat leather studded with brass. "He is a great man."

"He plunders and pillages, Guy. He is a pirate."

Guy jerked his thin shoulders forward. " 'Tis the way of the world. He has told me so himself. Take—or be taken."

Katherine stared at the boy, shivering slightly, for Liam was right, dear God, he was right. In this world, might made right, and she herself had learned that firsthand. Clearly Liam had learned such a painful lesson himself as well. And she wondered, then, when he had received his education in bitter reality. She began to suspect that it had been far too early in his childhood years, perhaps when Shane O'Neill had taken him from his mother.

It would explain so much. The contradictions in his character and personality, the duality, his being both savage pirate and charming gentleman—a man she feared to comprehend.

With a heavy heart, Katherine stole out of the castle in the same manner that she had a few days before. A message had been relayed by one of the dairymaids. The ship from Belfast had arrived.

She rushed to the village, jumping at every sound and shadow. She was half-afraid and half-hopeful that, at any moment, she would find Macgregor on her heels, or worse, come face-to-face with Liam. But the Scot had been nowhere to be seen all day, and Liam was still at sea.

Her rendezvous with the seaman would take place beside an alehouse which was on First Street, the dirt avenue fronting the docks. Katherine espied him lurking about kegs of beer that were piled against the wooden wall of the ordinary. Her glance moved on, taking in all the usual activity of the day, the few passing drays, some men moving briskly about their business, a woman hawking fish pies, a single painted whore lurking on the street corner. Two children played ball near the wharf, kicking it back and forth. But then her blood chilled and every air upon her nape prickled. Not far from the closest dock, the *Sea Dagger* bobbed at anchor.

Katherine's steps slowed and she stared at the pirate ship. Men were scurrying about the decks, preparing the ship for its berth, others unloading chests and barrels onto the docks. She strained her vision, then realized she hoped to espy Liam one last time before she stowed away on the supply ship destined to take her from the island.

"Lady?"

Katherine jumped in fright. A gasp of relief quickly followed when she face the sailor. "You scared me! When did the *Sea Dagger* arrive?"

"This morn."

Katherine gaped. Liam had arrived many hours ago— but she had not seen him. Was he still aboard? Overseeing the unloading of his booty? She should not be hurt that he had not come running to a reunion with her, she should be relieved. "Are we ready to go?"

"All the way to Belfast, my lady," the sailor said, smiling.

Katherine closed her eyes, overwhelmed with sudden confusion, with heavy doubt. She did not want to leave— but she had to. Yet she could not leave without a final good-bye to Liam. But if she really wished to escape, she knew she must not delay, must not return to see him, she must quickly go forward to the supply ship. Too easily she imagined herself in his embrace, and if she did not leave now, she suspected that she never would. "Where is Liam?" she asked very hoarsely.

The sailor looked at her, hesitating.

Katherine licked her lips, trying to summon up the will to leave—a will she had been so sure of until now. Her pulse was thundering in rhythm with her doubt.

"I am right behind you, Katherine," Liam said very softly—very dangerously.

Katherine felt the ground tilt wildly beneath her feet. She whirled around. Liam stood there, staring at her coldly. Dangling from his hand was the ruby-and-gold necklace with which she had bribed the seaman.

24

*L*iam tossed the priceless necklace to the seaman. "Keep it, Jacko. Well done."

Katherine's hand covered her mouth, her eyes wide, incredulous—fearful. Jacko grinned, pocketed the jewels, saluted Liam smartly, and turned away. Katherine's gaze lifted to Liam's. His regard chilled her to the bone.

He was very angry, and she should be afraid of him. But her pulse was beginning to subside now, not accelerate. In fact, Katherine was vaguely aware of feeling relieved.

He gripped her arm, jerking her up close. "I did not realize you were so unhappy, Katherine."

She stared up at his handsome face. Oh, God. She *was* relieved. She had not really wanted to leave him, she had not.

He shook her briefly, to get her attention, his mouth tight. "I did not realize you were so unhappy," he repeated angrily.

She hesitated, her eyes growing moist. "I . . . I was not *that* unhappy, Liam."

His laughter was harsh, unamused. "Then why?" he demanded. "Why this?"

She had the reckless urge to fling herself into his arms, yet she stood very still instead. "'Twas my duty—to myself."

He stared at her.

"I could not passively accept this circumstance," she said softly.

He eyed her. "You have never demonstrated the slightest tendency to passive behavior in my presence."

She knew what he was referring to and she blushed. "That is not fair."

"Life is hardly fair. And I am tired of your hypocrisy." He began to propel her back in the direction she had come.

Katherine hurried to keep up with him, trying to dislodge his hurtful grip. She gave up, for it was clear he wished to drag her about, and she was very aware that passing villagers were watching them with avid curiosity—with more than a few smiles amongst the men. She stumbled alongside him as he quickened his already long, brisk strides. His iron hold kept her upright. "What are you going to do?" She could not keep the anxiety out of her tone.

His eyes were chips of silvery ice. "We shall settle this issue once and for all."

"What do you mean?"

His answer was a dangerous smile. Katherine grew frightened. He was very angry, he did not understand that she had not really wanted to leave him, and she was not ready to bare her heart to him, not yet. She could not begin to imagine what he intended for her, now. Suddenly he veered right, turning onto a street going into the center of the village, instead of continuing on toward the castle on the hill above the town.

"I want to know where you're taking me," Katherine panted as his pace increased.

This time he did not look at her. "The church."

And suddenly, through a cluster of silver birch trees swaying in a summer-soft breeze, Katherine saw the freshly whitewashed church on the corner ahead of them, its tall gray steeple and golden cross piercing the air. Suddenly she began to fathom what he was doing—but surely she was wrong! "Liam, stop, this makes no sense," she cried, trying to pull her arm free of his iron grip.

His response was to propel her forward along the stone path bordered with blue pansies and up the chapel's three front steps.

"What can you be thinking?" she gasped as he crashed

his shoulder into the front door. It flew open, banging loudly on the inside wall.

" 'Tis time we are wed," he said.

Inside, the church was cool, the light dim. It was startlingly quiet. Stained glass windows graced each side of the nave where they stood, the altar in front of them. All the symbols of the mass were present, including a huge gold crucifix, and Katherine knew immediately that the church was Catholic, but that gave her no comfort at all. It only added to her confusion.

"Liam," she managed desperately. "I am already married. You know that."

His icy regard held hers. "And I also know that your marriage to Hawke was never consummated. I wonder if he has not already divorced you? In any case, surely you know that the Pope does not recognize marriages between Catholics and heretics. In the eyes of your own church, Katherine, you and Hawke are not wed."

"But you are Protestant," she said weakly, beginning to realize that he was deadly earnest. And of course, she knew that he spoke the truth.

"My beliefs are my own," he said flatly, "but Father Michael will not refuse me, for I built this church, brought him here, and I pay his stipend. He can convert me now, and marry us, too."

She opened her mouth to protest, but only managed a strangled sound. It quickly dawned upon her that a Catholic marriage was what she had always wanted—but not, of course, to a godless pirate.

"Liam," a male voice said from the other end of the nave.

Katherine half turned and watched the priest drifting up the aisle toward them, his dark robes flowing gracefully about his slim form. He was a young, dark-haired man, and he smiled at Liam as if he were pleased to see him. Katherine's pulse raced so fiercely now that she felt faint.

Would it be so terribly bad to marry Liam O'Neill?

"Father Michael," Liam said quietly. "I wish you to meet Katherine FitzGerald."

Father Michael turned to her, also smiling. "I have been

hoping to make your acquaintance, my lady,'' he said, his gaze holding hers. His blue eyes were both kind and serene. "To welcome you to our island, and to offer you my services should you have need of them.''

Katherine could not speak.

"I want you to marry us," Liam said, "I, of course, will take the necessary vows.''

The priest regarded him, not appearing at all surprised. "Am I to understand that you wish the ceremony performed now?''

"Aye," Liam said, his voice ringing out harshly in the empty church. "I wish you to wed us immediately.''

Katherine's knees gave out. But Liam caught her instantly and moved her forward, down the aisle, to the altar, holding her upright. His gaze captured hers. Katherine saw the stark determination there, and knew that nothing, neither man nor beast, neither devil nor God, would sway him from his path now.

Liam opened the door to their bedchamber. Katherine was careful not to look at him or touch him as she preceded him into their room. They were married; incredibly, they were man and wife. She walked to the room's far side and stood staring out of the narrow window at the courtyard below, not seeing a single thing.

She must accept her fate. And her fate, apparently, was Liam O'Neill.

In truth, was there any other choice for her? In all likelihood, Hawke had already divorced her. Was it not better, then, to be the pirate's wife instead of his whore? Had Liam not married her, had he set her free, no other man would have her, not after her sojourn upon his island, her father could not support her, and she would be homeless, a vagrant upon the streets.

And, truthfully, secretly, was it so bad to be his wife? When she yearned for him so? When she was, perhaps, on the brink of falling in love with him? Or even past it?

Tears blurred Katherine's vision. She was exhausted, so very exhausted, and so unsure of everything. Of him, of herself. She did not dare think about the past or the future, not now, not today. She hugged herself.

Katherine became aware of the utter silence filling the bedchamber. But she knew she was not alone. She looked behind her. Liam still stood in front of the door. His expression was very strained. He watched her intently.

Her pulse skipped wildly. She stared back.

His jaw clenched. He turned his face away, staring, apparently, at the floor. How beautiful his profile was. But should he not be elated? He had wanted this marriage; he had won. Why then did he appear so subdued? Why was he suddenly so restrained? Could he feel as uncertain, even as shy, as she did?

Katherine could not tear her eyes from him, wondering what he would say, what he might do, now that they were wed. Finally he lifted his head, his silver gaze searching. Then, uncharacteristically, he raked a hand through his hair. Katherine thought that it trembled ever so slightly.

She wet her lips. "Now what do we do?"

His gaze held hers. "What is it you wish to do, Katherine?"

"I do not know." But she was assailed by her old dreams, and in them she was so gay, so innocent, and so happy—a laughing bride. She wanted to be that bride now.

"I do not want to fight you," he said, his tone thick.

She jerked, her gaze flying to his. "Then perhaps you should change your forceful ways, Liam."

"Perhaps."

A silence thickened between them. Katherine became aware of the tension inside her own body, in her thighs and in her hips and in her mind. They were married now. It was their wedding night. He had every right to take her to his bed, when before he'd had none. Surely this night would end with seduction and lovemaking. Yet why did he stand there staring at her so gravely? What halted him from coming to her, as he had done so many times before?

He had folded his arms across his chest as well. "I wonder if a peace is possible, between us."

Something soared inside her breast. "I . . . don't know."

His jaw flexed.

Katherine wet her lips. "We could . . . try."

His eyes widened, his arms dropped to his sides.

She realized then how much she wanted a truce, how tired she was of constant warfare, and how eager she was for the sanctuary of his powerful embrace. How eager she was for his body, for both the comfort it would provide her, and the pleasure. She flushed. "We are married now. 'Tis insane . . . to war."

He moved forward, his strides eating up the space between them, halting abruptly in front of her. But he did not touch her. "I think that I am insane, Kate, to have done all that I have done, to have risked so much—for you."

A wild, heated, joyous emotion unfurled inside of her. Katherine tried to control it, to subdue it. "Perhaps this will work," she said. "We can make it work."

He inhaled, the sound loud and sharp.

Katherine felt tears rise swiftly and her vision blurred as she reached up and laid her hand against his cheek. Liam's eyes closed. A moment later he turned his face, opened her palm, and pressed a lingering kiss there.

Katherine smiled and moved into his arms. This time, when their mouths mated, it was the prelude to far more than a carnal union.

Katherine awoke as covers were placed over her naked body. She heard strange sounds in the room, which became less strange, and then familiar—servants filling a tub with bathwater.

Her weary mind began to function. She was in bed, in their bedchamber—a chamber they had shared for many days now. She recalled all of it. Liam had refused to allow her to leave, and passion had bred more passion. The first time had been amazingly gentle, amazingly tender, the second time wildly savage. She could not remember the rest. His hands, his mouth, his huge heated entry, his whispered words, sometimes endearments, sometimes lewd provocations, 'twas all a blur. Except for one thing, one thing which stood out in her mind, remaining crystal clear.

Not once had Liam given her his seed.

Sudden despair washed over Katherine, chasing away her sated contentment. She had always wanted children. She still did. And she was his wife now. Why would he still be resolved to deny her his children? What dark demons drove him in such an unnatural manner? All men wanted children. All men wanted heirs: immortality. All men except, apparently, this one. The man who was now her husband.

And suddenly his words came back to her, so loud and so clear it was as if he spoke in the room now. *"I am not so cruel, to bring my bastards into the world. I do not want children. I will not have children. I will not bequeath them this life."*

Katherine opened her eyes abruptly. Sunlight poured into the chamber, telling her that it was midday, and a fine afternoon, too. Dismay filled her, dismay and an aching sadness.

Was he so set against children that she would never have any? What caused him to have such a strange, dark determination?

Katherine had no answer, not yet. She turned and watched a servant adding sweet herbs to a tub of steaming bathwater, and the scent of rosemary wafted over her. Katherine tried to summon up some interest, but failed. She was fully awake, though, and she sat up, holding the sheets up over her chest. Then she gasped.

Liam stood by the doorway, regarding her intently. He was not smiling, but when their gazes collided, the slightest, most tentative smile formed on his face.

Katherine summoned up a smile that felt utterly shy and every bit as uncertain as his.

"Good morning, Kate." He moved to her, took her hand, and raised it to his lips. He kissed her palm, holding her eyes. The servant pretended not to see, quickly leaving. Katherine's senses rioted, her cheeks flamed. His eyes were so warm as they looked at her that Katherine could not help but believe that he cared for her far more than he had ever let on.

And she was jolted by the notion. Jolted and undone.

He sat down beside her on the bed. "What dark

thoughts do you entertain, that you wake up so serious and so gloomy?''

She studied him, but he seemed to want to know, so she blurted out the truth. "Liam, surely, now that we are wed, you want children?''

His smiled disappeared. Liam rose to his full height, staring down at her, his eyes stormy with emotion. "No, Katherine. I thought you understood. I will not bring *my* children into this world.''

Katherine gripped the bedcovers to her neck. "I do not understand.''

His jaw flexed. "I am sure that you do not.''

Dismay, and anger, filled her. "I am your wife. God knows, I did not ask to be such, but it is done now, and surely I have some rights.''

His gaze traveled over her features, returned to her eyes. "I do not want my sons to sail the seas, with no other world open to them. And God forbid we should have a daughter, for she would have even less choice than that. No. I will not have children.''

Katherine shook her head. "Please, Liam, this is very important to me. We must discuss this. We must—''

"No!''

Katherine flinched at the note of raw fury in his voice.

His eyes blazed. "No. *No*. I will not breed whores and pirates on you.''

Katherine cried out—as he slammed from the room.

25

*T*he letter came a month later, in August. Liam brought it with him when he returned from his second voyage, one that had lasted a mere week. Katherine recognized the seal instantly; it belonged to the earl of Desmond. Her heart seemed to still. Clearly the sealed missive was from her father, who still recklessly used the insignia to which he no longer had any right.

Liam regarded her searchingly as she stared transfixed at the letter. "I will rid myself of salt and grime in a bath upstairs," he told her. His smile appeared, soft and seductive. "Perhaps you will come up and help me in my bath after you have read the letter."

"Thank you, Liam," Katherine said softly. She watched him climb the stone stairs. She had missed him, but their reunion would have to wait. She understood that he was deliberately leaving in order to give her a moment of privacy in which to read the missive from her father. Katherine was grateful. In the several months since her abduction, in the few weeks since their marriage, she had become more adept at avoiding all thoughts pertaining to the world outside their island. Her father was a part of that world—and she was not sure she wanted to hear the tidings he now brought her.

Katherine moved to stand in front of the fire and she tore open the seal reluctantly, fearfully.

The first of July, in the year fifteen hundred and seventy-one. Dearest Katie, why have you not sent me word? What passes? The court was in an uproar over your abduction, the queen enraged, as was John Hawke. But she denied him his request to set chase after both you and O'Neill.

Have you heeded my wishes as I last made them clear? Is O'Neill an eager suitor? Will he support my cause? My situation has not changed. My worries have never been greater. I die slowly in this exile. In Desmond, FitzMaurice is as strong as ever. At court the queen pulls out her hair, despairing of ever catching the blackguard fanatic. Philip supports him more actively than ever, and from time to time, so does Catherine de Medici. The situation cannot continue, dearest Katie. Soon FitzMaurice will be so ensconced in Desmond, that only an act of God will remove him from Desmond lands. Katie, although you are wed now to Hawke, you must entice O'Neill to our cause if you have not already done so. We need O'Neill as our greatest ally. Send him to me.

> *Your loving father,*
> *Gerald FitzGerald.*

Katherine's hands shook as she quickly folded the letter and tossed the parchment into the fire. *She was still married to John Hawke.*

She was panting, her temples pounding. The letter had been dated July 1—perhaps by now Hawke had divorced her. *Oh, God.* Something was amiss. Liam had abducted her on the fifteenth of April—would Hawke not have divorced her immediately?

Katherine sank into a chair. She could hardly think. *Did she have two husbands?*

Oh, God. Katherine looked toward the stairs. Up above, in their room, Liam now bathed. How fond of him she had become.

No. Not fond. And not just enslaved. Far more than fond, and far more than enslaved. Katherine knew that she was in love with him.

Katherine fought for calm, and failed. But despite her near hysteria, she realized that she could no longer hide on Liam's island, pretending that the real world did not exist. She could no longer ignore her duty to her father, who was relying upon her to help him shift the scales of justice in his favor. The time had come for her to persuade Liam to ally himself with Gerald and his cause, no matter that she did not want to use Liam, no matter that she did not want any politics to become a part of their marriage.

No, she could no longer avoid her duty to her father, and she could no longer avoid the question of her own future—for the future had come to find her. Katherine ran to the stairs.

Liam was still in the tub, which had grown tepid now, when he heard her racing footsteps. His slight smile was instantaneous. He saw Katherine appear in the doorway, closing the chamber door behind her. His response to her was always the same—he marveled at her beauty, at her spirit, at her intelligence—yet with every passing day, his feelings became more intense.

He saw that she was distraught. What had her rascal father written to her? Liam had guessed that the tidings would not be good. He had not wanted to give her the letter. But he could no more deny her communication from her father than he could deny her any other thing. Liam sighed and rose to his full height, the water streaming down his hard body. "What is wrong, Katherine?" he asked softly.

She was very pale, and she swiftly came to his side, holding out a towel. Liam took her wrist before she could hand it to him. "What news has saddened you, sweetheart?"

Her gaze met his, her breasts heaved. She spoke in a rush. "Father is despondent. He worries about me. His cousin is usurping all that once belonged to him. If Fitz-Maurice is not caught by Perrot soon, it looks like he will be too powerful ever to be removed from Desmond." She wet her lips. "I have never asked much of you. I ask something of you now."

Liam was unmoving. His gray eyes were calm, watchful.

"I need you to help my father, Liam." Katherine's voice broke. "He is the victim of a grave injustice, surely you know that. Please, Liam. I beg you to help him."

Liam took her hands in his. Very softly, he said, "For you, I would gladly commit such treason, Katherine."

"You will do as I ask?" she cried.

"I am already helping your father," he said very gravely. But he felt a stabbing of guilt—and fear. He had met with FitzMaurice but once, many months ago, but that had been enough. Since that winter meeting, he had supplied the rebel and his band of soldiers well. Well enough that their resistance to the British thrived. They had never been better fed, better armed, or better supplied.

Liam was well aware of how dangerous his plan was. To plot to raise a man up, in order to bring him down, was a fragile scheme indeed. It was fraught with weak points, could so easily fail. And if it failed, FitzMaurice would reign supreme in Desmond, and he, Liam, would have been instrumental in achieving that. Katherine would never understand. She would be shocked by his apparent betrayal.

"H-how?" Katherine stammered, clearly stunned. "When?"

Liam touched her cheek, the lobe of her ear. His smile was gentle. "Katherine, my very existence is political. I sleep, eat, live, and breathe politics. I do not want there to be any politics between us." He tilted up her chin, looking into her eyes, and then he kissed her, half-soft, half-hungry. "I want naught but this between us, Katherine."

She returned his kiss, then remained within his embrace. "Liam, I am so grateful. But what are you doing? Do you thwart FitzMaurice at sea?"

He brought her hand to his lips and kissed it. "Ssh. I know you are very clever, Kate, but you should not dwell on politics. From afar, you have no hope of affecting them."

She surprised him, for her hand moved to his face, cupping his cheek. Although Katherine was wildly demonstrative in bed, out of it she kept physically aloof from him.

"I think you have just flattered me," Katherine said, her voice shaky. "Did you imply that if I were at court or in Ireland, I might be able to affect the actions of men like my father and FitzMaurice?"

He pressed her hand to his cheek, then studied her ravishing face. He did not tell that she already affected the fates of such men, because she had moved him to act in a conspiracy which, if successful, would shift all existing balances of power, and which would ultimately affect them all. Carefully but truthfully he said, "Kate, a woman like you could move mountains if she so chose."

Katherine gazed at him, flushed. "My mother was such a woman," she finally said.

"Undoubtedly you have inherited her tenacity, her intelligence, and her beauty."

"I am not a *great* beauty, Liam."

"The convent taught you modesty, but women who move men know their own worth. Modesty does not serve them well."

Katherine's brow furrowed. "Why are you telling me this?"

"Because unlike your mother, you are naive and too innocent. One day, you may need every weapon at your disposal. Modesty will not help you then, sweetheart." He was not sure why he had spoken so frankly, perhaps because he courted the gallows with his venture into treason. If he were ever caught and hung, Katherine would be left to fend for herself. He did not like that thought at all. "You are so seductive that men think of but one thing when they look at you. You can enslave any man that you choose. And once enslaved, that man will do your bidding, even against his own better judgment and his own self-interest." He thought of his commitment to FitzMaurice. He thought of the Tower and the block.

She still stared, now appearing uneasy as well as upset. "I do not like the sound of this. And Liam, I have not enslaved you."

He laughed. "No?" He pulled her hand down and wrapped it around his quivering manhood. "My cock has been swelling ever since you walked into the room and with every passing moment, continues to ripen."

She pulled her hand away, appearing very close to tears.

Liam cursed himself and his lust and put his arms around her. "I am sorry, Kate. Forgive me for being bold now, when you are so distressed. Tell me what has upset you so. There is more, is there not?''

"Yes! John Hawke did not divorce me," she cried against his wet shoulder. "My father's letter was dated the first of July. Why did he not already divorce me if that is what he planned? I am afraid we are still wed, Hawke and I.''

Liam stiffened, but chose not to lie. "I know."

"What?'' She pulled out of his arms, staring at him, aghast.

He let her go. Watching her. "He did not divorce you, but do not dwell on it. We are wed in your own faith, Katherine. Is that not enough?''

She regarded him for a long moment. "Hawke must still consider me his wife—as does the entire English world."

Liam grew angry, but fought his rising temper. "It is no easy thing, to be scorned by the world, Kate—I know that well." He saw her gaze soften. "Do not pity me, I hardly need it. Nor do you need pity, either—not even from yourself.''

She stared.

"We are wed now, legally, in the eyes of God and the Pope—no small thing. You belong to me, Kathcrine. Or do you still wish to return to England—to John Hawke?'' His gaze darkened, and for a moment, he lost the ability to breathe.

But she whispered, "No."

Liam stared into her eyes, his anger gone, wild exultation filling him. "You choose to stay with me, now, of your own free will?''

"Yes." Katherine gazed up at him, the expression in her eyes so warm and tender, so loving, that he was speechless. And then she said, in the manner in which one might speak a vow, "I am not leaving you, Liam. Not ever.''

His eyes widened. His grip tightened. A vein pulsed in his neck.

"I promise," she said hoarsely. "No matter what happens.''

Liam made a sound, one rich and deep, one harsh yet

joyous. He pulled her fully forward, captured her mouth, and then Katherine was against the wall, pinned there by him. She met his questing lips eagerly, opening for him instantly. Her tongue swept his. Liam tasted her tears, and understood that they were tears of joy. A moment later he lifted her off her feet and laid her on the bed, tossing her skirts up, and she wept, "Yes, darling, yes." His penetration was both swift and savage, a huge and sudden invasion. Their gazes met, locking.

He did not speak, overwhelmed now by both the feeling of her sheath and her recent confession, but as he thrust into her, again and again, he held her gaze, hoping she might comprehend the love he felt for her—a love he had harbored for so very long. Katherine clung to his shoulders, beginning to weep, and he knew her climax neared. He was almost undone. He gasped. Stiffening, he fought for control, fought for the strength to withdraw, so that he would not spill his seed inside of her warm, fertile body.

"Liam," Katherine gasped, clutching his face. "Please, don't leave me."

He froze, throbbing strongly, thickly, inside of her. Never had he felt such urgency before. How he wanted to explode, wet and hot, there inside of her tight canal. "No, Katherine," he gasped, "I cannot."

She tightened her muscles around him, and he saw from her expression that she was prepared to fight him to gain her way. Still holding his face, she cried, "I love you. I want your children. Liam, please!"

His body was rigid and unmoving as he held himself over her, except for the incessant pulsing of his penis. Liam was caught in the throes of agony. What man, flirting with the gallows as he did, would get his child upon such a noble woman? Sweat trickled down his cheeks.

"Liam, give me your children," Katherine cried. Tears streaming down her face. "Darling—I love you!"

Liam gasped then, covering her mouth with his—and instead of withdrawing from her, he plunged deep, not once, not twice, but many times, lost in pure ecstasy, and when his hot, potent seed finally spewed, shooting deep inside her womb, Katherine clung to him and wept in joy.

26

Richmond

*T*he queen's barge moved through the waters of the Thames, its gilt prow casting up a spray. Twenty-one oarsmen propelled it. It was a pleasant autumn afternoon and Elizabeth, clothed in gold, reclined upon her cushion, out of doors. The decks of the barge were strewn with flower petals, as was customary. Beside her were two of her ladies and several noblemen. One of the ladies was playing the lute.

Richmond Palace lay ahead. Its many towers, domes, and finials etched the skyline above a huge fruit orchard, past which the royal barge moved swiftly. Beyond the orchard the land was still lush and green, consisting of rolling meadows and timbered countryside.

Richmond Stairs lay ahead. Swans floated out of the barge's way as the boat was rowed to the dock. Elizabeth rose to her feet with the help of the gentlemen, thanking them most graciously as she alighted from the barge. Then, her pleasant expression changing, she hurried past the gardens and through the palace gate. Her ladies had to run now in order to keep up with her.

Elizabeth had not enjoyed herself this afternoon and she was grim of countenance. How could she? Earlier that day she had learned that Sir John Perrot was on his way to visit her. That bit of information had given her an instant aching of the head. The last thing she wished to discuss

was barbarian Ireland. She had so many other problems
now. Another plot to free her cousin Mary had been discovered, one which called for Elizabeth's assassination and
a Catholic rebellion supported by an invasion of the duke
of Alva from the Netherlands. Ultimately these plotters
intended to thrust Mary upon England's throne. The duke
of Norfolk was one of the ringleaders in the conspiracy,
but he was joined by the Pope and Philip of Spain. Just
last week Elizabeth had ordered the Spanish ambassador
out of the country. Norfolk was in the Tower. The Pope
she ignored.

And the plot against her was only the most recent, of
all her problems politic. Now she prayed that Perrot would
announce that he was about to deliver FitzMaurice's head
to her upon a silver plate, for the papist also intended to
overthrow her.

Elizabeth was sick inside, a sickness born of fear. No
one understood how difficult it was to be a queen. How
difficult, how demanding, and how dangerous.

Richmond was the largest of the royal palaces, and at
first glance the numerous buildings, courts, and gardens,
the many towers and onionlike domes, gave one the im-
pression of supreme disarray and confusion. Yet Elizabeth
did not waver from her course. She went directly to the
middle court and then into the hall on its western end.

Elizabeth swept through the hall. Courtiers dropped to
their knees as she passed. Upstairs, in her private apartments, she found the lord president of Munster awaiting
her impatiently. She ignored Cecil, now Lord Burghley,
and her cousin Tom, her gaze riveted upon Perrot's huge
form. The redheaded man dropped to his knees with surprising grace. "Your Majesty," he said. "As always, I
am your ever-loyal servant."

He was also her half brother, although it was never
openly acknowledged. "Sir John." Elizabeth waved him
up. "You bring Us good news, We hope."

John looked directly at her, unblinking. "Aye, for is it
not always good to learn who England's traitors are?"

Elizabeth was uneasy. She glanced at Cecil and Ormond. She noticed now that Cecil was as calm and com-

posed as ever, but her cousin was flushed with anger. "We know who the traitors in Ireland are, and We know their leader, that damnable lunatic, FitzMaurice. Are you going to capture him before the winter sets in and starves one and all?" It was exceedingly difficult to supply the British troops in the winter, and every year their numbers were decimated more by starvation and illness brought on by the wet and cold than by actual warfare.

"Oh, I shall capture him, I promise you that," Perrot said baldly. But he had made this promise many times before.

"We grow tired of this rebellion," Elizabeth snapped, losing her temper. "If you cannot catch this single man, perhaps We must put someone else after him."

Sir John turned red.

Cecil coughed and approached the queen. "I think you should hear Sir John's news. There is a good reason why we have not been able to touch him these many past months."

"Aye," John growled, still flushed. "He is being supported by a far more determined enemy than Philip."

"Anyone would be more determined than the Spanish king," Elizabeth snapped again. "He is beset with troubles everywhere, and his only interest in aiding the Irish is to wound me!"

"Prepare yourself, Elizabeth," Cecil murmured in her ear.

Elizabeth stiffened. "Who aids the papist traitor now? Who dares?"

Perrot smiled, as if relishing the moment. "The infamous half-Irish pirate, the Master of the Seas."

Elizabeth stared. And she did not understand.

She could not understand. She refused to understand. She forced a smile. "All that Liam has done, as annoying as it is, was to steal the FitzGerald girl and hie himself off to his island to indulge in debauchery and perversions with her. Perhaps that lends credence to the case Tom wishes to make, that Liam is allied with FitzGerald, that he seeks to marry Katherine, that he seeks to restore Fitz-Gerald. But that is the worst of it."

"Your Majesty," Perrot said coldly, "I have chased FitzMaurice up and down all of southern Ireland for almost an entire year. I know of what I speak. I care not that O'Neill has taken the FitzGerald girl as his mistress. I care not if she is even his wife. I know of what I speak. The bastard pirate supplies FitzMaurice with victuals and arms and everything else that he needs."

Elizabeth felt quite faint. She shot a glance at Tom, and saw that he believed Perrot. She turned to Cecil, who also was complacent. "No!" she cried, suddenly stabbed in her breast with a terrible, burning pain. "No, you are wrong! My golden pirate might support FitzGerald, but never, *never* would he support the man who has openly declared that he will dethrone me!" She was close to tears. For she knew Liam could not betray her in such a grievous manner, for he loved her a little—he did.

"I am not mistaken," Perrot almost shouted, red of countenance now. "I have a spy amongst the rebels, Your Majesty. He has seen them meet face-to-face, more than once. He has seen them shake hands. My God, he has seen the *Sea Dagger* being unloaded three times since last spring. *I know of what I speak.*"

Elizabeth turned away. Cecil guided her to a chair. Elizabeth was close to weeping. She reached out, but it was Ormond who knelt beside her, gripping her hand. "How can this be?" she whispered to her cousin. "How could he do this to me?"

Tom lifted her hand and kissed it firmly. "He has no soul," he told her. "He serves no master but himself, and you have erred, Bess, ever to think otherwise."

"But . . ." She covered her eyes with her hands, choked on a sob, then looked at Tom. "But he was fond of me. I am sure of it."

"No," Tom said forcefully, kissing her hand again. "I am fond of you, Bess, I have always been your greatest ally, and we are cousins. O'Neill is the spawn of Shane, and you must think on that, for it explains everything."

Elizabeth gripped Tom's hands, growing angry now. How could she have forgotten that the pirate was but the son of a savage barbarian and murderer? How could she have ever forgotten that first time she had met the father, when she was but a young girl and newly crowned? God! She had been betrayed, and soundly. As a woman and as a queen. She was a fool! She turned to Cecil.

"Why did you not know of this?" she cried, flushed. "Did I not give you all those thousands of pounds so that you might put your spies everywhere? Why did you not learn of this immediately, Lord Burghley?"

Cecil did not blink. "There were signs pointing to this alliance, Your Majesty, but I did not wish to alarm you unless it were true. And as it hardly makes sense, that O'Neill, Mary Stanley's son, would support a papist lunatic, I deemed it the first order to gain proof, and not present you with mere rumors instead."

Elizabeth stared. Cecil was right, as always. O'Neill might be a proven traitor now, but it made no sense. He was hardly godly, but he was staunchly Protestant. And if religion did not move him to support FitzMaurice, what else could?

"The man obviously was bought with gold," Ormond said. "We must bring FitzMaurice down, and we cannot do it unless we capture O'Neill first."

Elizabeth forced herself to think, no easy task when she was at once heartbroken and furiously angry. But she was queen. These fits could not be entertained. And Ormond was right. She reached for his hand again and squeezed it.

"Clearly," Elizabeth said, her voice shaking, "Liam O'Neill has not a loyal bone in his body, nor a loyal thought in his head."

Elizabeth shoved herself to her feet, welcoming the rage. "He is every bit a whoreson pirate, a bloody murderer, and loyal to no one but himself. He is a traitor to the Crown, a traitor to Us."

Perrot snorted in agreement. Neither Cecil nor Tom moved.

"I want his head," the queen said.

Perrot moved to stand before her. "Put a price on his head. Send Drake after him, or Frobisher. O'Neill is good, but Drake could bring him in."

Elizabeth swallowed, licked her lips, and could not re-

strain a shudder at the thought of setting her greatest sea-
man after Liam O'Neill. Who would win in such a fight?
Perhaps, in the ensuing battle, she would lose everyone.
The thought was distressing.

Elizabeth closed her eyes. It did not matter. She had to
capture her golden pirate, capture him and try him for
treason. And then . . . he would hang, a fate he more
than deserved.

Elizabeth cleared her throat. "You are right, Sir John.
Fifty thousand pounds will be the reward I give to anyone
who brings me Liam O'Neill."

Cecil's eyes widened. "Our budget is already strained,
Your Majesty," he murmured in warning.

"I do not care," she cried. She would worry about the
damned treasury another time. "I want his head!" Then
she imagined his golden head impaled on an iron pike.
Her stomach grew queasy. "I want him alive," she stated
harshly. For the woman who lived and breathed and
dreamed inside the queen must confront him privately,
make him explain his actions—for surely there would be
some explanation for these new foul deeds.

And then a new thought occurred to her. Elizabeth
froze. She wanted his head—but so did another man, a
man whose motivation would be far greater than greed. A
man whose motivation was revenge, a man who even now
harbored a deep and dark and personal fury against Liam
O'Neill. Surely such a man could bring her the Master of
the Seas.

"Send me John Hawke!" she cried.

Juliet pulled up her filly. The horse was but three years
old, hardly broken, and she danced about, yet Juliet sat
her as she might a rocking chair. She had been riding
upon the moors since she was a small child, and it was
second nature to her.

She had halted her mount upon a rise and below her
lay Hawkehurst. The stone manor had been built some
centuries earlier, and although some might have called it
run-down and dilapidated, Juliet thought it charming, far
more so than her own home, which was so gaudy with its

towers and turrets and stained glass windows. She swallowed. She told herself that, being Katherine's friend, there was nothing wrong with her going to the manor to visit John Hawke. She had just learned from Thurlstone's steward that he had arrived at his home yesterday afternoon.

Yet deep inside herself, she was aware that she lied to herself, that it was wrong to visit him—wrong and dangerous.

Juliet forced her thoughts away. Hawke was her best friend's husband. The last time she had seen him he had been consumed with rage over Katherine's abduction. Juliet wondered what his mood would be this time. Did he grieve? Had he heard from her in all this time? Over the months, Juliet had thought frequently about Katherine and Hawke.

Juliet urged the frisky chestnut filly down the slope. The young mare broke into a canter. Juliet became increasingly anxious as she approached Hawkehurst's stone entryway. She should turn around, go away, pretend she had never met him, pretend she did not even know of his existence. The filly clattered onto cobbled stone, through the tunneled entrance, and into the circular courtyard.

Juliet pulled the mare to a prancing halt. She made no effort to dismount. Her pulse was thundering now. She should not have come. She should gallop home. No one had espied her yet. She could still leave. The filly continued to dance, moving in small circles now, pirouetting as if highly trained. And the weathered and heavy front door of the manor opened, Hawke appearing on the threshold there.

Juliet's gaze went to his immediately. Dear God, she had forgotten how dark he was, how imposing. She had forgotten that he frightened her somewhat.

And she had forgotten just how handsome he was, as well.

He did not smile. He moved forward quickly, clad not in his crimson uniform, but in a plain tunic and a worn leather jerkin, in equally worn breeches and riding boots. He gripped the filly's bridle, instantly restraining her. His gaze caught hers again.

Juliet felt herself coloring. She reminded herself that he did not know—could not know—anything about her. He could not know her most secret thoughts. He could not know about the shameful dreams that came to her at night.

Nor could he know how carefully she had dressed for this occasion. Juliet had rejected one gown after another that morning, finally choosing a particularly lavish and beautiful taffeta, one whose dark green color enhanced her own ivory coloring and striking dark hair. The gown was richly trimmed with fur, with a matching cloak. John Hawke did not seem to notice how the fashion suited her. His blue gaze remained solely upon her face.

"Good day, Lady Stratheclyde. This is a surprise." He spoke curtly.

Juliet swallowed nervously. She should not have come. Not after all those terrible dreams, in which John Hawke, her best friend's husband, kissed her in the most shocking manner. Juliet could feel how high her color was. "I had heard you were in residence," she managed, but her tone was barely audible and she cleared her throat.

Hawke stared at her.

Juliet licked her lips. "I h-hope you do not mind that I have come to call," she managed.

His jaw was clenched. He did not appear pleased. His next words confirmed it. "In fact, I have great matters to attend to."

She froze. He had just made it clear that he had no interest in speaking with her. Juliet was hurt to the quick. So he would not see the tears that welled in her eyes, she looked down, fumbling with her reins. If only she hadn't come.

He muttered something to himself, and then his strong hands were on her waist and he was lifting her abruptly from her mount. Juliet could not breathe, paralyzed by his touch.

When he set her on the ground, she backed up against the mare, staring up at him mutely. Her pulse was rioting.

"Lady Stratheclyde?"

Realization was striking her with a full and brutal force. She had not come to Hawkehurst to ask after Katherine.

She had come to see John. She had come because she secretly, sinfully, coveted this man, her best friend's husband—in spite of the fact that she was betrothed now to Lord Simon Hunt.

She took a deep breath. She knew she must remount and go home. Before her real feelings became apparent to him, before she betrayed her dear and best friend in some small but genuine way, before she betrayed her own fiancé. "I . . . do not feel well. I am unaccustomed to riding," she lied. "I feel somewhat like swooning."

He eyed her. "Really? I have never seen a woman sit a mare as well as you. And this one's half-wild still."

She felt absurdly pleased with his praise. Then she started, because Hawke had gripped her arm.

"Come inside. Perhaps a glass of ale will fortify you."

Juliet could not think of how to refuse, and she followed him into the hall and allowed him to seat her at the table. He did not sit beside her. He ordered refreshments, then proceeded to stare at her. He made no attempt to converse.

Juliet took a deep breath. "Sir John, I have come to see you because Katherine is my best friend and I had hoped you had some word from her."

Hawke's expression grew more grim. "No."

"No word at all?" Juliet was amazed. "But surely, by now, O'Neill would allow her some communication with you!"

"No. There has been none."

Juliet was rooted to the spot. Dismay filled her. John stared past her, out the window at the moors, gray and purple now with the impending winter. She gazed at him, trying to discern what his emotions were. She felt his anger—he was still angry over Katherine's abduction—but she could not detect any grief.

Juliet gripped her gloved hands tightly in her lap. "I am sure that she is fine. I am sure he would not harm her."

Hawke turned back to her. "Yes, undoubtedly there has been no rape, and if he was displeased with her, he would have freed her long ago."

Juliet gasped when she realized what he implied. That

Liam had won Katherine by wooing her, and that she was pleasing him even now. Her cheeks burned.

Juliet did not know what to say to comfort John. Yet she wanted to comfort him. The urge overwhelmed her. Juliet stood up, moved to his side, and lightly touched his hand, gripping his fingers for an instant. Hawke's vivid blue gaze pierced hers. For another heartbeat, Juliet was at a loss, unable to look away, unable to speak.

"Katherine did not wish to be abducted, Sir John," she finally said. "She wished only to marry you. She told me so." That was the truth. Yet Juliet recalled seeing the doubt in her friend's eyes at the time. She would never tell John of it.

John regarded her without expression.

"If you hear from her," Juliet finally said, growing uneasy beneath his stare, "will you let me know?"

Hawke nodded.

Juliet realized that now she had no further excuse to linger. Yet she was loath to leave. She could not help wondering when she would ever see him again. "When are you returning to court?" she asked.

"Tonight."

She hid her dismay. But . . . she had hoped he might remain in Cornwall for a few days. Even though she knew that his immediate departure was best. For everyone.

Hawke's next words stunned her. "I have been commissioned to go after O'Neill by the queen herself. My men and ships are almost ready to depart. I plan to set sail within a week."

Juliet gasped. She had not heard of this new turn of events. John was going after Liam—and fear filled her. "What do you do?" she half cried, half whispered.

His gaze was direct. "The queen wants his head."

Juliet was more than frightened, she was terrified. "Sir John . . . he is a dangerous man! Please, take care . . . I wish you Godspeed."

He stared at her, his eyes widening.

Abruptly Juliet turned away, afraid that he had detected her concern for him, a concern she had no right to feel. She hurried to the door.

His large hands suddenly gripped her arm from behind, halting her. Juliet tensed, half turning. His blue eyes were like twin fires.

"Thank you, Lady Stratheclyde, for your prayers," he said.

She flushed with pleasure, her heart pounding so hard and so fast it felt as if it might burst.

"And if you wait but a moment, I will escort you back to Thurlstone."

She would have his company a little bit longer. Her pleasure knew no bounds. And then she thought about his impending departure, about why and where he would go, and all pleasure disappeared. Dear God, she was so afraid, afraid that Hawke would be killed when he finally cornered Liam O'Neill.

And she realized then that her heart would be broken should he die. Somehow, she coveted more than his kisses. Somehow, she had fallen in love with her best friend's husband—on the threshold of her own marriage to Lord Hunt.

27

Dingle Bay, Ireland

*T*he *Sea Dagger* bobbed at anchor while supplies far more precious than powder were unloaded rapidly into small rowboats and rowed to shore, where FitzMaurice's men awaited. Liam stood on the beach, having disembarked with the initial boatload of victuals, which would see the Irish rebels through the first months of the winter. And winter would soon descend upon Ireland. It was a cold, bluff day. Liam's breath formed puffs of vapor in the air, and he wore a heavy woolen cloak.

Hugh Barry stood beside him, both men watching momentarily as the *Sea Dagger* was unloaded under the supervision of Liam's first mate. "This will sustain us through the first half of the winter," Barry said.

"I am aware of that," Liam replied. "In January we will rendezvous again, but not here." He had already used Dingle Bay twice, and would not risk using it yet again. "There is a small estuary just south of Galway. Do you know it?"

Barry nodded.

Liam studied him a moment. The young man had aged considerably in the last year. There were lines in his face where before there had been none. And he had lost weight. He had not been a big man in any case, but now he was reed-thin. Liam had long since stopped hating Hugh Barry.

The rebel cause was almost hopeless, and Liam felt sorry for him.

"How is Katie?" Barry asked, surprising him.

Liam was careful not to smile, and not to allow the light to shine in his eyes, a light her mere name evoked. "She is well."

"Does she stay with you of her own will, O'Neill? Or is she still your prisoner?"

Liam contained a smile. "She stays of her own free will, Barry." He said no more, purposefully withholding the news of their marriage. If he were ever caught, it would be better for Katherine if the whole world did not know that she was more than willing—that she was also his wife. He understood the scandal—and repercussions—such a disclosure would cause. "You said FitzMaurice wished to meet with me. Where in hell is he?"

"I do not know," Barry answered, glancing up at the wooded hills behind them. "I was wondering that myself."

Liam was already somewhat uneasy, as he had been since he'd arrived at Dingle Bay earlier that day. Although his mission was not without danger, he had been on adventures far more dangerous, without feeling such a prickling sense of anxiety. Liam did not like the fact that FitzMaurice was late for a meeting arranged several months before. Liam tensed, wondering what had befallen FitzMaurice. "FitzMaurice will not come," he stated suddenly. Knowing as he spoke that it was true. And his hand closed upon the hilt of his rapier.

"What? How can you know that?"

Liam did not answer. Trouble was in the making, he was now certain of it. His gaze scanned the wooded and rocky hills. Seeing nothing, he turned nevertheless, barking orders to his men. He wanted the ship unloaded in record time, and even as they unloaded, he ordered her prepared to put to sea. "I will meet with FitzMaurice another time," he told Barry, silently thinking, *if FitzMaurice is still alive and free to attend such a meeting.* He was acutely aware of danger now. Already he was striding toward the roiling surf, intent on reboarding the *Sea Dagger.*

Barry strode beside him. "In two months," he said.

Liam nodded as someone screamed.

That scream was accompanied by a musket shot.

Liam whirled, rapier drawn, as British troops burst from the woods, running and tripping down the hillside, armed with both muskets and rapiers. "To the ship," Liam shouted to his men.

More firing sounded, some of the rebels fell. Others drew their swords and spears and charged the British soldiers. Liam winced as he saw cavalry, poorly mounted but on horseback nonetheless, charging down the slope on the heels of the infantry. The Irish rebels were clad in furs, not armor, and armed with knives and daggers, heavy swords and nearly useless spears. They would be slaughtered by the mounted troops. As he ran toward one of the rowboats, Liam wondered who had betrayed them.

Barry had drawn his own sword and was running to join his men and meet the attacking soldiers. Liam heard him cry out. He whirled to see Barry falling, blood blossoming high up in his chest, hit with a musket ball.

A savage fight was ensuing. The Irish valiantly tried to defend themselves against the soldiers, but their weapons were no match for those of the British, who chopped them down with razor-sharp, lightweight rapiers, or shot them in the back with their muskets. It was a massacre and within minutes it would be over. Liam ran back toward the melee.

Hugh was trying to get up, but could not rise above his knees. Liam jerked him to his feet, then saw the rider galloping toward them. He dropped Barry, whirled, his rapier ready, legs braced. The soldier had holstered his musket and now raised his rapier. Liam parried his blow but once, yet so powerfully that the rider was toppled from his horse. Liam darted forward, kicked him back to the ground as he tried to rise. An instant later he had skewered him in the heart.

Liam turned and found Barry staggering, just barely standing, trying to draw his own sword. Liam knocked the weapon from his hand and threw the smaller man over his shoulder. He ran into the surf. His men had already leapt into the rowboats and were shouting to him in encouragement. Liam plunged through the waves, the water lapping his knees, swirling about his thighs. He reached the closest boat and tossed Barry inside it, leaping in himself. Two men helped haul him over the side. Swiftly two others began to row the small boat away. A musket ball whistled past Liam's head. Everyone ducked.

Liam sat up, looking back at the beach. The battle was already over, most of the rebels lay dead or dying, but a few were escaping up the hill, into the forest. The British soldiers milled about, killing the rebels who still lived. Liam's eyes widened. A huge man had ridden slowly forward on a small horse, one which appeared pathetically abused by the man's vast weight, and now stood fetlock-deep in the water. He wore no helmet and his red hair gleamed. He stared directly at Liam. It could be none other than Sir John Perrot.

Even from this distance, he saw the man's rage. Perrot lifted one hand, shook his fist at the escaping rowboat. Liam's jaw set. And he stared back, knowing he had just escaped with his life—by an act of God, or of Fate.

Katherine was in the kitchens when Guy came running in. Her hands were sticky with syrup, for she had been candying sweetmeats alongside two kitchen maids. This past week had been a frenzy of activity, distilling cordials, drying fruits, and making jams. Katherine did not have to hear what Guy was saying so exuberantly to know that the *Sea Dagger* had come home. To know that Liam had come home.

She washed and dried her hands quickly, her pulse pounding in excitement—until she realized that Guy was telling her that the *Sea Dagger* had already berthed, and that there were wounded men amongst the returning sailors. Katherine cried out. "How do you know?" She could imagine Liam upon a pallet, pale and lifeless.

"I was there when the ship arrived," Guy said in a rush. " 'Tis not the captain, he is fine, but he is bringing a wounded man up to the house. He says you must get your medicines out and prepare a bed."

Katherine was briefly stricken with relief, but in the next instant she had turned to the two serving girls, ordering them to bring her medicinal basket, soap and water, and plenty of clean linen for bandages. She flew from the room.

Katherine ran upstairs, entering the unused bedchamber. She threw open the hides to let in the sharp winter air. Contrary to what physicians recommended, she believed fresh air to be healthy and invigorating.

She uncovered the bed. A servant appeared behind her. "Let me do that, my lady," he said.

"Make a fire, Ned," she ordered, then raced from the room.

As she stumbled down the stairs she heard Liam's richly timbred voice. Her gaze flew to him, clinging—inspecting every inch of him.

A servant had taken his cloak. His shirt was blood-stained, as were his breeches, but she saw no sign of any wound upon him. "Are you well, Liam?" she cried, rushing into his arms.

He smiled at her gently. "I like this greeting, this hot concern," he murmured. "Yes, Kate, I am well. But your old friend is not."

Katherine did not understand. She turned, finally seeing the man who lay upon a pallet stretched on two wood poles, an unconscious man sweating with fever. Her eyes widened when she recognized Hugh. "Good God!" She ran to him and knelt at his side, touched his forehead. How terribly hot he was. Then Katherine saw the wound. It was festering, and it needed to be taken care of immediately. Hugh opened his eyes, but only stared at her blankly.

Katherine nodded. "Take him upstairs." The two sailors instantly obeyed. She turned to Liam's steward, who hovered behind her. "Bring me vinegar, brandy, and moldy bread."

"Moldy bread? We have no—"

"Get me moldy bread this instant," Katherine cried. Lifting up her skirts, she hurried up the stairs, determined to save the life of the man she had once loved and intended to marry.

*   *   *

"I thought it was you," Hugh whispered several days later.

Katherine had just entered the room. She smiled, pleased to see him awake and without fever, but she had known for some time now that he would live. "Barry men are hard to kill off, it seems."

Hugh watched her. "At first, when I was out of my head with fever, I thought you an angel."

Katherine laughed, thinking of how wicked she had been last night. "I am hardly an angel."

Hugh looked only at her face. "You could be an angel, Katie. That is how beautiful you are."

She stared at him, no longer smiling.

"You have changed even more than when I last saw you," he said with a sigh, falling back on the pillows. "And I, I am still as weak as a newborn kitten."

"That is correct," Katherine said. "But you are mending well, and in a few more days you will be able to get up and out of your bed."

"How can I thank you?" Hugh asked. "For saving my life?"

Katherine did not hesitate. "I treated you as I would have treated anyone. You do not need to thank me."

Hugh stared at her searchingly. "Perhaps I will find a way."

Katherine shrugged. Then she started, for Liam stood in the doorway. She smiled at him, going to him immediately. He put his arm around her. "You never cease to amaze me," he said.

"While you stay with me upon my island, I ask but one thing of you," Liam said quietly. He and Barry were alone in the hall.

"You can ask anything," Barry said. "Because I owe you and Katie my freedom and my life."

Liam sat in a chair in front of the fire, as did Barry. They both sipped Irish whiskey. "Katherine does not know about my involvement with FitzMaurice, and I prefer that she remain in ignorance."

Barry started. "Has she not asked how I came to be upon your ship, and wounded at that?"

Liam stared unsmiling into his glass. "Aye, she has. I lied. I told her I brought *you* winter supplies, and that we were attacked by bandits."

"And she believed you?"

"Yes, she believed me," Liam said harshly. " 'Tis better that I lie to her. She would not understand the truth."

"Considering that FitzMaurice wishes to usurp what once belonged to her father, why, I would not blame her for feeling betrayed," Barry agreed.

Katherine stood frozen upon the threshold of the hall. She had heard their every damning word. In her hands was a trencher containing fresh meat pies. The trencher dropped from her hands. The pies splattered upon the floor; the trencher clattered and rolled away.

Liam was involved with FitzMaurice? No—it could not be!

Both men jumped; Liam turned and paled when he saw her standing there.

Katherine stared at his beautiful face, in absolute shock, absolute disbelief. "Tell me it is not true," she whispered hoarsely. "Liam?"

"I do not think you have heard me correctly, Kate," he said softly, and then he reached and touched her face.

She shrugged him off. "I heard you tell Hugh that you are lying to me. That you are involved with my father's worst enemy! How are you involved with FitzMaurice?"

Liam swallowed. "Dearheart, this is not as it seems."

She batted his hands away again, in disbelief, with rising fury—and with real panic. "No! Tell me now, tell me the truth, tell me I have misunderstood what I have heard—before I go down to the village and ask every single sailor who has sailed with you about your long, secret voyages!"

"You have misunderstood," he insisted.

Katherine saw the anguish in his eyes, and the fear, and her own heart was torn in two. She faced Barry. "Hugh?"

Barry's eyes widened.

"What is he doing, Hugh?" When he did not answer,

paler now himself, she shouted, "You owe me your life, answer me, Hugh!"

Barry got to his feet slowly. "I also owe Liam my life, Katie."

Katherine faced her husband, her fists clenched. Her heart hurt her now. Disbelief was giving way to pure, cloying fear. "How have I misunderstood you, Liam? How?"

" 'Tis but a ploy," he said, "my support of FitzMaurice."

Katherine stared at him. Her breast heaved. In that instant her entire world collapsed. His words were a crucifying admission of guilt. "So you do not deny it. You do not deny you are aiding my father's worst enemy?"

Liam flinched. "Katherine—I am aiding him, but 'tis hardly what you think. I have your father's interests at heart."

He was aiding FitzMaurice. "My father's interests?" she whispered, tears forming now in her eyes. *Oh, God, how could this be? How could Liam betray her like this? He was her husband!*

Liam began to speak now, in a low, soothing tone, but Katherine turned her back to him, covering her face with her hands, shaking. She did not hear a word he said. Liam, whom she loved, was aiding FitzMaurice. When only a few months ago she had asked him to aid her father. He had lied, telling her that he did help Gerald—he had told her to trust him. And she had.

Liam could not possibly love her.

Oh, God.

Barry moved past her and out of the room, leaving them alone, but Katherine was not even aware of him.

"Katherine," Liam whispered, gripping her shoulders from behind. "I am trying to explain this game to you. You must listen to me very carefully."

Violently Katherine shook him off, whirling to face him, her face contorted in rage—and hatred. "No! There is nothing to explain—bastard! Liar! Cheat!" And she began to beat him with her fists.

Liam did not move. He stood still and silent as she

began to sob and pound on his chest, weeping for the loss of a love that she had never had, that had never existed, and for a treachery too painful to bear. Because she wept uncontrollably now, she did not see the tears welling in his own eyes.

"I have been trying to explain to you why I have been supplying FitzMaurice this past year," he said flatly. "But you refuse to listen, refuse to trust me; you have not heard a single word I said."

Katherine stared at him, shocked again, flooded with new anguish. He had been supplying the papist lunatic for an entire year? That meant that he had allied himself with her father's cousin sometime shortly after he had first met her! "No." She held up her hands as if she could ward him off. She had never hated anyone the way she hated him. "Don't touch me!"

"You have no choice but to listen," Liam said, with a flash of anger, dropping his hands.

"I will never listen to you again," she cried, and in that instant, she wished to hurt him as he had hurt her. But she could not. Because she had loved him—but he did not love her.

"I have a plan, Katherine," Liam began, his expression so earnest, so deadly sincere, that Katherine backed away from him.

"No!" she screamed. How she wished she had not burned her father's letter. How she wished she could now shove it in his face.

"Katherine, my plan was dangerous, and not without flaw, and the very first step was to build FitzMaurice up," Liam told her, never taking his eyes from her face.

"No!" Katherine shouted again. A tiny voice inside her head—and her heart—warned his not to do this, to listen to him, but Katherine ignored it. "Let me tell you about my plan!"

His jaw tightened. "You are overwrought, which I understand." He turned from her, moving to the sideboard, pouring a glass of whiskey.

"You don't understand me—you could not possibly,' Katherine cried, having followed him.

He faced her, holding out the glass. "Drink this."

Katherine struck the glass from his hand. It shattered on the floor, whiskey spilling everywhere. They stared at one another.

"I do not want to hurt you," Liam said. "I have never wanted to hurt you."

"You cannot hurt me," Katherine said, her words so obviously incongruous, for her face was streaked with tears. "We are two of a kind, you see." She laughed bitterly. "Both adept at playing games, both adept at theatrics—both adept at using one another for purely selfish purposes."

Liam stared, his body tense. Katherine stared back defiantly, growing dizzy with the flood tide of pain washing over her. Liam finally said, "You are too honest to play the kind of game you speak of."

"Oh?" She laughed, hysterically. "Don't you wish to know of what I speak—darling?"

"I don't think so." His gray gaze had gone flat and watchful.

"Do you remember the letter my father sent me in July? The letter you brought to me?" Katherine asked harshly.

Liam nodded slowly.

"I burned it," she said. "Do you know why?"

"No. I don't want to know why, either." But he did not turn away from her, he was riveted in place. His eyes held hers.

And the room was so silent that Katherine's uneven breathing could be heard. "I burned it so you would never find it, never read it—never learn its contents."

Liam stared into her hostile eyes. "But now you are going to tell me what was in the letter, are you not?"

"Yes!" she cried, and one of her fists landed on his chest. Liam did not appear to notice the blow. "Yes, damn you, yes! Long ago, before I was even wed to Hawke, my father asked *me* to use *you*. To lead you a merry chase right to my bed—and right to the altar! He wished for me to enslave you with my body. He wished for me to play the temptress. He wished for me to entice you into marriage. Have you heard me, Liam?"

Liam's expression was one of growing comprehension—and growing horror.

Katherine half cried and half laughed. "And I did as he asked. It was a game, Liam, naught but a game, and every moan and sigh was pure pretense, intended to madden you with lust, to chain you to my side. I pretended that all I ever thought of was you and our lovemaking, I pretended that I could not live without you or your touch, and I pretended that I loved you!" Katherine realized that she was weeping again. "In return, you were supposed to aid my father—not FitzMaurice!"

"If it was but a game for you—then why are you crying?" he asked hoarsely.

"Because I have lost! Oh, God, I have lost everything, giving myself to you as I have! And you—God damn you to hell—you have played me false, aiding the papist traitor."

Liam stared at her as if she were a stranger—or a monster.

Katherine's smile, tear-streaked, was savage. "I was a fool, to think I could best you. But you are a fool, too. To believe that I could ever really love the son of Shane O'Neill."

Liam inhaled sharply.

Katherine turned away. But his cold, clipped words stopped her in her tracks.

"You are a bitch, Katherine."

She whirled.

Rage suffused his features. "A cold, deceitful bitch."

Her eyes widened.

"Hawke can have you." He turned his back on her and walked to the door.

"Go!" Katherine screamed after him, sobbing again. "Go! Go far away and never come back! I hope you and your damned ship are sunk to the very bottom of the sea! Do you hear me, Liam? Do you?"

But he did not answer her, disappearing into the corridor. And the next day, the *Sea Dagger* set sail.

Only this time, it did not come back.

III

THE TOWER

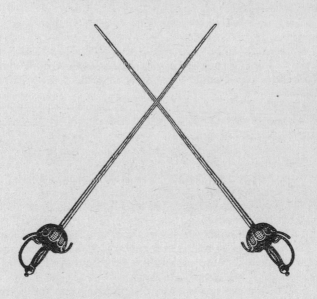

28

January, 1572—Richmond

*R*ichmond was the warmest of Elizabeth's many palaces.
It was her custom to spend most of the winter months
there. Now a fire roared in the hearth of the Privy Chamber. But through the windows, which looked east over the
Privy Gardens and the orchard, Elizabeth could see how
the leafless trees bent over backward in the constant wind.
The sky was dark and threatening overhead, and sometime
soon a storm would sweep down upon them. Rolling thunder could be heard in the distance.

Elizabeth had just sent her ladies from the chamber and
she was alone. She had received an urgent message from
Ormond, who was on his way to meet with her. Tom usually
had Ireland first and foremost on his mind, and she was
expecting the worst.

Elizabeth paced, her nerves frayed. Just yesterday she
had recognized Mary's brat James as the king of Scotland.
'Twas an action she had been resolved never to take; but
circumstance had forced her, finally, to this extreme. The
plots against her, favoring Mary, never ceased, nor did the
interference of foreigners, and the time had come to abandon one rightful monarch in favor of another. Elizabeth
felt the creeping fingers of fear around her throat, almost
choking her. Every time a monarch fell, she could imagine
herself in the same position. She had no wish to lose her
throne—and her head—at an early age—or even at an

elderly one. How tenuous life could be if one were a king or queen.

Ormond burst into the room. "He's gone mad!"

Elizabeth tensed. "Of whom do you speak? FitzMaurice?" A chill had taken her now. Perrot had driven FitzMaurice into the west, where he was now in hiding. Would the papist fanatic never be taken? Damn Liam O'Neill for supplying him so well that he would survive another winter!

"No, not the papist. I speak of your pretty pirate, Liam O'Neill!"

Elizabeth stiffened. "Now what has Liam done?"

"He has attacked another vessel, this one Spanish, but bound for the Netherlands, not Ireland. That is the second vessel he has seized in as many weeks. And in but a month, he has attacked four different ships, including one bound for the King's Lords in Edinburgh. He has truly gone mad like some slobbering, bug-eyed dog!"

Elizabeth wondered if it were true. In the past, Liam had been discriminating. No more. He was striking out blindly, it seemed, at each and every passing vessel that crossed his path. And to attack Spain, the very nation which had paid him in gold bullion and silver plate to supply FitzMaurice? It made no sense at all.

"Liam must in insane," Elizabeth said tersely. "In the past there was reason behind his actions at sea, no more. What do you think, Tom?"

Butler smiled without mirth. "I think he is a man with no master, a man without a country or a king. I think you should raise the price on his head—and pray that Hawke succeeds in capturing him."

"Can we not play tables, Katherine?" Guy asked.

Katherine stood staring out of the narrow window in the hall. She stared at the wind-whipped snow as it fell ceaselessly upon the island, hugging her mantle to her. The wind moaned incessantly. She hardly heard the small boy who stood beside her, and did not look down to see his face, pinched with anxiety and worry.

Katherine stared at the snow until her vision blurred.

Somewhere, out there in the winter storm, sailing the winter-wild northern seas, was the damned traitor, Liam O'Neill. She hugged herself harder, unable to swallow the lump of anguish in her throat.

She still did not understand. Katherine could not fathom how Liam could have laughed with her, wooed her, and loved her so insatiably for over nine months, while secretly dealing with FitzMaurice all that time. How very little he had cared for her, if he had cared for her at all.

He had been gone almost two months now. There had not been any word. Katherine was adamant with herself. She did not care where he was, or what he did. She did not care if his fate had been as she had prayed it would be—to sink with his ship to the very bottom of the sea.

Guy tugged on her hand. "If you do not want to play tables, do you wish to read to me instead, Katherine?" The boy looked worried.

Katherine forced a smile, bent and kissed his head. "Of course."

"I think, Guy, you can read with Katherine later."

Katherine turned to face Macgregor. The big Scot moved so soundlessly for a man of his size. She had not heard him approach. When Liam had sailed away, he had left Macgregor behind. To guard her if she tried to leave the island? Katherine almost laughed at the idea. Where would she go? To her father? To John Hawke? To the queen?

"Lady, I wish to speak with you privily."

Katherine's cheeks began to flush. Does he know? She thought wildly. No, she decided, she had been so very careful, he could not know. The only one who knew was her maid, and Katherine had sworn her to secrecy long ago. Katherine turned to Guy. "I will be with you in a few minutes. Why don't you meet me here a little later?"

Guy nodded, looking relieved, and he darted off. Katherine turned her back on Macgregor, facing the wind-driven snow. Would the wind never stop? She wondered. It howled constantly, sounding very much like a pack of lost and lonely wolves. How could anyone live on this island in the wintertime? And not go mad? Her grip upon her sanity felt so tenuous. Katherine stared at the swirling snow. She could not help wondering what it must be like to be at sea right then, upon the pirate ship.

Cold and lonely and dangerous.

"He is never gone at this time of year," Macgregor said from behind her.

Katherine tensed. "I do not care."

"You do not care if he has been captured? Or run aground? Or worse, run upon rocks by the winter storms and sunk to the very bottom of the sea?"

Katherine hugged herself. "Undoubtedly such is his fate, as he is but a bloodthirsty pirate."

"Does he know?" the Scot asked.

Katherine inhaled. The sound was loud and sharp; Macgregor must have heard it, too. She still did not turn from the window. "I beg your pardon?"

"Does he know that you carry his child?"

Katherine could not breathe. She felt light-headed and faint. Such a feeling was not new to her. There had been moments these past few weeks when she had become short of breath and dizzy. She had no experience in these matters, but she guessed it was because of the life growing inside of her womb. She did not answer Macgregor.

"Lady Katherine, I have known many women in my many years, and although you wear that cape as you would a shield, I have seen how your belly is expanding. And there are other signs as well. Please, let us talk frankly."

Katherine whirled, angry and frightened, hugging herself, tears trickling from her eyes. "This is my baby," she said fiercely. "Not his!"

Macgregor was gentle. "Does he know?"

"He has no rights," she shouted, flooded with hot anger, recalling his terrible betrayal. "None!"

"You refuse to answer me. But I do not think, no matter how angry and hurt he was, that he would leave you like this if he did know. When is the babe due?"

Katherine stared at him mutinously. "Liam, hurt? A man must have a heart in order to be hurt, and he has none!" Then she started to weep, but softly.

"Liam has a heart and if you do not know that, then you are not the woman for him," Macgregor said quietly.

"I am not the woman for him!" She glared at him. "I hope he is dead."

Macgregor held her gaze, and she was startled by the sadness in his eyes. "When, Katherine?"

Katherine took a calming gulp of air. "In July, I think. I am probably four months along, maybe more."

"There is a midwife in the village. I want her to examine you."

And suddenly Katherine was relieved, so very relieved, that her secret had been discovered. She had been afraid. Being pregnant and alone, having no one to ask the many questions she had, with no one to turn to, and no one to trust. "Yes." She nodded, the color returning to her pale cheeks. "The sooner the better, I think."

South of Galway, Ireland

Liam stared at the timbered coast of the inlet. Every instinct he had told him not to go ashore. These past two months at sea he had learned that he was a hunted man. Three times British ships had espied the *Sea Dagger* and had made chase. Three times Liam had successfully outsailed, outmaneuvered, and outraced his pursuers, engaging only in the shortest exchange of cannon fire.

He was a hunted man now, wanted for treason against the Crown. As he had, indeed, committed treason, he was not surprised. He had known that the game could boil down to this. He had been prepared to live the life of the hunted for a while. He had been prepared to live that way, and to successfully defy all pursuit.

Now he no longer cared.

Indeed, he welcomed anyone who dared to hunt him.

His instincts warned him strongly not to go ashore, but Liam climbed into the longboat and ordered the oarsmen to proceed. He itched to do battle. With any foe, imaginary or real.

His jaw tightened. Katherine's image invaded his mind.

He no longer cared that he had not explained his master plan to her; in fact, he was glad he had not explained how he had intended ultimately to aid her father in regaining Desmond. Damn her. The bitch. The treacherous bitch— his treacherous wife. Using him all along, feigning her love.

He stood in the prow, surveying the approaching shore-line. There was no sign of the Irish rebels, no sign of FitzMaurice, but his pulse was pounding now with excite-ment. He could feel the danger. He could feel the im-pending attack. How he welcomed it.

"Ready yourselves," he murmured to his five men. "We are not alone." He had seen the flash of metal in the trees.

The several longboats, containing a dozen men, all beached. His men leapt out. Everyone was silent and tense. Liam's hand moved to his sword. And when he saw the riders and soldiers bursting from the trees, he threw back his head and laughed.

In that single instant, it occurred to him that he had a death wish—but he would go down fighting to the very end.

As the mounted troops descended the slope, infantry behind them, Liam realized that he and his men faced no small force but some hundred attackers. As rapidly as it had come, his death wish vanished. He owed it to his men to live so he could lead them to safety. He could not allow this massacre, no matter how he wished to do battle himself.

"Put down your weapons," he snapped, sheathing his rapier. "Put your empty hands into the air."

Everyone obeyed. The troops thundered down upon them. Horses blowing, ears laid back, the soldiers with their rapiers drawn and held high. At the last moment, the cavalry skidded to a halt, surrounding them on all sides and cutting off any escape they might make to the sea by the boats. Liam's eyes widened when he saw John Hawke seated in the very forefront upon a black charger. Hawke smiled slowly at him.

Liam's surprise vanished. Silently he saluted Bess. For

setting against him the one man who most wanted him. His hand crept to the hilt of his weapon again.

Hawke moved his mount forward to face him. "Do you surrender without a fight, O'Neill?"

"Do you wish me to fight?" Liam asked calmly. In his mind he saw Katherine standing lush and nearly naked in the master's chamber of Barby Hall, awaiting Hawke on their wedding night. He wondered if Hawke had divorced her. He told himself he did not care. Hawke could have her now, if he still wanted her.

"You know that I do." Hawke said softly, his gaze locked with Liam's.

Liam no longer had any interest in death, but here, at last, was a real enemy with which to battle. He smiled back, menacingly. "Come, Hawke. Come."

Hawke slid from his horse.

Liam taunted, "Surely you wish to avenge Katherine? Surely you wish to kill me for the many endless nights she spent so eagerly in my bed?"

Hawke stiffened, his face paling. Then he ripped his rapier from its hilt. "Bastard. I will deliver your head on a pike, make no mistake about that!"

Liam also drew his rapier, laughing with real pleasure. The two men thrust and parried. Only the first blows came slowly. Swords crossed, Liam and Hawke strained at one another the way two stags might lock horns. As one, they broke and fell back.

Immediately their weapons rose and clashed again. Both men locked blades and withdrew. Neither Hawke nor Liam was able to take up the offensive, for they moved at one another simultaneously. Again their rapiers crossed. Both men were panting now, their expressions murderous.

Liam feinted, lunged, and thrust. Finally he suceeded in getting past Hawke's quick defenses, and he nicked a gash on Hawke's cheek. A line of red appeared there.

Hawke snarled and wielded another blow, which Liam blocked. They danced around one another, their blades striking back and forth. Suddenly Hawke's blade sliced open Liam's tunic, leaving a fine razor-thin gash down the center of his torso.

The two men withdrew, sweating and breathing harshly. But only for a heartbeat. As two mighty rams might charge at once, so too they lunged and thrust again, with even fiercer determination. Their rapiers rang, the fine steel blades vibrating. Steel screeched as the weapons were disengaged. Liam thrust again, almost blinded by sweat. And this time his blade was quicker than Hawke's, evading his blocking maneuver, the lethal tip piercing the soldier's chest dangerously close to his heart. But Liam did not thrust home.

Hawke stood unmoving, frozen.

Liam smiled savagely. "Do you wish to live?" he asked, his blade still pushing up against Hawke's chest.

Then Hawke's smile mirrored Liam's. "Do you?"

Liam realized that a dozen muskets, primed and loaded, were pointed at his head.

"Drop the rapier, pirate," Hawke commanded. "You have won the battle—but I have won the war. Drop your weapon, now—if you wish to live."

Liam slowly withdrew his rapier, then let the long, fine blade fall to the ground.

Hawke, ignoring the blossoming of blood on his chest from the light flesh wound, bent and picked up the blade. He handed it to another soldier and moved forward swiftly, removing Liam's dagger from its sheath as well. Liam stood as still as any statue. Two soldiers quickly pulled his hands behind his back as Hawke watched with savage satisfaction. A moment later steel manacles were snapped on his wrists.

"In the name of Her Majesty, Elizabeth, the queen of England," Hawke said, "I pronounce you my prisoner."

Another week had passed. Katherine found herself counting the days, but she told herself it was because she was eager to see the end of winter, the coming of the spring—and then the birth of her baby. The midwife had confirmed her suspicions. The babe would come sometime in July.

Katherine caressed her swollen belly, a habit she had taken to. Without her mantle, it was clear that she was with child, but her stomach was still a small mound, and hardly a protrusion. She hoped to comfort the unborn babe. Although she hated its father, Katherine loved the child. Once, she had hoped to have many children, but now it seemed as if she would bear this one single babe. It did not matter. She would love it all the more. And she was determined to do everything she could for it. But what could she really do?

She was forced now to think of the future. Her love for Liam was dead, murdered by his betrayal, and she could not stay on his island much longer. Yet she did not want to go to her father, and share or even compound his disgrace and live in exile. Obviously she would not return to John, nor could she go to the court. Only one thing was clear. Somehow she must get off this island. Somehow she must return to Ireland.

For Ireland beckoned her as a beacon light would a ship at sea. How she wished to go home. Surely her uncles would find some small place for her and her child in their homes, their hearts, and their lives.

But Katherine did not know how she was going to manage to leave, because Macgregor watched her like a hawk. The Scot was protecting what he believed to be Liam's interests. Katherine stubbornly, no, viciously, clung to her belief that the babe was hers and hers alone. Liam had no rights. He had forfeited all of his rights when he had betrayed her love for him by consorting with FitzMaurice.

Yet even though she knew she must leave, before the baby was born, before Liam returned, she did not seem to have the will or the strength to plan an escape from the island.

A sharp banging sounded upon her chamber door.

Katherine jerked, moving across the small guest room, the same chamber Hugh Barry had used when he had convalesced there. After having learned of Liam's betrayal, the very first thing she had done was remove herself from the chamber they had shared.

Katherine opened the door. Macgregor stood there, unnaturally pale. Instantly Katherine knew that something terrible had happened—to Liam. "What is it?"

"Prepare yourself," he said, but it was the big Scot who went to her room's single chair and sat down heavily there. Katherine saw that he was shocked.

"What is it!" she cried, rushing to him. "Is Liam dead?"

Macgregor looked at her. "No, but soon he will be." He paused for effect, staring straight at her. "He has been taken prisoner by your first husband, Katherine. Sir John Hawke engaged him and his men south of Galway last week. The *Sea Dagger* escaped. Liam did not."

Katherine stared. How light-headed she was—and how funny the floor had become, rolling beneath her feet like the deck of a ship.

"He is the queen's prisoner," Macgregor continued, beginning to sound strange and far away, "and even now, he is bound for the Tower—where he will be tried for treason, and, like all pirates, hanged at Hangman's Gate."

Katherine cried out. And as she fainted, she could see him, his neck broken, his face pale and lifeless, dangling from a noose.

29

Richmond

*C*ecil brought the queen the news. "Sir John Hawke has captured Liam O'Neill, Your Majesty. One of your vessels bearing them put into London this morning."

Elizabeth gasped. "You are sure, William?"

Cecil waved a small scroll of parchment. "This missive came from Sir John himself. After depositing O'Neill in the Tower, he comes to you posthaste. He gives no details of how or where he caught the pirate."

Elizabeth was reeling. For, deep within herself, she had never really thought it possible for any man, not even Sir John, to capture the wily Irish scoundrel. But it had been done. O'Neill had been captured. He was in the Tower, where all traitors belonged. She should be thrilled, wildly so. She *was* pleased. Yet . . . she could not identify another emotion, one which was causing the rapid beating of her heart. "These are good tidings, indeed," she finally said.

Cecil approached. "I advise that we think very long and carefully on what we do next," he said in a low tone of voice.

Elizabeth gazed at him, grateful for his words. Already she could see O'Neill hanging from a gibbet. Somehow she did not like the image—yet the man was the worst scoundrel possible, a traitor to the Crown—and he *must* meet his fate. An example must be made. If only the mere notion did not upset her so. "What do you think, Cecil?"

"I think O'Neill *is* the Master of the Seas. Over the years, he has been invaluable to us. I think we must unravel all the complications of the Irish issue, and decide if hanging the pirate serves us best."

Elizabeth nodded, relieved in spite of what she knew she should do with her golden pirate. "FitzMaurice has gone so far underground Perrot does not even know where he is," she commented.

"Yes, and he has been so well supplied by the pirate that he will not come out of his winter den until the weather turns again."

Elizabeth grew fierce. "We *must* capture him this spring! We cannot bear another year of war with that miserable man! I *hate* having to spend another farthing on the bloody Irish!" If only she could wish that miserable land of papists and savages away, she thought. How worthless it was. Yet she did not dare allow another nation a foothold there.

Cecil inclined his head. "FitzMaurice is damnably clever. If this new treaty comes about with Spain, we must make it clear that we will no longer tolerate their interference in Ireland."

"Or Scotland," Elizabeth added vehemently, thinking of Mary and all of the plots that had been seeded about her.

"Yes. But the picture brightens, Your Majesty. With O'Neill imprisoned, and without Spanish support, Fitz-Maurice will begin to lose ground."

"I pray so," Elizabeth muttered.

Looking her in the eye, Cecil said a most peculiar thing. "FitzGerald never gave us half as much trouble as his lunatic cousin."

Elizabeth met his gaze, suddenly realizing that her councillor was right. FitzGerald had been much like an annoying gnat, forever buzzing about one's head, taking small bites until swatted away. All that man had wanted was to control Desmond in a despotic fashion, without outside interference.

How Elizabeth now rued the day that she had agreed with her Council to strip Gerald FitzGerald of all he had.

Even then, Cecil had opposed the others, afraid of what would happen in southern Ireland with the earl of Desmond gone. He had been right. FitzMaurice had moved into the breach, seeking not power over the other Irish lords, but the restoration of the Catholic Church and the overthrow of England's queen.

How sorry Elizabeth now was for destroying Desmond's earl.

There was no window, no light. The cell was absolutely black. And it was foul with the odors of the many prisoners who had been entombed there before him. The walls were so thick that, although straining to detect any noise, he could hear nothing at all. He finally gave up. He was several stories below ground in the dungeons, and he was not going to hear anything or anyone.

He wondered if his life were about to end. He had been brought to this impasse by a woman. How ironic it was. He, *Shane O'Neill's son,* had been brought to this moment in his life by a woman—by a woman he had once *loved.*

That single thought generated a terrible stabbing in his breast and Liam rubbed his chest. He closed his eyes. No, 'twas not love, he thought. It had never been love. It had only been lust, a lust that knew no bounds. He had confused his insatiable need for her with love, but it was not, had never been, would never be, love.

Liam forced himself to think clearly. He must not dwell upon Katherine, there was no point. He was finished with her. He had waged a dangerous game for her sake, never realizing the kind of woman that she was. No, it was over, and he must think of naught but his own future—of how to avoid the hangman's fatal noose.

For Liam did intend to escape the hangman, he did intend to live. He had not made his final move yet. It was a very powerful play, one he had anticipated the moment he had decided to join this game, and delay merely increased its value every day that FitzMaurice lived. But he could not play alone. He needed a partner; he needed the queen.

And it was only a matter of time, Liam thought. For

surely Bess would send for him, to chastise him, to berate him. Liam knew women, and he was betting his life upon his knowledge of the female gender. She had been fond of him, and she would be sorely angered now by his treachery. He must have patience, he must survive the days or even weeks that she might make him await her pleasure in his hellhole of a dungeon. And then he must woo her as he would woo the most beautiful, provocative siren he had yet to see—he must woo her as he had once wooed Katherine.

Liam shoved himself to his feet and began to pace the room, planning the best way to gain his release. But there was no thrill anymore in the play. It had become mundane. For the stakes had changed. It was only his freedom he sought—the freedom to return to his life as Master of the Seas—a life he no longer wanted. What a fool he had become.

Not too long ago the stakes had been Katherine's hand in marriage and their return to Ireland—the future had loomed before them, sunny and bright. No more. Now he sought only his miserable freedom and his equally miserable life.

Katherine arrived in London with Macgregor and Guy, exhausted from the madcap trip. For as soon as she had learned that Liam had been taken prisoner, she had departed the island. All had changed. Liam's life was at stake.

Liam had betrayed her, but he did not deserve to die. She had been living for a full week now with heartrending anxiety and crushing fear. She could never forgive him his terribly treachery, nor could she ever forget it, but she did not wish him dead after all. Somehow, she must prevent his execution; she must plead his case with the queen.

The White Bear Inn was popular with foreigners, and they took rooms there. They quickly learned that the Court was at Richmond, Liam imprisoned in the Tower, his fate yet undetermined. But the street gossip was filled with expectation; the common folk looked forward to another pirate hanging at Hangman's Gate.

Katherine faced a looking glass. She was pale with fright, huge circles under her eyes. Indeed, she was exhausted. But she had a mission now, the mission which had brought her to London—and it was to free Liam O'Neill. And she would do whatever she had to do in order to succeed, even though she could never return to him as his wife.

Elizabeth paced the Presence Chamber. Her heart raced. She had ordered the pirate brought to her because she could no longer wait to confront him about his treacherous ways—and his treacherous heart. She could no longer wait to have him on bended knee, begging her pardon—and offering her some pitiful explanation for his horrendous behavior.

"Relax, Bess," Leicester murmured in her ear.

"I cannot," she snapped, annoyed with his unruffled calm. But then, Robin hated rivals, and he had known that she favored Liam from the start—and he was so vastly pleased that Liam had turned traitor. These past weeks he had been advocating that she try Liam immediately, try him, convict him, and hang him.

Now Elizabeth wished he were not present, just as she wished that neither Ormond nor Cecil was present, as well. Yet she knew she needed their judgment on this matter. For she did not trust herself.

The doors to the chamber were thrown open. Elizabeth froze. She faced a dozen members of the guard, all clothed in crimson. But she did not see them. In their forefront stood John Hawke, whom she also failed to notice. Beside him was the prisoner.

Elizabeth's heart lurched, her eyes widened. Briefly she was shocked by his appearance, and for an instant, her heart was wrenched with pity.

His tunic, once white, was bloodstained and charcoal gray. His breeches were as stained and as filthy. Even from the distance separating them, Elizabeth could smell his dirty, unwashed body. He was unshaven, of course, his beard short but wild and unkempt. Their gazes locked.

Any pity she might have entertained died in that moment. How proud and unafraid he was. Elizabeth looked into his cool gray eyes and thought him as magnificent as ever. This was a man no mortal could defeat. This was a man who would bow only to Death. And even then, he would die wearing the cloak of both his lion's pride and his lion's courage.

Elizabeth began to notice many things at once. He stood very tall, his shoulders straight, despite the manacles, which held his wrists behind his back. His head was high. There was even the slightest smirk on his beautiful mouth as he looked far too boldly into her eyes—the way he might at a woman he wished to bed.

No, he was not afraid, not of death—and not of her.

Elizabeth was at once excited and dismayed. As a woman she would never be immune to him—but as a queen, she demanded his fear and his respect.

The fact of his betrayal stabbed her yet again. How could he have turned traitor upon her? Had he no care for her at all? She thanked God—and her own iron will—that she had not invited him into her bed that one night last year—when she had been so tempted. To hide her agitation, she smiled as coldly as she could, yet her mouth quavered. "Come here, pirate."

Liam walked forward, held her eye, and had the audacity to say, "I beg your pardon, Your Majesty," and only then did he drop to his knees at her feet.

"Oh? You are a foul rogue. You do not seem in the least bit repentant."

"I am very repentant." He looked up. "I beg your pardon not just for my perceived crimes, but for coming into your presence in such a malodorous state."

She stared at him as he knelt before her, wondering what he was up to now, not missing his use of the word "perceived."

His gaze was too bold, too male, and filled with too much promise.

Elizabeth trembled. She felt far less a queen and far more a young and anguished virgin girl. She studied him and saw that the manacles caused him pain. But she would not order them removed—he deserved to suffer for what he had done to her. "You may rise."

Liam rose to his feet quite gracefully, a feat few men could accomplish while their wrists were bound behind their backs. "Thank you."

Elizabeth was disturbed by their small audience, not liking the fact that their every word was overheard, their every gesture watched. Yet she told herself she must not dismiss her advisors. To be alone with Liam O'Neill was far too dangerous. "Next time you are brought to me you must bathe first, for I am offended by the horrid sight you make, and the horrid smell," she said frankly.

"I hope there is a next time." He inclined his head. "I cannot tolerate being in my own body," he said affably, meeting her gaze, "and I am sure I look like a Bridewell wretch."

"I might send you to Bridewell," Elizabeth said, wringing her hands. Did he think to seduce her with his too-direct gray gaze?

He lifted a brow quite arrogantly. "But only vagabonds and whores serve in that place."

"Ahh, then perhaps I should send your strumpet there." Elizabeth smiled grimly at the thought.

His arrogance was gone. Something not quite cool flickered in his eyes. "A mistress is hardly a whore."

"Oh? I did not realize there was a difference," Elizabeth said. "You care for her still?" Elizabeth fought to hide her flaming jealousy.

"She was good bedsport."

"Where is John Hawke's wife?"

"Upon my island."

And Elizabeth wished them to be alone. She had to learn the truth. "Everyone, leave us," she commanded.

Ormond had been glowering throughout, and with a final murderous glare at O'Neill, as if he had some care for his half sister, he tromped out with William Cecil. Leicester did not rush to obey. Concern plain upon his face, he came close to them. "Your Majesty," he began in protest.

Elizabeth turned a glacial gaze upon him. God's blood,

she had no time for Robin now! She had no time for anyone but the pirate. "You, too, my lord. I wish to speak with the renegade alone."

" 'Tis not wise," Dudley said, flushing with anger.

"But I am queen, and if I wish to be a fool, so be it," Elizabeth snapped.

Dudley turned on his heel, furious, and marched out.

Then Elizabeth realized that Hawke still stood by the doorway, unmoving and grim. "You too, Sir John."

Hawke bowed, as red-faced as Leicester, but Elizabeth thought some of his coloring was due to shame. "I beg your pardon, Your Majesty, but the pirate is a dangerous man. I do not think you should remain alone with him." He hesitated. "And I would learn more of my wife, if I could."

"The pirate might be a traitor, but he will not hurt me. You may learn of your wife later. Out," she ordered Hawke.

His heels snapped together. Mouth pursed tightly, he turned and obeyed.

Elizabeth gripped her palms, which were damp now that they were alone. Her gaze fused with Liam's. "Would you hurt me, rogue?"

He smiled softly. "No."

Her heart, already wavering, melted. This was the Liam she knew—and was so very fond of. Oh, damn his rascal, mercenary, treacherous hide! She began to pace. "You mastered the seas many years ago, and we have always had an understanding, unspoken, but one you abided by," she said. "You never attacked except where it did not hurt my own causes at the time, or somehow furthered them— even if those causes were highly secret." She paused, facing him now. "Why? Why, Liam, why did you turn traitor to me?"

Liam's expression became grave. "I ask you to listen to me closely, Bess, very closely."

She did not like his use of her familiar name. She stiffened. "I am listening. I am waiting. I have been waiting for this explanation a very long time."

"My intention was not to hurt you."

Elizabeth was frozen. No longer a queen, merely a woman who had never dared to live her dreams.

"I am no papist and you know it. Indeed, you are aware I saw too many burnings during your sister's reign ever to support a fanatic like FitzMaurice."

"I know this. Which is why I fail to understand you now, Liam," Elizabeth cried. "You betrayed *me*, Liam. Your friend and your queen!"

"No." Liam approached her. "I have not betrayed you. You have been pursuing the rebels in Ireland for many years now, without success. Lord Perrot cannot capture FitzMaurice, and this everyone knows. But I," he paused dramatically, his gaze glittering, "I can capture the papist, Bess, and if you but free me, I will."

Elizabeth gasped. "What further treachery is this?" she cried. "What crockery is this? You ask me to free you? You are a *traitor*. Traitors *must* hang."

No fear showed in Liam's eyes. Patiently, he said, "You are not listening, Bess."

Elizabeth was shaking. "What could you possibly say to make me think to free you?"

He smiled slightly. "I have never been a traitor to you. Instead, at great risk to me and mine, I have allied myself with FitzMaurice—so that I can deliver your worst Irish enemy to you."

Elizabeth stared, frozen.

"Do you not have other spies, Bess?" he said very softly. "Is it so surprising that I have played the spy for you, now? Who is better prepared, or better positioned, than I—to ensnare and entrap FitzMaurice?"

Elizabeth said nothing, her mind racing frantically, suspended between logic, which dictated disbelief, and her love for him, which blossomed with excitement and hope.

"I have raised him up only so I can bring him down," Liam O'Neill said calmly. And he smiled, the smile of a victor, the smile of a master of the game. "And when I do, I expect a great reward from you." And his gaze held hers.

Elizabeth turned away, imagining what he might ask of her—a reward no other man would dare request, one far too personal, one far too intimate. Already she could taste his kisses, feel his caress. She wet her lips, tried to clear her mind of such female nonsense. She was a queen. She had no business allowing him to seduce her now.

But the question raised itself. Did she dare? Did she dare trust her golden pirate now, after all that he had done?

Katherine wore the hood of her fur-lined velvet cloak in order to hide her face as she passed through Richmond's northern gate. Macgregor walked beside her, as did Guy. Wedged as she was between the huge Scot and the small boy, Katherine hardly felt unremarkable.

Someone was going to recognize her soon. Katherine had been too distraught over Liam's impending fate to think about her own reception at court until the past hour, on the barge that had taken them from London to Richmond. She could imagine the shock, excitement, and torrid speculation her appearance would cause, and she hoped to delay the inevitable.

Her first priority was learning all that she could about Liam—and gaining an audience with the queen.

She would deal with the rest afterward.

As they traversed the small gatehouse and climbed a broad flight of stairs that entered the hall directly, Katherine was well aware of the utter irony of her defending the man who had so thoroughly betrayed both her and her father. She would defend his support of FitzMaurice. How laughable it was. How sad.

Katherine and her companions entered the hall. Her heart began to race with fear. She must gain a royal audience, but that would surely be the most simple of her tasks. How would she convince the queen to spare Liam his life? Katherine had brooded upon little else in the past days since learning of Liam's capture, and had not found any worthy argument to make in his defense.

She had debated very carefully, too, as to how to represent herself. Unless Liam had told someone of their marriage, the whole world thought her John Hawke's wife. Katherine would tell no one of her second marriage. It would not help her cause. For she had no intention of ever living with him again if he should survive this circumstance. For Katherine had faced her deepest, darkest feelings. A part of her still loved Liam, foolishly, stupidly, and it always would. But she would never be able to trust him again.

His treachery was a scar upon her heart, to be worn forever.

Katherine paused on the threshold of the hall. The large chamber was crowded. Cautiously Katherine looked about for a familiar face, holding the neck of her hood with one hand. Her eyes widened when she saw several ladies she knew, including Anne Hastings, with whom she had been the most friendly. "Wait here," Katherine murmured to Macgregor and Guy. She pushed her way forward, coming up behind the baroness.

"Anne," she whispered nervously.

Anne whirled, her blue eyes widening as they met Katherine's. "By all the saints! Katherine! What are you doing here!" Then her eyes widened even more with some inner comprehension Katherine did not understand.

"I must speak with the queen," Katherine said tersely. "But we will speak later, privily," she added, knowing Anne wished to learn all about her stay with the notorious pirate these many past months.

"Her Majesty is in the Presence Chamber," Anne said quickly.

Katherine squeezed her hand, turning away.

"Katherine!" Anne cried. "Wait! There is more that you must know!"

But Katherine ignored her. She caught Macgregor's eye, then hurried through the hall, pushing past the gentlemen and gentlewomen, keeping her head lowered and her eyes downcast. Her heart thundered now. Only when she had left the great hall, and stood in the antechamber outside the Presence Chamber, did she raise her head and lift her gaze. Her heart skipped a beat. The two massive wooden doors were closed, and a dozen gentlemen and courtiers, as well as a dozen Royal Guard, milled about them. The Queen was giving private audience to someone.

She would have to wait her turn. Katherine's anxiety raced unfettered now—as did her fear.

Suddenly the doors began to open. The courtiers and gentlemen stiffened with attention. Conversation ceased. The guard moved forward, as if to escort the petitioner who was closeted with the queen.

But it was no petitioner ensconced within, no petitioner at all. It was a prisoner. Liam appeared on the threshold, disheveled, his wrists manacled behind his back—incredibly proud.

Katherine gasped. In the utter silence of the antechamber, the sound was loud and shocked, and many gazes shot her way.

He heard her, too, and as if he recognized the sound of her voice, his gaze sliced directly to her. It turned fierce and bright.

Her gaze locked with his. And despite his treachery, her heart wept for what he must be suffering. Slowly, her gaze filling with tears, no longer caring to hide her identity, Katherine released her hold on her hood, allowing it to fall back from her face.

Gasps and exclamations sounded as one and all recognized her—followed by a series of hushed, shocked whispers.

And Katherine realized then that the queen stood behind Liam, staring at her with the same stunned surprise as everyone else. And then her heart lurched. For the crimson-clad man who had moved to Liam's side was none other than John Hawke.

30

*K*atherine's gaze riveted upon Hawke. His expression was rigid with shock. She met Liam's gaze again. If he was surprised by her appearance at court, he did not show it.

Katherine wished she could disappear. She was ashamed to face John Hawke now. She had behaved shamelessly with Liam when Hawke had been her true husband, before she and Liam had wed. She had never ever dreamed she would encounter him like this, publicly, surrounded by the tittering court—as he escorted Liam back to the Tower. While she prepared to go to the defense of the man who had abducted her out of her wedding bed—the man the entire world thought to be naught but her lover.

Katherine was very careful not to allow her gaze to flick to Liam again, not even once. She was resolved to ignore him, acutely aware of a hundred stares trained upon her—and of the heated whispers surrounding them. Had Liam revealed the fact of their marriage to anyone? She stole another glance at John, wondering if he still believed himself to be her husband—wondering what he would say and do if he knew the truth. In any case, Katherine was quite certain that one and all were accusing her of being a whore, and condemning her as such. It was undoubtedly the most horrible moment of her life.

To make matters worse, Katherine now noticed the earl of Leicester standing behind John, his expression as surprised as everyone else's. But how quickly his surprise became something more, his dark gaze piercing. Katherine quickly looked away, noticing that her half brother, the earl of Ormond, was also present, and looking far from pleased.

Katherine felt dizzy.

Then the queen pushed past Hawke and Liam. Immediately Katherine dropped to her knees.

"This *coincidence* is unseemly," the queen said sharply.

"Your Majesty," Katherine murmured, her pulse racing.

"Rise. We shall speak privately. *Now.*"

It was a command, one Katherine was glad to obey. Not only did she wish to exit the antechamber filled with gawking gentlemen and gentlewomen, and her two husbands, she had come to court for this very reason—to have a private audience with the queen. Very awkwardly—and very carefully, Katherine got to her feet. Someone—Macgregor—reached down and aided her. She kept her cloak tightly closed. Her state of pregnancy would be another shock to everyone.

"Take the prisoner to the guardroom," Elizabeth said to Hawke.

Hawke nodded, but then his gaze found Katherine's again. There was no mistaking his disbelief that she had come to court at all. His anger was also clear. Did he guess her purpose? Or did he blame her for her fall from virtue? Katherine did not blame him, whatever the cause of his anger, it was justified. When he realized that she was pregnant with Liam's child, he would be even angrier.

Hawke wheeled, pushing Liam forward. Katherine's heart lurched hard against her breastbone and for a moment, Katherine could not help herself and she gazed after him. If only he had not betrayed her—if only he loved her—it would be so much easier to beg for his freedom, for his life. But if that were so, he would not be a prisoner of the Crown. If that were so, her own heart would be whole, instead of aching and broken.

Katherine flung one last glance in his direction. His shoulders were squared, his head high, yet his clothing was in tatters. The steel cuffs on his wrists gleamed, catching the light streaking through the windows, as he was led away. He was so proud, so cool and so unafraid—as if he were in control, and not at the mercy of the wrathful queen or unkind Fate. He acted as if he were master not of the seas, but of this dangerous game, yet that he could not be. He was a victim now, no master at all. Katherine shuddered at the thought.

The queen was staring at her. Katherine jerked, praying that any remaining feelings she still had for him did not show upon her face. "Come," Elizabeth said.

Katherine followed her into the Presence Chamber. When they were alone, Elizabeth said, "I am not surprised, Katherine, not anymore, to see you here. I should have known that you would come." Her gaze glittered.

Katherine said nothing. Trying to marshal her thoughts into some form of coherent argument. But her mind was scattered. Did the queen know of her marriage to Liam? Had he told anyone? She must proceed with caution.

"So you have followed your lover to court. Do you wish to make a plea for the traitor?" Elizabeth asked, her fists on her hips.

Katherine was relieved. Liam had not told anyone of their marriage. "Yes. I wish to plead his case, your Majesty."

Elizabeth's stare was cold. "You are just like your shameless mother."

Katherine flinched. The queen was frozen with disapproval—indeed, she seemed furious. Katherine swallowed, frightened. She had not expected this. The last time she had seen Elizabeth, the queen had been kind and friendly.

Now the queen was flushed, and she shook her finger at Katherine. She did not give Katherine a chance to speak. "I also should have known the moment I laid eyes upon you that you would be a temptress exactly like your mother was!"

Katherine gasped. "I am no temptress," she whispered, stunned by the queen's vicious attack.

Elizabeth laughed. "Do not deny it now! You led O'Neill a merry chase, did you not, before your betrothal

to John Hawke? You incited his manly appetites! You
drove him to abduction, and in all likelihood, you drove
him to conspiracy as well.''

Katherine cried out, shocked.

But the queen was not about to stop. ''Your mother was
a slut!'' she shouted. ''She took your father to her bed
when her own husband lay dying! You are exactly like
her! Giving yourself to a pirate lover despite the fact that
you are wed and bound to an *honorable* man.''

''No,'' Katherine said. She almost defended herself by
telling the queen that her marriage to Hawke had never
been consummated, and that Liam was her husband now.
She restrained herself. One did not argue with one's sovereign—and Liam was only her husband in name now, not
in any other way—never again in any other way.

''No?'' Her expression livid, Elizabeth struck Katherine
across the face, hard. ''Get down on your knees!''

Katherine reeled but did not fall. She held her cheek,
felt the seeping of blood from where the queen's rings
had gouged her. Tears filled her eyes, not of pain, but of
fear—and of helpless fury.

''Get down,'' the queen said again.

Katherine inhaled, trembling, no longer clutching her
cheek. Having no choice in the matter, nor daring to disobey, she dropped to both knees.

The queen began to pace. ''I blame you for it all,'' she
stated. ''You seduced my pirate, just as you tried to seduce
Leicester and Ormond.''

Katherine bit down hard to remain silent. How unfair,
how cruel, Elizabeth was.

Elizabeth paused in front of her, staring down at the
top of her bent head. ''Ormond was set against you when
you first came to court. But you worked your wiles upon
him and now he has some small feeling for you! And
Robin! When you walk into a room, Robin looks at you
like he will jump on you as fast as any stallion upon a
mare! Have you let him bed you?''

Katherine's breathing was shallow and fast. She tried to
speak and failed, shook her head no.

The queen towered over her, shaking uncontrollably. "If you dare to sleep with him, I will have your head."

"No," Katherine croaked.

"I will not allow sluts in my court."

Although on her knees, Katherine squared her shoulders. "Your Majesty, I did not seduce my own brother, nor did I seduce Dudley."

"For your sake, that had better be the truth." Elizabeth stared coldly at her. "No, I cannot blame Liam or any man for trying to gain what you so freely give. You are the culprit here, the one who must be sent away."

Her heart shrinking, Katherine whispered, unthinkingly, "I loved Liam."

"Oh?"

Katherine met the queen's furious gaze. Her pulse raced. How could she have said such a thing after Liam's betrayal? Yet how could she not, when it was her only defense against the queen's slanderous attack? When it was the truth?

The queen spit, "And what is it about him that you loved? His sweet flattery—or the size of his manhood?"

Katherine started, flaming.

"Answer me," the Queen snapped.

Katherine was painfully dry. "What are you asking me to say?"

"Did he please you in bed, Katherine?"

She held the queen's gaze. She knew better than to respond, fully aware that her cheeks were flaming—providing all the answer the queen needed.

"Slut," Elizabeth hissed. She turned away.

Katherine closed her eyes, fighting tears of helpless rage. She did not understand why the queen hated her so. And it was nigh impossible for her to defend herself against such malicious slander, to protest her innocence to the queen. Yet what innocence? For in fact, the bulk of Elizabeth's accusations were true.

Katherine despaired. She had no weapons to wield now, none, and she had no allies. All she had was herself. She must be very clever.

"Your Majesty," Katherine said, licking her lips, "I accept all blame for enticing Liam, for inflaming him. Like my mother, I could not control myself. You are right. And . . . I am so sorry.'' She bowed her head, shaking, her pride warring with her common sense. "I beg your pardon.''

Elizabeth was unmoving now, and Katherine felt her staring at her. "I am not disposed to give it,'' she finally said, but her tone was much calmer and far less rancid now.

Katherine dared to look up and meet her gaze. "As I am the one at fault, 'tis unjust and nonsensical to blame Liam, is it not?''

Elizabeth's eyes gleamed with sudden respect. "I did not know you were capable of debate, Katherine.''

Katherine held her gaze. "I would not dare to debate you, Your Majesty.''

The queen's gaze was piercing. "Your mother was very astute, very clever, and very determined, too. She knelt before me more than once, much as you do, begging for my leniency for her lord.''

Katherine regarded her steadily, not daring yet to hope or be assured by the queen's new tone of voice and by the dialogue now taking place betwixt them.

"Liam is a traitor, even if his lust made him lose his mind, and traitors must hang.''

Katherine remained very still, her face impassive, even though the queen's words were like the lash of a whip. She must make her argument now, and it must be flawless if Liam were to be saved. "You have known Liam since he was a squalling newborn babe. Surely you still have some small fondness for the boy you grew up with and raised in your very own household?''

"Perhaps,'' Elizabeth said, her eyes agleam.

"Does not the history you have shared entitle him to a second chance?'' Katherine asked.

"No,'' the queen said flatly. "It does not.'' Elizabeth was grim. "That sad and lonely little boy is now a dangerous man. One who committed treason against me! The boy I was fond of. The man I abhor!''

And Katherine suddenly realized the cause of the

queen's hatred for her. "Abhor?" she asked softly. "Or adore?"

Disbelief and then rage transformed the queen's face.

Before Elizabeth could speak or strike, Katherine cried, "He is a man many women adore, Your Majesty, because of his manliness, because of his nobility, regardless of his pirate ways. I am but one woman in the long line of women he has had, and there will be many more women after me—I do not delude myself. No woman can be immune to such a man, not even a great monarch."

Her anger gone as quickly as it had come, Elizabeth looked at her with open respect. "You are no green child anymore, are you, Katherine?"

Katherine did not bother to answer. "Your Majesty, once Liam served you well. He can serve you well again. He is, after all, the Master of the Seas. I beg of you, pardon him his crimes. Do not put such a man to death. Punish him, yes, but do not hang him. Think on his value."

"I cannot trust him," Elizabeth said.

Katherine was stabbed with fear and dismay and complete understanding. How well she understood Elizabeth now, who was also suffering from Liam's betrayal. "You have many wise advisors. Surely one of them can devise a scheme where Liam would give some kind of surety to you in return for his worthy behavior."

The queen did not respond.

Katherine rose to her feet somewhat awkwardly. "He is far more valuable to you alive than dead."

"He will be a valuable example to other would-be conspirators if he swings from the noose," Elizabeth replied, but her eyes were darkened by the thought.

Katherine sought desperately for a response. "If he is executed, you will never be able to bring him back—the ending is final. Can you live with that?" And she prayed the queen loved Liam far more than Katherine suspected.

But the queen did not answer—did not even hear her. She stared at Katherine, gasping.

And suddenly Katherine realized that she had forgotten to hold her cloak together when she rose to her feet, and that now it hung loosely open about her—revealing her pregnancy. She blanched.

Elizabeth's wide gaze fixed upon Katherine's rounded abdomen. "You are with child. I should have guessed. It would have been far more astounding had O'Neill proved himself less than a man."

Katherine had pulled her cloak together instinctively.

Then the queen said, "It is *his* child?"

Katherine gasped. "Yes!"

"When is the child due?" Elizabeth demanded. As unfriendly as before.

"In July."

"Shameless—you are shameless, as I said. And I will not have a slut here—strutting about my court carrying a bastard babe!"

Katherine fought despair—and fought the impulse to shout that her child was no bastard. "You were Mary Stanley's friend."

"I was not a queen then," Elizabeth snapped.

And Katherine knew she had lost. When, for just a moment, it had seemed as if she might win.

"The child complicates matters," Elizabeth said darkly. "Liam never mentioned any child."

"He does not know."

Elizabeth's eyes widened. Then she smiled slightly, to herself.

Katherine did not care for her expression, and unease claimed her. "Your Majesty, will you not spare Liam so that he might know his own son?"

Elizabeth's gaze was piercing, her laugh was cold. "If I choose to spare that rogue, my reason will have naught to do with his bastard babe." Then her gaze narrowed. "Is it a son? Have the astrologers said so?"

"I have not tried to determine the babe's sex," Katherine said slowly.

"You will see an astrologer immediately," Elizabeth said. "I want to know if your bear Liam a son."

Katherine tried to fathom why. The queen was devious, what did she plan? Katherine could not decide.

Then the queen said, "Does John Hawke know yet?"

Katherine grew rigid. "No."

The queen smiled again. "Then we must summon him. For he must be told."

Dismay swept through Katherine. John Hawke had been the very last of her concerns—but suddenly he was the most immediate.

"Enter, Sir John," the queen commanded.

Katherine stiffened as Hawke walked into the chamber, his gaze not on Elizabeth, but on her. He stared at her swollen stomach, which she made no attempt to hide. His own healthy color had faded.

Katherine desperately wished that she had had time to meet with him privately, to break the news gently, to learn what his real thoughts were. This time she refused to meet his gaze. She stared at his buckled shoes. Her pulse raced so forcefully that she felt faint.

"Look at me, Katherine," Sir John said.

Katherine had no choice but to obey. His mouth was turned down, in bitterness and distaste. "I am sorry," she said unsteadily. She did not think her fragile nerves could stand too much more.

"Tell me one thing," John said as shakily. "Tell me that you regret every moment you have spent in his arms—in his bed."

Katherine's gaze flew to his. Her breath escaped. She opened her mouth to respond—to lie—but could not manage a single sound.

His jaw ground down. He looked away. " 'Twas a foolish question, was it not?" he said to the room at large, or perhaps to himself.

And Katherine almost hated herself. Hawke was a good, noble man. He did not deserve this. He did not deserve her. He deserved someone who would love him, someone sweet and good, someone loyal. Yet she could not lie about what she had shared with Liam. She felt trapped in an impossible place—one with no escape.

The queen snapped. "A very foolish question, John. It makes no difference what Katherine felt then. What matters is that she is here, now, carrying another man's seed—but she is your wife.''

Katherine began to shake. But she said not a word. Surely he would divorce her soon enough, now that he knew the truth.

Hawke inclined his head, then turned to Katherine, his mouth tight. ''Are you well, Katherine? Considering the circumstances?''

Katherine wet her lips. ''I . . . I am distressed.''

''A not surprising state,'' Hawke said. ''The child—when is it due?''

''In July.''

He nodded, staring again at her stomach. He turned his head away.

''Sir John,'' Elizabeth said sharply. ''What do you intend to do with Katherine?''

Hawke's expression was sardonic. ''What would you have me do, Your Majesty? Divorce her? So she can take to the streets, perhaps as a strumpet—in order to feed her babe?''

''The lesson would serve her well,'' the queen said.

Katherine was frozen. ''I will go to my father,'' she whispered.

John turned toward her. ''FitzGerald is no better than a pauper. He can hardly feed his wife and son—but you would go to him? I think not.''

''She can be sent to France, from whence she came,'' Elizabeth remarked. ''We do not object should you send her to a nunnery to have her child, or should you wish to keep her there for her lifetime. We will gladly find a foster home for the babe.''

Katherine cried out. She faced John, seeking his gaze, a desperate plea in her green eyes. ''No.''

''She will go to Hawkehurst,'' John stated, staring at her, his jaw tight. ''Where she belongs.''

Katherine gasped. She could not believe what she had heard. He did not intend to cast her aside? Surely she misunderstood him!

His brow lifted. ''What did you expect, Katherine? For me to divorce you and allow you to beg for—or steal—

your bread? You are my wife. You may have enjoyed the damned pirate's seduction, but you did not plan to be abducted by him—and had I not been so negligent that day, had I posted proper guards—the abduction would not have succeeded—and it would be my child you now bear.''

Katherine clasped her hands together. "You will not divorce me?'' she gasped.

"The one thing I understand is duty, madam,'' John said harshly. "My duty is to you—and to your child, as well.''

In spite of her shock, Katherine knew she was a lucky woman because even if Liam did not hang, she would never return to him—and she had a child to raise. A child she must feed, clothe, and rear at all costs. But, dear God, she did not feel lucky; she felt shameless and amoral, desperate and confused. She felt dismayed.

And her traitorous mind whispered, *How can you live without Liam?*

Katherine sucked in a sob, refusing to listen to such madness.

The queen was applauding John's words. "Well said, Sir John. But then, you are a very noble man.''

Hawke bowed his head again. "I wish to take my wife to Hawkehurst myself, on the morrow, with Your Majesty's permission,'' he said.

"Granted,'' Elizabeth replied. "But with one condition.''

Both Hawke and Katherine turned to the queen, Katherine still stunned with disbelief.

Elizabeth smiled. "She is to remain far from London, in Cornwall. I do not wish to see hide nor hair of her, Sir John. I am most displeased with her conduct, and have no wish to set a contagion amongst my other good ladies of the court. Do you understand?''

Hawke nodded grimly.

Katherine stared. Exile. She was being condemned to an exile in Cornwall as punishment for her sins. She would reside there—as Hawke's wife.

Hawke held out his hand. Katherine saw it but couldn't touch it. Comprehension finally filled her. If she remained with Hawke now, she would be breaking God's law. No woman could have two husbands.

His mouth tightened and, very firmly, he took her arm. "And now I will take you to your lodgings," he said. "I think it best if you stay in your chamber, Katherine, until we leave tomorrow."

And as John led her away, Katherine flung a last, desperate glance over her shoulder, and met the queen's triumphant and hostile gaze.

The queen had won. Yet Katherine had never dreamed that the outcome of their battle would be a forsaken exile for herself in Cornwall as Hawke's wife. And it was Liam she thought of, disheveled and foul, bound in manacles, imprisoned in the Tower. Panic filled her breast.

How could she go with Hawke, when she was married to Liam? And if she left the court, how could she help Liam?

Outside the queen's doors Katherine balked, spinning to face John, gripping his uniform. "John! There is something I must tell you," she cried. "I . . . I am married to O'Neill—and I have the signed documents to prove it."

31

*H*awke stared at her, frozen.

Katherine realized what she had said. Her heart raced wildly, and she tried to think, but logic failed to come to her now. She did not know if she should have told him the truth, especially here and now, just outside the Queen's Privy Chamber, with the ladies and gentlemen of the court staring at them and whispering to one another about them. But it was too late to take back her words, and somehow, she was relieved that she had declared the truth.

Hawke gripped her arm. "We will not talk here," he ground out, and he moved her forward. Almost miraculously, the crowd parted to make way for them, and just before they exited the antechamber, Katherine's glance found Anne's. The baroness appeared genuinely sympathetic to her plight.

Then Katherine stumbled as she realized who stood behind Anne. Leicester stared at her.

Hawke held her firmly so she did not fall, saying, "Do those two belong to you?"

Katherine saw that Macgregor and Guy were following them. "Yes." She hesitated. "I am fond of the boy, and Macgregor escorted me here. I was afraid to come alone."

Hawke sent a quelling glance at Macgregor. "I have no need of pirates, and neither does Katherine. Not anymore."

Katherine began to shake, realizing that she was going

to be truly alone now. "It's all right," she said softly to Guy and Macgregor. "I will be all right."

Hawke said nothing as they hurried down a long corridor, leaving Macgregor and Guy behind. Once through the hall, Hawke's grip upon her eased somewhat. They paused at the entrance to one of the covered walkways that led to other parts of the palace. His stare was impossible to read, but his blue gaze was powerful, immobilizing hers. Katherine could not look away from him. A lump seemed to have wedged itself in her throat.

"Tell me if I am wrong. You were as shocked as I was by O'Neill's abduction of you on our wedding night."

Katherine nodded slowly.

His stare was angry. "So he seduced you with his handsome face and ready smile."

Katherine did not dare agree. She did not dare speak.

"And when he asked you to marry him, you eagerly agreed."

Tears blurred her vision. "No, John," she said softly. " 'Twas not like that at all."

"Then how was it?" he demanded.

"He dragged me to the church, ignoring my protests. He claimed that in all likelihood you had already divorced me. The Catholic priest there married us immediately." Katherine did not continue. She hugged herself. She would never tell John that she had already been half in love with her captor, and had readily accepted their marriage once it was done.

"He forced you to marry him?" Hawke asked sharply.

She bit her lip. Hawke did not understand—and she could not explain. She blinked back tears. "Do I have two husbands? What shall I do?" she cried.

John took her arm again. When he spoke, his tone was soothing, kind—firm. "Does anyone else know of this marriage?"

She shook her head.

"Do not speak of it."

"Why?" Suddenly she was panicked, afraid.

"Because we were legally wed, Katherine, regardless of your other, forced marriage, and the pirate will hang. I have no intention of abandoning you now, in your time of need. What kind of man would I be?"

Katherine stared up at him, stunned.

"Do not mistake me," he said grimly. "I am not pleased by any of this. But eventually, when the pirate is dead, we will be able to put all of this behind us: If I did not believe that, then perhaps I would abandon you as a lesser man would."

Katherine was crying, shaking her head.

"Why do you weep?" John asked angrily. "For him? Do you love him?"

She pulled her arm from his and hugged herself again, uneasily, telling herself that she must not answer truthfully. "He is the father of my child. I do not wish to see him hang."

"He will hang," Hawke said firmly, "for the queen cannot show any leniency in this case. And it is for the best. It is best for everyone involved, and if you think carefully, if you think of the child, you will agree."

Her child. A pirate-traitor's babe. One the whole world would condemn as a bastard, and worse, condemn as Liam O'Neill's son. Suddenly Katherine understood Liam completely, too late. Suddenly she understood what it had been like for him growing up, and what it was like for him living now, carrying the ugly burden of the fact of his paternity, unable ever to escape being Shane O'Neill's son. Suddenly Katherine recalled every time she had taunted him, scorned him, and condemned him for being Shane O'Neill's son. And she recalled their last vicious argument, when she had told him, untruthfully, that she could never love him because Shane O'Neill had been his father.

Katherine was sick, in her heart, in her soul. How could she have been so cold-hearted, so cruel?

And would her own child suffer as Liam had, for the sins and crimes of his father?

Katherine wiped her eyes, and looked up at John. "Will you raise my child?" she asked unevenly. "Will you be a good, kind father?" Her heart was breaking all over again. *Oh, Liam. I am sorry, but now I protect our child— I do!*

"Not only will I be a good father to your child, Katherine, I will give him my name," Hawke stated. "Even if it is a boy."

A huge sob burst from Katherine's throat. She could not speak, and was blinded now by her tears.

"And you, of course, shall give me my own sons," he said.

Katherine turned her head away, unable to stop crying, nodding. She was a mother, and like any mother, would do whatever had to be done to protect and nourish her child. But God, how hard it was to accept her fate, how hard, how painful. Yet there was no choice. Not anymore, not for her. Because even if a miracle occurred, even if Liam escaped or were freed, she could not return to him— no matter that she knew now that she still loved him with all of her heart.

But Katherine had to face the heartrending face of reality. It did not appear that Liam would be pardoned, and no one escaped from the Tower. Only a miracle, it seemed, would save him.

And Katherine had stopped believing in miracles long ago.

She must do everything in her power to save Liam, she realized, everything—anything—it would be her parting gift to him, a gift of eternal love—the gift of life.

Katherine decided to remain in her room rather than go down to supper in the dining hall. She needed time to think and to plan, and had no wish anyway to face the curious and lewd stares of the court at the dinner meal. She and John had also agreed to postpone their journey to Cornwall for another few days, because of Katherine's obvious exhaustion. Katherine was relieved. She had some small amount of time, then, to find a powerful ally to aid her in her cause to save Liam's life.

And Katherine was seized with more determination now as well. For she could not survive if she did not see him before she departed for Cornwall. She did not know what she would do, or what she would say, if she succeeded in finding a way to visit him secretly, she only knew that she must see him one more time. But how?

She did not dare turn to John.

A dark, handsome, saturnine image filled Katherine's mind. His smile was seductive and dangerous, his intention bold, amoral, and amorous. Robert Dudley, the earl of Leicester. One of the most powerful men at court, nay, in all of England. He could help her—if he but chose to do so.

And Katherine knew exactly what price she would have to pay to gain his support. But pay it she would, in order to see Liam one more time—in order to save Liam's life.

Katherine could not approach Leicester directly. She did not dare, recalling too well the queen's threat to behead her should she ever slip into his bed. There was only one person Katherine trusted to serve as a messenger for her. She had already sent a message to Anne Hastings, asking her to come to her room.

Katherine jumped when she heard the knock upon her door. She was both relieved and terrified to espy Anne, who was smiling widely.

Anne entered her room; Katherine bolted the door behind her, and the two women hugged. "Katherine," Anne exclaimed, "I am so glad to see you—how I worried about you this past year—how beautiful you are!"

"Thank you for coming to see me, Anne."

"How could I not?" Anne was arch. "Katherine, you have spent close to a year with one of the most dangerous—and reputedly the most virile—of men! And you have followed him here despite your knowing the reception you would meet!"

Katherine sat down on the bed, staring at her friend.

Anne studied her. "Well? Is he as virile as it is said? Is he unsurpassable? Insatiable? You do not seem the worse for wear. And soon you will have his child."

Katherine was disappointed with her friend. "Perhaps you should find out for yourself, Anne."

"Oh! I have upset you! But can you blame me for imagining what he is like? My husband is old and fat and a lecher as well. There, there, dear, you are distraught. I am happy for you, Katherine—to have enjoyed such a man. How I wish the pirate had abducted me.''

Katherine's disappointment faded. Anne meant no harm. "I am afraid he will hang.''

"You have cause to fear. The queen detests traitors, and on principle will hang the most petty conspirator.''

"You are not soothing me.''

"I do not wish to soothe you. If you love your pirate, then you must be as clever as your mother was—you must politick for your cause, my dear. I can tell you this. Her advisors are divided. Cecil does not wish to see O'Neill hang.''

Katherine felt hope spark in her breast. "Lord Burghley often sways the queen!''

Anne held up a hand. "But Leicester despises O'Neill. He is pleased with this turn of events. He is advising Elizabeth to try him immediately, and he reminds her at every turn of the anarchy elsewhere in the world, and of the rebels plotting against her here in England—knowing that her fear of conspiracy will lead her to use Liam as an example to deter those others.''

Katherine's heart lurched. *Leicester.* How right she was to have conceived of this plot. "Anne—I beg a single boon of you.''

Anne patted her hand. "If it is in my power, you know that I shall do it.''

"I wish for you to deliver a message to Leicester for me, immediately.''

Anne started, then stared. "Katherine!'' Her eyes widened, filled with comprehension. "You know not what you do!''

"To the contrary, Anne, I know exactly what must be done.''

The chapel bells tolled the midnight hour. Nervously Katherine counted each ring. Her palms wet with sweat, her mouth dry, she sat upon a bench in the Privy garden, wrapped in her fur-lined cloak, shivering.

She saw him coming through the bare trees a moment later, the garden walls behind him. He was a tall, powerful, black-cloaked figure, moving swiftly toward the arbor where she sat. Katherine's nails curled into her palms. "My lord," she called.

He changed direction and strode to her. Katherine rose to her feet. He stopped before her. She wore her hood and now she held the neck of it tightly at her throat.

Leicester smiled slightly. "Do you know what it did to me, to receive word that you wished to meet me—clandestinely?"

Katherine trembled. She did not speak. Moonlight spilled from the parting clouds, and she could see his handsome face quite clearly.

He reached out. Katherine stood still, not flinching no matter how she wished to move away, and he pushed back her hood. "God, you are so lovely," he said harshly. His hand touched her cheek.

Katherine forced herself to stand utterly still. "I am fat now."

Leicester's dark gaze held hers. "You bear his child. 'Tis no surprise. I always knew you were made for taking a man's seed, for bearing a man's children."

Katherine did not respond.

Leicester's gaze roamed slowly over her face. "Did you think of me, sweetheart? When the pirate sheathed his cock inside your lovely body—did you think of me?"

Katherine tensed.

"I have thought of you often," Leicester said. "I still want you. More now than before." He smiled slightly, took her hand, pressed it against his groin. He was rock-hard.

Katherine pulled her palm away. "I am with child!"

"Some women enjoy a man more in such a state."

Katherine was shocked and afraid. She had not thought he would be ardent, not now, not while she was so heavily pregnant. "Not I."

"I do not believe you." Leicester pulled her close. Katherine stiffened but did not resist, and was acutely aware of his manhood against her hip. "You are a woman of passion. I knew it from the first. But the proof is that O'Neill did not tire of you, that he kept you on that island for almost an entire year. I imagine he has taught you many interesting ways to please a man." Leicester's mouth brushed hers. "But he has been imprisoned now for several weeks. Your body must be hot. I intend to take his place, Katherine."

Katherine twisted to remove her mouth from further contact with his. She was short of breath. "Stop. Please."

"But you summoned me," he said too lightly. Then his gaze pierced hers. "What do you want of me, Katherine?"

Her hands pressed against his chest, a futile effort to put some small distance between their bodies. "I need your help."

"I know. And I can guess in what manner you wish me to help you."

Katherine stared at him.

He smiled at her. "The queen told me you begged quite prettily, quite capably, for your pirate lover's life. Katherine, you are right to come to me. I alone can help you gain what you seek. The queen cannot refuse me."

"Then you will convince her to spare Liam his life?" Katherine managed hoarsely.

"Are you prepared to pay the price I will demand?"

She nodded, her heart sinking with dread.

He smiled and rocked against her. "Tonight?"

"No!" She pushed away from him, consumed with panic.

He let her go, watching with interest. He was cool and confident, a predator stalking easy prey.

Panting, Katherine faced him. "First you must succeed in gaining Liam's release. Afterward I will come to you. After my child is born."

He laughed. "I don't know. I must wait to have you until after the pirate is freed? And then have you but once? The stakes are so high, Katherine. The queen would be furious with me if she ever learned of our affair. And we talk about your lover's life. I do not think one time is enough."

Katherine shook her head, telling herself not to cry, to remain strong. "After Liam is released, I will come to you but once." She was firm. She hugged herself to try to stop her body from trembling. She hesitated. "Before the baby is born then, if that is what you truly wish."

He eyed her. "And if I refuse?"

"Then you shall never have me," Katherine said far more calmly than she felt.

He did not laugh. "I could take you now, and you would never dare complain, would you?"

Katherine gasped. "Then you shall not have me willingly," she cried, frightened now. "I am offering you an endless night of pleasure, Dudley. I will show you each and every one of my temptress's tricks." Her voice broke. Tears streaked her cheeks.

He stared at her. "Done."

Katherine hardly felt any relief. "There is one other thing."

His brow rose.

"I want to see Liam, one single time, in case you fail to arrange his release."

"I see." His jaw flexed, and his tone was harsh.

"If you do not arrange a visit for me, in the next two days, then we have no pact," Katherine cried, bluffing.

Dudley's smile was dangerous. "And when you visit him, will you give him what you have just denied me?"

Katherine looked at him. " 'Tis not your affair."

He stared. "Two deeds require two prices, Katherine," he finally said.

Katherine understood. She nodded and turned to leave. He grabbed her sleeve. "Not so quickly."

Katherine faced him with vast reluctance.

"Come here," Leicester said, "I wish to seal our bargain with a kiss."

A noise awoke him.

It was a scratching noise. At first, as he stiffened upon his pallet on the floor, Liam thought it was a rat. He prepared to kick the beast should it come near. Kick it and kill it.

But the scratching sound faded. Now he heard a distinct clicking sound. Liam jerked into a sitting position. The door to his cell was being unlocked.

There was no light in his cell. It was always dark, but he was brought gruel and water twice a day, and these meals aided him in keeping track of the time. He knew it was well past suppertime, perhaps as late as midnight. He rose to his feet, fully alert, ready to receive a friend—or an assassin.

The door was pushed open wide. Blinding light spilled into the cell. Liam raised his arm, blocking the torchlight, blinking madly. But he had glimpsed a jailer, and the cloaked, hooded figure of an unknown visitor standing behind him.

There was the rustle of stiff fabric, a sound only a woman could make. Liam froze, dropping his arm, afraid that he was dreaming. Or that he had gone mad.

Katherine moved into the cell.

She carried a lantern, saw him, and became as rigid as he. They stared at each other. Neither one of them saw the jailer leer, nor did they see him close the cell door smartly behind Katherine.

"Liam," Katherine said huskily. "Oh, God, Liam—are you all right?"

She was a vision of ethereal loveliness. At once a heavenly angel and an earthbound temptress. Liam did not move, did not breathe. Her presence caused a stabbing anguish. He reminded himself that she had been using him to aid her father. That she was treacherous, a deceitful bitch. That she could never love the son of Shane O'Neill. She had told him so herself.

"What do you want?" he said, his tone ringing harshly in the small stone cell. Trying to ignore her beauty, and worse, the open concern he saw in her eyes. That and something more, something that could not be.

Her whisper was raw. "I wanted to see you."

"Why?" he demanded.

She ducked her head away. But he glimpsed the sparkle of tears in her eyes.

"Why?" he demanded again. "Are you not pleased, Katherine, that I shall soon meet a pirate's fate?"

She looked up, blinking back tears.

He raised one fist. "Are you not pleased, wife, that your

husband—Shane O'Neill's son—will soon die? Leaving
you free to entrap the noble and saintly John Hawke? If
you have not already done so?''

She bit her lip, staring at him sadly, a tear trailing down
her cheek. "I am sorry."

He froze.

She turned her back on him, raised her fist, about to
bang on the door, for the guard.

"Don't!" he cried, leaping forward. Catching her wrist
before she could knock. She did not move.

"Katherine," he whispered, agonized. He no longer
cared about her treachery. Not now. He only cared that
she was there, a flesh and blood Katherine, not the figment
of his imagination, not an unearthly apparition—and that
she had said she was sorry. He was a romantic fool after
all, for his breast filled with hope. "Katherine—why did
you come?"

She turned slowly, facing him. Only a blade of grass
could have fit between them. Her tone was low and barely
audible. "I came to tell you . . . I don't want you to die."

The hope overwhelmed him. "You care."

She sucked in her breath, trembling. "Liam . . . yes."

He reached out and cupped her face—her extraordinary
face. A face that had haunted him for years—ever since
he had first glimpsed her that day long ago at the convent.
He was foul and dirty, but he could no more stop himself
from kissing her than he could have stopped himself from
thinking about her in all the days and hours and minutes
since that day at the Abbé Saint Pierre-Eglise, so many
years ago. He touched her lips with his. Aware now, of
the hot, powerful force of his love, a love he had refused
to believe in, a love he had never wanted, a love that had
enslaved him then and still did now, a love that had moti-
vated his most significant actions, that had precipitated this
game, and had brought them both to this point in time,
together and aching in the dungeons of the Tower of
London.

Katherine's lips trembled beneath his.

Lust seized Liam, hot and hard, huge. He shook with
it, seized Katherine's shoulders, and thought of little else

now but taking her, mastering her, and enslaving her to him with the force and power of his body, as she had enslaved him with her beauty, her pride, her determination and intelligence. "Katherine. I want you."

She clung to his shoulders, swaying against him, her loins soft and inviting against his. She met his gaze, whispering his name, whispering, *"Yes."*

He wrapped his arms around her, groaning, pressing his face into her neck, savoring the pulsing heat that coursed between their bodies for one more instant. He was huge now, ready to explode, but that was unthinkable, even though her invitation was clear. Even though, despite his determination to live, he might very well die.

"Liam, I am so afraid, please." She undulated against him, kissing his forehead, and running her fingers through his hair. "I want you, too, darling. *I need you.*"

He had no defenses left. Every single last one of them, erected to guard his heart, were shattered by her words. Liam gazed into her sea green eyes. This was no pretense; there were no theatrics. Desire shimmered in her eyes, desire and something much more powerful. Something irrevocable, something eternal. Something that was meant to be from the very start. Something ordained by fate, that two human beings could not defy.

The words were there, on the tip of his tongue. *I love you. I always have. I always will.*

He caught her mouth with his. Katherine cried out. His lips sucked her, his hands as greedy, touching her everywhere, exploring her curves, relishing them. Then, his palm flattened upon her belly and he froze.

It was hard and round and protruding.

Katherine half laughed, half sobbed. "Yes, Liam, I am going to have your child."

He raised his head and gazed into her eyes with disbelief, while his hand slid over her swollen belly a dozen more times. He was stunned. His gaze slid to the mound he caressed. "My child," he whispered hoarsely. And through the haze of shock came a piercing pleasure—Katherine was giving him a child.

Her gaze met his, and although she was crying again, she was smiling, too.

And then his pleasure died. He stared at her, remembering his childhood—all of it. "Oh, God," he said, torn between utter joy and sheer hopelessness.

Her smile faded. "You are not pleased."

He stepped back from her. "You do not understand." Suddenly he was that boy again, filled with pain, and he could hear the taunts, cruel and mocking, *Shane O'Neill's bastard son.*

She touched him. "I do understand. Liam—I will protect this child. He will not suffer as you have suffered, I swear it to you."

"You cannot stop the world from cursing him, and you can not change the fact that he is my son."

She said nothing.

He jerked. "What do you plan?"

She turned pale. Except for two bright spots of pink upon her cheeks, the signs of her guilt.

And he recalled her treachery again, and thought of how clever she was—how determined. "What do you plan Kathcrine?"

"The queen is furious. Hawke says you will hang."

Hawke. John Hawke—her other husband. "I am not dead yet, Kate. Nor do I intend to die anytime soon—or have you already buried me?"

"I do not want you to die!"

"And I will not die. I will escape this prison, return to the seas, and finish the game I have begun. Do you hear me, Katherine?" he shouted. "And you will be with me. You and the child," he cried.

She did not answer him. Her silence told him everything that he needed to know. "You are my wife," he said, his chest heaving. And suddenly he could not stand it, not his captivity, not the powerlessness of it, and he was consumed with rage. He gripped her chin, forcing her to face him. She was shaking her head no. "Has he taken you to his bed, Katherine? Has he?"

"No!" she cried, frightened.

Liam did not relax. She was deceiving him now, damn

her soul. Suddenly the walls of the cell felt as if they were closing in on him. He was acutely aware of being reduced to a state of impotent wretchedness. Frustration made him shake. "You have not answered me, Katherine."

"Hawke says you will hang. I am doing everything in my power to prevent that, but I do not know if I can succeed," she cried in a rush. "Hawke says . . ." she stopped.

Hawke. Hawke. Hawke. "What else does he say?" he snarled.

"He will give your child his name—even if it is a boy!"

He saw it all then. The future—her future with John Hawke. The two of them ensconced cozily in Barby Hall, his child growing up a little English lord, clad in plumed hat, doublet and hose, taught by the best tutors, conversant in English, French, and Latin, moving with ease from the London court to any country hall. And undoubtedly there would be other children as well, little boys and girls—the children Katherine would eventually give John Hawke, as any wife must do.

Liam hated him.

In that moment, he hated her.

He turned with a cry of rage and smashed his hand into the wall. Katherine cried out in fright. Liam punched the wall again. And again, and again. Until he realized that Katherine clung to his back, weeping, weeping and shouting that he must not do this, please, please stop.

Panting, his fist bloodied and hurting terribly and probably badly broken, Liam leaned his face against the wall. Katherine sagged against him from behind. She sobbed softly. He felt his own tears streaking down his cheeks. And for the first time in his life, he doubted himself.

He was going to lose everything. His woman, his child, his life.

Fear almost paralyzed him.

And then some inner strength surged forth. The fear remained, but determination pulsed now in his veins, roiled in his blood. He must gain his freedom, and he would. Before Katherine did the unthinkable and returned to John Hawke. Before she gave herself to John, or any other man, in the hopes of using them while they used her—in order to free him. Before she became a political sacrifice, her altar his life, and before he truly succumbed to madness.

32

Hawkehurst

*I*t was exactly one year since Katherine had first visited Hawkehurst. Then she had been John Hawke's betrothed, soon to be his bride. It seemed an eternity ago. She remembered how naive and innocent she had been, both of the ways of the world, and of the ways of men. She felt as if she had aged a decade since that time.

Now she was returning to Hawkehurst in circumstances which she would have never dreamed even remotely possible.

They traveled slowly along the rutted, muddy road that wound down through the moors toward Hawkehurst. Although Katherine had spent much of the past week traveling in a carriage, today she had insisted upon riding astride. Hawke had conceded. Last year Katherine had found the windswept, gorse-covered moors picturesque and somehow romantic. This year she found them desolate and inhospitable.

The stone walls and slate roof of the old manor, with its several limestone chimneys, was already visible below them, and Katherine felt a bubble of panic rising up in her. Her life was pure madness. How could she carry on as Hawke's wife when she yearned so desperately for another man? When she carried that other man's child? When that other man might very well hang? How?

Pain pressed in on her heart unerringly, very much like

a huge vise. She was counting on Leicester being successful in persuading Elizabeth to pardon Liam, dear God, she
was. He had to succeed, but if he did, then she would
have to uphold her part of the sinful bargain she had made
with him. How powerless she felt. How desperate. How
alone.

They clattered into the cobbled courtyard, a dozen men
following them. Hawke helped Katherine to dismount.
"My parents are not in residence. They are in their London home, so you will not have to face them quite yet."

Katherine was relieved. But she had been too anxious
about Liam's fate even to think about the unpleasant reception Hawke's parents would undoubtedly give her.

"I know you are tired," Hawke said. "Why do you not
go upstairs to your chamber and rest? You need not join
me for dinner if you are too fatigued to do so."

Katherine met his troubled gaze. Why did he continue
to be so kind when he was, it seemed, as unhappy as she?
"Thank you." She turned to go into the house.

"Katherine."

Katherine paused.

Hawke's regard was grave and searching. "We must
put the past behind us," he said slowly. "I know it will
not be an easy thing to do. Not for me, and certainly not
for you. But we must try." He forced a smile, still holding
her eyes.

Katherine could not reply. In that instant, standing there
in the courtyard beneath the warm spring sun, she realized
it was going to be impossible for her to put the past—and
Liam—behind her.

"We must try," Hawke said firmly when Katherine did
not speak. "I think it best you bear the child here in
Cornwall, far from the court, and my motives are not the
queen's. And even after the child is born, you should remain at Hawkehurst, where you will have few visitors, if
any. In time the scandal will die down."

Katherine could not agree. "The scandal will never die
completely. Like my mother, they will whisper about me
after I am dead."

"No," Hawke said flatly. "The scandal will die down,

although it may take some years. But after you have given me children, when we are happy, people will forget.''

And Katherine was stricken. She could not do this. John Hawke was a good man, but she would never be happy if she remained with him as his wife.

''I want your promise, Katherine,'' Hawke said, ''that you will put the past behind you, forget the pirate, and in good faith, abide with me as my loyal wife.''

Katherine hugged her swollen belly. Logic told her to say the words, to tell the lie, but somehow, she could not. She would never forget Liam. Never.

Hawke's right eye ticked. ''You will not give me the promise I have asked for—knowing all that I will do for you and your child?''

Katherine could hardly speak. Tears filled her eyes. ''You ask me to promise the impossible,'' she whispered.

He cried out.

''I'm sorry,'' she cried back. ''I'm sorry, so sorry! But I cannot forget him, I will never forget him, I love him— in spite of all he has done. God help us all!''

Hawke stared at her as her face crumbled and she wept, silently, in great anguish. When he spoke his voice was harsh. ''He will hang, Katherine. And what will you do then? Dream of a ghost?'' He strode away.

And Katherine covered her face with her hands. Knowing that even if Liam were hanged, she would, always, yearn for a dead man.

Hawke shook with anger and disbelief. He moved across the courtyard with no destination in mind. He spotted a horse and rider cantering toward Hawkehurst's front gates. He recognized the chestnut filly instantly—just as he recognized Juliet.

Immediately he tensed.

Juliet slowed to a trot and rode into the courtyard.

It had been several months since he had last seen her. He became wary. Not of her, but of himself. If only she were old and ugly and mean-tempered. If only she did not look at him with such big blue worshipful eyes.

In fact, he had forgotten that she was Katherine's dear

friend. Now he realized Juliet might become a constant presence at Hawkehurst. He did not care for that thought—not at all.

But of course, although Katherine and the child would live in Cornwall, he would remain with the queen and her Guard at court.

Juliet had stopped her frisky mount beside him. Two bright spots of color marred her otherwise flawless face. And her blue eyes seemed to spark as they settled upon his face. He could not help but wonder if she had ever been kissed. He shoved the very thought aside the instant it occurred to him.

"Sir John," she said unevenly. Her flush was more pronounced now. "I am pleased to see you again."

He ignored the remark. "You have come to visit my wife?" He wanted to be rude, he wanted her to leave.

Her gaze slid away. "Yes."

"She is in the hall. I am sure she will be glad to speak with you."

Juliet stared at the ground, appearing dismayed and at a loss.

Hawke felt like a boor. He bowed. "Excuse my poor manners," he said stiffly. "We have traveled for many days now, and we are all overtired."

"I should not have come," Juliet said, and she gathered up her reins and began to whirl her mount around. But before Hawke knew what he was doing, he had caught the filly's bridle with one hand—and with his other he gripped Juliet's knee.

At the contact, she froze, her eyes wide.

Hawke grew rigid too, and their eyes darted together, held, then skipped apart.

Hawke took a breath. What kind of adolescent behavior was this? He forced a semblance of a smile to his lips. "Lady Stratheclyde, please, dismount. Katherine is in need of a friend right now."

Juliet studied him for what seemed an eternity, and then she was slipping from her mount, sliding to the ground. Hawke steadied her, and told himself it was not because she was so pleasant to touch.

Juliet drew back. "How is Katherine?"

"Better than one would expect," he said gruffly, unable to tear his gaze from hers. And her next words rocked him. "And you, Sir John? How do you fare?"

He stared at her, knowing she did not ask after his health. And suddenly he wanted to pour out all of his anguish, and all of his need, to her, a girl just sixteen. And she gazed at him out of huge blue eyes as if she wanted nothing more than to comfort him, but surely he imagined her sympathy, her caring, her concern. He said awkwardly, "I am well." A lie. "And pleased that Katherine is back." Another lie. Dear God, he was not pleased, not anymore, not at all.

Her eyes widened, her small face tensed, and then she smiled gamely. "I am glad Katherine is back, too," she whispered. Her smile became far too bright. Her voice quavered. "Now she will be able to attend my wedding to Lord Hunt in December."

Hawke flinched as if struck. For a moment he could not speak. "You are marrying Simon Hunt?" An image of the fat viscount assailed him—an image of him covering Juliet with his soft body, slobbering kisses upon her.

Juliet looked away, providing him with a striking view of her perfect, suddenly expressionless profile. "Yes."

And Hawke was engulfed with red-hot jealousy.

They did not speak again. Instead, careful not to look at her, not even once, he escorted her into the house so she could visit with his wife. But he could not stop thinking of her in Simon Hunt's arms, as Simon Hunt's beautiful wife.

Elizabeth's favorite summer residence was Whitehall, and with the cheerful advent of spring, she had moved her court there. Outside, trees budded along the Thames, daffodils bloomed. Inside, Elizabeth paced her Presence Chamber. It was time to deal with the issue that lay unresolved and hanging over her like a shroud.

She turned to face those closeted with her, whom she had summoned to aid her in making what could be a horribly painful decision—her cousin, Tom Butler; the earl of Leicester; and William Cecil. She said without ceremony, "I must try O'Neill or pardon him. I cannot allow him to rot in the dungeons of the Tower indefinitely."

Everyone began to speak at once, offering their fervent opinions upon the controversial subject. Clearly Ormond was aghast at the thought of a pardon, but Leicester was suddenly speaking against a trial when so far he had been for one. Cecil did not utter a single word. Elizabeth cried out, silencing the two younger men. "If he claims he can deliver FitzMaurice, should I not free him?"

Ormond was incredulous. "Surely you do not think to trust him!"

The queen regarded her cousin. "If he would bring me FitzMaurice, his pardon would be worth it."

Ormond was angry. "He will not bring you FitzMaurice. He dissembles and lies. He is the papist's ally! And *you* would trust him now, Bess? You are allowing his handsome demeanor and manliness to interfere with your judgment!"

Elizabeth paled. *How close to the mark was Tom?* She was frightened to think that he was right. No matter how often she brooded upon hanging Liam, her heart always rebelled at the thought.

Ormond continued, a tirade. "You forget he is Shane O'Neill's son. Yet how you could forget *that* when my sister arrived at your court, swollen with his child, God's blood, I do not know! You were there, Bess, not too many years ago when poor Mary Stanley came to court, carrying Shane's son! It is ironic, it is not, that Mary's son has now inflicted the same grievous crime upon Katherine as his father inflicted upon his mother? You are mad to think to trust O'Neill."

Leicester remarked, "Are you accusing O'Neill of rape, Ormond? I hate to say it, but Katherine did not appear hate-filled toward the pirate when I last saw her."

Ormond had no chance to respond. Elizabeth moved in front of Leicester. "And when was that, Robin?"

He started. "I beg your pardon, Bess?"

Elizabeth did not repeat the question. A gossip had told her of a strange rendezvous a week ago in the Privy Gardens of Richmond. A rendezvous at the midnight hour.

The witness swore that the woman was Katherine. The spy had not glimpsed the man's face, but swore he was very tall, broad-shouldered, and very dark. Elizabeth stared at Robin, wondering if he betrayed her with Katherine FitzGerald. She shook even to think of them together. Was it not enough that the slut had worked her wiles upon O'Neill? Was it not enough that Elizabeth had exiled her to Cornwall?

Leicester spoke, as if Elizabeth had never questioned him. "If O'Neill can deliver FitzMaurice, he should be freed."

Elizabeth raised her brow. "You have changed your tune, dear Robin. Why, just the other day you were advising me to try him swiftly—and hang him just as swiftly."

Leicester smiled. "We can not afford these Irish wars. FitzMaurice is too capable a leader. If O'Neill can bring him down, it is far better to free him than to hang him. No one else is capable of capturing the papist and you know it, Bess."

Elizabeth stared coldly. Something was going on—she was certain of it. Dudley had changed his mind too quickly—and too fervently. Now he was an advocate for the pirate's freedom. The girl was behind it. Elizabeth sensed it—just as she sensed that removing the girl from court was not enough to dull Leicester's desire to have her. It flashed through Elizabeth's mind that she could have the girl hanged as a traitor alongside her pirate lover.

"Your Majesty, please," Cecil intervened. Elizabeth turned to him with relief. "We must give up on Sir John Perrot. He cannot catch the wily papist. The best he could do was to challenge him to a duel, and make an utter fool of himself."

Elizabeth met Cecil's direct brown gaze. "I have already given up on Sir John," she said. "Since hearing that most incredible tale."

Both Leicester and Ormond snickered, unable to help themselves.

Elizabeth sent them both a quelling glance. "Clearly he has gone mad," she said. "To challenge FitzMaurice to meet him in a duel! Dear God! Sir John must have lost his wits if he thought a private duel would end a public war."

Leicester still grinned. "At his age, and bulk, too."

Ormond also chortled. "And FitzMaurice, the fox, failed to show up, making Sir John twice the fool."

"Thrice," Leicester said, and both men erupted into laughter.

"Cease this at once," Elizabeth cried. "How cruel you are to make fun of a man who has served Us well, then loses his mind in Our cause!"

" 'Tis a difficult land," Cecil said softly, an apology for Perrot's failure and apparent madness.

"Should I trust the pirate?" Elizabeth asked him.

Cecil smiled slightly and when he spoke, it was only to her. "If O'Neill can deliver the papist, we are indeed very fortunate. Of course, that leaves us with a whole new rotten carcass."

"What mean you by that?" Leicester demanded.

Cecil barely looked at Leicester. "With FitzMaurice gone, who shall rule the south of Ireland and the Irish there?"

"I will rule the south of Ireland," Ormond said.

Cecil looked at him. "You are more English than Irish and a staunch Protestant. The Irish lords tolerate you—but they will never follow you."

Ormond ground down his jaw. "I know what you will say next."

"Indeed?" Cecil mused.

"You never wanted FitzGerald removed from Ireland in the first place!" Ormond cried. "But it is too late. He has been removed, stripped of all that was his, he is half-mad now, and destitute. The Irish will have to accept me as the most powerful lord amongst them. There *is* no other choice."

"There is always another choice," Cecil said calmly.

And Elizabeth knew that he had already decided what to do if she freed the pirate and he brought her FitzMaurice. Silently she thanked God for Cecil, a man she had known since she was but a young princess, a man she had trusted ever since. "What choice do we have, William?"

"Free the pirate," Cecil said, "Let him finish his game. Allow the fox to run. And let us watch where all the pieces fall, and be poised to pick up the ones we must use again."

"You can not trust Shane O'Neill's son," Ormond insisted angrily.

Cecil smiled. "Trust him? I do not know. But we can certainly control him."

Silence.

Cecil spoke to the room at large. "After all, the royal astrologer has said his mistress bears a son. What better way to control a man than with his only child, his only heir?"

No one moved. Smiles formed. And then Elizabeth clapped her hands. "How clever you are," she cried, beaming.

And Cecil smiled, thinking that he was hardly as clever as the pirate, who, if all went as Cecil expected it to, would indeed prove himself master of the game.

33

*L*iam knew that his fate drew near.

He had been told to bathe and shave, and had been removed from his foul cell to a spare but far more hospitable chamber on one of the higher floors in the Tower. He had been given clean clothes and a decent meal. He realized that a meeting with the queen was near at hand.

He prepared himself. He prepared himself to outwit and outmaneuver the queen and her advisors—including the very shrewd William Cecil. Everything he cherished hung in the balance—Katherine, his child, his life.

And then Liam was escorted to the queen.

She awaited him in the antechamber of her Privy Apartments, and for the first moment, Liam thought she was alone. Then he espied Cecil standing behind her. Despite his determination to gain his release, he was also relieved. For it had crossed his mind that he might have to seduce—and bed—the queen if all else failed.

"You appear in better spirits, pirate," Elizabeth said sharply.

Liam bowed, getting down on one knee. "I am thankful that you allowed me to bathe and don fresh clothing, Your Majesty. More grateful that you can possibly know."

"I had no wish to entertain a foul wretch in my apartments," she said. "You may rise."

Liam got to his feet.

"What am I to do with you, traitor?"

"Have you not thought upon my proposition?" Liam asked.

"Indeed, I have, but my Council is divided. Some suspect it is but another ploy." Elizabeth moved closer, peering up at Liam's face. "Is it a ploy? Would you betray me yet again?"

"Dear Bess, I did not betray you before, and I would not betray you now."

She stared at him searchingly. "I have thought long and carefully on this matter," she finally said. "And your word is not enough."

Liam inclined his head. Tense now, waiting.

"I must have some hold upon you, some great hold, to make you adhere to your part of the bargain."

His heart lurched. Katherine. Would she try to use Katherine against him—or offer Katherine to him as an enticement? That last possibility was exactly what he wanted. "What do you think of, Your Majesty?" he asked softly.

"The child," she said.

Liam started. His mind raced. Hundreds of years ago, for many centuries, children had been used frequently as political pawns, yet he could not believe that this was the queen's intent. Not in this modern age.

But he was very wrong. "After the child is born it shall be removed to my household," the queen stated. "And your son will be a hostage for your good behavior. When you deliver FitzMaurice to me, I shall deliver your son to you."

Liam stared, stricken. He recalled growing up at court. He had never dreamed his own child might be raised here—and endure the exact same cruelty as he himself had. He could not bear the notion.

"Liam?" Elizabeth asked, her tone puzzled.

He did not really hear her. Visions of his small son— or daughter—surrounded by a crowd of mocking English youth, assailed him, tormented him. He wet his lips. Afraid. He had never doubted his ability to entrap and capture FitzMaurice before, but suddenly now, the possibility raised itself. It frightened him. And then what would happen to his child? "If I fail to deliver the papist?" he asked, his voice rough, sounding strange.

Elizabeth squinted at him. "If you do not deliver Fitz-Maurice, I will find some proper Englishman, one loyal to me, to foster the babe."

He found it difficult to breathe.

"And I will send my best sea captains after you," Elizabeth added, "to return you to the Tower, where you will stay."

He had no choice. For the child's sake, an innocent life that must not suffer because of him, he would win. Trying very hard not to show his distress, certain that he failed, he said, "I will deliver FitzMaurice. But you will return Katherine to me, along with the child."

"Oh ho!" the queen cried. "Nay, I will not!"

Liam stiffened.

"Katherine remains with her husband, John Hawke. And this is not a negotiation, rogue, this is my single offer to you. Bring me FitzMaurice, and I will give you your child."

His heart beat hard. Painfully so. He had come so far, risked so much, in order to gain the woman he loved. The child alone was not enough—would never be enough.

Liam took a deep breath. The game was not over yet. There was much play still to be had. After all, Gerald was still in exile in Southwark, so the delivering of Katherine to him, Liam, was yet premature. And he did not inform Elizabeth of the fact of their marriage, because if he wound up hanging, then John Hawke would provide for her and his son.

And suddenly Liam's gaze met Cecil's. He knew instantly that Burghley comprehended him completely, yet somehow, he was not surprised. He also sensed that he had an ally. There was a hint of encouragement in his eyes. Liam recalled how, five years ago, William Cecil had been adamantly against the dispossession of Desmond's earl. Their gaze held for another moment, and then Liam returned his attention to the queen. "Hawke does not wish to divorce her?"

Elizabeth said, "He is a noble man. He will do his duty to her. Nor will I try to persuade him otherwise. *You* cannot have her. I will not change my mind on that score.

Already I suspect that somehow she is the one who has led you astray. You will have to forget the girl, Liam, and direct your manly appetites elsewhere.'' Elizabeth had grown flushed.

Liam said nothing. Then, casually, he shrugged. "You misunderstand. I want the woman for the child, not for myself. My own pleasure can be taken anywhere."

"Indeed?" Elizabeth stared at him, but her mouth had softened. "Do you tire of her already?"

"Bess, come, do you think me a man capable of love?"

Elizabeth regarded him. "I do not think any man capable of love," she finally said. "I think all men are ruled by what they cherish beyond all else, that unruly appendage kept in their codpieces. But she is very beautiful, and very wicked. She has seduced both Leicester and Ormond. And, of course, you."

Liam refrained from a rebuttal, but his pulse quickened. Did Elizabeth speak literally? He was sickened at the thought. But it no longer mattered. He would forgive Katherine anything that she had done in order to aid him. But he remarked closely the queen's rampant jealousy—and her evident fear of a beautiful rival. He realized then how easy it would be later to lead Elizabeth—exactly where he wished her to go.

"Well?" Elizabeth peered at him. "Do you accept my terms or not? After the babe is born, I will take him into my household. Then you shall appear to escape. When you bring me FitzMaurice, I give you the child. Not a moment sooner."

Liam nodded. "I accept," he said. He took the queen's hand, bent over it, kissed it. "And I promise you that I will not fail you. As always, it is you I serve."

"I doubt that," she said, but her cheeks flushed with color.

He looked into her eyes. Seeing not the all-powerful queen, but the jealous, desperate woman. He could still win. For he had one more move up his sleeve, yet he would not use it until the very end. Then he would play her fear of Katherine's ability to seduce her favorite, Leicester against her—when it was time to collect the prize.

Hawkehurst

Katherine screamed. And screamed and screamed.

Juliet held her hand and stroked her hair, talking to her. "It will pass. Be brave, Katherine. Be brave."

Katherine hardly heard her. She had known there would be pain, but she had never dreamed it could be like this. Long and constant, like the brutal stabbing and twisting of a knife blade inside her womb. Oh, God. Liam. How she needed him.

Finally the pain began to dull, and Katherine wept. She knew that within too short a time it would return, worse than before. She did not think she could endure much more.

She had been trying to deliver the child since dawn. The labor pains had started after suppertime, and had begun in earnest around the midnight hour. By sunrise Katherine had already been exhausted. Now it was close to noon. Sunlight streamed into her bedchamber. How much longer could she last?

"Katherine!" Juliet cried excitedly. "The midwife sees the babe's head! You must push now, dearheart, push as hard as you can!"

But Katherine was sobbing again, racked with yet another brutal pain.

"Push, lady, push," Ginny cried. "The babe cannot stay in such a condition!"

Fear filled Katherine as she comprehended the midwife's words. She had no strength left with which to push, yet the babe was no longer safely in her womb, but caught in her birth channel instead. What if she failed to push him out? Surely he would die!

She panted, knowing she must summon her strength now, strength she did not have, in order to expel the babe. Liam's babe must live. She forced herself to bear down, clawing at Juliet's hand.

"That's good, Katherine, that's good, I can see his entire head!" Juliet cried.

Katherine gave up, collapsing back against the pillows,

sobbing. She had no strength left, nothing. "Liam," she cried. "Oh, God, I need Liam!"

Juliet paled.

Katherine wondered if this was the first time she had called his name aloud, and then she ceased to care. It should be Liam with her now, holding her hand, encouraging her through the worst trial of her life, not Juliet—and Hawke should not be the man standing outside her bedroom door.

"Push, lady, push now, and let the poor mite be born," Ginny cried, her plump breasts swinging.

Liam's image swam before her, concerned, demanding. Katherine knew she must succeed in giving him his child. This was the most important act of her entire life. Groaning, raised up on her elbows, she panted and pushed. And for one single instant it was his face she saw so close to her own, and his hand she felt upon her brow, not Juliet's. She could do it—for him! She could, she would! The midwife cried out triumphantly, and in that same moment, Katherine knew she had managed to expel the babe.

The pain was gone. Katherine was flooded with relief. And as suddenly as her agony had ended, her weakness turned to strength. Katherine stared at the midwife, who was working between her legs. "Is it all right?" Katherine gasped, straining to see. She saw a mop of brown curls, and the babe's body, which was covered with a whitish afterbirth and blood.

" 'Tis just fine," Ginny smiled, cutting the cord between mother and child.

"Is . . . is it a boy . . . or a girl?" Katherine gasped, on her elbows, desperate to see her newborn baby.

Ginny lifted the child for Katherine to see. "A boy, my lady, you have delivered a fine son to your lord."

Tears streamed down Katherine's face as she beheld her child, Liam's son. The babe's face was round, his nose somewhat flattened from the birthing, his arms and legs seeming surprisingly long; his tiny fingers were curling, and his blue, blue eyes were wide open—he was staring directly at her. He was the most beautiful sight Katherine had ever seen. Instant, all-consuming love washed over Katherine, and she held out her arms.

" 'Tis a big boy, too," the midwife said. "Here, let me clean 'im up a bit fer you."

"Oh, Katherine," Juliet cried, her eyes swimming with tears. She gripped Katherine's hands. "You have a son. A lovely, healthy son."

Katherine sagged against the pillows, but never took her gaze from her son. Ginny was now wrapping the child in clean linens and a lightweight blanket. She held out her arms again. "Bring me my son," she commanded softly, smiling, her eyes shining.

Ginny turned, the child in her arms, grinning back.

John Hawke stepped between them. "No."

Katherine froze, turning her head toward the stern sound of Hawke's voice. "My son," she whispered, confused and uncertain. "I want to hold my son."

Hawke's jaw was rigid. "No," he repeated. "Ginny, take the child downstairs, now."

"I want my son," Katherine cried, raising herself up with difficulty. "I want to hold my son. Why do you deny me?"

Juliet stared at Hawke, pale and wide-eyed.

Hawke looked only at Katherine, his face set in stone. " 'Tis better that you do not hold him—that you do not know him. It will be easier for you, in the end."

"Wh-what?" Katherine cried, struggling to sit. Juliet propped her up. "Hawke! I want my son!" She turned to stare at the midwife, who was bustling out of the door, the child in her arms. Tears filled Katherine's eyes. "My son! Bring me my son!"

"Katherine, listen to me," Hawke said.

"No!" Katherine screamed, kicking at the sheets and forcing her feet to the floor. She had to grip the bed for balance as a wave of dizziness swept her. Panic, huge and terrible, terrifying, filled her. "Did you lie! Did you lie! *I want my son!"*

"I did not lie, but my plans mean naught now," Hawke said grimly. "The queen has decided to take the child into her own household, for reasons she has not declared."

Katherine stared at him, panting, speechless.

"And because she said it was most important, I agreed," Hawke said. Then, flushing, "I am the queen's man, Katherine. I could not refuse her."

Katherine shrieked. Terror engulfed her. "She is taking my son away from me? And you have let her? You cannot do this—you cannot!"

"He will be well cared for, Katherine," John said. "I promise you that."

Katherine screamed, doubling over in pain that felt physical and was far more severe than all that had gone before. When she finally straightened, her face was ravaged with rage, with fear, and with grief, making her appear old and ugly. "I want my son!" she screamed. "Give me back my son!"

"I cannot," Hawke said. He hesitated. "I am sorry." And he turned and walked away.

Katherine gasped, lunging to her feet. Juliet caught her before she could topple to the floor. "Let me go," Katherine cried. "Let me go before they take my babe away! Oh God! *God!* Help me, *please!*"

Tears streaming down her own cheeks, Juliet held Katherine upright, preventing her from leaving. "Katherine, dearest, there is naught you can do, not if John has allowed this."

Katherine ignored her. She found superhuman strength and managed to break free of Juliet. She staggered to the door, pulled on it. The wood seemed to weigh a hundred pounds. Panting, Katherine wrested it open. She stumbled into the corridor, clung to the railing at the top of the stairs. "Ginny! Come back! Ginny! Help me! They are stealing my son!"

But no one responded to her cries, and Katherine collapsed upon the floor. Juliet, rushing after her, found her prone, clawing the parquet with bloody fingernails, moaning like an animal.

Her tormented whispers filled the hall. *"They have no right! They have no right! God help me—I want my son!"*

Hawke stared blindly at the moors, which were almost

lushly green and dotted with yellow wildflowers. The sky was so blue overhead that the day appeared idyllic. Yet it was an illusion. Hawke could still hear Katherine's screams. Not her screams during her labor, but her screams afterward, the anguish far greater, when he had ordered the midwife to take the babe away.

The courtyard was filled with saddled horses and soldiers. A covered cart had been prepared for the wet nurse and the child. Elizabeth had stressed how important the child's safety and survival were, and she had ordered Hawke to bear the babe to London personally.

He was sick. He was sick from it all. His wife loved O'Neill fiercely, and on this day, he had finally realized that she was the kind of woman to go to her grave still yearning for the other man. Oh, she might do her duty toward him, she might never discuss the pirate again, she might run his household willingly and warm his bed, she might bear him half a dozen sons, but she would always love Liam O'Neill. Hawke wondered what it was like, to love another so much, so completely.

And now he was denying her not just her lover, but her child, as well. Bile rose up in his gorge. God's teeth. He had become weak. To tear a child from its mother's arms was one of the most grievous crimes he could think of—one he wished never, ever to have to perform again, not even for his queen.

But Katherine would survive. She was made of strong stuff. Yet his confidence in that did not chase away his anguish.

"How could you!"

Hawke turned around to face an enraged angel. It was Juliet.

"I thought you a noble man, a decent man, a good man, but what you have done is monstrous!" Juliet was crying.

Hawke had stiffened. Her accusations stabbed him hurtfully. He knew he did not need to defend himself to this moon-eyed chit. "I could not refuse the queen."

"Yes, you could!" she cried.

He saw that her fists were clenched. "You do not understand."

"I understand," Juliet said bitterly. "I understand that I have harbored a great illusion about you. I understand that you are not half as noble as you appear. I understand that you are jealous, yes, jealous, because Katherine loves another man. Perhaps you planned this all along!" she cried furiously. "To rid yourself of O'Neill's child!" She held her head high, daring him to refute her.

He did not. She would not believe him if he tried. "How is Katherine?"

Juliet's laughter was sharp. "How is she? She has finally collapsed—damn you."

Hawke blanched.

Juliet wheeled around and, lifting her skirts, raced back to his house.

His mouth downturned, Hawke received his horse from a groom and mounted. "Send for the child and wet nurse," he told one of the soldiers. "We are ready to depart."

Katherine refused to speak to anyone, not even Juliet. She lay in bed for two full days, regaining her strength. Not completely. But she could not wait until she was in fine form to do what had to be done.

She took no one into her confidence, not Juliet, not Ginny—both of whom were almost as aggrieved as she. On the third day after her babe had been born, Katherine dressed in a servant's clothing, clothing she had ordered a slow-witted kitchen girl to bring to her in the middle of the night. Underneath her gown, she strapped an Irish dagger to her thigh, careful to make certain that it could not be discerned by any observer.

That night, when the manor was asleep, including Juliet, who had refused to return home to Thurlstone, Katherine slipped from her bed and left the house, wearing a plain gray mantle over her borrowed dress. She stole into the stables, which were deserted, all the grooms and horseboys asleep in their adjacent quarters. She chose the mount she had ridden on her last journey, when she had left London for Cornwall, that spring. Savage determination gave her strength, and within moments she had saddled the docile mare herself. It was not until she was in the saddle, and through Hawkehurst's front gates, that weakness assailed her. She felt so faint that she clung to the saddle, telling herself she must not swoon, not now, not when she had a long journey to make.

She was going to London, to confront the queen. She was going to London, to recover her babe. And nothing and no one was going to stop her.

Whitehall

"I must see the queen!"

It was early morning, and the queen was still closeted in her Privy Chamber with her maids. Numerous noblemen, including the Gentlemen Pensioners, several Guardsmen, and other retainers milled about her antechamber, awaiting her. Katherine faced the two uniformed soldiers in front of her closed doors. "I must see the queen!" she repeated.

The desperation in her hoarse voice caused many heads to turn her way. "How did you get in here, wench?" one of the soldiers asked. "Get on with you. Commoners don't petition Her Majesty."

Katherine squared her shoulders. Her cloak was torn and caked with dust; her hair had come loose long ago, and it was tangled and snarled, her coif lost; her hands were dirty, her nails torn, and her face was pale, sweat-streaked, and ravaged. She had not eaten in days, and she was terribly weak. But she had made it to court, and she would not be deterred. Not by these louts, nor by anyone else. "I am no common wench," she spit. "I am Katherine FitzGerald, daughter of Gerald FitzGerald, the earl of Desmond!"

The courtiers who had overheard her cried out, shocked, staring. Katherine knew she had become the object of everyone's attention, but did not care. "I demand to see the queen," she gritted, her fists clenched.

"You cannot be an earl's daughter," the soldier said. "What crockery is this? Leave! Leave now before I have to heave you out of here myself."

Katherine's face contorted in rage and she began to push between the two soldiers, reaching for the door they barred. The soldiers instantly closed rank, forcing her back quite roughly. Katherine stumbled and almost fell, but someone caught her from behind and steadied her. She did not look at the man standing behind her, who even now gripped her shoulders. "I am Katherine FitzGerald," she cried, her voice high, cracking.

"Katherine." Leicester turned her away from the closed doors of the queen's bedchamber so that she was facing him. His eyes were wide and shocked. But his voice when he spoke was low and concerned. "Dear God! What has happened to you?"

"Dudley!" Katherine shouted, clawing his arms. "I must see the queen, I must! She has stolen my child! I want my child!"

Leicester stared at her. Then, his jaw ticking, he nodded imperiously at the guards. Instantly the first soldier turned and knocked. The doors opened ever so slightly. The soldier spoke in a hushed tone to one of the queen's ladies, who remained out of sight. And a moment later Elizabeth herself stepped into the doorway, her face lined with curious concern. The earl of Ormond appeared behind her. "Robin? What is so urgent that you cannot wait another moment to—" Abruptly she broke off her words. Her eyes fixed on Katherine. Comprehension dawned in them. She gasped. And Ormond had paled.

"I want my son," Katherine cried, her breasts heaving. "You have no right, none! I demand my son—this instant!"

They were surrounded now by onlookers, every single person in the room a witness to this bizarre confrontation, everyone paling in shock at hearing Katherine's bold tone and even bolder words. His legs brushing her skirts, Dudley murmured a warning in her ear, which Katherine ignored.

Elizabeth stepped forward. "Robin, remove your hands from her."

Dudley dropped his hands, reluctantly.

The queen faced Katherine. "You will not make demands of Us."

"She is distraught over the child, she knows not what she does," Ormond said quickly.

"Quiet," Elizabeth snapped. And the entire chamber became deathly still, as if the royal command were directed at everyone.

Katherine touched her dagger through her skirts, for Leicester had loosened it from its binding. The seething, murderous rage she had been nursing ever since the queen had abducted her child roiled in her veins. She pressed the dagger against her thigh. "You have stolen my child, like any ordinary thief," Katherine cried accusingly. "Does not your court know?" She laughed hysterically. "Why not, Your Majesty? Do you not want your people to know what you really are? A stealer of children—a thief of innocence?"

The crowd gasped. Fury mottled Elizabeth's countenance. Ormond was deathly white now. "You are impudent beyond belief," Elizabeth cried. "Take her away, now. Throw her in Bridewell Prison—where all strumpets belong!"

Instantly a group of soldiers moved forward toward Katherine. But Katherine had not come to court to be locked away with whores and vagabonds. She fumbled with her skirts, lifting them.

And Leicester gripped Katherine's right wrist from behind, preventing her from finding—and wielding—her knife. "Do not do it!" he cried sharply.

Katherine shrugged free of him, managing to grip the dagger and pull it from beneath her skirts. Even as she did so she saw the five approaching soldiers, Ormond at their forefront, and in her dazed mind, she understood that they would stop her from doing what she must do, that they would force her to leave Whitehall, send her to Bridewell Prison.

Ormond realized what she intended. He broke into a run. "No, Katherine," he cried, reaching for her.

Leicester also saw, and from behind, he tried to grip her wrist. But her madness made her move far faster than

either man, and Katherine darted to the side, away from
them all, brandishing the blade.

And the queen screamed. "She has a knife! She thinks
to murder me!"

Pandemonium erupted in the antechamber. Elizabeth
backed up, instantly surrounded by her Gentlemen, while
a dozen soldiers descended upon Katherine. Suddenly
Katherine was afraid. Leicester shoved her in the direction
whence she had come. "Katherine, flee!"

And Katherine whirled, shoving past Ormond, who
made no attempt to stop her—who even blocked the corridor, momentarily deterring any others from pursuing her.

"She is mad!" the queen cried from behind the men
guarding her. "The girl has gone mad! Seize her! Seize
her!"

Metal shrieked as the soldiers drew their swords and
gave chase. Katherine pounded down the corridor, heard
loud, racing footsteps and looked over her shoulder. Her
eyes widened when she saw that two soldiers were gaining
on her—and that one of the two men almost on her heels
was none other than her husband, John Hawke.

It flashed through her mind that she was doomed. In
another second Hawke or the other soldier would be close
enough to grab her, and even if she fought them with
her knife, they would ultimately subdue her, they would
ultimately win. And she would be sent to Bridewell, where
whores were imprisoned—never to be released, never to
know her own child.

Katherine waited for the feel of a hand upon her shoulder. But nothing happened.

She glanced back again. And saw John Hawke, an inch
from her now. Their gazes seemed to met. And in his eyes
she saw a silent message, a message that could not be.
And then he mouthed—*"run."*

And then John Hawke lunged for Katherine—and
tripped and fell. He fell in such a manner that he took
down the soldier beside him as well. And as he fell and
rolled, he became tangled up with the other soldier, and
the two men succeeded in blocking the entire corridor.

The three soldiers following them crashed into them and also went flying to the floor.

Katherine ran.

* * *

Katherine crouched behind a pile of garbage outside of a timbered warehouse just across the street from St. Leger House. She was on her knees, for she did not have the strength to stand. She clawed the rotten wood in the refuse heap, peering across the street. She was exhausted, so exhausted that her head throbbed painfully and her insides heaved. She had been running through London all afternoon, eluding her pursuers.

Dusk had fallen, for which she was thankful. The sky was pink and gray, and the long shadows hid her well. She licked her dry lips, which were cracked and swollen. She watched the queen's soldiers, led by John Hawke, as they sat their mounts in the cobbled courtyard of the manor, speaking with her father. She could not hear their exact words, but she knew what was being said. Hawke wanted to know if she was there, and her father was telling him that he had not seen her—truthfully.

Several soldiers dismounted and entered the house. Katherine supposed that they would search the entire manor and the grounds very carefully to see if she were hiding there.

Katherine choked on her despair. She was so tired. She did not think she could last much longer. If a soldier saw her now, she would not be able to run away. She prayed to God for His help.

And then the soldiers returned, mounted, and the dozen or so troops turned around and left St. Leger House. Katherine's heart began to pound. She watched them riding away, down the street, toward the Tower Bridge. And then Hawke suddenly turned in the saddle and stared back— not at the manor but toward the depot—toward her.

Katherine shrank down, out of sight. Her pulse rioted. But he had not seen her, for he gave no command to his men to turn around and seize her.

Panting, Katherine slowly stood. She swayed a little; the soldiers were no longer in sight. She crossed the street slowly, pulling up her hood. She saw her father standing in the courtyard still, staring at her as well.

And then Gerald went to the manor's guards, posted at the gates, and began to speak. The guards listened, and turned, looking toward the east—away from Katherine. Gerald pointed and gestured. Then he shot a brief glance at Katherine, and it was a command. Katherine sucked up her courage and ran through the front gates just as Gerald and the two guards walked toward the back of the house. No one in sight now, she entered the house—and collapsed in the entry hall.

She did not know how long she sat there on the floor, too weak even to move a muscle, but the next thing she knew her father was there with her, crouching beside her. "Katie? Dear God, Katie! What's happened to you?" He touched her dirty, scratched cheek.

Katherine began to cry, moving into his open arms. He held her and stroked her hair. Hysterically, almost incoherently, she told him what had happened. "What am I to do, Father? I have lost my child! Liam will soon hang! And now it appears my fate is the same, for I tried to kill the queen!"

Gerald helped her to her feet and held her upright. "We must think on this, darling, carefully. But all is not as horrific as it appears. I do not think your cause is lost."

And hope sparked in Katherine's breast. She should have known to come to her father. He had always been a hero, a man capable of moving mountains, and even his exile could not change that. She gripped the lapels of his faded, much-mended doublet. "What do you say, Father? What do you mean?"

Gerald smiled at her. "Clearly you have not heard the latest news."

"What news?" she whispered dryly.

"Your lover is no longer in the Tower, Katie. Two days ago, Liam O'Neill escaped. And the *Sea Dagger* was spotted off the Essex coast, sailing north, toward Ireland." Gerald smiled at her. "The Master of the Seas is free, Katie. Liam O'Neill is free."

And finally, Katherine swooned.

IV

THE PRIZE

34

*M*any hours had passed since the FitzGerald girl had tried to murder her, but Elizabeth was still terribly shaken, and terribly enraged. There had been numerous plots against her since she had ascended the throne in 1558. But never had she been faced with an assassin's blade. And never had she dreamed an assassin would be a woman she knew, a woman she had befriended.

"Please, Bess, pacing like a caged tiger will get you nowhere."

Elizabeth jerked as Leicester entered her bedchamber as if he shared it with her. She ran to him, heedless of her women, who huddled together by her bed, having given up trying to calm her when she had slapped Anne Hastings for her efforts. Elizabeth rushed into Leicester's arms, clinging to him. "Have they caught her? Have they caught that treacherous slattern?"

"Ssh, dear, sssh. I think some brandywine is in order." Leicester smiled at her, stroking her back. His regard grew sharp and imperious as he looked over her shoulder at her ladies. Understanding his silent command, they all ran from the room. With one velvet-tipped toe, Leicester slid the door closed.

"Did they catch her?" Elizabeth cried. "Did they catch Katherine FitzGerald?"

"No."

Elizabeth gasped. "How stupid can everyone be. To allow a mere girl—and one maddened at that—to escape after such an attempt at murder."

Leicester had moved to a sideboard to pour his queen the brandy she so needed, and now he handed it to her. "Drink," he ordered.

Her gaze riveted upon him, Elizabeth obeyed.

Leicester waited until she had taken a healthy dose of the liquor. "As you have said, she is mad. Who knows where she would go?"

"Undoubtedly she has gone to her rascal father."

"Hawke was at St. Leger House. She is not there."

Elizabeth jerked on his doublet. "And you, Robin? Did you get a good look at her? Caked with mud and slime, her hair like a bird's nest? Did you see her eyes? The mad, wild light therein?"

"Elizabeth," Leicester began softly.

"Answer me!" she cried.

"Yes."

"And do you still wish to bed her?"

His stare was unwavering. "Do you truly expect me to be a monk when it is you who denies me what I really want?"

Elizabeth flung her glass to the floor, unmindful of the splinters which sprayed about them. "She has probably run to him! To O'Neill! Now I will never capture her! Even now, they are probably in one another's arm! When I told the rogue that he could not ever have her!"

Leicester said sharply, "Who is it you really love, Bess? Him, or me?"

Elizabeth's jaw clamped down hard. She said not a word.

He sighed. "O'Neill was spotted at sea. Katherine is undoubtedly still near London. They cannot possibly be together."

"I want her caught and hanged," Elizabeth cried.

"Dear, you are not thinking clearly. The girl was in great distress. She was mad with grief—she knew not what she did. She—"

"Stop. Do not dare take up her defense, Robin—I warn you."

Leicester became still.

Elizabeth faced her window, looked out at the gray, sluggish Thames, dotted with rowboats and barges. "She will be tried for treason, Robin. I want her hanged and it will be so."

"She tried to kill the queen. She cannot stay here!"

"She is my daughter, her husband is gone, and I don't think Hawke will be back soon. She is staying here, Eleanor, at least until I think of a safe place to send her."

Katherine listened with little interest to her father and Eleanor as they argued. She could not move, for she was more exhausted than she had ever been in her entire life, so much so that she could not lift her head from her arms, which rested on the dining hall table. Liam had escaped. How glad she was. Liam would live. She laughed softly, then tears filled her eyes. Now she would have to fulfill her part of the bargain she had made with the earl of Leicester.

"She is mad—look at her!" Eleanor spit.

Gerald glanced at his daughter, who was laughing strangely even as she wept. "She has just given birth to a babe, and you know how terrible that ordeal is. Leave her be."

Katherine clawed the wood table, having heard them. Was she mad? She herself could not understand why she had tried to kill the queen. Her rage had been so great and so uncontrollable. Then she remembered—she had a son. A tiny, needy infant son who had been stolen from her. She heaved with the dry sobs which now racked her body.

For, as much as she missed the baby, she was afraid now, so afraid, that the child would suffer for the crimes of both of its parents. Liam had escaped, but he was a traitor. And she herself had almost murdered the queen. What would Elizabeth do with her child?

Perhaps Leicester would help her yet again.

"Katie," Gerald said softly, bending over her, "you must go to bed. Before you become truly ill."

Katherine smiled at her father through her tears. "Will I ever see my child again, Father? Will he be nourished, taken care of, and loved? Oh dear Lord, how shall I live?"

He stroked her tangled, dirty hair. "We will speak of this tomorrow, darling, when you are rested."

Katherine allowed him to pull her to her feet. "And Liam? Will I ever see him again?" she choked out.

Gerald smiled at her as if the pirate had hardly betrayed him. "I have little doubt," he said.

"I know that she is here."

Gerald stood facing the earl of Leicester in his dark dining hall, holding one candle aloft, unblinking. "The queen's troops were here, several times. They searched every nook and cranny of this house and all the grounds, and turned up nothing. Katherine is not here, my lord."

Leicester smiled. The candlelight danced across his dark, striking features. "Gerald, you forget that I am your friend," he said softly. "And I am also Katherine's friend." His dark eyes burned. "I seek to protect her. I do not wish to see her hang."

Gerald hesitated. He understood what Leicester's interest in his daughter was, it was obvious. But Katherine had confided in him before she had lapsed into the deep sleep of utter exhaustion, and he was aware now that she had married Liam O'Neill last October on the pirate's island. He considered the alternatives. Was it better if Katherine left with Leicester and became the earl's mistress? Without question, Dudley was the most powerful man in England. Or should she eventually return to O'Neill and carry on as his wife—keeping O'Neill allied with Desmond?

A moment later Gerald's mind was made up. Leicester, although influential, had failed to thwart the queen when she had decided to try and convict him for treason four years ago—and now he was dispossessed and powerless, in exile at St. Leger House. No, Liam O'Neill could do more for his cause than the earl of Leicester, Gerald was certain of it.

"I know that she is here," Leicester repeated with growing impatience.

"She is exhausted, asleep, and ill."

Leicester's eyes gleamed with satisfaction and he nodded. "I shall return for her in another week or two, when all has quieted down. I have a very small, isolated estate in Northumberland, the perfect place for her to go. Meanwhile, keep her well hidden, and I shall warn you if the queen sends her troops to you again.''

Gerald nodded, smiled, and shook the earl's hand. Leicester turned and crossed the hall, his dark cloak flying about his broad shoulders, and he disappeared into the black night shadows outside.

Katherine was so exhausted that, the moment her aching body touched the soft down mattress of the bed, she was asleep. She slept deeply, dreamlessly, without moving even once, for an entire day.

Eventually she began to awaken. But there was such a fierce, burning pain inside of her breast, an unspeakable anguish, that she sought sleep again, desperately. On the edges of her mind, she knew that untold horror awaited her should she awaken.

''Katherine?'' he whispered.

Katherine smiled. She dreamed of Liam now, and that was far better than to be threatened with understanding the bursting pain in her heart. How quickly the pain turned to joy.

''Katherine.'' His voice was low and hoarse. He touched her face, butterfly soft.

It was so real. Katherine sighed.

''Wake up, Kate.''

Katherine did not want to wake up, not now, not when she dreamed of being with Liam again. But her eyes seemed to flutter open. Her vision searched the darkness and found him immediately. He sat there beside her hip, on the side of the bed, unsmiling, his expression filled with tension. For a moment Katherine was confused, because she was dreaming—yet it was so real.

''Katherine!'' he cried, bending over her, cupping her face in his strong, warm hands. His hands were shaking. ''I heard the news in Bristol, that you attacked the queen. Are you all right?''

She stared at him. She was very, very tired, but it occurred to her that she was not dreaming, that she was not hallucinating, that Liam was there in her bedchamber, sitting beside her upon her bed. "Liam?"

A moment later they were in one another's arms. He crushed her to his chest. Katherine clung to him. He was her haven, her refuge, her rock against all things insane, unjust, and evil. She was safe now, and loved.

His shaking hands roamed over her back. "I wasn't there for you," he choked. And he gripped her face, tilting it up toward him. "Darling, forgive me."

"Liam," she whispered, still dazed.

His jaw flexed. Their gazes locked. His eyes were suspiciously moist.

Suddenly his mouth claimed hers. His kiss was restrained, yet the hunger in it was unmistakable. Katherine gave him her tongue. Liam entwined with her, then thrust deep. A moment later he tore his lips from hers, gasping.

"Liam," she protested, reaching for his face.

But he pushed her hands aside. "Kate." He was hoarse. "You have just had a babe." He managed a smile, but it was rueful.

She blinked at him. She had just had a babe? Comprehension began to dawn, but she did not want to remember, so she buried her face against his chest. She rained kisses there, on the broad slabs of his flexed muscles, on his hardening nipples. Her breathing had become shallow.

"Don't," he whispered, moving onto his side and taking her with him. He tucked her head beneath his chin, her cheek to his chest, and began to stroke her back lightly. "Katherine," he murmured. "How I have missed you."

Katherine slowly relaxed, soothed by his body's warmth and strength and by his soft, gentle caresses. Her lids became heavy, and it was almost impossible to open them. But she did, glancing at his handsome, flushed countenance. "Liam. I love you." Her fingernails slid across his ribs, underneath his shirt. Her lids seemed to close of their own volition.

"Katherine, do not sleep. I must talk to you."

She could not seem to force her eyes to open. "Later," she murmured, sighing.

"Katherine." He cupped her chin.

Somehow she opened her eyes. Almost immediately the lids sagged.

"I want to take you with me, but I cannot," he said quickly. "I have much work to do. I must entrap and capture FitzMaurice. Do you understand me?"

FitzMaurice. Katherine did not want to discuss politics now. She closed her eyes.

"When I have captured him, when your father is restored, I will come for you. And then we will be together, always. Do you understand me?"

She blinked at him. It was hard to focus. What, exactly, was he saying? His voice sounded far away.

"And when I do come for you, I will bring you our child," he said loudly, disturbing her sleep. "Katherine?"

Sighing, on the threshold of a dark void, she murmured, "I trust you, Liam."

"Katherine, you must listen. In the interim, it is not safe for you here. I am sending you to Stanley House in Essex."

She tried to nod.

His hand stroked her brow, her hair. Tenderly. "Have you heard a single word I said?" he whispered.

She could not find the strength to respond. But she thought he added, "I love you, Katherine," just before sleep finally claimed her.

Morning sunlight was streaming harshly into Katherine's chamber when Eleanor awoke her. A part of Katherine felt as if she could sleep forever, but that was hardly wise. As she obeyed her stepmother, her body protested mightily. Her muscles were stiff and aching, her body felt battered and sore. It took Katherine a full moment before she comprehended exactly why she was in such a wretched condition.

Oh, God. She had birthed a child, but the queen had taken it away from her. And then she had attacked the queen in a maddened fury.

Gingerly, she tested her muscles. She still felt fatigued, but she had some strength now, strength she needed in order to survive. And survive she must. Somehow, someway, she must regain her child, and she also needed to hide from the queen's troops.

It seemed a monumental task.

Eleanor helped her bathe and dress. Finally gowned, Katherine faced herself in the room's single, chipped mirror. She was far too pale and far too thin. She no longer looked healthy, strong, and robust. Perhaps, finally, men would cease to regard her as a possible plaything. And Katherine wondered if Liam thought about her at all. Undoubtedly if he saw her now, he would hardly look at her. The notion was too painful to bear.

Her glance darted to the bed. Had she not had a dream of Liam last night?

"That's right, you're not so comely now," Eleanor said, breaking into her thoughts.

Katherine glanced at her, but saw no malice in her stepmother's expression.

"You had better stop grieving," Eleanor said firmly, "and think about living. Aye. There's women who have suffered far more than you. You can grow old now—or you can choose to live." Eleanor stared. "Your mother was a fighter."

"And I must be strong like her," Katherine murmured.

"Aye. Think of what you want, what you need. Then put the past behind you and go forward toward your goals." Eleanor's mouth firmed. "The queen wants you hanged, Katherine. You can not stay here with your father and me at St. Leger House."

Katherine realized that Eleanor was correct in all that she had said. Not only must she recover her wits and resolve and continue to fight to regain her child, she must leave London. But where would she go?

The answer was simple. To Liam.

He was free now, having escaped the Tower. She did not want to live without him, and the time had come to face the fact. She *could* not live without him. She realized that she must go to him, tell him how much she loved him, and ask him to take her with him, wherever he now thought to go. And could he not help her regain their child? How ironic it was, she thought suddenly. They were both outlaws now, wanted by the Crown.

Katherine glanced at the bed again. It was coming back to her. She had dreamed of Liam last night, a wonderful dream in which he had held her and kissed her and comforted her. It had been so very real. But she knew better—didn't she?

"I've put together a few things for you that you might be needing," Eleanor said to Katherine's reflection in the mirror.

Katherine turned, confused.

"Oh, did I not say why I've wakened you so early when you're still needing to heal from the birthing and the rest of your ordeal?" Eleanor asked bluntly. "Your father is sending you to Mary Stanley in Essex."

Katherine froze.

"O'Neill came here last night. 'Twas his decision. He wants you out of London, and we all agree. 'Tis not safe for you here, Katherine," Eleanor said in a kind manner.

Katherine could not move. She was trying to unscramble her wild, racing thoughts. *In the interim, I am sending you to Stanley House.* Oh, God. Liam *had* visited her last night. But she had been half-asleep. She had mistaken his visit for a dream.

Why hadn't he taken her with him?

Katherine strained to remember his words—for nothing he had ever said to her before was as important as what he had said to her last night. Had he not said that he would come back for her? She clasped her warm cheeks with cool hands. Yes, he had promised to return for her—with their child—after he captured FitzMaurice and restored her father!

Oh, God.

Katherine closed her eyes and prayed to God for His goodwill and intervention. And with all of her might and all of her heart she prayed that her dreams would come true—that Liam would be successful in all that he endeavored to do—that he would bring her their son—that he would return for her. And if any man could achieve such a mastery of fate, Katherine knew that that man was Liam O'Neill, the Master of the Seas.

35

*J*uliet had insisted that she accompany her uncle when he announced he was going to London on business. He knew just how anxious she was about her upcoming marriage, and hoping to improve her spirits, he agreed. Juliet did not tell him the real reason she wished to go to London now. That reason was Katherine.

The rumor of her attempt to murder the queen had traveled like wildfire, reaching Cornwall within a few days of the event. Juliet feared her friend had gone mad and desperately needed her help.

Juliet had to go to London to learn what she could of her friend. Richard had obtained rooms for them at a popular inn, and left her with several servants. She claimed that she wished to go shopping. But the coachman did not bat an eye when Juliet ordered him to Whitehall instead of to the market of Cheapside.

Now, as Juliet stood uncertainly in the Banquet Hall, ignoring the astrological decorations and the strange pendants and fruits hanging everywhere, her gaze searched the crowd. It was the dinner hour. But she did not see John Hawke. Indeed, she saw no one that she knew or even recognized, but she was not familiar with the court or the ladies and gentlemen who attended it.

Juliet hailed a passing soldier, ignored his snicker when she asked for Hawke, and was told he could be found in the Guard Room. Given directions, her pulse pounding, Juliet left the Banquet Hall and crossed the Sermon Court.

It was a blustery November day, damp and chill and gray, and she held her fur-lined cloak tightly to her. How bold and brazen she had become.

Hawke was leaving the Guard Room as she approached. Juliet faltered and paused. His eyes were wide—he had remarked her immediately.

Juliet could feel her own blush. Oh, God, what was she doing? Ostensibly she had come to court because she wanted to learn if Katherine were well, and if the baby was being well cared for. But in truth, she had come to see John Hawke.

They stared at one another across the length of the corridor. Juliet recalled the last time she had seen him, when she had acted like a mad shrew, shrieking at him and attacking him for doing his duty to the queen. She regretted her wild, unladylike behavior. But there was no taking it back.

Hawke finally moved forward, his spurs jangling with each strong step, his high boots gleaming. Juliet glanced aside, for he was such a handsome, stirring sight in his taut breeches and crimson uniform. How could Katherine have preferred the pirate? It made not one whit of sense.

"Lady Stratheclyde," he said stiffly, and he bowed as he took her hand. But his lips did not even come close to kissing it.

Juliet pulled her hand away, trembling. "Sir John. I . . . I have heard about Katherine," she cried. "Please tell me it is not true."

He took her elbow. "Let us walk in the gardens."

Juliet was acutely aware of his touch. She did not want to be so affected by him. As it was so raw outside, they were completely alone. She glanced up at him when he finally paused by a bench in a deserted arbor. "Did Katherine attack the queen?"

John's gaze pierced hers. "Yes."

"Oh God!" Juliet cried.

John's expression was anguished. " 'Twas not her fault. She was maddened by her grief. Thank God Her Majesty was unharmed—and that Katherine escaped."

"Thank God," Juliet echoed. "Sir John, is Katherine now all right?"

His jaw flexed. "I do not know, Juliet. I do not know where she is."

Juliet bit off a sound of despair.

"But I would not worry too much if I were you," Hawke said, taking her hand in his. Juliet knew he only meant to comfort her, but she stiffened perceptibly, and he flushed and dropped her palm. "I beg your pardon."

Juliet wished she had a small share of Katherine's experience where men were concerned, so she might be more coy and adept. Then she reminded herself that Hawke was Katherine's husband, that she herself would marry Simon Hunt in another month, and her despair grew. She forced her feelings aside. "How can I not worry about her? She is alone out there somewhere, alone and, perhaps, mad."

"I do not think she is alone."

Juliet looked up at him. Hawke knew something he was not telling her. Relief swept through her.

He turned his gaze away from her, toward the large, faded bowling green just visible on the other side of the gardens. "O'Neill escaped shortly before Katherine came to London."

Juliet wondered if they were together. And suddenly she realized that they belonged together, and if they were not yet together, knowing the pirate, they soon would be. And instantly she was glad, so glad, that Katherine was not alone in this dire time, that she had someone to take care of her, to love her. Then, too late, she recalled the man she stood beside. Oh, God! Juliet's gaze shot to Hawke's. But she could see no terrible reaction in him to the possibility that Katherine, his wife, had returned to the other man. "John, I am sorry."

His gaze moved across her face, lingering on every single one of her features. "Are you? I think not. Katherine loves him. I believe he loves her. It was wrong of me to try to keep her as my wife."

Juliet began to feel choked up inside. "The last time we met," she whispered, her cheeks warm, "I accused you of being selfish and dishonorable. I am so sorry. How wrong I was. You are selfless, and entirely noble. Forgive me, Sir John."

His regard held hers. "I did a terrible thing," he said, and his anguish was both stark and visible. It shimmered in his eyes, strained his features. "I took the newborn babe from her arms. I can never forget it. I will never forget it. Not her screams, not her sobs." His voice was thick. "I dream of it at night. Every night."

Juliet cried out. "You were obeying the queen!"

John faced her, and she saw tears in his eyes. "But it was wrong, and I knew it was wrong. And now Katherine is wanted for treason, her child in the care of another." He was hoarse. "That Katherine attacked the queen, it was not her fault."

"It was the queen's," Juliet cried, furious. "For being so cruel!"

"It was also mine," John said. He sucked in his breath, his expression ravaged, and looked away from her.

Juliet felt his anguish as if it were her own. "John," she whispered, stepping closer and touching his arms.

He turned back to her, startled.

Juliet realized that she was embracing him. But she did not care. He was hurting so. She loved him, and she had no choice but to comfort him. She smiled at him through her own tears, and then slowly she laid her head upon his chest. She slid her palms around his back, gently hugging him to her, as if he were no great, big man, but a fragile thing.

John Hawke did not move. Not at first.

And Juliet thought, *This is heaven. To hold such a man.* And she could not help but add a selfish wish—if only he loved her, as she loved him.

Hawke suddenly groaned and his powerful arms crushed her to his chest. Juliet cried out, stunned, looking up. She cried out again. His blue eyes were ablaze, the anguish gone. And for the first time in her life, Juliet both saw and understood male desire. And she froze.

"Juliet," John said thickly. One of his hands, shaking, slipped up into her coiled tresses. Pearl-headed pins scattered. A fall of her thick dark hair cascaded over his hand.

Juliet could not move, could not breathe. She could only stare up at him, mesmerized . . . and hoping.

He cried out, caught her face in both of his large, warm hands, and suddenly his mouth was on hers.

In her dreams, his kisses had always been tender, soft, and barely there. This was nothing like her dreams. It was far, far more.

His mouth moved passionately over hers. Instinctively Juliet opened her lips beneath his, and suddenly his tongue was inside her, twisting with hers. Juliet clung to his strong shoulders. Her body had come gloriously alive in a way she had never even imagined possible. She shook, she was on fire. On tiptoe she strained feverishly for him as their mouths mated and fused.

It was Hawke who finally raised his head, tearing his mouth from hers. He was panting. Juliet made a small mewling sound of protest.

"Oh God," John gasped when he could speak. He touched Juliet's face reverently, then brushed back her hair, which was wild and loose now, hanging to her waist. He began stroking her face with the fingertips of his right hand, which was shaking. "Juliet," he said.

Juliet still leaned against his magnificent, hard male form. She still clung to his crimson uniform. Breathless, dazed, she managed to smile at him. "I love you," she said softly, meaning it with all of her heart and all of her being.

He froze.

Juliet suddenly realized what she had said—and what she had done. Reality intruded. John Hawke was not a free man. She was not a free woman. Stricken, she dropped her hands from his chest as if burned, and backed away, stumbling.

Oh, God—what had she done!

"Stop!" he cried, grabbing her by her shoulders, and pulling her close. "Do not turn from me now," he commanded.

Juliet could not speak, and as he held her so forcefully, she could not move away even if she had really wished to.

"Katherine belongs with O'Neill," John said. "I am going to petition Canterbury for a divorce."

Juliet gasped. Her mind reeled. No, this could not be

happening. No, her dreams could not possibly be coming true.

But his next words proved that dreams did come true. "Juliet," he said huskily, hesitating. "Juliet—I wish to marry you—if you will but have me."

Juliet cried out. "Yes, John, yes."

Hawke smiled. "I think I have loved you for a very long time," he said.

"And I have loved you since I first saw you," she said daringly.

He took her hand. "I will speak to your uncle today. I think I can convince him of the merits of this marriage, of the joining of our two neighboring estates."

"And if he refuses?" Juliet asked with some fear.

Hawke smiled tenderly. "Then we will run away."

It was daring, it was romantic. And Hawke was so strong that she was not afraid. Juliet laughed. And then she saw the look in his eye and she became utterly still.

His head lowered, hers lifted. And they moved together in a dance as old as time, there in the arbor beneath the gnarled oaks and the ancient elms—a dance which would last them a lifetime.

Katherine was eager to leave London. No one would ever think to look for her at Stanley House. But even more importantly, Gerald had revealed to her that Leicester knew she was hiding at St. Leger House—and that he planned to remove her to one of his own estates in northern England within days. Katherine could not depart London soon enough.

She was well aware that she owed Leicester for his part in obtaining Liam's freedom. Nonetheless she sought to avoid him, and postpone what she must eventually do. Yet it did not take much thought for her to know that it would be better to pay back Leicester now, before Liam returned for her, than afterward. Yet Katherine could not linger. Panic propelled her, and she ran not just from the queen's men, but from Her Majesty's powerful lover.

Mary Stanley was expecting her. As soon as Katherine entered the small courtyard of the manor house, the front door opened, framing a slender blond woman in an elegant dress.

At once, Katherine saw that Liam resembled his mother. She was blond and gray-eyed and very beautiful; her face was but a softer, female version of her son's. From all accounts, Mary had suffered greatly in her lifetime, yet this woman appeared as elegant and self-contained as any noble lady.

Katherine slid from her mount, aided by one of the men sent to escort her. She had been uncertain of what Mary's greeting to her would be, but when she realized that the other woman was smiling warmly at her, she was relieved. Mary embraced her and escorted her inside and upstairs to the small bedchamber she would use.

"My son has told me much about you, and I feel as if we are old and dear friends," Mary said as she opened the door.

Katherine was amazed. What had Liam said about her? And had he really talked to his mother at length about her? "I wish to be your friend, Lady Stanley."

Mary smiled at her. "Please, Mary is fine." She moved briskly about the chamber, opening an armoire, hanging Katherine's cloak on a wall peg, throwing back the heavy down coverlets on the four-poster bed. Katherine stared out of the window, which looked out over the rolling Essex countryside and a pretty bubbling stream. There sheep grazed and lambs played.

Her gaze returned to Liam's mother, who now regarded her as well. "Liam said to care for you as I would care for him," Mary remarked.

It felt so good to be accepted like this by this woman. "You are being more than generous. Thank you," Katherine said, moved. But her thoughts remained on Liam. "Do you see Liam often?"

"No, I do not." Mary's smile faded. "He lives such a difficult life. It is not always safe for him to be in England. Now more so than ever. But we correspond. And he is a good son; he comes when he can."

Katherine stared at Mary, whose voice was full of love when she spoke of Liam. Katherine was glad, fiercely so.

She had wondered if his mother cared for him. Some women would hate the child they had been forced to bear by a savage rapist. But not this woman. "You do not mind, that I am here?" Katherine had to ask.

"You are Liam's wife. The mother of his son. The woman he loves. No, I do not mind."

Katherine stared at Mary. Liam had never told her that he loved her, yet Katherine believed now that he did. But believing just wasn't enough. "Did Liam tell you . . . that?"

Mary appeared amused. "Katherine, all that he has said to me over the years would fill up a book. Since my son first saw you, he has been in love with you."

Katherine was frozen. "Perhaps he loves me now. I hope so. But he did not love me before—when we lived together upon his island. He betrayed me. He acted as if he loved me, but he was aiding my father's enemy, FitzMaurice." Although Katherine had forgiven Liam, there was a lingering sadness at the memory of his past treachery.

Mary no longer smiled. "There were many burnings here in Essex, Katherine. During Bloody Mary's reign, we lived in terror of being accused and imprisoned and burned alive ourselves. We all witnessed the burnings. I did not want Liam to watch such torture, such bestiality, he was so young—but the priests insisted that he watch, too."

Katherine was sickened by the thought of any child seeing people burned alive, but especially Liam. "What are you trying to tell me?"

"FitzMaurice is not just a Catholic, as you are. He is a *madman*. He burns those who dispute his faith, just as Bloody Mary's people did. Liam would never support him. He took vows in order to marry you—but he would *never* support FitzMaurice."

Katherine whispered, "But he did."

Mary snorted. "My son is terribly clever. His plan was then what it is now. To raise FitzMaurice up only to bring him down. Even now, he has told me that there are factions at court eager to restore your father to Desmond, when the time comes to replace FitzMaurice."

Katherine gripped the table. Trying to understand and dizzy with the impending realization.

"Life is naught but politics, my dear," Mary said firmly. "I lived at court for many years; I know it first-hand. Men come and go. Positions of power are filled and emptied and filled yet again. Liam has vowed to capture FitzMaurice. Someone will have to take that man's place."

Katherine stared speechlessly.

"FitzMaurice became too strong and too successful in his rebellion, Katherine. Everyone now realizes that it would be far better that your father be in power in Desmond."

Katherine cried out. How clear Liam's actions were now. She should have trusted him. *Oh God.* But she had not. How clever, how bold, how remarkable Liam was!

Katherine clung to the table. " 'Tis bold and daring beyond belief," she whispered hoarsely. "But why? Why would he do this? Why would he commit treason in order to restore my father to Desmond? I would understand if this game began but recently, after we were wed. But he admitted to me on Earic Island that he began his liaison with FitzMaurice much earlier, immediately after he captured me on the French ship that took me and Juliet from Cherbourg when we left the nunnery. Liam had only just laid eyes upon me when he became allied with FitzMaurice."

Mary's gaze was sharp. "Tell me, my dear. Why would a powerful and rich man like Liam seize a small, politically insignificant French trader, one with an apparently worthless cargo?"

"I do not know."

Mary smiled again. "Because the cargo was only worthless to the world, Katherine, it was hardly worthless to him. To Liam, it was priceless."

Still Katherine did not understand.

"My dear, you were on that ship—and my son wanted you."

Katherine knew that Mary was mistaken. For Liam had not even known of her existence then. And suddenly she wondered, *or had he?*

36

*L*iam stood upon the forecastle, holding the spyglass to one eye, training it across the frothing Atlantic Ocean. He knew they sailed just hours ahead of another deadly winter storm. But he would not turn around just yet and seek the safety of a protected harbor. Not until he had determined the identity of the vessel his watch had espied many hours since, a vessel clearly bound for the south of Ireland.

Liam had spent the past three months blockading the island, preventing any supplies from reaching FitzMaurice. Two weeks earlier reports had reached him that the rebels were a ragged, starving lot, hiding in the ravaged mountains of Kerry. Periodically they swooped down upon the locals, raiding for what little food they could find, uncaring that those they took from would starve as well—uncaring that those they took from were also Irishmen, women and children, the long-suffering, innocent victims of this heartbreaking war.

It was a nasty business. Liam steeled his heart against feeling any sympathy for FitzMaurice or his men, and he could hardly prevent the widespread famine which affected all of southern Ireland, as a result of years of the vicious maurauding of both the Irish rebels and the English armies. No, he focused on but one thing. He must bring FitzMaurice to heel; he must have his son. And Katherine.

Liam finally determined the identity of the small ship

racing ahead of him. It was Scottish. He smiled, lowering the spyglass. And ordered the *Sea Dagger* brought about so that they might race for the safety of the harbor on Valencia Island.

For he wanted the Scottish cargo to reach FitzMaurice. Unbeknownst to the Scots, the powder they carried was defective. It would fail to explode, rendering useless whatever muskets it was loaded into. Liam was well aware that FitzMaurice desperately needed this gunpowder, just as he desperately needed the victuals so far denied him.

The *Sea Dagger* came about, plowing now through rising, heavy swells, intent on outracing the impending storm.

Richmond—March 1, 1573

Sir John Perrot's messenger was an exhausted boy of perhaps sixteen. His red uniform was black with mud, torn in numerous places, and threadbare everywhere else. He stood before the queen shaking with exhaustion and fatigue. "Your Majesty, the lord president of Munster commands me to give you this," he said, handing Elizabeth a sealed missive.

She already knew what it contained. Rumor flew faster than any messenger or document could ever travel. Her heart beat wildly. She tore the letter open, read its three lines and looked up. " 'Tis true?" she cried. "FitzMaurice surrendered to Sir John at Kilmallock last month?"

"Aye," the boy said. "And a sorry sight he was, too. Bony and white, more naked than not."

Elizabeth threw back her head and laughed loudly.

Leicester came forward to wrap his arm around her. "What good news this is!" he said.

She embraced him briefly but hard. "Oh, yes! One papist traitor dispatched—at long last!" She studied the last line of the letter again. Perrot had written that O'Neill had indeed played a most important role in forcing the rebel leader to his knees. Elizabeth smiled again. Her golden pirate had not betrayed her this time. Her heart quickened as she imagined seeing him again, and rewarding him perhaps with a lingering kiss.

Elizabeth dismissed the messenger, and quickly realized that Cecil wished to speak with her. By the look in his eyes, she knew he had something serious upon his mind, and that he wished to speak with her privately. She sighed. Could she not just enjoy this victory? It had been so long in the coming. "William?"

Cecil murmured, "We have matters to discuss."

Leicester stepped forward to stand at the queen's side. He smiled, but his gaze was challenging.

"Speak. I do not wish to send Robin away. To the contrary." She sent him a warm glance. "I wish him to sup with me this night."

Leicester's expression brightened. His tone seductive, he murmured, "As you wish, Bess, always as you wish."

Cecil was annoyed and made no attempt to hide it. "Southern Ireland is without a leader. Another papist traitor might move into the breach left by FitzMaurice. We *must* forestall that."

Elizabeth scowled. "I know what you will say next."

"Indeed? FitzGerald should have never been removed, Your Majesty. He might be wayward, but he is a petty lord, interested only in his own power. Send him back, now, before another, more dangerous man comes forth."

Elizabeth began to pace. She felt like ranting and raving about the injustice of it all. In truth, she could not stand the impudent, arrogant Irish lord, she could not—and she had always detested him. Too, Ormond, who was in Leinster on his own business now, would not be pleased should his ancient rival be returned to Desmond.

Leicester moved to her side. "For once I am in complete agreement with Burghley, Your Majesty. FitzGerald is basically harmless, especially now, with Desmond destroyed. Return him to his home immediately, before another FitzMaurice rises up with Spain's encouragement against your authority."

Elizabeth sighed.

"We will structure an agreement where he is beholden to you," Cecil said. "In restoring him, we will make him your great ally." Cecil smiled then. "Let *him* fight any more wars in southern Ireland. Let us concentrate ourselves elsewhere as we have longed to do."

Cecil was so right. Ireland was a constant problem, but so damned insignificant. Elizabeth nodded then, sharply. "So be it. That cocky little traitor shall be pardoned and returned. God's wounds! How this annoys me!"

It was Cecil's business to know the movement of significant personages about the world, much less about the court. The moment he learned of Liam O'Neill's arrival at court, while Elizabeth flew upstairs to her royal apartments to ready herself for the audience she would grant him, Cecil secluded himself in the Privy Chamber and ordered the pirate brought to him.

O'Neill's expression was impossible to read as he entered the room. His gaze was perfectly blank. Cecil ordered his clerks and secretaries to leave them alone. They faced one another, Cecil smiling faintly.

Finally Liam smiled slightly in return. "My lord, you wish to speak with me?"

"Indeed," Cecil said. "I wish to congratulate you, O'Neill, on a game well played." Admiration had crept into his tone.

Liam blinked at him innocently. "And of what game do you speak?"

"Oh, I speak of games politic, of deadly, dangerous games politic."

Liam's eyes widened, his brows lifted, but otherwise, his expression was quite bland. "Indeed?"

"Tell me but one thing. For there is one thing I fail to understand."

Liam waited.

"How did you know that Katherine FitzGerald was upon the French trader when you seized it?"

Liam cocked one tawny brow. "What makes you think that I was aware that she traveled upon that ship, my lord?"

Cecil laughed. "Oh, come. No more pretense. You would not have seized that ship otherwise. You seized the ship knowing she was on it, beginning the game."

Liam inclined his head. For a moment he did not speak. Then he said, softly, "Yes."

Cecil was pleased. "I thought so. You were already determined to wed with her and restore FitzGerald."

Liam met his gaze. It would not hurt for Cecil to know the truth. "I had already decided that Katherine was mine, but I did not decide to wed her and restore her father until shortly after capturing her."

Cecil's brows rose. "You captured her in order to amuse yourself?"

"Have you never wanted a woman so badly, my lord?"

"No," Cecil answered flatly. "I would have never guessed. But how did you know of her movements? Her father was in contact with her?"

"No. Her father did not know that she was leaving the convent."

Cecil waited.

Liam smiled. "The abbess alerted me to Katherine's departure with Lady Juliet Stratheclyde. You see, for many years, I was Katherine's anonymous benefactor."

Liam awaited the queen in the antechamber of her private apartments, ignoring the flurrying of her ladies about him, ignoring their interested and seductive looks. Finally Elizabeth appeared, having made him wait almost an entire hour. He saw that she had dressed with great care, entirely in white. Even the jewelry she had chosen was virginal—she wore naught but pearls.

"Everyone, begone," she ordered. And then she looked at Liam and beamed.

He wondered at her fashion choice. Did she think to remind him that she was untouched and innocent? Or did she wish to appear as one untouched and innocent? One thing was clear. She was too old to wear white, and this particular shade was unkind to her. Still, Liam moved to her, smiled, and bowed.

They were alone now and she said, "Please, Liam, rise."

He straightened. "Hello, Bess."

Her gaze flitted over his face, then down his body, very quickly—before returning to his eyes.

"Have I proved myself?" he asked quietly.

She smiled at him. "Yes. Yes, you have. Liam, you naughty rogue, to give me such a fright!" She took his arm and pressed close. "You are still my favorite pirate." She gazed into his eyes.

"And I am still your loyal servant," he murmured. "Always."

"Then you do care for me," she whispered, holding his gaze. Her small breast was pressed against his arm. Her invitation was clear.

Liam thought of Katherine. How carefully he must play this final match. He tucked her hand under his arm and then slid three fingers over one of her cheeks. Her skin was stiff from the cosmetics she used. "What passes, Bess?" he asked softly.

She started. Then, as honestly, trembling, "You have never kissed me, Liam."

"Is it a kiss you wish from me, or something more?"

She flushed. "What do you mean?"

There was no avoiding her now and he knew it. He must hope that a single kiss would satisfy her lust for him. He bent his head, touched her rouged lips with his. Elizabeth softened instantly. He put his arms around her and plied her mouth gently. She gripped him desperately. Her mouth opened immediately. Responding as he must, Liam deepened the joining of their mouths. Elizabeth trembled, her entire body pressed up hard against his, her tongue seeking his. Sometime later he finally released her.

She gazed at him with starry, dazed eyes, suddenly appearing every bit as innocent as she claimed to be. She touched her swollen mouth. Her glance slid to his loins.

Liam was not aroused and would only pretend so much.

Elizabeth sighed, wistfully, then said, "You should have kissed me years ago, rogue."

Her bantering tone relieved him. She had no intention of losing her virginity now. He laughed. "Your Majesty, I was afraid to risk my neck."

"I doubt it." She eyed him. Her tone no longer arch, her eyes gleaming now with something other than desire, she said, "How is Katherine?"

He jerked. Katherine, who was still a fugitive for having assaulted the queen. Katherine, his wife. "I do not know."

"No?"

"No."

"Come, rogue, surely she is with you on your island. My soldiers cannot find her anywhere, there has been no sign of her here in London or in the south of Ireland."

"She is not on my island."

Elizabeth stared, wide-eyed. "Why not? Do you not still lust after her?"

Liam did not answer.

Elizabeth's tone became sharp. "I am returning your son to you, as you have expected me to do. You have not married her in anticipation of that event?"

"She is married to John Hawke, remember?" Liam was wary. He said no more. Not about to tell Elizabeth that Katherine had married him long ago on Earic Island. At least, not yet.

But Elizabeth appeared amused. "She is hardly married to Hawke. John Hawke divorced her months ago. In fact, he is about to marry Lady Juliet Stratheclyde."

Liam stared, stunned. And exhilaration swept through him.

Elizabeth said, "Will you marry her?"

"Yes."

Elizabeth inhaled hard. "She tried to kill me. She is an outlaw. She deserves to hang. She is a strumpet!"

Softly Liam asked, "Can you not forgive her, Bess? Knowing as you must that she was mad with grief over the loss of her child? Can you not forgive her, pardon her—for me?"

"Regardless of whether I forgive her you will marry her, won't you?" Elizabeth challenged.

How jealous and petty she was, Liam thought, and knew the time had come to make his second to last move. "You have sent FitzGerald back to Ireland. How is that man to hold the south together without allies? Have I not proved myself, Bess? Can you not think now of the advantages to a union betwixt FitzGerald and myself? Think clearly. I have no love for wars. I would do my best to keep him out of all forms of intrigue."

She stared, her expression unhappy. "How clever you are. Of course I would rather have FitzGerald allied with you, than with some wild Catholic lord like Barry or MacDonnel."

And Liam played his final, most powerful card. "With Katherine as my wife, you will never have anything to fear from her again, Bess. I assure you of that."

Elizabeth jerked.

Liam said softly, "I do not speak of Katherine's way with a knife."

Elizabeth was silent, her breasts heaving.

"I keep what is mine," Liam declared softly. "And no other man will dare even to think of trespassing onto territory that is clearly Liam O'Neill's. Not even the earl of Leicester."

Elizabeth paled. "He wants her still," she cried after a moment. "He has been in a rage over her disappearance—my spies have told me so!"

And Liam felt inexplicably sad for Elizabeth, who spied upon her own lover. But he shoved his sentimentality aside. "I would kill Leicester," Liam added, "should he even think to try to coax her to his side."

Elizabeth was flushed now. "Take her then! Marry her! And I shall pray you keep her pregnant with a dozen children, by God!"

But Liam was not through. "The pardon, Bess. Will you pardon her?"

Elizabeth's angry expression became distinctly mulish. "Do I not do enough already? Returning your son to you, sanctioning your marriage?"

"Long ago you told me to come to you freely with any petition. You promised me you would reward me for my service. I have served you well. I petition you now, Bess. I want a pardon for Katherine."

Elizabeth had turned red. "Very well! I will pardon her! But let me tell you this! If she ever appears in my sight again, I will have her seized immediately! Do you understand me, Liam? Keep her away from me and my court!"

"Yes." Liam smiled.

He had won. The prize was his. Katherine was his.

37

Liam had also obtained an official pardon from the queen for his own crimes, as well as a commendation for his efforts on her behalf against FitzMaurice. She had also hinted at other future rewards should he be successful in maintaining the status quo in southern Ireland. Liam was stunned. Elizabeth had practically promised that one day she would ennoble him with his own lands and title, so he would have a patrimony to bequeath his son.

Now he strode toward the *Sea Dagger,* which rode at anchor in the Thames not far from Richmond Stairs. A buxom young woman strode beside him, hurrying to keep up. In her arms was his son.

Liam could not take his eyes off the small, blond babe. How blue his eyes were. How blue, how alert, and how obviously intelligent. What a fine son Katherine had given him. Now Liam was going to bring her child to her, as he had promised her he would do.

When he had last seen her, she had been more asleep than awake. Yet she had told him that she loved him, that she trusted him. Had she not, then, spoken from the heart?

Liam hoped that it was so. He missed her so much and loved her even more, and he did not know if he could stand it if she did not feel the exact same way about him. But if not, he would continue to woo her until he had won her heart, just the way he had, so long ago, won her body.

He could not rest easy until they had been reunited, until they were living together again as man and wife.

"O'Neill!"

Liam paused, recognizing the voice of the man who called to him from behind. He turned and waited as Ormond strode toward him. Liam was tense and wary. This man was now his enemy.

Ormond halted. "Do you return to Katherine?"

"Aye."

"She has joined her father, you know. In Bristol. They left for Ireland last week."

Liam already knew this. Mary Stanley had sent him a long, informative letter.

Ormond hesitated, then thrust a small bundle at him. "Give this to her. I believe that she would want it."

Liam stared at the earl of Ormond, but could not fathom what emotion he harbored, for his dark eyes were hooded, his visage impassive. "What is this?"

Ormond's face contorted with emotion. "My mother, in her quieter moments, kept a journal. 'Twas returned to me upon her death. Now I thought Katherine might want it."

Liam was stunned.

Ormond looked away. "Do not mistake me," he growled. "I am forever FitzGerald's sworn enemy, and I am poised now to break his back as I did at Affane so many years ago lest he dare to try to offend me or mine— or my queen! It matters not to me that Katherine is my half sister!"

Liam believed him, but he couldn't help but smile.

"You find my words amusing?" Ormond snapped.

"Come, Tom, admit it," Liam taunted quietly. "You have grown fond of my Katherine."

Ormond's jaw clenched. "Just slightly. So hear this, too. If you do not marry her and make a proper wife of her, I will chase after you, as well. And drag you to the altar."

"We are already married," Liam told him quietly.

Ormond's eyes widened. "You have already wed my sister?"

And Liam grinned. "Aye. But for reasons politic, we have kept it a secret."

Ormond grunted. His eyes gleamed. "Yes, of course. I

will keep your secret too, O'Neill.'' Then he smiled. "But do not think, now that you are my brother-in-law, that aught is changed. You are exempt no more than any other man from my determination to protect the queen.''

Liam inclined his head. "Honor suits some men well."

Ormond started. "You have just flattered me?''

But before Liam could reply—had he wanted to—the babe began to squall.

Instantly both Liam and Ormond turned to stare at the crying infant. The wet nurse turned aside, putting the child to her breast, hushing him. Liam and Ormond looked at one another, their gazes locking. "Your son,'' Ormond said, a small quaver in his tone. Then, "My mother's grandson.''

"Your nephew, Ormond,'' Liam said calmly.

Color flushed the man's cheeks. "Do not think to weaken me with these family ties!''

Liam laughed. "I would not dream of it,'' he said. He saluted the Irish earl. "My lord, I am sure Katherine will be overjoyed to receive this gift from you. On her behalf, I thank you.''

But Ormond did not seem to hear, for he was staring at the suckling child.

Kylemore Forest

Gerald FitzGerald's progress from Dublin Castle was triumphant. Swarms of Irishmen flocked to his side as he journeyed, cheering him mightily, both kern and lords alike, and by the time Gerald had reached the great forest which stretched for miles into the Galtee and Ballyhoura mountains, he was surrounded by hundreds of joyous followers. He stood in his stirrups then, clad now in the clothing of a Gaelic chieftain, preparing to speak. In great expectation, the crowd hushed.

Katherine sat her mount beside Eleanor, her heart pounding with happiness, tears in her eyes. She and Eleanor exchanged warm glances, then clasped hands. Gerald began by lifting his arms high in the air.

"My people," he cried, a pale, wraithlike figure, "I have returned. The earl of Desmond has returned."

Cheers erupted, filling the glen, echoing.

"Never again will Desmond be taken from you," Gerald promised, while the roars of his men drowned out his voice. When they had quieted he cried, "Never again will Englishmen dare to chase you into the forests and bogs, across mountain and glen! The earl of Desmond protects what is his! For Desmond, hurrah!"

Katherine froze, dropping Eleanor's hands. She could not believe that her father would speak so defiantly of the Crown's authority—that he would dare to pick up exactly where he had left off eight years before. Beside her, Eleanor had turned pale, as disbelieving as she.

But the lords and gallowglass, peasants and kern were screaming now, wildly, enthusiastically, waving spears and daggers, waving pennants and flags.

"*Never again!*" Gerald roared. "There is no prince here, no queen, no God, there is no ruler here but the earl of Desmond!"

Pandemonium erupted in the glen.

And Gerald beamed, standing in his stirrups, and his eyes glittered feverishly.

Katherine stared out of the window of her old bedchamber across the rushing waters of the river below Askeaton Castle, which was perched on a small island. On the opposite bank she could just make out the bell tower of the abbey where her mother was buried. Lush green meadows surrounded it, and beyond stretched dark forests of elm, oak, and pine. Katherine was as familiar with the view as she was with the reflection of her own face in a looking glass. How good it was finally to be home.

But it was not enough. Askeaton would never be enough for her, not anymore.

Liam. How she loved him. How she missed him. How she missed him and their son. How irrelevant all of the past now seemed. Where was Liam now? Hadn't he said that he would return for her—with their child?

He had delivered FitzMaurice. Her father was restored

to Desmond. What was keeping him—why hadn't he come?

And was it truly possible? Had he abducted her so many years ago purposefully? Had he known of her existence even then, when she had not known him at all?

"Katherine?"

Startled, she turned to face her father, who had come into her room without knocking. Her smile of greeting died, because he looked so somber, and that was a rarity since his return to Ireland. "Father? Is something amiss?"

"You have a visitor," Gerald said.

'Twas Liam. Katherine cried out, her hand clasped to her breast.

" 'Tis the earl of Leicester," Gerald said.

Katherine started. And when she did finally understand, she understood completely. He had chased her all the way to southern Ireland, to Askeaton, to collect what he was owed. *Oh, God.* Dread overwhelmed her and she could not move.

Gerald's stare was hard. "Leicester is one of the most powerful men in England. Do not anger him, Katherine. Do not oppose him."

"Father," she began weakly.

"No!" he cut her off. "Do not fail me now. Do what you must do." He turned and strode from the room.

Katherine stared after him, her chest tight, unable to move. *Do what you must do.*

Leicester was waiting for her downstairs, in the great hall, alone. He stood when she entered, his dark gaze sweeping over her thoroughly. His mouth was set in a firm, serious line.

Katherine's heart thundered in her ears. She felt weak. Faint. She halted before she came too close to him, wondering with real panic if he intended to take her then and there, in the hall.

"Did you think to deny me my due?" he asked.

Katherine could not speak. She wet her lips.

"Let us walk in the garden," he said abruptly. And he moved to her, taking her arm firmly in his.

The garden. He intended to take her in the garden. Katherine said not a word as he led her outside, into the courtyard, and then into one of the castle gardens. By the time they paused beneath a blossoming apple tree, Katherine had managed to get a grip on some of her panic and fear. Leicester released her. Katherine faced him cautiously.

"You ran away from me," he said, his gaze sliding over her features, her mouth.

"Yes."

"So you think to cheat me?" Anger flared in his eyes in spite of his mild tone.

Katherine lifted her head. "I do owe you. And if you insist, I will give you what you want. But ..."

"I insist."

She inhaled hard. "Please. Robin, do not do this." She had never addressed him so familiarly before.

He cocked his head. "I have wanted you for a very long time, Katherine. You are mad if you think to convince me to desist. You may come to me willingly, tonight, or I will come to you, and take what I want—even if you think to resist me."

She trembled. Closing her eyes. "You will not have to rape me." She glanced at him. "But I love Liam."

His jaw clenched. "I do not care." He turned and strode away.

And Katherine watched him go, telling herself that she would survive the coming night. Yet she could not help but think of Liam, and wish for a miracle.

The afternoon was endless. Katherine stood at the window in her bedchamber, staring blindly out of it at the river and the surrounding countryside. Leicester sat with her father in the hall below, and their laughter rang out frequently. She could hear bits and pieces of their conversation, and knew that Gerald was getting thoroughly drunk. But Robin Dudley, unfortunately, seemed intent upon remaining sober.

The bright blue sky began to fade in hue. The sun began to gently lower itself.

Below, the men laughed uproariously, and a maid squealed.

Katherine clawed the stone windowsill. The sky was turning mauve now, the sun a flaming orange ball hanging over the thick forest.

She could not go through with this. Yet she would have to, because if she did not, he would rape her. Her mind was filled with panic. Perhaps she should poison him?

The sky was violet now, and a crescent moon, pale and incandescent, had appeared.

It was then that Katherine saw the ship. Black and sleek, its silver sails unfurled and proud, racing upriver toward her.

Katherine cried out.

The Sea Dagger. *Liam. Liam had come.*

And then she remembered who sat downstairs with her father, and her excitement and joy disappeared, turned to real fear. Abruptly Katherine whirled and raced from her chamber, flying down the narrow, slick stone stairs.

Katherine froze in the middle of the hall. Her father also stood, swaying a bit. "Who comes?" he demanded, slurring the two words somewhat.

Katherine's gaze met Leicester's. "Liam," she whispered.

Leicester's expression hardened. Slowly he rose to his feet.

Liam strode into the hall.

Katherine cried out, joy piercing her breast. Clad in his breeches, high boots, and naught else but an unlaced tunic, he was the most magnificent sight she had ever seen. She was afraid of what was going to happen, but exhilaration swept through her, too, rendering her breathless.

And he had eyes only for her. "Katherine."

With a glad cry, Katherine ran to him, into his arms.

Liam held her, hugged her, rocked her. Then he stiffened, and she knew he had just noticed Leicester standing behind her.

She looked up at Liam and their gazes locked. "Nothing has happened," she whispered urgently.

"What does he want?" His tone was very, very dangerous.

"I . . . I promised him the use of my body—for his help in convincing the queen to free you." Katherine clung to Liam's broad shoulders, feeling his shudder of rage—terrified by it. "I love you so, Liam, that I would do anything to save your life."

Briefly his gaze softened. "Katherine. How I have missed you." His embrace tightened, and then his gaze grew dark and hard again. "You are not going to fulfill your part of the bargain." He set her aside, turning to Leicester.

Katherine could not move.

Liam's smile was cold. "Did you hear me, Dudley? I don't care what pact you made with my *wife*. I break it, now."

Leicester's gaze widened. "And when did that deed occur?"

"Long ago," Liam said softly, menacingly.

Leicester's gaze slid to Katherine, and she nodded.

But Liam was not through. "Have you touched her?"

Leicester understood the challenge, and he stiffened, his hand going to the bejeweled hilt of his rapier. Looking only at Liam now, he said not a word.

Liam snarled, and in the blink of an eye, his rapier sliced the air, hissing softly. "Perhaps I will rid you of a certain package you are so fond of. And then you will have no way of terrorizing women."

Leicester wielded his rapier now, too. A trickle of sweat gleamed on his temple. "You are insane. Katherine approached me. She herself agreed to our bargain. But she has never warmed my bed, O'Neill."

"Stop," Katherine whispered, as Liam began to stalk Leicester—who moved backward, away.

"Did you touch her?" Liam demanded, and suddenly he lunged and his rapier cut the air, back and forth, hissing loudly now, angrily, and then a long strip of Leicester's doublet appeared on its tip.

Leicester paled. "No," he said.

And Katherine screamed, rushing forward between the

two men. "Liam, please!" Her back to Leicester, she faced Liam so boldly that the tip of his rapier briefly brushed her breast. He deflected it immediately, before it could cut her dress, but she advanced upon him, begging. "Liam, stop this madness! Nothing has happened of any significance! Liam, please! You cannot hurt Dudley! Oh, God! Think of me, think of your son! The queen will hang you this time certainly!"

Liam stared at her. His eyes were wild, filled with a light she had never seen before.

Katherine stared back, into his eyes, and finally saw the bloodlust fade and die. "Liam," she choked out.

He sheathed his rapier and held out his arms. Katherine rushed into them. She laughed now, burying her face against his chest while he held her, hard. Then he turned her against his side, so that they faced the earl of Leicester together. Dudley was staring at them.

His mouth twisted in a smile that was sardonic and biting. "I will leave on the morrow. But beware, O'Neill. I do not take lightly losing what is my due."

Liam trembled, but Katherine gripped his arm tightly, in warning, and he remained silent as Leicester turned away. Gerald now rushed forward, appearing far more sober than before. He threw an arm around the earl, leading him back to the table, speaking rapidly, thinking to appease him, no doubt.

"We have just made an enemy," Katherine said in a hushed tone of voice, shaking now that the confrontation was over.

Liam held her close. "Leicester is shrewd. He may think himself our enemy now, Katherine, but in the end he will remain our grudging ally here in Ireland—for he hates Ormond far worse than us, as they vie with one another for the queen's favor."

He stroked her back, her hair, and finally cupped her face. His gaze held hers. "Will you return to me, Kate? Rest at my side, keep my home, bear my children, live with me—love me?"

"Yes," she whispered. "Yes!"

He laughed, the sound rich and rough and free, and then

their lips caught and held in a deep, melting kiss. When he raised his face he was smiling. "I have brought you something, darling."

Katherine froze, gripping his shirt. "Our son!"

Liam's smile was gentle and tender. He nodded, glancing past her shoulder.

Katherine whirled, and saw a woman standing by the door, holding a bundle in her arms. Crying out, Katherine lifted her skirts and ran to her.

She felt faint. Tears poured down her face. The woman smiled at her, handing her the babe. Katherine clutched the small, warm body to her breasts, gazing down at the sleeping child. "My son," she whispered, choking.

Liam stood beside her. "Her Majesty did not name him," he said. " 'Tis your choice, darling."

Katherine sobbed, kissed the baby's downy cheek, rocking him. The baby stirred, and his lashes fluttered open. Their gazes suddenly met. Mother and son, for the very first time since the child had been born.

Katherine wept harder, in joy. "How beautiful you are—like your father." She blinked at Liam. "I wish to name him Henry—in honor of the queen's father—in honor of the queen."

Liam laughed. "Why, Kate—you have become political!"

Katherine laughed, then, too, their voices blending together, as Henry O'Neill yawned.

Moonlight filled the dark stone chamber.

Katherine and Liam paused in its center. Her heart pounding, already weak-kneed, Katherine sent Liam a long, sideways glance.

Instantly she was crushed in his embrace. His mouth claimed hers. There was nothing gentle or soothing about his kiss. It was frantic and hungry, long and deep.

His hands molded and crushed her breasts. Katherine tore the laces of his shirt open, thrusting her hands inside. His chest muscles jumped beneath her fingertips. He tore his mouth from hers. "Greedy wench," he rasped, stripping off his shirt and tossing it aside.

Katherine laughed, the sound throaty and wicked. "I am very greedy this night, my lord, with just cause," she whispered. Her fingers slipped below the waistband of his breeches, brushing the heavy erection straining there. "I do not think you can possibly please me."

His eyes widened while his flat stomach tensed. Liam murmured, "A challenge, mistress? Do you not know that pirates love to duel?"

"Indeed?" She smiled seductively, caressing the area of his navel with her thumb. Her palm brushed his swollen tip again.

Liam growled a low warning and then Katherine found herself flat on her back on the bed. She shifted restlessly as he loomed over her, his gray eyes glittering. "Come to me," she whispered.

His mouth curved, but he ignored her soft entreaty. His glance was dark and bold, holding hers, and then he worked her bodice down, bringing her chemise with it, baring her breasts. Katherine tensed in expectation, breathless.

Liam smiled at her, and ducked his head.

The moment his tongue touched her nipple, Katherine arched up off the bed, crying his name, gripping his head. As he suckled, his hands were pulling her skirts up high around her waist. Katherine half laughed and half sobbed when he ripped the linen drawers off her body and cupped her slick, slippery sex.

His thumb rubbed up against her cleft immediately—expertly. Katherine thrashed, moaning, swelling.

"I cannot please you this night, darling?" he whispered, bending over her.

His tongue fluttered in the path his thumb had taken. Katherine locked her hands around his nape as he buried his face there. She cried out—again and again.

Suddenly limp and dazed, she began to float—until Liam nipped her thigh. Their gazes met. His was bright and feverish, but his tone, although raw, was teasing. "What, pray tell, was that?" he inquired.

She managed a smile, suddenly achingly aware of how he was poised between her open thighs. Her pulse picked up its beat. "Perhaps you have pleased me," she conceded, "but I am hardly satisfied."

His jaw flexed, his eyes darkened. An instant later his mouth was fully occupied again. Katherine gasped, holding his shoulders, his tongue causing havoc upon her already sensitized skin. Her hips began to undulate urgently, brushing up against him. Suddenly his strong fingers were there, inside of her, thrusting deep repeatedly. Panting, she cried, "Liam, please! Come inside of me now!" But it was too late, for already she was spiraling out of control and keening wildly.

When she opened her eyes, he was stroking her face, staring down at her, his eyes a brilliant shade of silver. His hot, hungry look caused Katherine's entire body to tighten. "I admit defeat," she whispered, reaching out and cupping his cheek.

He smiled, but the muscles in his face were tense, and then he guided her hand down to his chest, and then lower still, to his abdomen. Their gazes locked now, he waited, and Katherine reached lower, tracing his heavy outline through his breeches with trembling fingertips.

Her body had become feverish with desire again. Holding his gaze, she said simply, "I want you, Liam."

He laughed, the sound heavy with excitement, with triumph. A moment later he was moving on top of her, his strong arms around her, his mouth upon hers. His tongue thrust swiftly inside. Katherine did far more than meet it—she sucked it deep into her mouth.

And she curled her ankles around his calves, locking them in place. Her aggression shifted their bodies so that his throbbing loins were intimately wedged between her thighs.

He broke their kiss with a groan. "Kate, it's been so long—too long—I cannot wait." Already he was tearing at his breeches.

Pearl buttons hit the floor and scattered. Katherine's hands delved into his breeches, finding him, gripping him. Her fingers brushed and teased the ripe tip she found there. Liam cried her name, shoving hard up against her palms, his back arched, all of his weight up on his heavily corded arms.

Both laughing and sobbing, tears streaking her cheeks, she guided him inside of her.

He needed no encouragement. Liam growled and plunged deep, so forcefully that Katherine was pushed back on the bed against the headboard.

She did not care. She cared about one thing—the man on top of her, the man inside of her—this man that she loved.

Clasping her buttocks, he lifted her higher, so he could thrust more deeply into her. Katherine clamped her legs around his waist. His frenzied pumping continued. She cried out, he gasped; her muscles convulsed, again and yet again, light blazing through the darkness, and then she felt his manhood thicken and stretch a final time, becoming impossibly huge and hard, and his hot, wet seed was shooting deep into her womb.

He held her in his arms, panting harshly, then turned to his side, taking her with him. They lay in one another's embrace. Liam kissed the top of her head.

It was a while before Katherine could move. She shifted, came up on one elbow, caressed his chest, his face. Her eyes were shining. Liam's eyes opened, the light in them as brilliant, and he smiled at her. Her heart turned over. "I love you," she whispered.

His smile died. "How I have yearned to hear those three simple words."

"I do," Katherine said. "I always have—and Liam—I am sorry I ever doubted you."

"Sssh." He touched her mouth with his fingertip. "Do not apologize. Perhaps I should have told you of my game from the very beginning. Perhaps I am to blame for what we have suffered these many months past."

"Do not blame yourself," Katherine said fervently. "Let us truly put the past aside. I can forget it all now, Liam."

"And forgive all, as well?" he asked, up on one elbow now.

She turned coy. "But there is nothing to forgive."

He leaned forward and claimed her mouth, very tenderly.

"Katherine," he said afterwards, "although I intend that we spend most of the time here in Desmond, would you mind very much if we passed a few months in the summer on Earic Island? In the manor house, of course?"

Katherine's heart swelled. "Of course not," she whispered. "I would love it." Then she grinned impishly, although her very soul was singing. "Actually, there is one thing that bothers me."

Liam tensed, until he saw her grin. "And what might that be, Kate?"

Katherine sat up, very serious now. "Liam, did you know that I traveled upon the French ship when you seized it?"

He sat up as well. "Of course."

Katherine gazed at him. "Did you seize that ship because of me?"

He looked guilty. "Yes."

She was amazed. "I do not think I understand!"

"No, of course not, how could you?" He put one arm around her. "I first saw you, Katherine, when you were but sixteen. I spent a single night at the convent after returning from some business not far from there. I saw you and was smitten. My obsession began at that moment—my love began then and there."

Katherine stared.

"The abbess resented my questions," Liam told her, "and I asked many about you. 'Twas clear that she feared my interest in you. However, when I offered to pay your pension, she could not refuse, as your father had failed to provide the funds. And once I became your benefactor, she wrote me regularly to keep me informed of your well-being."

"You paid my pension to the abbess?" Katherine whispered, dazed.

He managed to look even more guilty. "I am a man, Katherine—and a pirate. You were a beautiful woman without protection—desperately in need of a protector. I wanted you then almost as badly as I want you now. But you were so young that I was prepared to wait. Of course, at the time my motives were not so noble as they now are." His smile was brief, rueful. "I intended to make you my mistress once you were older, not my wife. Yet after I met you, soon after, I realized that a brief liaison could not be enough." He bent and brushed her mouth with his. "That it could never be enough, Kate."

Chills were sweeping up and down her spine. She managed to say, "You pretended you did not know me when we first met face-to-face."

"How could I tell you my plans for you? I quickly realized you would resist my seduction even more strongly if you knew I had abducted you intentionally."

"Yes," Katherine breathed, thinking that he had been in love with her from the start—before she even knew him. "I would have been furious."

Liam hugged her. "Can you forgive me, Katherine? For my taking your fate into my own two hands? For my guiding it? Shaping it? Mastering it?"

She laughed then, hugging him back. "Liam, it dawns upon me now that everything you have done since you abducted me was because of me—because of your love for me."

He smiled into her eyes. "Yes, Katherine. You are right."

"Once," she whispered, "you told me that you were my destiny. Now, finally, I understand." She cupped his face in her palms. "I truly love you, Liam, and I thank God for your pirate ways."

His gaze, suspiciously moist now, locked with hers. A moment passed. "I love you, Katherine," he finally said, rough and low. "I always have. I always will."

AUTHOR'S NOTE

*T*his book is a work of fiction, but wherever possible, I have tried to adhere to the actual course of historical events. However, as I am a novelist, my overriding goal has been to provide my readers with a fast-paced and compelling drama. Therefore, I have exercised poetic license whenever necessary for the sake of my story and characters.

All of the main characters in this book, with the exception of Hugh Barry, Mary Stanley, Katherine, and Liam, did exist, and I have enjoyed portraying them as I thought they might have actually lived. Please note that I took great liberties by using the Barry family name in the manner that I did. But while Mary Stanley is a fictional character, the Stanley family, with its connection to Queen Catherine Parr, is not.

Leicester and Ormond were both the queen's favorites, and possibly her lovers, too. Elizabeth frequently called Tom "my Black Husband." Leicester finally married Lettice, the countess of Essex, in 1578, and weathered the Queen's great wrath, although his wife was not allowed at court during the rest of her life.

Ormond's mother, Joan, did indeed marry FitzGerald, a man twenty years her junior, after carrying on with him much as I have described. Joan and Queen Elizabeth were, at one time, good friends.

Gerald FitzGerald did attempt to rule southern Ireland in a despotic fashion, without interference from the queen. He was captured by Ormond after the battle at Affane. Historians are divided about whether he was returned to Ireland after being brought in chains to London in 1565 or remained a prisoner there for almost eight years. He was tried and convicted of treason, and exiled to St. Leger House in Southwark in 1568.

FitzGerald married his second wife, Eleanor, less than a month after Joan Butler FitzGerald died. Eleanor was a headstrong, capable beauty who spent most of her time lobbying at court to gain support for Gerald's cause.

FitzMaurice was Gerald's cousin. Eleanor claimed to all who would listen that he sought to usurp her husband's authority in Desmond. Some historians have suggested that FitzMaurice and FitzGerald were secretly allied. In any case, FitzMaurice quickly proved himself a far more capable leader and antagonist than Gerald ever had been. By the time he was captured in the spring of 1573, it was obvious to Elizabeth and her advisors that Gerald was the lesser of two evils and that he should be restored.

FitzMaurice continued to wage his war against the queen and her heretic religion from the shores of France and Spain. Eventually he invaded Ireland with a small force and continued his campaign of guerilla warfare. In 1579 FitzMaurice was killed by a peasant in an argument over a horse.

Gerald FitzGerald resumed his defiant ways almost immediately upon his return to Ireland. He had not learned his lesson from his long imprisonment. By the time of his cousin's death, he had taken over full command of the rebellion and was up in open arms. The British retaliated with a scorched earth policy that was so devastating that thirty thousand Irish died from starvation. In 1583 the great Desmond rebellion ended—for Gerald FitzGerald was finally run to ground and killed. His head was sent to Kilkenny for Ormond to view, and then to London, for the queen to see, too.

Shane O'Neill was clan chieftain and a barbarian who spent most of his time hunting down O'Donnells and murdering them. He submitted to the queen in 1562 much as I have described. Historical records do not show that he had a wife or children. He probably had many bastards—sons like Liam forced by circumstances to live on the very edges of civilization or even outside of it. Shane was finally murdered himself in 1567—by an O'Donnell.

The records also seem to indicate that Gerald and Joan FitzGerald did not have any children. Which is not surprising, for when they married, Joan was about forty years old. However, even if they had had a daughter, it is unlikely that her birth would have been recorded, for the birth of daughters was often ignored by noble families—and thus forgotten by history.

Brenda Joyce likes to hear from her readers. You may write her at P.O. Box 1208, Wainscott, New York 11975.

Dear Reader,

My next novel is BEYOND SCANDAL, on sale early September 1995. It is my first novel to incorporate romantic suspense. Set in Victorian England, orphan Anne Stewart has been in love with Dom St Georges, heir to the dukedom of Rutherford, since she arrived at her uncle's house as a child. But he has never noticed her. Then, one hot summer night, Anne and Dom succumb to a mad passion—during Dom's engagement party to another. And dutifully he weds her—only to abandon her the next day.

Dom does not return home for four years, and when he does, Anne finds herself irresistibly attracted to him despite his horrible betrayal—and despite the series of strange little accidents that occur, leading her to believe that someone wishes to frighten her, or harm her—or even kill her. And soon Anne must face the fact that her fear is not misplaced and that she is in jeopardy, but surely not from her own husband, Dom…

And Dom, meanwhile, is trying desperately to find out who is trying to hurt his wife—and as desperately, he is trying to ignore a mystery that could change his entire life forever, rocking society with its biggest scandal yet…

Come join Dom and Anne, the Marquis and Marchioness of Waverly, as they defy the plots and intrigues of the St Georges and Collins families, overcome their own suspicions of one another, solve two mysteries, weather a shattering scandal…and finally find the happiness they truly deserve!

Best,

Brenda Joyce